Luck of the Draw

Also by William Scott Morrison

Novel
The Energy Caper,
or Nixon in the Sky with Diamonds

Short Story
A version of "Draft Night" was published as a short story in the anthology *Veterans of War, Veterans of Peace* © 2006 Koa Books

Acknowledgment

I would like to thank my wife, Padma Catell, for her patience and forbearance in correcting the many flaws in my writing and in my life.

LUCK
OF THE DRAW

a novel

William Scott Morrison

CASTALIA COMMUNICATIONS
Petaluma, California

Published in the United States by
Castalia Communications
Petaluma, California

Publisher's Cataloging-in-Publication
(Provided by Quality Books, Inc.)

Morrison, William Scott.
Luck of the draw / William Scott Morrison.
pages cm
LCCN 2015904973
ISBN 978-0-929150-31-4
ISBN 978-0-929150-30-7
ISBN 978-0-929150-32-1

1. Male friendship--Fiction. 2. Man-woman relationships--Fiction. 3. Vietnam War, 1961-1975--Fiction. 4. Historical fiction. 5. Baseball stories. I. Title.

PS3613.O7779L83 2016 813'.6
QBI15-600112

Cover illustration: Duncan Long

Manufactured in the United States of America

For the victims of
the war in Vietnam

Chapter One

Nicknames

Pittsburgh, 1959

JENNY WAS ONE OF ONLY TWO GIRLS IN HER SIXTH-GRADE CLASS TO GET stuck with a nickname. Linda Tanner got "Bubbles" because of the breasts she'd grown over the summer, which wasn't too bad as nicknames go, but Jenny got "Honker" because of her nose. Now that her three older brothers had all moved on to junior high, there was nobody to defend her if the boys made fun of her—they would never have dared to even think about it if her brothers were around.

It started one day at recess under the basketball hoop when she beat Rusty Limbergh at four-horses and he got so furious at losing to a girl that he chased her around the playground going "honk-honk-honk" like an old pick-up truck. After that, the boys were always honk-honk-honking at her—loud, on the playground, or muffled, under their breaths, so the teachers couldn't hear as they passed her in the halls.

Having a big schnozzola wasn't so bad for her brothers. They were guys, and everybody knows that on a guy a big nose is directly proportional to you know what. But Jenny was the first Abruzzi girl in two generations and the only thing anybody ever seemed to notice about her was her dill pickle of a nose.

Jenny had her dad's Mediterranean complexion and his glistening, coal-black hair, and she was always being told how lucky she was to have her mom's blue eyes and prominent Irish cheekbones. But grownups were much too polite to come right out and tell the truth—it was all ruined by the Abruzzi nose.

All her life she had wondered if she might be just a little bit pretty if she only had a normal nose, but since she'd been stuck with that horrible nickname, "Honker," she didn't care if she were to be ugly for ever and ever if only the boys would stop honking at her.

Right after Halloween, the school district's roving music teacher, Mrs. Scott, who came around every Tuesday to lead the class for an hour of singing, held tryouts for the Christmas pageant. Once again, Mrs. Scott picked Jenny, the third year in a row. Jenny was surprised at the first rehearsal when Mrs. Scott asked her to come see her after school.

What could she have done wrong?

But it wasn't like that at all. Mrs. Scott said, "Jennifer, you have a wonderfully pure, angelic voice. How would you like to be the soloist on 'Silent Night' this year?"

"You mean...all by myself?"

"No, I'll play piano, and the choir will sing harmony, but you'll sing the melody."

Every Tuesday after school Mrs. Scott coached her on articulation, breath control, and how to breath from her diaphragm. Jenny already knew how to play it from her piano lessons, and she practiced playing and singing for hours on end. The week before the pageant, Mrs. Scott rehearsed them every afternoon; the full choir came in at "sleep in heavenly peace," but the rest of the song was all Jenny's.

Her mom was even more excited than she was and gave her an early Christmas present of a velvet dress, very plush, deep green with a white lace collar and ruffles on the sleeves, good enough for Sunday mass and perfect for a Christmas pageant solo performance.

Her turn came toward the end, when Mrs. Scott announced, "Jennifer Abruzzi will sing 'Silent Night.'" The audience applauded as she stepped out from the choir and walked to the front of the stage into the bright spotlight. The house lights came down, and as she took a deep breath she heard a "honk" from way in the back of the darkened gym, then one from up front, and the whole place erupted in honk-honk-honking like it was downtown at rush hour.

In one more second she would have run right off the stage, but Mrs. Scott crashed down hard on the piano, jolting the room quiet. She gave Jenny her cue, and began to play. Not even Rusty Limbergh would dare honk during "Silent Night."

Somehow she sang as if nothing had happened and got a standing ovation. Later, when she was helping at the cookie table, many parents and teachers told her how much they liked her voice, but on the drive home she curled up in a ball in the back seat of her mom's Ford station wagon and cried the whole way.

The next night at bedtime, Jenny was reading a Nancy Drew mystery when her mom came in, shut the door, and sat down next to her on the bed. "Jennifer, would you like to get your nose fixed?"

Jenny clapped her hands. "Oh Mom, do you really mean it?"

"Don't get your hopes too high. First, we have see what Father

Zyhowski says, so promise you won't breathe a word to your father or your brothers—and especially not to Mama Antonia."

"Oh I won't, Mom, I promise."

One snowy morning right after Christmas they went to see Father Zyhowski in the parish rectory. He listened intently, nodding his head from time to time as her mom told him about the nickname and the horrible honking at the pageant. When she finished he shook his head, sighed, and turned to Jenny. "I know it's hard, my child, but you must understand that boys will be boys. I'm sure they don't really mean it."

Her mom scowled, not at all happy with his answer. "Father, does the Lord not help those who help themselves?"

He seemed to be taken aback. "Yes, surely."

"Good, because we need God's help to get Jenny's nose fixed."

Old Father Zyhowski sputtered like he'd swallowed a pretzel the wrong way. "You…you want God to perform a miracle…*on her nose*?"

Jenny had never seen anybody so completely flummoxed, not even on *I Love Lucy*.

"Oh no, Father," her mom said. "Nothing like that. We only want Him to lend us a little support, that's all. You should hear the way her grandmother goes off when I bring it up…."

Jenny couldn't help but chuckle at how her mom got Mama Antonia's fractured English and quick little hand gestures just right. "God make'a da nose. She born with it, she die with it. She Abruzzi!"

Father Zyhowski seemed perplexed. "I'm not sure I understand. What exactly is it you want God to do?"

"We don't want God to do anything, Father. We want you to have a little talk with Mama Antonia, that's all. Just tell her that plastic surgery is not a sin."

Father Zyhowski frowned, his countenance very grave. "It may not be a mortal sin, my child, but false pride can lead to the deadliest of the seven deadly sins…the sin of vanity."

Her mom gasped. "You're not saying it's a sin for Jenny to want to be normal, are you Father?"

Father Zyhowski peered at her mom through his horn-rimmed glasses, let out a heavy sigh, then turned and faced Jenny directly, his lips pursing tight, his face crinkling up like used aluminum foil. As he leaned close to her she smelled some kind of alcohol on his breath, and when he laid his icy hands on top of hers it gave her the shivers.

"The Lord works in mysterious ways, my child," he intoned as he poked his bony finger in her face. "Vanity is the root of pride, and false pride has led many of God's children into the arms of Satan, and to the eternal damnation of the immortal soul."

Her mom leaped out of her chair. "But Father—"

His hand shot up like a traffic cop's, right in her mom's face. "I know your intentions are good, and you only want what is best for your daughter. But the road to Hell is paved with good intentions. It is not for us to question the will of God."

Father Zyhowski seemed to think that settled the matter; he looked at his watch and straightened up as if he expected them to accept his answer as God's will and leave.

Her mom would not let it go. "But Father...."

Father Zyhowski slumped back, resigned to being quizzed on the distinction between deadly sins and mortal sins and whether a simple nose-job in Pittsburgh was any different than fixing a cleft palate in Nigeria or a clubfoot in Bolivia. Back and forth they went, her mom never winning, yet never quite giving in. Jenny had seen her argue with the good Father before about the nature of sin. He was well-practiced in the art of telling his flock what they didn't want to hear, and he always seemed to win in the end. Despite her mom's logic and heartfelt pleas, the good Father declined to intercede with Mama Antonia on behalf of a nose-job.

Jenny and her mom bundled up tight and put on their gloves. Father Zyhowski held the door as they grabbed the railing and started carefully down the snow-covered stairs. "Watch your step...it's slippy," said the good Father. "And remember, my children—God made His creations with a purpose. False pride is the root of vanity, which is the deadliest sin of all."

As they trudged up the sidewalk in the new-fallen snow Jenny wiped back a tear. "Father Zyhowski isn't going to help us, is he, Mom?"

Her mom stopped, put her arm around Jenny's shoulder, pulled her tight and said, "No, dear, I don't think so."

"Does that mean God doesn't want me to have a normal nose?"

"Father Zyhowski didn't say that, Jennifer."

"But he said it was a sin to want one."

"No...not exactly. If you listened very carefully, what he really said was that it's only a sin if you become too prideful. You wouldn't be like that, would you, Jennifer?"

"Oh, no, Mom. I would never be prideful, I swear. Never. Cross my heart and hope to die."

"Maybe we'll have a talk with a psychologist and see what he says."

"A psychologist? But aren't they for crazy people?"

"Not always, dear. Sometimes they're for normal people, too."

A few weeks later she and her mom took the trolley downtown for an appointment. Jenny's ears popped as an elderly black man in a red uniform whooshed them up in the polished-copper elevator to the thirty-fifth floor of the forty-four story Gulf Oil Building, which all of Pittsburgh knew was the tallest structure between New York and Chicago. The waiting room overlooked what in colonial times was known as "the forks of the Ohio," the confluence of the Allegheny and Monongahela rivers where they join to form the Ohio. The early French explorers thought the Ohio to be the most beautiful river in the world, calling it "La Belle Riviére."

What a sight, so high up! The hazy disc of the late afternoon sun glowed just above the horizon, bathing the snow-covered hills in the day's last light like a pale orange blanket the color of children's aspirin. It was the end of January, and it had been a very cold winter; not a single barge or boat was moving on the frozen rivers. The weatherman on TV had been warning of flooding next spring if rain melted the snow-pack in the mountains before the ice-dams broke up.

Her mom had promised a psychologist like Dr. Westcott would be very scientific and would not have the same concern for her immortal soul as had Father Zyhowski. He certainly looked and sounded like every psychologist she'd ever seen in the movies: curly-haired with flecks of gray, glasses, pipe, goatee. He told her to stand in the middle of the room while he appraised her, circling, staring while thoughtfully pulling on his goatee, going hmmm...hmmm. "Yes, there's no question that an operation would vastly improve your daughter's appearance, Mrs. Abruzzi, no question at all. That, in turn, will raise her self-esteem, regardless of what else may be troubling her. Is there anything else wrong, Jennifer? Anything you'd like to talk about?"

"Oh no, Dr. Westcott."

"Are you absolutely certain?"

"Oh yes, Dr. Westcott. Absolutely."

And that was that. As to the problem with Mama Antonia, the wise

Dr. Westcott proposed a simple solution. "Why get into a fight with your mother-in-law? Don't tell her, just do it. Make it a *fait accompli*. She'll be mad for a while, but in time, since she loves her granddaughter, she'll come to accept that it's for the best."

Armed with the opinion of a Doctor of Psychology, they took the elevator down twelve floors to keep an appointment her mom had made with Dr. Emery, a famous plastic surgeon. Jenny felt comforted as the doctor used his long, slender fingers to probe all over her face and explained the procedure, called a "rhinoplasty."

That night Jenny looked up the new word in her Webster's; she looked everything up. Rhinoplasty came from the Greek: rhino meant "of or pertaining to the nose," and plasty was "the act or means of forming." Using her French textbook and her English/French dictionary, she figured out that in English "fait accompli" meant "accomplished fact," a done deed that was too late to change.

Dr. Emery's nurse lent them a book with photos of hundreds of possible noses to choose from. Jenny suggested that the best place to hide it was under her mom's panties and bras, the only place her father and brothers would never dare to look. Her mom agreed, and every night at bedtime for the next week they thumbed through the nose-book like they were shopping for the perfect gift in a Gimbel's catalog.

It wasn't easy choosing which nose would turn out to be the best—Dr. Emery promised she would learn to "grow into it," no matter which one she chose. In the end, they decided she couldn't go wrong with a nose just like her mom's, since it was only bad luck that she'd gotten her dad's nose instead of her mom's in the first place.

They planned everything as if it were a C.I.A. spy operation, scheduling the procedure for late August, so Jenny wouldn't miss a whole summer of swimming. That way, her bandages would come off just in time for a fresh start in junior high school. She had trouble sleeping from keeping the secret for so long and wondering how her life would change. When the day finally came, she packed a suitcase like she was going to Camp Tioshango for a week, just like she had done for the last two years. It was a perfect alibi. Nobody suspected anything.

She was only in the hospital for a night, and when she left her nose was bandaged up like a mummy. Grampy Jim and Grammy Liz let her hide out in her mom's old room at their house up in Beaver Falls. Nobody but the four of them knew she wasn't at Camp Tioshango.

Grampy Jim bought her a Made-in-Japan transistor radio so she could listen to her own music, while Grammy Liz took her to the library, where she checked out *Gone With the Wind, Little Women*, and *Black Beauty*. She tried to check out *Lady Chatterley's Lover* and *Peyton Place*, but Grammy Liz wouldn't hear of it.

Jenny spent her time recuperating by reading and listening to the Pirates' pennant-drive on the radio with Grampy Jim as the Bucs kept winning on their way to the World Series. At dusk, she caught lightning bugs in a mayonnaise jar, and when the stars came out and reception got good, she tuned in stations from Boston to Chicago as "The Twist," "Chain Gang," and "Itsy Bitsy Teeny Weenie Yellow Polka Dot Bikini" battled for Number One on the Top 40 countdowns. She watched the Olympics on TV, and was captivated by the women's diving. She loved going off the high dive—all the Pittsburgh pools had one—but she had never seen a competition with judges holding up scorecards and the divers trying for a perfect ten. If she couldn't play in Little League because she was a girl, she would be a diver instead.

The entire Abruzzi clan was at Mama Antonia's big table for Sunday dinner when Jenny and her mom came in, a little late, just back from "camp." As Jenny took her usual seat all the Abruzzis froze in place like concrete cinder blocks, gaping in astonishment. Mama Antonia squinted from across the table, shuddered, and burst into tears.

To everybody's surprise, Papa Carlo leaped up and wagged his finger in Mama Antonia's face. "Hush'a you up, woman. It a good thing, a good thing." He leaned close to his wife and touched his finger to the tip of his own giant schnozzola. "Whad'a you know? You no gotta see in da mirror. You think I marry you if you gotta da nose? Ha!"

Papa Carlo, having taken charge, came around the table, smiling and spreading his arms wide. He took Jenny by the shoulders, planted two big old-country kisses on her cheeks, and gave her a grandfatherly hug. "Now you bella, mia cara. Molto bella!"

The previous September, Arthur Bolton McGill III, called "Arthur" by his parents and "Art" or "McGill" by everybody else, had been in the sixth grade at Calvin Coolidge Elementary School in Milltowne, an industrial city of about 30,000 an hour's drive outside of Pittsburgh. It was a hot September day, just two weeks into the school year, when he began his first serious day-dreaming about girls.The teachers assembled the boys from the sixth-grade classes in the gym and the girls in the cafeteria. They showed each group the same educational film about the birds and the bees. McGill was astonished by the amazing journey of the sperm, which leaped from the gonads through the vas deferens and burst into the vagina, where they struggled upstream, like migrating salmon, fighting their way into the womb. Millions of the squiggly little suckers engaged in an epic battle, fighting it out, winner-take-all, over the single female egg that coyly dropped down from the ovary.

McGill learned a lot from that movie. All those fancy anatomical words were new to him. He had never heard of a penis; his mom insisted he had a "weezer," although the guys called theirs "cocks," "dicks," or "peckers," and their testicles were "balls" or "nuts." The boys called the girls' most secret parts "pussies," "cunts," "twats" or "beavers." Some girls loved shooting "beaver shots," nonchalantly spreading their legs so you could see all the way up to the whites of their panties as they pretended to work on arithmetic problems before they clamped their knees shut and snatched your heart away.

In addition to shooting beavers, accidentally or not, most girls, once they got to junior high, acquired another anatomical feature—breasts. Of course the guys never called them that, instead calling them "titties," "bazooms," and "knockers," while the girls who didn't develop as quickly were snickered at for being "flat." McGill never did learn what terms his mom would have thought appropriate to describe a girl's hidden body parts, as she preferred to never talk about hidden body parts at all. Vaginas and breasts might have been acceptable, but his mom would never have approved of pussies, cunts, twats or beavers.

Before then, McGill had not thought about girls' anatomies very much, but once he started getting a few pubes on his crotch he thought about very little else. It started in earnest in that fall of 1959, a year and a half after the Russkies sent up Sputnik, the first man-made satellite. That enemy triumph freaked out the American military-industrial establishment, which proceeded to enlist the nation's schools to help win the Cold War. Working together, the generals and the principals came up with a crash program to get more science into the schools and keep America safe. The call went out: America needed rocket scientists to close the missile gap!

At Coolidge Elementary, this meant duck-and-cover drills to keep the future scientists safe. The entire school would scramble under their desks when the air raid siren blared, and everybody made sure to cover their faces so they'd be safe from flying glass when the shock wave from the H-bombs hitting Pittsburgh blew out their windows. Everyone knew the tune to the corny song in the TV cartoon from the Civil Defense Administration starring Bert the Turtle: "Duck...and cover, duck...and cover," which had instantly been changed by the older guys to "Fuck...your mother, fuck...your mother."

All over town, even more bomb-shelter signs—three black triangles on a yellow background—popped up on brick and stone buildings such as churches and schools to let people know they had a safe refuge when the H-bombs started falling. The Sputnik threat also meant that a science lab was installed in one of Coolidge's sixth-grade classrooms.

McGill's teacher, Miss Deale, just two years out of college, had the boys in her class enthralled in a collective crush...and boy did she ever seem to enjoy it. "Built like a brick shit-house," was the highly-complimentary term for her anatomy.

One day, Miss Deale was sitting on the top of the teacher's desk facing the class, her legs carefully crossed. It was only her second year, and she was already called "Sexy Mary." Perched on her desk, knees at eye-level, the lucky guys in the middle aisles had the best seats when she parted her legs; everyone knew she did it on purpose.

"You'll be glad to know," Miss Deale said, "that we get two hours a week in the new science lab. Since our turn is tomorrow, after lunch we'll trade classrooms with Miss Williams class and she will give you a tour of the new lab, so we won't have recess today."

McGill raised his hand and complained, "It isn't fair to cut out recess, Miss Deale. Let's cut out arithmetic instead."

It didn't do any good, and after lunch Miss Deale led the class down the halls, the girls in one line, the boys in another, short to tall, and left them at the mercy of "Witch" Williams.

McGill took the seat he always tried to get in every class, way in the back of the room, as far away from the teacher as he could get. Because he was tall, it usually worked. But the first thing Witch Williams did was point to him and say, "You, Arthur, there in the back. Come up here."

He hadn't even had a chance to do anything.

"Hold out your hand," she ordered. Then, with a fat eighteen-inch wooden ruler, she gave him a stinging RAP across his palm. "That's just to let you know I've heard all about you."

Then Witch Williams gave the class a pep talk about how everyone was to take turns exploring the lab, get to know it well, because they would be there every Friday afternoon for the rest of the year. McGill was still mad they'd stolen recess, so he hogged one of the microscopes, checking out the legs, wings, and compound-eyes of a dead fly.

After a while, some of the girls were buzzing around a microscope, giggling and pleading for Candy Riley, who was looking through the eyepiece, to hurry–hurry–hurry up. They were making a lot of noise, and nobody made noise in Witch Williams' class. "What's going on over there?" cackled Witch Williams.

The girls went instantly quiet.

"I said, what's going on?"

"Nothing, Miss Williams," one finally answered.

"Then what has you all riled up?"

The room was hushed; nobody said a word. Everybody was frozen, except for Candy, who was still looking through the eyepiece, oblivious to everything around her. Witch Williams said, "Candy, what are you looking at?"

Candy glanced up for an instant, ignored the question, and put her eye back down to the lens.

"Candy!" shouted Witch Williams. "Answer me! What are you looking at?"

Candy blurted out, "Sammy Duncan's sperms! Want to come see? They're really cute."

Witch Williams turned pale and sat slowly down in her seat. She'd probably never come so close to any live sperm before.

Candy, who still had her eye to the lens, asked, "Miss Williams, why are all the sperms swimming in circles? The movie said they always swim in the same direction, like salmon."

Witch Williams could only manage a gasp as Candy answered her own question. "Is it because they don't have any place to go? Is that right, Miss Williams?"

Sammy was older than everyone else in the class, almost fourteen, and he hadn't flunked two whole grades for nothing. He was smiling like a football hero as the girls giggled and grinned when he strutted to his seat after his three-day suspension.

Chapter 2

Growing Pains

September, 1960

THE FURTHER THE BUS FROM THE SOUTH-SIDE CLIMBED UP THE STEEP North Hill, the more Nixon signs Mulligan saw. In his own part of town, Kennedy signs dotted the small front yards. He didn't know of any with a Nixon sign. Up here, as the yards got bigger, Nixon signs sprouted everywhere. For the first time he realized that Kennedy could lose.

The bus driver, a thick-necked, burly man with a balding head and a badge on his jacket, drove past the front of the school, where dozens of students were milling about as they waited for the bell. He parked the bus in the lot by the football field. When everybody started to get up at once he pulled out a whistle—TWEEET!

"Get back in your seats and be quiet! Y'uns don't get off 'till I tell y'uns to get off."

The bus fell silent. Everybody fidgeted, anxious to get out as the driver checked his manifest, looked up and said, "Now listen up. I'm Mr. Pickens and this is my bus. I'm also assistant custodian. You'll see me around."

"You mean assistant janitor," cracked a voice from the back, and everybody laughed.

"I'm a custodial engineer," he said with a smile. "Now, before y'uns go, remember we leave here at a quarter-to-four, on the nose, every day. There's a late bus at four-thirty, and another at five-thirty for y'uns in sports and detention, but they don't go direct. Any questions?"

Nobody had a question. They just wanted out so they could get to their homerooms on the first day of the school year.

Pickens pointed to the set of double doors at the corner of the building and said, "Okay, y'uns can go. Use them doors right there."

Michael Patrick Mulligan, twelve years old, with curly red hair and a noseful of freckles, was full of excitement as he got off the bus and looked over the athletic fields. He couldn't wait to go out for football. He and thirty-five other seventh-graders whose last names began with "M" were assigned to homeroom #109, the domain of Miss Crowne, a seventh-grade English and singing teacher. Older guys had warned him how tough she was.

George Washington Junior High stood three stories tall with classrooms built for nine hundred students. Constructed in 1922 with thousands of top-grade yellow bricks, it had an octagonal brick chimney a hundred feet high and lightning rods shooting into the sky. An American flag waved atop a steel flagpole in the middle of the front lawn, and a row of dogwoods lined the semi-circular front driveway. Championship pennants hung all around the large foyer just inside the main entrance. Big oaks, pines, maples and elms were scattered along paths and in groves around the thirty-acre campus. The grounds also doubled as the only public park on the North Hill and had two big swing sets, climbing bars, a pair of see-saws, two horseshoe pits and a tether-ball pole. Two stone bridges over a tiny creek that ran along the edge of the campus served as hangouts for smokers and troublemakers. In addition to the football field, Washington boasted two baseball fields, six tennis courts, two outdoor basketball hoops, an indoor swimming pool with a diving board and a gymnasium with roll-out bleacher seats. Everything about the building and the grounds was solid, muscular, built to last.

Washington was one of two junior highs in Milltowne, in the heart of western Pennsylvania's steel country. In the fall of 1960, it was overflowing with the first wave of "war babies" from what demographers called a "baby boom" who were surging into puberty. Four public and two parochial elementary schools funnelled students into Washington's melting pot for seventh, eighth, and ninth grades. On school days, a fleet of yellow buses fanned out from the parking lot to pick up students who lived over two miles away, about half the school.

Mulligan went inside and found his new homeroom. He looked around, hoping to see a familiar face or two, but he didn't know anybody. At eight-thirty sharp the tardy bell went off and a tall, skinny kid slipped in the door a second before the final clang.

Miss Crowne scowled at the kid but only said, "Sit anywhere and be quiet." All the desks had a piece of paper taped to the top, each with a different number. Mulligan took the last seat in the back, by the windows, and the skinny kid took the last seat in back by the door.

Miss Crowne said, "You will now stand for the 'Pledge of Allegiance' and the 'Lord's Prayer.'"

The class rose as she turned to face the American flag hanging above the blackboard. She put her right hand over her heart and led them in the Pledge. Then she faced the class, folded her hands, bowed her head, and began the Lord's Prayer.

Mulligan mumbled along, glancing around to check out the other kids. Most had their heads bowed and their eyes closed. Half the class were girls. This was completely new. Except for the nuns who taught at St. Vincent's, he had never been in a class with girls before.

There were also three Negroes, two boys and a girl; he had never been in a class with Negroes and didn't know any, though he had played against some in Little League. He wondered why their skin was dark, but the palms of their hands were white. Did the color rub off, like paint? He noticed two boys and one girl staring straight ahead, their heads unbowed, their mouths closed, their eyes wide open, not even pretending to pray. He figured they must be Jewish, though he had never met any Jewish kids and he had no idea if he'd played against any in Little League. Halfway through the prayer, a few kids began glancing around; one girl passed a note to another, and the skinny kid was leaning forward and peeking over the shoulder of the girl in front of him trying to see down her blouse.

"I am Miss Crowne," she told the class after the "amen." "Welcome to George Washington Junior High and your homeroom for the next three years." Then, with a firm and well-practiced solemnity, she informed them, "You are no longer children. This is junior high. You are young adults. You will behave as such, and if you don't, you will be punished like children. Now, I want the boys to line up along the windows, the girls along the wall, the shortest in the front by the blackboard, the tallest in the back by the closets."

Disputes broke out over who was taller. Mulligan and the skinny kid moved to the end of the line. The kid looked Mulligan up and down and said, "You got me," then turned to the kid next to him and said, "and I got you."

"I want you to count off, front to back," Miss Crowne said. "And remember your number. Girls first."

The girls counted off, one to seventeen; Miss Crowne frowned, shook her head and said, "Somebody's missing."

Then the boys counted off; Mulligan was number eighteen, the last boy.

"When I call your number," Miss Crowne said, "I want you to step forward and say your full name, and tell us where you went to school last year. Girl number one."

"Barbara Ann Mabellini," said the shortest girl. "I went to Saint Mary's."

"Very well, Barbara Ann," Miss Crowne said as she found the name on the roll and wrote something down. "Sister Agnes is a dear friend of mine. Have you ever been in class with boys before?"

"No, sister, I...I mean, no, Miss Crowne."

"You'll find it very different. Please take desk number one." Then Miss Crowne called boy number one, and gave him desk number two. Gradually the desks filled up: girl-boy-girl-boy, left-to-right, front-to-back, short-to-tall.

As he waited his turn Mulligan sized-up the skinny kid next to him. In seventh grade, size mattered. Like Mulligan's dad said, "You've got to know who can kick your ass and who can't." He didn't know anybody his age who could kick his ass.

The skinny kid wore his hair with a wave on his forehead kept in place by heavy dabs of Brylcream or Wildroot and he smelled of English Leather cologne. Mulligan would have no trouble handling him if it ever came to that. A NIXON-LODGE button was pinned on the pocket of the guy's Madras shirt. Madras was "in."

The guy nudged him with his elbow and said in a whisper, "Who you for?"

"What do you mean?" Mulligan whispered back.

"Who you for? Nixon or Kennedy?"

Mulligan's dad was a shop steward for the United Steelworkers Union at Babcox Tubing, the biggest factory in Milltowne. His was a Democratic family.

"Kennedy, who else?" Mulligan said, irritated by the Nixon button. Then he noticed the skinny kid wore the ugliest shoes he'd ever seen in his life—red suede loafers. Mulligan snickered and said, "Do you always come to school in bedroom slippers?"

Miss Crowne's sonar picked up the talking; she gave them a stern glance, pointed at them and said, "You are young men now. Talking in class is not allowed. Is that understood?"

"Yes, ma'am," the skinny kid said.

She introduced Mulligan to her infamous glare. "How about you? Do you understand?"

"Yes, Miss Crowne," Mulligan said.

When Miss Crowne called number seventeen, the skinny kid stepped forward and said, "Arthur Bolton McGill the third. I went to Coolidge."

Calvin Coolidge Elementary School, on the upper North Hill, was the only elementary school in the only Republican ward in heavily Democratic Milltowne. To kids from Mulligan's South Side, anybody from the North Hill was "rich." Mulligan recalled the radio ads with the slogan: "McGill Motors, home of Cadillacs, Chevrolets, and quality used cars. When it comes to cars, Milltowne is McGilltown." This kid had to be related to those McGills.

Only Mulligan was left; Miss Crowne checked her roster and asked, "Does anyone know Susan Ann Milton?" Nobody did, and Miss Crowne said, "Very well. We'll leave her seat vacant for now. That leaves only you. Tell the class your name, young man, and where you went to school."

"Michael Patrick Mulligan. Saint Vincent's."

"Congratulations, Michael. You get seat thirty-six, by the door. It is your job to make sure it is quietly closed, exactly one minute after the bell, every morning. I'll be counting on you."

Miss Crowne was trim and silver-haired, with thick bifocal glasses that made her look bug-eyed. The room had an upright piano between her desk and the windows. It faced sideways, at an angle, so she could play while keeping a watchful eye on the class from her low seat on the piano bench.

Miss Crowne had graduated from Slippery Rock State Teachers College in 1925 and started at Washington the same year. Only Mrs. Newmark, the Latin teacher, had been there longer. Photographs on the history wall by the trophy case as well as shots from yearbooks showed that while she had not been ravishingly beautiful as a young woman, she had been attractive in a strong-willed, prim-and-proper kind of way. From the Roaring Twenties through the Great Depression, World War II and the Cold War, every Washington seventh-grader had endured Miss Crowne's singing class, one period a week, for the entire school year.

Those generations would forever know by heart the patriotic songs of World War I. Whatever the season was—Christmas, Easter, Thanksgiving—it didn't matter, Miss Crowne always had her classes sing at least one World War I song, every class, every time, decade in, decade out. By the end of the year her seventh-grade classes knew them far better than the Doughboys themselves. When she played those songs on the piano, she would stare at the ceiling, misty-eyed. "Over There," "My Buddy," "Give My Regards To Broadway"—even the bawdy "Mademoiselle from Armentieres" carried her away into her own private wonderland when she banged out chords on her piano while singing "Inky dinky parlez-vouz" at the top of her lungs. Legend had it that Miss Crowne had lost her one-true-love "over there" during the Great War, which was why she never married, but most people thought she never married because she was such a bitch.

All seventh-graders reported back to their home rooms at the eleven-thirty bell. "We will walk in single file," Miss Crowne said. "And there will be no talking in the halls. Other classes are in session."

At eleven-thirty-five, she led them up the stairs to their assigned tables in the third-floor cafeteria. Miss Crowne went a step further than most other teachers, assigning seats at lunch in the same order as homeroom. She strongly disapproved of allowing pupils to sit wherever they pleased as it led to cliques, which always led to trouble.

Mulligan and McGill picked up trays and moved down the line as the cooks—middle-aged women in powder blue aprons, candy-striped blouses and sanitary hair nets—dished out the daily fare: a box of milk, a pizza-burger or hot dog, a scoop of macaroni-and-cheese or potato salad, and a big spoonful of green beans with tiny bits of bacon. For desert, they could choose between two gingersnap cookies or a jiggly bowl of red Jell-O with fruit cocktail chunks.

As they pushed their trays along the shiny metal rails toward the register the McGill kid kept standing up on the balls of his feet, looking all over the big room, and said, "There she is. Oh shit."

"Who?"

"Cindy Seymour, over there, with the long black hair. See her, in the red skirt? I'm going to go see how she's doing."

"Better not," Mulligan warned him. "You know what Crowne said."

"She knows what she can do," McGill said with a dismissive sneer.

On the way back to their table McGill said, "Come on, let's cut over," and he veered out of the main aisle and threaded his way through the aisles to the girl's table. Mulligan followed, watching as McGill stopped behind the girl and said, "Hi, Cindy, how was your summer?"

"Fine," she said, not bothering to look up, or asking how his summer had been, or even to mention his name. Instead, she opened her box of milk, carefully slipped the wrapper off her straw, dipped it in, and took a big sip.

Mulligan stopped long enough to check the girl out and continued on to his and McGill's assigned table, watching as McGill made a fool of himself while the girl ignored him. Miss Crowne was also watching, and quick as a cat she darted across the room, snuck up behind McGill and filliped the back of his ear with the nail of her middle finger—SNICK!

McGill yelled, "OW!" and jerked his head around, shrivelling into silence when confronted by Miss Crowne's withering stare.

"No talking to other classes at lunch!" Miss Crowne ordered in a high, shrill voice, making sure everyone in the cafeteria got the message. "You're grown-ups now, and we can't have you running around willy-nilly, talking to whomever you please. Is that understood, young man?"

"Yes," McGill answered.

"Yes what?"

"Yes, Miss Crowne."

"That's better. Now get back to your own table!"

Cindy and the other girls at the table giggled as McGill flushed in embarrassment and slunk away.

In addition to homeroom and lunch, Mulligan and McGill had one regular class together—social studies. The teacher was the young, radical and flamboyant Mr. Branch, who drove a yellow Karmen Ghia sports car and always had a bright silk, perfectly folded three-point handkerchief in his sportcoat pocket. He had not one but two masters degrees, in Education and in Social Science, and he was gaining a reputation among his peers for actually educating his students.

"You all have heard about the presidential debates coming up between Vice President Richard Nixon and Senator John Kennedy," he told them that first day. "Well, we're going to have our own debates."

Mr. Branch divided the class into eight teams. There would be four different debates, each on a different topic of current interest, both pro and con. He had written the topics and positions on pieces of paper, one for each student, placed them in a goldfish bowl and walked around the room as they all picked one out. Mulligan got the negative side of the question: Resolved: Right-to-Work laws should be repealed. McGill pulled the affirmative on the topic: Resolved: Earl Warren should be impeached. The debates would begin in four weeks. Every student left Branch's class that day in total fear. Nobody had ever been in a debate, or done research in a library, and everybody was scared about being forced to speak in public.

The second day of school, Mulligan wore a Kennedy button he got from his dad. He flashed it at McGill at their adjoining lockers outside homeroom; McGill glared and said, "Bet you a buck Nixon wins."

"You're on!" Mulligan shot back.

They shook hands to seal the bet, but before they released the shake they were gripped by an iron-fisted force that spun them around by their jacket sleeves.

"Michael! Arthur! Come with me!" Crowne commanded as she clenched tight to their jackets and dragged them down the hall through crowds of students, shouting, "Get out of the way, get out of the way!"

Crowne released her grip at the office reception counter. She pointed to a wooden bench along the wall and said, "Sit and be quiet." She knocked on a door with a frosted-glass window with "Daniel R. McCracken, Principal" written in gold letters. Everybody knew "Whackin' McCracken" would just as soon swat you as look at you.

The McGill kid asked him in whisper, "What'd you do?"

"Nothing," Mulligan whispered back. "What'd you do?"

"Nothing. I put my cigarette out before I came in. They can't get me just for having 'em."

"Want to bet?" Mulligan said.

"Yeah, maybe they can," McGill said. Then glancing all around to be sure no one was looking, he took the pack of Old Gold filters he had sneaked from his mom's carton out of his jacket pocket and stuffed it down the front of his underwear.

Miss Crowne opened the door; a man's voice barked, "Get in here!"

McCracken was in his forties, about five-ten, with a stocky build and a graying flattop that bristled up from his scalp like a shoe brush. Behind him on the wall, next to pictures, plaques and diplomas, was a wooden paddle, about two feet long, the kind known in college fraternities as a "pledge-paddle."

All the male teachers had paddles of one style or another, many of them hand-made by Mr. Byers, the woodshop teacher. But only McCracken's had a red-and-gold Marine Corps insignia by the handle, and "Semper Fi" stacked vertically, top to bottom. It was rumored the other side of the paddle, the side he got you with that nobody ever saw, had USMC burned into the wood—right at the sweet spot—but backwards, like a branding iron.

"Boys," McCracken said, "I know this is only your second day, so I'll go easy on you if you tell me all about it."

Neither of them had a clue what he was talking about. Mulligan noticed a photo on the wall of McCracken in a uniform with General Douglas MacArthur pinning a medal on his chest. Anybody who got a medal from MacArthur couldn't be as bad as everybody said.

"Well, I'm waiting," McCracken said.

"But…I don't know what you mean," McGill said.

"Gambling," McCracken said. "Have you been gambling?"

"Oh, no, Mr. McCracken!" McGill blurted out. "Absolutely not!"

Mulligan kept silent, but it didn't matter. They were about to learn just how serious the problem of gambling was in the football-crazy towns of western Pennsylvania. First and second generation immigrants from places like Italy and Poland had not given up the old ways simply because all forms of gambling—from cards to dice to dominoes to horses to pool to football parlays—had long been made illegal by the blue-nosed Quaker legislature of the Commonwealth of Pennsylvania.

Of particular concern were the weekly "parlay sheets" handed out by bookies in the local Mafia. The game was to beat the Las Vegas point-spreads by choosing the winners among some fifty college and pro games: Pick three winners, win five to one; pick four, win twenty-five to one; pick five, win fifty to one and so on. Parlay sheets could be obtained under the counter at barber shops or from clerks at newsstands, bars, and gas stations, as well as from co-workers and fellow students who sidelined as "runners" in lunch rooms, offices and factory assembly lines.

To play, you picked up a sheet on Monday or Tuesday and kept it for a couple days, figuring which games you wanted, how many to play, and how much to bet. By Friday afternoon, your cash and completed slip had to be in with your runner. You kept a stub as proof on the chance you won, and the runner got ten cents on the dollar from his bookie for handling the transaction. In America's industrial heartland, gambling was a passion, right down to junior high. Police estimated that some weeks as many as two hundred Washington boys put up a dollar, and often much more, on the football parlays. Girls just didn't seem to be interested.

"In this school," McCracken informed them, "gambling is not

tolerated. Now, I'll give you one more chance to come clean."

McGill had been in a poker game Saturday night and had lost his two-dollar a week allowance and the twelve dollars he had saved from mowing lawns all summer. He was broke. Maybe that's what McCracken meant?

"But I only played poker on Saturday," McGill said. "That doesn't count. It was still summer vacation."

Miss Crowne's face turned the color of Dentyne chewing gum. "Arthur, you placed a wager with Michael. I heard you with my own ears."

"You mean…you mean on Kennedy and Nixon?" McGill said.

"Yes," Miss Crowne said with her famous glare.

"But that's not gambling," McGill said, throwing up his hands in disbelief. "It's the election!"

"Not gambling?" McCracken said, his voice rising. "Ha! What would you call it? You wagered money on an event. It's the same as dice or cards or the parlays. Bookies take bets on elections, just like football. It's against the law and you were caught. Do you deny it?"

It looked like McCracken had them. "We didn't know," Mulligan said. "Nobody told us."

"There's an old saying that ignorance of the law is no excuse," McCracken said as he leaned forward in his chair to emphasize the point. "It's a lesson best-learned when you're young. So, you admit it?"

"I…uh…I guess," Mulligan said.

"And you?" McCracken said to McGill.

"No! It's not fair. It's just the election," McGill said waving his hands back and forth like a policeman signaling for traffic to stop. "It's not gambling. It doesn't count. I didn't even give him odds. Honest."

"You stand at attention when you're in this room!" McCracken yelled, startling McGill into motionless silence.

McCracken stared, trying to figure out if the kid was a wise-ass or just young and stupid. He zeroed in on the Nixon button, then glanced at the other kid's Kennedy button, and shook his head. "Okay, I'll go easy on you two this time. Only one swat each. You'll be an example for the rest of the school."

McCracken stepped into the main office, went to the intercom, flicked the switch for the teachers' lounge and said, "This is McCracken. Anybody there?"

After a moment a woman's voice squawked over the speaker. "Dorothy Hiflinger here."

McCracken, said, "Dorothy, is—"

"Did you have a nice summer?" she said. "We went—"

"Dorothy, I have a disciplinary situation. I need a witness."

"Pug here, Mac," said a man's voice. "Be right over."

A minute later the boys' gym teacher, football and basketball coach and local sports legend Romeo Pugliano, who even the mayor called "coach," swaggered in. He was decked out in the school colors—an orange and black T-shirt, a black nylon windbreaker with orange trim, black gym shorts with orange trim; even his white socks had black and orange trim. A silver whistle and a stopwatch hung on straps around his neck. A pack of Camel cigarettes poked out of his breast pocket, and there were yellow nicotine stains on the inside of the middle and index fingers of his right hand. He was about the same age as McCracken but a little shorter, and his belly stuck out over his gym shorts like a basketball. To see him in street clothes, nobody would have guessed he taught physical education, but his teams had a great record.

"We'll take it from here, Lyla," McCracken told Miss Crowne. "Thank you for bringing this to my attention."

The bell rang, and Pugliano held the door and smiled as Miss Crowne hurried back to take roll and lead the Pledge and the Prayer.

McCracken ordered, "You, both of you, wait on the bench. I'll get to you after announcements."

They went out and sat on the bench and waited for the daily announcements, which always came at eight-forty. It was the busiest time of day for the secretaries and the office was buzzing with the comings and goings of students with problems, couriers with attendance reports, guidance counselors, bus drivers with manifests, parents and teachers, even the school nurse, who was checking her mail slot. The adults who saw them on the disciplinary bench stared with disapproval while kids smirked with a "What'd you do?" fascination.

Right on time a secretary switched on the intercom and said, "May I have your attention. Band tryouts will be held tomorrow, so...."

McGill kicked Mulligan on the leg and whispered, "Look what you did to us."

"Me? You're the one made the bet."

"You shook on it."

The door opened and they shut up as Pugliano and McCracken went to the intercom station. The secretary said, "Coach Pugliano has an announcement about tryouts."

Pugliano spoke for a minute about the school's athletic policy, how any boy was welcome to tryout for any sport. He read off the tryout schedules, from football this week to cross-country in the spring. He ended by saying, "Miss Spandau will have an announcement tomorrow for you girls who want to go out for cheerleading. Now, here's Principal McCracken."

McCracken sat down at the mic. "I am sorry to report that we have just had our first case of gambling. Now you older students know I say this every year: Gambling is not permitted on school grounds. Period. No exceptions. Cards, dice, flipping coins, all of it. And that especially means the parlays. Many of you might not even know what they are, but all of you be warned—just having a parlay sheet in your possession is against the laws of Pennsylvania and the rules of this school.

"Now some of you may be surprised at this, but it is also against the law to place bets on elections. I am only going to say this once. Do not place bets on the election, or you will pay the price. That is all I'll have to say on this. You have been informed. McCracken out."

Then he stood up, took off his sport coat, and barked, "Both of you, on your feet!"

At George Washington Junior High, boys were always punished the old-fashioned way—by swats with a wooden paddle in a well-established procedure. To ensure that no boys were ever abused, every swat had to be witnessed by a second male faculty member. Girls never got swats.

Neither Mulligan nor McGill could have known that McCracken always made sure to administer his swats in the halls, during class, when things were quiet. He believed the CRACK of a well-placed swat echoing up and down the cavernous halls served as a warning to troublemakers. It certainly never failed to get the students' attention. The cries and moans that usually followed a CRACK made his point far better than any lecture ever could.

"You first," McCracken said pointing to McGill. "What's your name?"

"Uh…Art McGill."

"Are you right or left handed?" McCracken asked.

"Uh...right."

"Okay. I want you to take off your jacket, empty your pockets, put everything right there on the floor. Then face the wall and bend over, brace yourself with your left hand, and stick your butt out. Now, we don't want to do any permanent damage," he said with a chuckle, "so take your right hand and grab your private parts and pull them up in front as high as they'll go. Okay. Assume the position."

Sometimes if a swatter's aim was low, or if a boy flinched at the last instant, the swatter could miss and hit the sensitive backside of the upper thigh and any private part dangling nearby. All male teachers were required to use the same tried-and-true procedure in order to maximize student safety.

McCracken loosened up with a few practice swings, like Babe Ruth in the on-deck circle—the Sultan of Swats.

"These your first this year, Mac?" Pugliano asked.

"Yeah. I'm a little rusty," McCracken said as he approached McGill, who was still just standing there. "I told you to assume the position."

As he turned around to face the wall McGill said, "Uh, what do you mean 'private parts,' Mr. McCracken?"

"Your testicles, stupid! Cup them in your hand, and pull them up in front of you."

"My testicles?" McGill said. "Oh, you mean my *balls*?"

Mulligan couldn't hold in it and a laugh leaked out. "Hmmmffff!"

"And just what's so funny?" McCracken demanded.

"Uh, nothing," Mulligan said as he wiped his nose with his hand. "I was just trying to hold in a sneeze. I have a cold."

Like many boys, Mulligan had little control over what made him laugh. Especially when the subjects were body parts or bodily functions.

"One more sound and you'll find out the hard way what I can really do with a paddle," McCracken told him, then he turned back to McGill. "Now, bend over and grab 'em and pull 'em up."

McGill seemed confused. "I don't under—"

"God you're dumb," Pugliano said with disgust. "Like this, stupid."

Pugliano demonstrated the position by arching his back, sticking out his butt, and balancing in a three-point stance, his left hand against wall. Then he cupped his nuts in his right hand and pulled them up in front of his bulging abdomen. "See, pull 'em tight, so they don't dangle. Keep 'em high, way up, and don't flinch or stand up till you're told. It's your own damn fault if you get hurt."

Mulligan watched as McGill leaned over and tried to balance himself against the wall with one hand and grab his nuts in the other.

"Lower, get down lower," McCracken ordered. "No, no, not like that. Don't bend your knees. Christ you are dumb. Keep your legs straight, and stick your ass out."

Watching McGill attempting to balance against the wall with one hand while trying to move the pack of cigarettes in his underwear off to the side so he had room to pull his nuts up was funny enough, but then Pugliano, pointing at McGill's feet, said, "What's with the red shoes? You some kind of a fruit?"

Mulligan couldn't hold it. "Haw, haaa haaa ha," and then McGill cracked up too and neither of them could stop guffawing.

McCracken was furious. "Shut up, both of you. So, you think this is some kind of a joke?"

"Well, look at this," Pugliano said, pointing to a pack of Old Golds that had appeared on the floor between the red suede loafers.

"Those yours?" McCracken demanded.

"Uh…no," McGill said.

"Then whose are they?"

"They're my mom's. I'm keeping them for her."

"You mean you stole them from your mother," Pugliano said as he reached down and confiscated the pack. "What a jerk."

McCracken said, "This will cost you, one swat each—*extra*. You for laughing, and you for the cigarettes. Care to try for more?"

McGill tried to protest. "But it's not fair. I didn't—"

McCracken wasn't having it. "Shut up and assume the position!"

McGill braced himself against the wall, cupping his nuts as tight as he could. The most important thing was not to scream or cry out, so nobody could call him a sissy. No matter what, he must not cry out.

Like a golfer addressing a ball on a tee, McCracken lined up the paddle, tapping the sweet spot of the paddle to the fleshy part of McGill's cheeks. Then he took a deep breath, addressed the target one more time, cocked his arm and teed off on McGill with two rapid-fire power swats.

WHACK!

"Unfff!"

CRACK!!

"Unhhhh."

McCracken lowered the paddle and said, "Stand up."

McGill straightened up and turned around, still holding his nuts, his eyes tearing, his ass searing. He had not cried out.

"*You*...assume the position," McCracken ordered, and Mulligan took his turn. WHACK—CRACK. He did not cry out or grunt, even a little.

Pugliano escorted them to Miss Crowne's room. She said not a word as they went to their seats and sat down, gingerly, trying not to grimace or give her any sense of satisfaction.

When the bell rang they zoomed to the boys' room. Most of the other guys followed, eager to see if the stories about McCracken's paddle were true.

Mulligan and McGill pulled down their pants while the guys looked on. Everybody had something to say.

"Wow!"

"Fuck me!"

"Look at that!"

"Holy shit!"

Standing with their pants down, they could see each other's asses, but they could not see much of their own. The mirrors above the sinks were too high for self-ass inspections; they would have had to stand in the basins of the sinks and then bend down to see their own.

The guys made them bend over side-by-side and took a vote. They agreed that Mulligan's welts were fatter, with a flaming, orange-red, almost neon glow; McGill's were narrower, as if the paddle had hit the exact same spot both times. McGill's were a deeper red, with two purplish-green ridges swelling up where the edges of the paddle had sunk in. Thanks to the bumpy red ridges, the guys voted McGill's ass the winner. A few guys swore they could see a US on one of Mulligan's cheeks and an MC on the other. While it wasn't as purple as McGill's, there was still a lot of swelling so it was hard to tell for sure. Not everyone agreed, but enough guys saw it to confirm the legend of McCracken's paddle.

Chapter 3

Peanuts & Crackerjack

October 5th, 1960

IN THE NORTHEAST QUARTER OF AMERICA THE EARLY WEEKS OF OCTOBER can be the most vibrant days of the year. Days shorten, pumpkins ripen, and at night Jack Frost paints the mapled landscape in brilliant hues of red and gold, yellow and orange as Mother Nature eases into her rest cycle and the smoky, pungent fragrances of autumn invigorate the air. And sometimes, in the very best years, Indian Summer comes around and warms up early October like it was the middle of May. The opening game of the 1960 World Series, between the upstart Pittsburgh Pirates and the mighty New York Yankees, was to be played such a day, a glorious afternoon filled with cotton-ball clouds that roamed the bright blue Pennsylvania sky like an endless herd of white buffalo.

Neither Jenny nor her brothers nor even their mom suspected anything until that morning when her dad, in his blue terrycloth bathrobe, walked into the kitchen at breakfast and, like a magician doing card tricks, fanned out six tickets and said, "How would you like to skip school today?"

As they rode the crowded trolley to the game her dad, "Sal" to his friends, sat in the middle, an arm around each of "his girls," Jenny and her mom, Jean. Her obnoxious older brothers, Tony, Jimmy, and Nicky, were making their usual ruckus a few rows back.

Jenny sat next to the window, studying her reflection in the glass, worried that her make-up might smear and then everybody would see the spidery red and purple discolorations on her new nose. Dr. Emery had promised everything would be normal by now, but he lied. It still hurt, especially at night, and she had to sleep on her back and use a special pillow to brace her head. But the worst was sitting and watching everybody else have all the fun playing in the pick-up baseball games down at the corner. At her last check-up she asked, "Dr. Emery, when can I play baseball again?"

"Not for at least another month," he sternly warned. "The risk of permanent damage to the reconstruction is too great."

"But baseball will be over and all the boys will be playing football."

Her mom had been standing off to the side, smiling, like she'd planned the whole thing. "It's good timing, Jennifer. Now that you're becoming a young lady, you have to stop being such a tomboy. Baseball is much too rough. It's not at all ladylike."

"But I'm really good, Mom. I get a lot of hits, and I'm faster than stupid Nicky or Rusty Limbergh or Joey Corvano. Everybody says I don't throw like a girl."

"How good you are isn't the point. The point is you *are* a girl. But isn't it nice Dr. Emery says you can still take your dance lessons?"

"But baseball's a lot more fun."

"I took dance lessons when I was your age and I had plenty of fun."

It was no use arguing. Her mom had never played baseball, not in her whole life, not even once.

The bell clanged and she forgot all about Dr. Emery as the car lurched down the line with the comforting clackety-clack-clack of steel wheels on steel tracks. Newcomers squeezed in, standing up and swaying back and forth to keep their balance as they gripped the silvery poles or the leather hoops dangling from the ceiling. Twenty blocks. Stop. Nineteen. Stop. They'd never get there.

As the trolley clacked down Fifth Avenue past the grand mansions of "Millionaires Row," she wondered what it would be like to live in a house where butlers served breakfast in bed on silver trays and maids did the ironing. They were still too far away to see Forbes Field, the Pirates' baseball park, but it was directly across the street from the Cathedral of Learning, "Skyscraper U," the University of Pittsburgh's forty-two-story gothic-style classroom campus, which loomed bigger and bigger at every trolley stop. The Cathedral stood guard like a solitary gray giant over the Oakland district, the city's cultural center, which was filled with museums, universities, concert halls, and the university's football stadium where both Pitt and the Steelers played.

She was double-checking her reflection for make-up smears on her new nose in her reflection in the trolley's window when somebody yelled, "*Look*! The Goodyear blimp!"

Everybody craned their necks to see. She had only seen the blimp on TV, and now there it was, in real life. She watched as it lazily circled the Cathedral, just high enough to keep a pinprick from the needle-sharp lightning rod tip from popping the blimp like a party balloon.

There were lots of black-and-gold Pirate caps and jackets, and kids with ball gloves hoping for a souvenir. She caught two boys staring at her. They quickly glanced away, pretending to be innocent, but she'd caught them all right. It was driving her crazy the way boys were always staring at her now. On her first day of junior high, it was as if her popularity switch had flipped from OFF to ON. Even Rusty Limbergh started being nice. A few girls who she thought were her friends tried to convince the boys that her new face didn't count because it wasn't natural, but the boys didn't seem to care.

When the trolley skreeked to a stop, the conductor called, "Forbes Field," and everybody hurried off. The old ballpark, which had been built in 1909 and for many decades had been famous as the most beautiful park in all of baseball, was dressed up and decked out like an elegant grande dame for her first World Series in thirty-three years. The facade was festooned with pennants and draped with banners, and the very air seemed alive with excitement as the leafy tang of Indian summer mixed with the salty scent of fresh roasted peanuts and the sounds of vendors calling, "Programs, here. Get yer programs, here!" For the next few hours this would be the most enchanted place anywhere on Earth, and she would be a part of it.

All her life both her grandfathers, Papa Carlo and Grampy Jim, had told them tales of the glorious season of 1925, the year the Pirates took the World Series from the Senators. She tried to imagine what it must have been like to be alive in the Roaring Twenties when the whole city went crazy all at once. Her mom hadn't even been born yet, and her dad was too young to remember much about it. They also told sad tales about the disastrous Series of 1927, the year the Babe set the all-time home-run record, and the Murderers' Row Yankees crushed the Pirates four games to none. She read in the *Post Gazette* that sports writers back then claimed that the Pirates had given up before the Series even started, chickening out before the first game after watching Babe Ruth and Lou Gehrig take batting practice. When she asked if it were true, Grampy Jim said it was a New York lie, but Papa Carlo just shrugged and said it didn't matter because "Nobody could'a beat da bastards anyway."

This year the smart money was on the Yankees to take the Series in five, maybe even blow the Bucs out four straight, just like in '27. The Pirates had not been back to a World Series since, while the Yankees seemed to win it every year. It didn't seem fair that the Yankees got to win so much, but nobody ever did anything about it.

Every year their dad took them to a few games, but they were usually in the cheap seats in the right-field bleachers. Today, their seats were just a few rows behind the Pirate dugout. "What did you pay for these, Sal?" her mom asked as they settled in.

"It's a bennie from the new job," he answered with a straight face. He had just been promoted to lieutenant in the fire department and Jenny was certain he wanted her mom to believe the tickets were like the new red Plymouth with a siren and P.F.D. in gold letters on the doors the city of Pittsburgh had given him to use. She would have bet a month's allowance that the tickets weren't a bennie at all, that he was fibbing so her mom wouldn't find out he'd been playing poker down at the Sons of Italy lodge again; Jenny couldn't help wondering what kind of hand her dad had drawn to win such great seats.

They only had tickets for today's game, so she was determined to take it in slowly, like a chocolate milkshake she wanted to last forever. She watched the groundskeepers dragging a hose along the edge of the grass by the ivy-covered brick wall in deep center field near the 440 sign, the deepest outfield in baseball, spraying the warning track with a fine mist of water and making a perfect little rainbow.

Everybody looked up as a biplane came along, did a few loop-de-loops, and began skywriting BEAT 'EM BUCS! in flowing streams of black-and-gold smoke across the sky. She borrowed her dad's U.S. Army binoculars and could see the pilot's leather helmet and funny goggles, looking just like a World War I fighter ace with his black-and-gold Pirate scarf fluttering in the breeze.

They had come early to see the modern-day Yankees—the Bronx Bombers of Mickey Mantle, Roger Maris and Yogi Berra—take batting practice. She especially wanted to see the most famous athlete in all of sports, Mickey Mantle, "The Mick," America's baseball heartthrob. She *ooohed* and *aaahhed* with the rest of the crowd as Mickey's mighty swings sent ball after ball rocketing into the upper-deck bleachers in right, or soaring into the trees beyond the ivy-covered wall in left. She hoped that the Pirates were not watching, so they wouldn't chicken out before the game even started, like they did back in '27.

When Mickey's turn was over, Jenny scanned the stands with the binoculars, looking for anybody famous. Her dad pointed to boxes in the first row. "There, with the governor. That's Lyndon Johnson."

As she focused the binoculars Nicky asked, "Who's he, Dad?"

Jenny knew. "He's Kennedy's running mate."

"Who's Kennedy?" Nicky asked. "And what's a running mate?"

Nicky was a whole year older than she was, but he didn't know anything. What an idiot.

"Look," her mom said, pointing to men coming on to the field from the Pirate dugout. "There's Bing Crosby!"

Jenny wasn't surprised. Everybody in Pittsburgh knew that the world's most famous singer owned twenty-five percent of the Pirates and came all the way from Hollywood every year to see a few games. She wondered how many other famous people were here today?

Just then a boy carrying a bag of peanuts and a ball glove came rushing down the steps, stopped two rows in front of them, checked his ticket stubs, backed up, looked at the numbers on the seats, and screamed, "Dad! Grampa! I found them. Hurry!"

A man wearing the same kind of fedora hat that Grampy Jim always wore yelled, "We'll be there in a minute, Arthur. You get in first, then your father. I need to be on the end to use my new Polaroid."

The boy rushed in, flipped down the upright wooden seat next to hers with a BANG, plopped himself down, looked at her and said, "Hi."

He was kind of cute, and about her age, but much too immature. "Hello," she said, polite and ladylike, careful not to encourage him.

Suddenly she felt her mom's hand shake her by the shoulder. "Jenny, look—with Bing. Isn't that Bob Hope?"

She cried out, "*Bob Hope*!" Nobody but nobody could make her laugh like Bob Hope. She loved his hilarious "road" movies with Bing Crosby almost as much as her mom did, and his monthly comedy special was her favorite TV show, better than *I Love Lucy* or *The Honeymooners* or *Lassie.*

She had just focused the binoculars on Hope when a group of men came along in the row in front and blocked her view as they made their way to their seats. She jumped to her feet, but still couldn't see, so she hopped up on her wooden seat, stood on her tip-toes, and at last was able to see over the men and focus on the world's most famous comedian. Who could believe it—Bob Hope, right here in Pittsburgh!

She watched for a minute or two until Hope and Crosby disappeared into the dugout, and as she went to climb down she saw that the boy was scrunched down low, in his own seat, his eyes just inches from her knees—*peeking up her skirt*!

She pulled it tight to her legs, jumped down and demanded in a fierce whisper, "Just what do you think you're doing?"

"Huh?"

She leaned in close, right in his face. "You were looking up my skirt."

He slumped back, stammering, "I…I…I was not."

He was guilty all right. "You're lying. I *caught* you."

"You…you…jumped up…and I…I couldn't help it. But I hardly saw anything. Honest."

Hardly saw anything? *Couldn't help it*! Of all the nerve. She had never been so completely mortified. She sat down in a huff, furious. She must try to be what sophisticated people called "nonchalant," and calmly ran her fingers through her hair.

After that, she ignored him completely…only checking him out with quick sideways glances when she was certain he wasn't looking. He was dressed okay, in a plaid Madras shirt. But when he took a NIXON-LODGE button out of his pants and pinned it on his shirt she almost broke out laughing. How could anybody be for Nixon? Then she noticed the ugliest things she'd ever seen in her whole life—red suede loafers, and an uncontrollable giggle leaked out. He looked at her funny, but she stared straight ahead and pretended the giggle had nothing to do with him or his corny red shoes or his stupid Nixon button. What a goof!

"What grade you in?" the goof asked.

"Seventh."

"Hey, me too. Where you from?"

"Shadyside."

"Where's that?"

"You don't know? Where are you from?"

"Milltowne."

"Where's *that*?"

"About an hour. You going steady with anybody?"

She was too flabbergasted at his audacity to even know if she should answer.

He said, "I am…want to see?" and before she could say no he whipped out his wallet and was showing off a school photo, the kind classmates trade every year. "Nobody's as pretty as Cindy Seymour. Not even Annette Funicello in the Mouseketeers."

The girl in the photo was cute, but she didn't care about that. She was curious why any girl would go steady with a goof with red shoes and a Nixon button. He was lying. She could feel it. Maybe she could trip him up, like Perry Mason on TV, and said, "Take it out and let me see."

He looked at her like he didn't trust her, so she gave him an innocent smile and said, "I'm not going to hurt it. I just want to look."

"Uh, well, I guess it's okay," and he slipped the photo out of the wallet's plastic sleeve and handed it to her.

When her girlfriends gave their pictures to their boyfriends they always wrote something on the back to make them special. She flipped the photo over. There was nothing special on the back; in fact, there was nothing on it at all. She had him. "If you're going steady, how come she doesn't say how much she likes you?"

His face reddened as he took the photo back from her. "Uh…it's from last year. She didn't like me then."

"You're lying. I can tell." She almost always could tell, having learned from her stupid brothers that boys lied and made things up all the time. Grown-up men too, especially her dad, but even Papa Carlo and Grampy Jim. They all did it.

He said sheepishly, "I am not," lying again—now she was absolutely sure. He slipped the photo back in his wallet and offered her his bag of peanuts. "Want some? They're still hot."

She liked hot roasted peanuts, so she took a few, but not so many as to be unladylike, and remembering to be polite, said, "Thank you."

"Arthur, look," said the boy's father, pointing to the very best seats in the very front row. "That's the Mellon's box. Looks like it's just their kids here today."

"Who are they?" the boy asked.

"You've never heard of the Mellons?" the grandfather asked.

"Are they famous?" asked the boy.

"They're just about the richest family in the whole world," the grandfather said with admiration, "and that's better than famous. They control Gulf Oil, Alcoa Aluminum, Mellon Bank, half the coal mines in America and not even God knows what else."

The boy was confused. "You mean those kids own our bank?"

"Their family controls it," his grandfather explained, "and that's almost the same thing. The Milltowne branch finances the floor-plan that puts the new cars in our showroom. They gave us our tickets today."

The boy cocked his head, perplexed. "You mean the Mellon kids gave us our tickets?"

"Not exactly," the grandfather said. "Their bank gave them to us because they can write it off."

"What's write-it-off mean, Grampa? And what's a floor-plan?"

The father laughed as the grandfather said, "It's a line-of-credit to put new cars on our showroom floor."

"Huh?" said the boy.

"You'll understand when you're older, Arthur," said the father.

Jenny's dad had also noticed the activity in the Mellon's box, and he didn't trust Mellons one bit, no matter how young they were. "Look, Jean—Mellon kids," he said to her mom in a wary undertone. "The adults must be at their fancy races. Serves 'em right to miss the game."

As luck would have it, the World Series conflicted with the annual Rolling Rock Races, which were being held that very afternoon at the Mellons' exclusive Rolling Rock Club in the Ligonier Valley in the mountains east of Pittsburgh. The featured race was the King of Spain Gold Cup, the most prestigious steeplechase in America. The *Pittsburgh Press* and *Pittsburgh Post-Gazette* society pages were filled with stories about the week of races and black-tie parties that the Mellons hosted every year for a few hundred horse-breeding friends with names like DuPont, Rockefeller, Whitney, Harriman, DeWolfe, Biddle, Morgan and Vanderbilt. The Rolling Rock Races were the social event of the year for Pittsburgh's high-society, as well as for the horsey set from all over America and Europe. The Rolling Rock races could not be postponed, not even for the World Series.

The grandfather took a picture of the boy and the father with his Polaroid, then pulled a strip of paper out of the back of the camera and held it gingerly while he checked his old-fashioned pocket watch. When he said, "That's sixty seconds," he pulled the paper apart and watched with his son and grandson peered over his shoulder as the photo materialized like magic.

Jenny's father held up their Kodak Brownie and said to the boy's grandfather, "Hey, mister, you look like you know cameras. Would you take a picture of us?"

"Sure," said the grandfather, and he took the Brownie from her dad. "It's just like my old one."

He stood up and put the viewer up to his eye. "Now everybody smile and say 'cheese.'"

The Abruzzis cheesed on cue, the shutter snapped, and as he handed the Brownie back to her dad he said, "Want me to take one of your family with the Polaroid, so you don't have to wait to see it?"

"Sure, that'd be great," said her dad.

The grandfather put his Polaroid up to his eye and said, "Let's see those smiles again."

The Abruzzis cheesed again, the shutter clicked, and the grandfather yanked a paper out the back and checked his watch. "We have to wait sixty seconds."

This was exciting. When a minute was up, the grandfather peeled off the backing, and holding the photo very gingerly by pinching the edges, passed it to her. "It has to finish developing, so don't touch the front until it's dry or you'll leave fingerprints."

At first she saw only brown blobs, then shapes began to materialize, like ghosts, becoming clearer and clearer as the seconds ticked by. As soon as she could recognize herself she checked the make-up on her nose. Oh my God, could the girl in the photo really be her? It was the first picture of herself she had seen since getting her new nose. If it was true that a camera didn't lie, she was pretty, and not just a little bit pretty—*really* pretty.

Her most obnoxious brother, Jimmy, yelled, "Pass it down, dum-dum." She ignored him as always, but as she stared at the picture an icy chill crept over her as she caught herself in the deadly sin of vanity old Father Zyhowski was always preaching about. She took a last, sinful look, tingling with fear and excitement, and passed it down.

Out on the field, sportscaster Howard Cosell was by the pitcher's mound with a TV camera crew. Suddenly Bob Hope and Bing Crosby walked out. She watched through the binoculars as Cosell interviewed them. When it was over, to her great surprise, Hope and Crosby came into the stands and started up the aisle—*right towards them*!

The boy's father saw them coming and got all excited. He stood up, and as they came close he stepped into the aisle, stuck out his hand and said, "Bob, remember me? I was your liaison officer on the '44 Christmas tour."

Hope stared for a moment, then his face lit up. "Captain McGill?"

"Yes. It's great to see you again."

"No, it's great to see *you* again," Hope said as he pumped the boy's father's hand like he'd found a long-lost brother. "What a tour that was."

The boy's father said, "Remember that time we lost an engine over the Channel?"

"Ha ha, yes," Hope laughed. "And Dorothy Lamour panicked and inflated a lifeboat right there in the cabin and got pinned between the seats. Ha ha."

The two of them cracked up in belly laughs as Crosby watched, a puzzled look on his face. "Wait a minute," Crosby said. "I was on that tour, and I don't recall anything like that."

"You and Ethel Merman had gone on in the plane ahead of us," the boy's father said.

Hope dead-panned like he did on TV, "Bing was already liberating Paris," and everybody in earshot laughed.

The boy's father was radiating with pride—Bob Hope had remembered him—*by name*! "Bob," the boy's father said, "I'd like to introduce my father, Art Senior, and my eldest boy, Arthur. Say, could we get a picture? My wife will be thrilled."

"Sure," Hope said. "Bing, you get in here too."

Jenny's dad stood up and volunteered. "Want me to take it for you?"

"Thanks," said the boy's grandfather, and handed her dad the Polaroid. "It's all set. Just aim and press the button."

Her dad snapped the shot, and as he passed the camera back, Jenny knew he was about to tell one of his own war stories. Nobody ever mentioned the war without him getting in at least one war story.

"I was a sergeant in the Ninth Armored Division with Patton," he began, "and you two did a show for us that was the best thing I ever saw in my entire life. It's an honor to meet you. I'd like to introduce my wife, Jean, my daughter, Jennifer, and my sons, Anthony, James, and Nicholas."

Crosby smiled and gave a little wave, but Hope bugged out his eyes in feigned amazement, touched his finger to the tip of his famous ski-jump nose, and joked, "I've never seen so many honkers in one place before. Almost makes me feel normal."

Hope was famous for having the second-biggest nose in all of show business, behind only comedian Jimmy Durante's gigantic snozzola, and self-deprecating nose-jokes were a staple of Hope's comic schtick. The Abruzzis laughed along with everybody else, flattered that the world's most famous comedian would share a nose-joke with them. What a day!

Then Hope looked right at Jenny, beamed and said, "You have a beautiful daughter. It's a lucky thing for her she takes after her equally beautiful mother."

It was the most exciting moment of her entire life, and it lasted exactly one-tenth of a second, vanishing like a dream when her brother Jimmy shouted out, "She just had a secret nose-job, Mr. Hope!"

She wanted to die, to melt away, to disappear. She hung her head, closed her eyes, and heard Hope crack a joke. "A secret nose-job? Where can I get one of those?"

Everybody was laughing—ha, ha, ha—everybody but Jenny. She kept her face down, totally crushed. There was an awkward silence that seemed to last forever, until she felt a gentle finger under her chin, tilting her head up. She opened her eyes and saw the comforting face of Bing Crosby, trustworthy and wise, like in the movies, when he played a priest or was singing "White Christmas." He smiled kindly and told her, "Try to be gentle on the boys, young lady. You're going to break a lot of hearts before you're through," and with an spiraling flourish of his other hand he crooned to her in his famous baritone, "Vaa vaaa vaaaa vooom."

She heard a camera shutter click, and just then the loudspeaker boomed out, "Ladies and gentleman, the New York Yankees...."

"C'mon, Bing," Hope said, beckoning in mock desperation as he started up the steps. "We've got to see a man about a horse or they'll be out of the gate without us."

Hope and Crosby waved good-bye, and as she watched them bounding up the steps she asked, "Dad, why do they want to see a man about a horse when the World Series was about to start?"

"They need to go to the men's room, Jen," said her father.

A minute after they left, the boy's grandfather leaned over and said to her, "Here young lady, this is for you," then peeled the backing off a Polaroid and handed it to her. "Remember, don't touch it until it's dry."

Her mom peered over as they watched the image come to life. "Oh my, Jeniffer, look, oh, it's you and Bing—and he's singing to you! Oh, what a wonderful picture. Oh, thank you, thank you, thank you."

The grandfather smiled. "My pleasure."

After the excitement of meeting Hollywood's two biggest celebrities died down, and her mom had tucked the photo safely in her purse, Jenny felt a nudge on her arm as the boy whispered in her ear, "What's a nose-job, and how come it's a secret?"

She wanted to die all over again and whispered back, "It's none of your business."

"Did they chop some off and not tell anybody?"

"I said it's none of your business. And quit looking at me like that."

The loudspeakers blared, "Ladies and gentlemen, please rise for our national anthem."

Jenny sang with her hand over her heart, all the while sensing the boy's eyes were examining her nose as if it were under a microscope, a million times worse than looking up her skirt.

The Pirates took the field and the first Yankee came up to bat. The Buc's ace pitcher, Vernon Law, nicknamed "The Deacon," got the Yankees to make two quick outs. Then the loudspeakers sent a buzz through the stands as the announcer said, "Batting third and playing center field, number seven, Mickey...*Mantle*!"

Mickey might be a Yankee, but he was awfully cute in his pinstriped uniform. She leaned over and said, "Daddy, can I see the program?"

Her dad passed it as Mickey settled into the batter's box and took some warm-up swings. She was leafing through to find his page when she heard a loud *CRAAACK*—

The next thing she knew, she was flat on her back, her ears ringing like cathedral bells, with hundreds of colored lights shooting around her head like sparklers on the Fourth of July. Her dad was crouched over her, and everything was in *s-l-o-w* motion.

Her mom was yelling, "My baby! My baby! Jennifer!"

A voice was calling, "I'm a doctor. Let me through!"

The boy was screaming, "It was an accident! It was an accident!"

She couldn't move, couldn't feel a thing. Her dad moved aside and the doctor bent over, lifted up one of her eyelids, then stuck something horrible under her nose. She gagged and pushed the awful stuff away.

"That's a good girl," said the doctor. "What's you're name?"

"Jennifer," she answered in a squeaky voice, surprised at how hard it was to speak.

"Now you just lie still, Jennifer," the doctor said. He took a flashlight from his bag and gently lifted each of her eyelids with his thumb, and shined the light in for a better look. When he finished, he put the light away and said, "Now tell me how many fingers you see."

He stuck his hand in front of her and popped up some fingers. She counted and said, "Three."

"Good, good. Now follow my finger with your eyes. Don't move your head, just use your eyes." She did her best to follow his moving finger, and when he was finished he said, "Let's sit you up."

He put his hand behind her back to help, and as she sat up she began to feel something very bad. Oh, it hurt so much, like her face had caught on fire. When she was upright, she saw everybody staring at her. My God, she was on TV, and she burst out crying.

The doctor put the tip of his middle finger to the tip of his thumb, making the OK circle sign, and held it up high for all to see, and a huge cheer went up throughout the ballpark.

"It's going to be all right, sweetheart," her dad assured her. "That's you they're cheering for. You had everybody worried."

She felt like heavyweight champ Rocky Marciano had punched her out with his bare knuckles. But she must stop crying. She hated anybody to see her cry. She wiped her eyes and took a deep breath, like her singing teacher taught for stage fright. "Daddy, what…happened?"

"Mickey Mantle almost took your head off with a foul ball. You're lucky to be alive, but you're going to be all right."

Her dad was a fireman and knew just about everything, but he lied a lot, so it was hard to tell when to believe him. Just then her mom shouted, "Doctor, she just had a rhinoplasty!"

Why couldn't she just have died?

"Oh my," said the doctor in a grave tone, and he felt all around her face for a minute. "She's lucky it caught her on the cheekbone. I see no signs of a concussion, or of any damage to her nose."

Her mom crossed herself and prayed, "Oh thank God, thank God."

"She's going to have one heck of a shiner, though, there's no doubt about that," said the doctor. "Let's get some ice on it," and he gave her dad two pills, one white, one blue. "These will get her through the game, but talk to her surgeon right away and have her X-rayed, just to be sure." He put a few more pills in an envelope, handed it to her dad, and wrote out a prescription on a pad.

A pop vendor called over, "What's she like?"

"Orange," said her dad, and the vendor passed him a cup, which he held to her lips as she washed down the pills with two little sips. Then the vendor gave her mom another cup filled to the brim with ice, and a souvenir vendor handed her mom a gold Pirate towel to wrap it in.

As they helped her back into her seat she heard the boy say, "Honest, mister, I just tried to catch it."

"Don't worry about it," her dad told him. "It could have been a lot worse if it had hit her head on. You might have even saved her life." Then her dad leaned over and said something she couldn't hear to the boy's father and grandfather, and they all shook hands.

Her stupid brothers were shouting at her all at once about how the ball came screaming off Mickey's bat so fast the boy barely snagged it in his webbing as the momentum carried it smashing into her face and that he made a great catch and it was her own fault she hadn't ducked.

Throughout the rest of the game, the boy kept turning his prize over in his hands, working it into the pocket of his glove, showing it off. Twice, between innings, he let her hold it.

She kept the ice-towel on her face, and even with the ice and the pills it hurt too much to cheer very loud when Bill Mazeroski hit a two-run homer to give the Bucs the lead, or when Roberto Clemente made a diving catch to snuff out a Yankee rally. When Bucs' relief ace, Elroy Face, got the last Yankee out in the top of the ninth inning, she jumped up and down and cheered along with everybody no matter how much it hurt. For the first time in history, the Pittsburgh Pirates had defeated the mighty New York Yankees, six to four, and she had been there. What a game!

The boy's father was in a hurry. "Come on, Arthur, we've got to get a move on to beat the traffic."

The boy looked over to her. "Bye."

"Bye," she said in a whisper, trying to smile through the pain.

A few minutes later she was shuffling along behind her mom on the exit ramp when she heard the boy's father calling, "Arthur! Where'd you go? Come back here! Arthur!"

She felt a tug at her elbow, and turned to see the boy, looking like he was about to burst into tears. "Here," and he grabbed her wrist, pulled it toward him, and slapped the prized Mickey Mantle foul ball into her hand. "You deserve it more than me."

He zoomed off, like he was trying get away before he could change his mind. As he was about to disappear in the rushing crowd, he spun around, cupped his hands to his mouth and yelled, "I hope your secret nose-job's okay."

Chapter 4

Sticks & Stones

THERE WERE NO OFFICIAL FIGURES AS TO HOW MANY GEORGE WASHINGTON seventh-graders were lucky enough to go to the first game of the World Series, but McGill hadn't heard of anybody else. The next day, he brought the ticket stubs, the scorecard, the souvenir program and the Polaroid of him and his father and grandfather with Hope and Crosby and showed them around and told the story of the foul ball.

As he was showing off in his Algebra I class Frankie Dombrowski, who sat behind hi said, "So how come you didn't bring the ball?"

"I, uh, I gave to the girl who got knocked out."

Somebody said, "You gave away a Mickey Mantle foul ball? Are you crazy?"

"Uh...my glove hit her in the face when I caught it and she'd just had a secret nose-job."

"A secret nose-job," Frankie said. "What's that?"

"She wouldn't tell me. I think they made her nose smaller."

A few girls he knew seemed to believe him, or at least pretended to, but none of the guys believed he'd caught a Mickey Mantle foul ball at the World Series and then gave it to some girl he'd never seen before and would never see again. Nobody could be that dumb.

A week later, in game six, the Yankee's ace pitcher, Whitey Ford, shut out the Pirates, twelve to nothing. The game ended before school even let out, and nobody was in a good mood. When Mulligan went to the bus, Mr. Pickens had the hood open and was muttering to himself and doing something with a wrench. "Y'uns listen up. It'll be an hour, maybe more. Y'uns might have to take the late bus."

So one of the ninth-graders, Tiny Tuzinski, led Mulligan and some of the other guys from the South Side bus over to the ballfield and challenged the North Hill guys to a game.

When Mulligan came up to bat, McGill was warming the bench and hoping the older kids would let him in. Somebody from the South Side said, "Go get 'em, Mulligan."

In a spontaneous inspiration, McGill imitated the *Hey, Culligan man!* slogan that everybody knew from the Culligan water-softener commercials on radio and TV.

"Hey, Mulligan man," he called out, mimicking the same weird, nasally voice as the Culligan lady. "When you need an out, call your Mulligan man. Hey, Mulligan man."

Mulligan glared at him, and realizing he was on to something, McGill razzed louder as Mulligan stepped to the plate. "Hey, Mulligan man. If you need an out, who do you call? You call your Mulligan man. Hey, Mulligan man. If you need an out, call your Mulligan man. Hey, Mulligan man."

Mulligan took some practice swings, ignoring the stupid catcalls. McGill kept up the razzing as the pitcher went into his windup. "Hey, Mulligan man. If you need an out, call your Mulligan man. Hey, Mulligan man."

Mulligan popped out weakly to short.

"Nice swing, Mulligan man. If you need an out, call your Mulligan man. Hey, Mulligan man."

McGill had the guys on his side laughing pretty good over it, and next time Mulligan came up to bat, McGill yelled, "If you need an out, who do you call?"

Their second baseman shouted from the infield, "You call your Mulligan man!"

Then the whole North Hill team, the outfielders, infielders, and everybody on the bench, were catcalling, "Hey, Mulligan man."

Mulligan gave McGill the finger, took two swings for strikes, and hammered a pitch over the fence into the oak trees for a home run.

The next morning as Mulligan walked into home room, there was a loud shout, "Hey, Mulligan man."

"Cut it out."

"Cut what out, Mulligan man?" McGill said.

"I said cut it out!"

"Cut out what, Mulligan man?"

"Cut it out, or I'll kick your ass."

"Kick my ass for what, Mulligan man?"

"You know what, Stickman," Mulligan said, getting in a dig at McGill's skinniness.

McGill gave him a fat grin. "You mean sticks and stones can break my bones but names can never hurt me, Mulligan man?"

"I mean it, cut it out!" Mulligan shouted, way too loud, "or I swear

I'll kill you. It'll be you and me, after school!"

Miss Crowne's shrillest voice rang out, "Michael!"

Silence gripped the room.

"Yes, Miss Crowne."

"What did I hear you say?"

"Uh, I—"

"You made a threat. I heard you plain as day."

Mulligan was too angry to watch his step. "He started it, he—"

"I don't care who started what," Miss Crowne said, cutting him off. "You said you'd kill him."

"But I—"

"Don't you play games with me, Michael Mulligan. We all heard it. How many heard it?" Crowne demanded. "Raise your hands."

A bunch of girls' hands shot high in the air and Miss Crowne said, "Do you think the whole class is deaf, Michael?"

"Uh—"

McGill jumped in, trying to keep them both out of trouble. "He means he was gonna kill me in the baseball game after school. But don't worry, Miss Crowne. We're a lot better than them."

The furrows on Crowne's forehead deepened, her bug-eyes darting back and forth. "That's not how I heard it. How about the rest of you?"

Nobody said a word.

"Lisa!" Crowne said, putting the question to her pet, a mousy girl who always volunteered to stay after school to clean the erasers. "I want to know exactly what you heard. All of it."

The girl hesitated for a moment, then blurted out in a single breath, "When Michael came in Art started calling him Mulligan man, like the Culligan lady, you know, hey, Mulligan man, then Michael told him to stop, and Art did it again, and Michael told him to stop, and Art did it again, then Michael called him Stickman and Art said sticks and stones can break my bones but names can never hurt me and Michael said he was gonna kill him after school."

Rearing back like a cobra about to strike, Miss Crowne hissed, "So, you're both guilty! Talking, gambling, disrupting class, and now, insults, threats and fighting. I've had enough of you two."

She pushed the red intercom button on the wall. "This is Miss Crowne. I must speak with Mr. McCracken."

A secretary's voice answered, "He's at a meeting with the

superintendent. He won't be back until after lunch."

"I have troublemakers who need to be disciplined. Give me Mr. Vago."

"I'm sorry, he's there too. Have them report to the bench for ninth period," the secretary said.

"You heard her," Miss Crowne said, shutting off the intercom.

"But I'm supposed to be at basketball tryouts," Mulligan said.

"Oh, really, Michael?" Miss Crowne said, turning the knife, "I thought you were going to kill Arthur after school in a baseball game."

By second period, word was out that Mulligan and McGill had punched each other out in Crowne's home room, McCracken was going to swat their asses good, and they were going to finish it behind the far tennis courts after detention. Nobody gave McGill a chance against Mulligan. Word was also out: Mulligan hated "Mulligan man."

Seventh-graders had physical education twice a week, gym one week, swimming the next. This week, it was swimming, and as Mulligan undressed among the rows of clattering metal doors and the usual raucous locker room antics someone yelled out, "Hey, Mulligan man."

He looked around to settle it right then and there, but McGill wasn't even in his class.

"Okay, who's the wise-guy?"

Mulligan was big and not used to being ragged. Everybody around gave him an innocent "not me" look.

Then from the next row of lockers came, "Hey, Mulligan man."

He ran around the corner only to hear, "Hey, Mulligan man," behind him.

"Hey, Mulligan man," from across the aisle.

"Hey, Mulligan man," from in the showers.

He yelled as loud as he could, "Knock it off or somebody's gonna get hurt!" But that just made it worse.

"Hey, Mulligan man."

"Hey, Mulligan man."

"Hey, Mulligan man."

It didn't matter how big he was, he couldn't fight everybody.

TWEET went the whistle as the gym teacher, Coach Pugliano, opened the double-doors that led to the pool. "Okay, move out, single file, but first pick up your towels at the equipment-cage."

The girls wore one-piece bathing suits when it was their turn for swimming class, but the boys always swam in their birthday suits. Nobody ever explained why.

The class lined up at the equipment-cage window to get their towels. Then they continued in single file, no running or horseplay allowed, into the long, narrow tunnel made of shower tiles and smelling heavily of damp chlorine. As forty bare-assed boys stood shivering in the narrow tunnel, waiting for Pugliano's whistle, the ragging just kept coming, like bullfrogs croaking in a summer pond.

"Hey, Mulligan man."

"Hey, Mulligan man."

"Hey, Mulligan man."

All Mulligan could do was to stand there, seething, and take it.

At lunch, Miss Crowne kept a close watch, stationing herself by their table in case there was trouble, but there wasn't much she could do to keep Mulligan from glowering and McGill from grinning whenever a nasally "Hey, Mulligan man" wafted through the cafeteria.

A seventh game of the World Series didn't happen very often, only about once every five years, so when it did it was the most dramatic moment in all of sports. This year, one of those rare seventh games began at one-thirty that very afternoon. In the first six games, the Yankees had outscored the Pirates 46 to 17, yet by some miracle, the Series was tied at three games each. After kicking the Bucs' butts the day before, the smart money was on the Bronx Bombers to finish off the Pirates in high style.

Many teachers brought their own radios and found legitimate educational reasons to tune in during class. Mr. Zenter, a math teacher, reviewed the principles of percentages that afternoon as his classes calculated batting and earned run averages. Mr. Osborne, a history and geography teacher, used U.S. Geological Survey Maps to teach his classes how to find Forbes Field's exact position on the Earth's surface, latitude and longitude, in degrees minutes and seconds.

As luck would have it, coming up that very night, Oct. 13, 1960, was the third historic meeting between Nixon and Kennedy in the first-ever series of televised presidential debates. Unfortunately for Mr. Branch's social studies class, they were going to stick to the scheduled debate and would not listen on the radio to the most important game in Pittsburgh history.

Mr. Branch had his seventh-grade debating teams doing library research, writing footnoted, bibliographied papers, giving speeches and rebuttals and thinking on their feet, just like in college, and changing the schedule would have meant throwing the rest of the semester completely out of whack. The topic that day was: Resolved: Red China should be admitted to the United Nations. The debate could not be postponed, not even for the seventh game of the World Series, not with the final historic debate between Kennedy and Nixon coming up that very night at which the same question would surely be addressed. For Mr. Branch, who cared little for sports of any kind, it was a chance-in-a-lifetime for a truly teachable moment.

The room was set up with a table and chairs for each team, facing the class with a podium in the middle for whoever's turn it was. There was a step-stool for anyone who needed a boost. Branch closed the door to shut out the noise as the rest of the school followed the game on their teachers' radios, but it was hopeless. The class endured the debate over Mao Tse Tung and the Red Menace in total agony as cheers and groans echoed through the hallways whenever something happened in the game.

After the 2:55 bell rang, Mulligan and McGill reported to the office. The secretary ordered them to sit on opposite ends of the troublemakers' bench—no talking. It wasn't so bad, as now they could finally hear the last innings of the game on the office radio.

"You two again," McCracken said as he and Pugliano came in.

"What's with the red shoes, McGill?" Pugliano asked. "You can tell me. Come on, what is it? You think you're in show business? You trying to be some kind of clown?"

"No, Coach Pugliano," McGill said.

The deluge of war babies had made Pugliano's job much easier. This year, he had one hundred twenty-six seventh grade boys from which to choose the junior varsity teams, way up from just a few years earlier. There were so many warm bodies he could cherry-pick and not have to waste time on second and third-raters. He wanted boys who were big, quick and coordinated.

Pugliano had singled out Mulligan and forty others as being potentially good athletes, and he was going to make sure they tried out for the teams. The McGill kid was not one of them. Far from it. Pugliano sized him up as a kid who, despite his height, would never be good enough for any his teams. Watching McGill stumble through basketball drills in gym class and seeing his hairless body in swimming class, Pugliano pegged McGill as a kid who dropped the pop flies and missed the easy lay-ups. He wouldn't need to shave for years. And then there were those red suede shoes.

"May I have your attention," McCracken said, holding the microphone and waving to Pugliano for quiet. "This is your principal. Now that it's homeroom period, I think those of you who want to hear the game should have that chance. I know I do. After-school activities, including band practice, cheerleading, chess club, sewing club and basketball tryouts will be held as usual. I've asked the bus drivers to turn their radios to the game, and we'll keep the intercom open until it's over. Beat 'em Bucs!"

YAAAY! rang out through the school, and McCracken put the microphone down next to the radio and pointed his finger at Mulligan and McGill. "You two stay right there. Don't move a muscle. I'll deal with you later. Come on, Pug," and he and Pugliano hustled down to the teachers' lounge to watch the game on the snowy black-and-white portable TV with rabbit ears.

"I'm gonna get you, Stickman," Mulligan said after they left.

"What for? You're the one got us in trouble with your big mouth."

"Me? You're the one calling me names."

"Oh, gimme a break. Sticks and stones, Mulligan man. What's the matter, Mulligan man? Can't take it, Mulligan man?"

Mulligan checked to make sure none of the secretaries were looking and punched McGill in the fleshy part of the upper arm, *hard*, got him good with a sharp knuckle.

McGill hadn't seen it coming. "Owww!"

In an hour it would be black and blue. A secretary looked up, so McGill backed off, waiting to get even, biding his time and listening to the game.

In the top of the sixth inning, Yogi Berra, who was famous for sayings like "It ain't over 'till it's over" and "When you come to a fork in the road, take it," hit a homer and put the Yankees ahead, five to four. In the bottom of the eighth, a Pirate pinch hitter smashed a three-run homer to put the Bucs back in the lead, nine to seven, and the school erupted in a cheering frenzy.

The Bucs just needed to get three lousy outs, but the Yankees would not die, and scraped back with two runs on three singles. The Pirates finally got them out just as the school's 3:30 bell rang, and the game went to the bottom of the ninth inning, tied nine to nine.

If the Pirates could score, the game was over. But if the Yankees held, the game would go to extra innings, and everyone knew the Yankees always won in extra innings. Always.

The first Pirate to come to bat was Bill Mazeroski, known for his flawless fielding but weak hitting. The announcer called the play, "Here's the swing, and…" suddenly the voice turned urgent, "…it's a high fly ball going deep to left…this may do it…back to the wall goes Berra…it is—OVER THE FENCE! The Pirates win! The Pirates win!"

Whoops, catcalls, hoots, hoorays, yahoos, all-rights and we-did-its boomed through the halls. Kids went crazy, jumping up and down, banging on desks and lockers, making as much noise as possible.

Outside, the streets were filled with honking horns and people hanging out of car windows and waving. Firecrackers were exploding everywhere, booming and banging and crackling like the Fourth of July. In the parking lot, the bus drivers were furiously BEEP–BEEP–BEEPING their high-pitched school-bus horns.

Coach Pugliano strode down the hall blowing his silver whistle: TWEET–TWEET–TWEET and squeezing off shots with his .22 caliber starter's pistol: KAPOW–KAPOW–KAPOW. Principal McCracken was right beside him and making more noise than anybody as he blasted a hand-held air-horn: WHOOP–WHOOP–WHOOP.

Fifty years later, sports writers would vote that the seventh game of the 1960 World Series was the most exciting baseball game ever played. For the only time in baseball history, the World Series had been won by a walk-off home run in the bottom of the ninth inning.

McCracken and Pugliano came into the office, where Mulligan and McGill were jumping around on the detention bench and waving to kids outside.

"Get down from there!" McCracken shouted, startling them good. "What are you here for? Gambling again?"

"Oh no, Mr. McCracken," McGill said as he sat right down. "Miss Crowne made a big mistake. Honest, we—"

"Now I remember—fighting."

McCracken was not totally without compassion, and while the victory celebrations continued to ring out, he had to decide what to do with these two. "It looks to me like you've made up," he said.

"Oh, yes, Mr. McCracken," McGill said. "It was nothing at all, was it, Mulligan Man? Miss Crowne had it all wrong."

"You sound like a goddamned lawyer," McCracken said. Then he looked each of them in the eye. "So, do I have your word that there will be no fighting?"

"Oh, yes, Mr. McCracken, you can count on us, can't he, Mulligan Man," McGill said, nodding his head up and down.

"And you…?"

It was too late to do anything about the nickname. He was stuck with it. Beating up McGill would only make it worse. "Uh, yes, Mr. McCracken."

"Good. If either of you shows up looking like you've been in a fight, you're both going to pay," McCracken said. "You're friends, right? *Right*! So shake." Mulligan and McGill shook half-heartedly.

"Good. Now both of you, turn around and face the wall."

They faced the wall and started to empty their pockets to take their swats, but McCracken said, "Don't bother." Then he aimed the air horn in the direction of their butts, one at a time, and pulled the trigger–WHHOOOOOPP–WHHOOOOOPP.

"Now, get the hell out of here, and if that old biddy Crowne asks, you tell her I whooped your butts good," McCracken said with a laugh. "And if I ever see either of you on the bench again, you'll be sorry you woke up that morning. Got it?"

Mulligan and McGill would forever remember the day the Pirates won the World Series as the day they got their nicknames. McGill was "Stick," for being skinny. "Mulligan Man" stuck much harder. Soon, nobody outside his family called him Mike or Michael any more. When he went on to play tight end for Milltowne High's championship football team, the stands would erupt in rhythmic chants of "Hey, Mulligan Man, Hey, Mulligan Man," every time he made a big play. The nickname and the chants even followed him after high school when he went on to star for the football team at the United States Naval Academy.

Chapter 5

The Summer of Love

Wildwood, New Jersey
Labor Day Weekend, 1967

FOR MANY YOUNG PEOPLE THE SATURDAY NIGHT OF LABOR DAY WEEKEND was the best party night of the whole year, the last big fling of what would be recorded in cultural history as the "Summer of Love." Unfortunately for nineteen-year-old Arthur Bolton McGill III, if he didn't score tonight, it would mean that the Summer of Love had come and gone, and he would still be a virgin.

McGill and five fraternity brothers had rented a beach house in Wildwood for the summer. They expected to get laid all the time because, with their nifty beach house and TKΩ Penn State T-shirts, they were convinced they were the coolest guys on the shore. They were Tau Kappa Omega, "Tokes," and modesty was not a Toke's strongest virtue.

They had jobs waiting tables in the busy tourist restaurants, and McGill, with his skinny six-foot-two frame, looked like a gangly penguin in his tuxedo-like uniform. He showed up every afternoon at four for the dinner-shift at Murphy's Surf 'n' Turf, which was famous for the best twice-baked potatoes on the shore. He went through the daily drill: arriving at four to set tables; eating at the employee table in the kitchen; ingratiating himself with patrons for tips and getting off around nine-thirty.

After work, he headed out to the bars in the 1962 Triumph sports car his car-dealer father let him drive for the summer. Coming back alone, night after night, made him feel degraded, incompetent, a failure. It was torture listening to the squeaking bedsprings and female yelps and squeals through the plaster walls. He had taken so much ragging from the other guys that twice he slept in the car at a rest stop on the Garden State Parkway and said he'd spent the night down in Cape May with a chick from Rutgers.

It was his last Saturday shift before heading home and then back to his sophomore year in college. He picked up his paycheck and said good-bye to the crew, planning to make the six-hour drive to Milltowne the next day.

He changed out of his waiter's uniform and put on his party uniform—T-shirt, cut-off jeans, and Topsiders with no socks. He carefully put on his GOLDWATER '68 button, then headed to Pelican Bill's, the most happening bar on the Jersey Shore, famous for its seven-mini-drafts-for-a-dollar special. It was rumored to have an arrangement with the cops, and even with a half-assed fake ID you could get in without a hassle.

McGill squeezed up to the bar and ordered a line of mini-drafts, and when the band took a break he saw a girl with long, dark, silky hair sitting at a table, the kind of girl who usually shot him down without a glance. He drank his mini-drafts while checking out the scene, but his eyes kept wandering back to her. She wore a casual black top with white fringe like she stepped right off a magazine cover. When the band came back from its break, he chugged the last draft, walked over and tapped her shoulder. "Would you like to dance?"

She looked up at him with her sparking blue eyes and said, "No thanks."

Getting shot down hurt, but he was used to it. As he turned to leave he was surprised to feel a tug at his T-shirt. He turned around as she said, "You can sit and talk if you want to."

Jenny had seen the skinny guy come in, but didn't pay him much attention. Later, she caught him eyeing her, but then guys were always eyeing her. Besides, he wasn't her type. He was tall and kind of cute with his straight brown hair, with a part down the left side, a style called a "Princeton." But he was way too scrawny, and the Penn State T-shirt meant he wasn't Ivy League like all Bryn Mawr girls expected.

When he asked her to dance she said, "No, thanks," as a matter of course. Then she noticed his GOLDWATER '68 button and she just had to find out what kind of a dork was still cheering for Goldwater three years after Johnson buried him in the '64 landslide.

"My name's Art," he said as he sat down. "What's yours?"

"Jenny."

She liked to think of herself as a good person and disliked people who thought too much of themselves. She felt guilty when she would walk into a room and guys would stop whatever they were doing and stare at her. Some girls had no power over guys at all, while others loved to flaunt theirs to get guys all twisted around. Jenny tried not to abuse her power, but sometimes she just couldn't help it. Guys often told her she reminded them of glamorous Audrey Hepburn, but with longer hair, or sultry Natalie Wood in *Gypsy*, or Mrs. Peel, the sexy, karate-kicking heroine in the TV show *The Avengers* played by Diana Rigg.

About to start her sophomore year on a partial scholarship, Jenny was intent on going on to law school so she could make a difference in the world. She was very political, and was overcome with curiosity about the Goldwater button; she never really expected the guy would have anything interesting to say.

The first thing he asked her was where she went to school and what she was studying.

"I'm majoring in psychology and trying to decide whether to minor in French or music."

"Music?" he said. "What do you play?"

"Piano, but I really like to sing."

"Wow, that's great. I write songs and play guitar."

"You write songs? What kind?"

"Mostly Bob Dylan, Paul Simon, stuff like that. But in high school I played in a band, Frankie and the Dynamos, so I do some rock and roll too. We were hot. Have you ever been in a band?"

"No, but I've always sung in choirs, and I had singing parts in 'South Pacific' and 'The King and I' in high school."

"Wow, you're an actress too. So are you going to Hollywood or Broadway after you graduate?"

"No, I'm too practical for that. I'll be going to law school."

"I know what you're saying. I figure on going to law school too and doing music on the side. I mean, you never know."

"I agree completely," she said. "After law school, I'm going to work for peace and justice, maybe with Martin Luther King or Bobby Kennedy." She reached over and flicked his Goldwater button with her finger. "So do you really want Goldwater to run again?"

"Oh, yes, absolutely," and he got all wound up about how Democrats were ruining the country and how only a conservative Republican like Goldwater could get America back on track. "Goldwater said, 'Extremism in the defense of liberty is no vice,' and he was right."

His ignorance got her dander up, and they debated for an hour about Red China, right-to-work laws, Vietnam, civil rights, John Wayne,

LSD and a host of other topics without even a hint of small talk, sometimes agreeing, mostly not.

"You know, Jenny, we've got the same dream," he told her, boldly taking her hand in his from across the table. "We both want to make the world better, we just come at it from different angles."

The singer called out, "Sorry, folks, but the state of New Jersey says it's time for last call, so suck 'em up and hit the bricks. This is the last dance," then the keyboard player cranked up the organ intro to the monster hit of the Summer of Love, "Light My Fire," by a new group called The Doors.

"Let's dance," Jenny said, "we can always argue politics."

The band played the long version, and when the song was over everyone on the dance floor was drenched in sweat.

"Do you need a ride?" he asked.

"No, but you can walk me to the car."

"So what are you doing tomorrow?" he said. "It's my last day and I really want to get to know you."

McGill was stunned when she agreed to meet him on the boardwalk by the snow-cone stand at noon. He went back to his room but he was so over-the-moon smitten he tossed and turned all night, unable to sleep.

He brought his Guild guitar hoping to enchant her with its magic. He was half an hour early, and nearly jumped out of his skin when she showed up just two minutes late. She was carrying a straw basket and wearing a sun-visor and a beach robe over a two-piece bikini, revealing a modest bit of cleavage, and when she moved just right the top pulled away showing the whites of her breasts beyond the tan line. Her legs reminded him of what World War II GIs said of Betty Grable's famous bathing-suit pinup: "Her legs go all the way to the floor."

He said, "Hi, I was worried you wouldn't show up," then flushed at having said something so totally uncool and stupid.

"Why? I keep my promises."

"Well, not everyone does."

They went body surfing and listened to Top 40 hits on his radio: "Groovin'" by the Rascals; "With A Little Help From My Friends," from the Beatles' *Sgt. Pepper* album; "Soul Man" by Sam and Dave; and "Apples, Peaches, Pumpkin Pie" and "A Little Bit o' Soul" by one-hit wonder groups. It had been a great summer for music.

When she said, "I think I'm getting too much sun," they moved to a spot under the boardwalk. He took out his guitar and played her one of his original songs. She applauded politely and said, "Play something we can both sing, maybe something by Peter, Paul and Mary."

After a few false starts to get the harmony right, they made it through "Blowin' in the Wind" without any mistakes and he said, "Damn, Jen, we sound great together. We should start a band."

That evening they strolled up and down the busy boardwalk, eating sticky cotton candy and greasy onion rings and playing carnival games. He won her a huge pink teddy bear with his deadeye, never-miss shooting at the .22 booth, and insisted they have their picture taken in the three-shots-for-a-quarter photo booth. As the sun set and the beach cleared they walked over the still-warm sand and climbed up in one of the lifeguard chairs. They cuddled and necked for a bit, and McGill had to fight not to put his hands anywhere that could get him in trouble. After the most wonderful hour in his entire life, a white jeep of the Wildwood Beach Patrol drove up, shined a spotlight on them, and the cop, using a megaphone, ordered them to leave.

"Where to?" he said, and hoping against hope, suggested, "There's always a party at our beach house."

"No," she said, her voice filled with caution, "I don't think so. I want to dance."

So they went back to Pelican Bill's and joined the throng on the dance floor until they were soaked and exhausted. After the last song, the killer Jimi Hendrix version of Dylan's "All Along the Watchtower," he drove her to her motel. They exchanged numbers and addresses, and kissed a tender goodnight while her girlfriends giggled inside.

The next morning, he packed up his Triumph and put down the convertible top, but instead of the early start he had planned, he drove to Jenny's motel and knocked on her door. One of her girlfriends opened the door, and squinting sleepy-eyed in the sunlight said, "Jennifer, it's the Goldwater guy."

He heard sounds of shuffling inside the room and Jenny, still in her nightgown, peeked around the door and said, "Oh, hi, Arty. I thought you were leaving."

"I am, but I've been thinking. You're going back today too, right?"

"Yes," she said with a yawn.

"Well, lets spend the day together, then I'll drive you back. Bryn Mawr is right off the turnpike, so it's no trouble at all. It'll give us a chance to get to know each other better."

"Oh, I don't know. It's all planned."

"Oh, come on. You've got four girls squeezed into a Corvair. I'll get you back safe. Come on, Jenny. You'll have an extra day at the beach, and I'll drop you at your dorm before curfew. We can just laze around under the boardwalk and play music, or we can rent a skiff and do some sailing. Whatever you want to do is fine with me."

He was charmingly persistent until she finally gave in. "Okay."

He strapped her suitcase and the big teddy bear on the luggage rack and they drove down to the boardwalk for breakfast. They were amazed when they saw the surf; the usual wimpy three-foot waves typical of the East Coast were higher than either of them had ever seen before. An early-season hurricane far out in the Atlantic was generating waves along the Jersey shore like it was the beach at Waikiki.

"Wow, Jen. I've never seen waves that big."

"Me neither."

"Have you ever been surfing?"

"No, never."

"Me neither. What do you say we rent a couple of boards?"

"Sounds like fun."

They spent the day laughing and falling off their surfboards into the roaring surf until they were both good enough to get most of the way to shore without dumping. After returning the boards, Jenny said, "Arty, I don't think I've ever had so much fun. I'm so glad you convinced me to stay."

They rinsed off the salt under the boardwalk's cold-water showers, and he took her to dinner at Murphy's to show her off to his frat brothers who were still waiting tables there. As is always the case when a waiter dines at his own restaurant, they were treated like royalty. He introduced her to everyone, savoring the intense jealousy on their faces.

McGill wanted the day to go on forever, and he never once went over the speed limit as he drove with the top down through the pine forests of New Jersey and the traffic of Philadelphia. When they got to Bryn Mawr, he carried her bag and the teddy bear up to the steps of her dorm and set them down. He took her in his arms, said, "Jenny, I really mean this," and then he gave her a sincere, bottom-of-the-heart kiss.

"Jenny, I really want to see you again."

"I like you too, Arty. Write me if you want."

Jenny and McGill dated others frequently, even seriously, but every month McGill would drive four hours down to Philly from Penn State to spend an evening with Jenny. His routine was to take her to some event, drop her off at her dorm, then crash in his sleeping bag in the Howard Johnson's parking lot on the nearby turnpike where the cops wouldn't bother him and he could use the men's room.

He made progress on every trip. Starting with simple necking on the first date, on the second date she let him get to first-base—sweater petting—and, on the third date all the way to second-base—bare titty!

But the very best time was when he convinced her to find a ride up to Happy Valley for the last football game of the year against Pitt, Penn State's archrival. She registered as a guest with some high school friends in the women's dorms. For all the talk of the "sexual revolution," America's colleges in the Sixties were still governed by the Victorian Age rules of *in loco parentis* to protect defenseless girls from male treachery, and most colleges had a "ladies curfew" that was strictly enforced. McGill felt like James Bond, sneaking her out the dorm window after curfew and up the TKO fire escape to his room.

Jenny let him take her bra off, and didn't seem to mind when he got naked, but she insisted on sleeping with her jeans on, which made dry humping excruciatingly painful. But he could tell she enjoyed watching him get hard, although she would never have admitted it. She never of her own volition touched him down there, but he kept guiding her hand down, where it would stay for a while, letting go when she got too excited, and he would gradually start the process all over again.

Sunday morning she made him drive her to mass at the campus chapel. He showed her where he would be parked a couple blocks away, then dropped her off so he could catch some ZZZs in the car.

"So tell me," he said later over Sunday breakfast at the crowded diner, "did you confess to the priest what we did last night?"

"We didn't go far enough for it to be a sin."

"Will you tell him when we do make love?"

She evaded the question like the lawyer she wanted to be. "I don't want to talk about something that may never happen. But, Arty, tell me, why don't you ever go to church?"

"Me?"

"Yes. You never talk about church at all."

"That's because I'm a Presbyterian. We don't have to go to church."

She had never heard of such a thing. "Presbyterians don't have to go to church?"

"It's true, Jen. It's our doctrine of predestination. Comes up from Saint Augustine through John Calvin. Reverend Maylan told us about it in communicants' class, seventh grade. The way he explained it, God is all-powerful and all-knowing, you know, omnipotent and omniscient. That means you are either predestined to be among what Calvin called the 'elect,' saved by His grace and guaranteed a spot inside the Pearly Gates, or you are destined for eternal damnation in the fiery brimstone of hell. It's set in stone, from the moment of creation, and there's no way to change it, no matter what you do."

"You mean you have no free will?"

"That's how Reverend Maylan explained it. You see, if God didn't already know your fate, He wouldn't be omniscient, and therefore, He wouldn't be God...right? It's totally logical. What it comes down to is your reward in the next life is not affected by your actions in this life, one way or the other, good or bad, because God already knows what's going to happen. So I figured, if God doesn't care if you brown nose up to Him in church, what was the point of sitting through all those god-awful hymns and sermons if it doesn't get you anywhere? Now you, as a Catholic, you could make love to me and all it would mean might be a little extra time in Purgatory. With us Presbies, we're either in, or we're out, whether we make love or not. So I say, enjoy life while we're here."

Neither Father Zyhowski nor any of the nuns had taught her how to argue with anything like that. Still, it didn't matter, because even with Arty's logic, and his persistent charm, premarital sex was still a sin.

She always tried to be a good Catholic, but questioned things like the Inquisition, which had been sanctioned by many Popes and had never been acknowledged as an error by the Church, an inconsistency which led her to question the concept of papal infallibility. There was no question in her mind that killing millions in search of heretics had been wrong, but according to doctrine, the Pope could never be wrong. How could that be? It was a question she had been unable to reconcile.

In eighth grade, she had posed the question to Sister Mary Grace.

"Sister, we're taught that the Pope can never be wrong, but what about the Pope who condemned Copernicus for saying that the sun was not the center of the universe? They were going to burn him at the stake until Copernicus confessed he was wrong. But science proved that the Pope was wrong, the Earth is not the center of the universe, and the church still hasn't admitted that the Pope was wrong."

Sister Mary Grace had fielded similar questions many times in her long career. "The Pope was referring to the spiritual universe, Jennifer, and the Earth is the center of the spiritual universe."

Jenny found that hard to swallow, and as she grew older many things about church doctrine made no sense. It didn't seem fair that God would allow someone else's sins to be passed on to someone else who had done nothing wrong. Nor could she understand why the path to salvation relied on the rote repetition of prayers. Did God really count how many rosaries she said before she could be forgiven for a particular sin? And she had never received a satisfactory answer when she questioned why women could not be priests.

Arty, with his nonchalant, you've-got-to-be-kidding-me attitude toward religion, began to have an effect on her. She took a bus up to see him for his twentieth birthday in the middle of March, 1968, to go to a concert by Big Brother and the Holding Company featuring a hard-living blues-singer named Janis Joplin. The big news that week was what history would call the Tet Offensive, with huge battles all over Vietnam dominating the TV news, but far, far away from a Big Brother concert.

After ladies curfew, Arty smuggled her out of the dorm and up to his room. They had barely snuggled up when there was a loud rapping and a voice yelled, "Room check. Open up."

It was the enforcers of the dreaded IFC, the Intra-Fraternity Council, making a raid. If they found a girl anywhere in the house, they'd slap the whole fraternity on probation, which meant no parties for the rest of the year and woe to the guy who ruined it for everybody.

McGill slipped her into his bathrobe, handed her the spare blanket, and helped her out the window onto the portico, covering the noise by swearing and bitching like he was roaring drunk. He closed the window, unlocked the door, and the IFC inspectors left after checking under his bed and shining a flashlight in his closet.

As Jenny crouched below his window on the snow-covered portico she had images of Janis Joplin running through her mind. She had never seen a woman more alive than Janis was up on stage belting out songs of love and lust. She was flat out jealous that any woman could have so much fun singing, and as she shivered in the snow while he bullshitted the investigators she made a decision. Her period had just ended, so she was safe. Tonight she would give in to his fumbling advances.

McGill was shocked when he got her jeans and panties all the way off. She had let him get them down to her ankles before, but never all the way off. The soft, furry triangle between her legs was the most beautiful sight in the universe. He was utterly panic-stricken. He wanted her more than anything, but she had drunk more than her usual couple of beers, and he didn't want her to think he had taken advantage of her.

"Jenny, honey, I…I don't want you to hate me tomorrow."

She laughed at his quaint sense of chivalry, gently grabbed his hard-on, and eagerly guided him in. When she woke up in the morning, she felt she was finally grown up—a free, liberated adult.

McGill snuck her down the hall to the bathroom and stood guard until she was finished. Then he went downstairs and woke up one of the pledges who was crashed under a winter overcoat on the living room couch. He didn't normally haze pledges, or have them do his personal chores, but this was a very special occasion.

"Pledge, get the fuck up. What's your name?"

The pledge leaped off the couch and came to attention. "Pledge Bowman, Brother McGill, sir, and I am lower than whale shit on the bottom of the ocean, Brother McGill, *SIR*!"

"Consider yourself lucky, Bowman, because you have a chance to get on my good side. My guest and I feel like a big breakfast, and you are going to serve it to us. And you're going to keep your mouth shut about it. Nobody else is to know. Understand?"

"Yes *SIR*, Brother McGill, *SIR*!"

He ordered Bowman to put on his coat and tie and have the house cook make eggs-over-easy, bacon, and home fries for two, along with orange juice and coffee. Bowman's eyes bugged out when he brought the tray in and he saw the gorgeous girl under the covers. If this was how it was at TKO, Bowman had joined the right fraternity.

Jenny's friends kept telling her that with her looks and brains and personality she could do much better than Arty, somebody Ivy League,

Princeton, or Penn, but she really enjoyed being with Arty even when they disagreed. They had spirited debates on many subjects, but no subject was more serious than the war in Vietnam.

She sometimes thought back to that first meeting at Pelican Bills, the way he mocked and debunked everything she had to say about the war. He was so sure, so absolutely, positively certain, that America always did the right thing. She felt she could turn him around, like she was trying to do with her mom and dad. Even though he claimed to be a conservative, Arty seemed to be open to new ideas. Not so her parents, who believed no Democratic president would ever lie to the country and send American boys, including perhaps her three older brothers, off to war if the nation's very existence were not at stake.

She always chuckled to herself at Arty's grandiose dreams for the future, which went something like this: after graduation, he would join the Navy, go to Officer Candidate School, win some medals, then go to law school, join the diplomatic service and hang out in nifty foreign capitals outwitting the commies, become an ambassador, then Secretary of State in a Republican administration, and finally, he would be drafted by a grateful Republican party to run for President.

McGill had grown up in a household steeped in Republican tradition, where FDR was "that damned Roosevelt" and Truman was "the bankrupt haberdasher." When the spring quarter of 1968 began, he was a card-carrying Young Republican, a Goldwater Republican, proud to call himself a conservative. McGill was thrilled when Lyndon Johnson said he would not seek reelection. McGill still hoped Barry Goldwater, and not the wimpy Nelson Rockefeller or the sure-loser Richard Nixon, would once again be the Republican nominee. McGill was convinced that if Goldwater ran again, he would be vindicated for his landslide defeat in '64 at the hands of Johnson, who had run as the "peace" candidate but then immediately sent 500,000 troops to Vietnam with nearly 30,000 already killed and no "light at the end of the tunnel" in sight. If Goldwater had won in '64 he would have blown the commies right off the map and the Vietnam problem would have long been over, unless, of course, the infamous "daisy bomb" ad had been right, and Goldwater started World War III.

McGill and Jenny didn't know it then, but 1968 was to become known to American historians as "the saddest year of the twentieth century." In January, a U.S. Navy ship, the *Pueblo*, had been captured by

North Korea, a crisis that threatened to reopen the Korean war; in February, the Tet offensive in South Vietnam shook America's confidence in the war, and led to President Johnson's announcement that he would not stand for re-election. Four days later, on April 4, civil rights leader Martin Luther King was assassinated while standing on the balcony of a motel in Memphis, which set off riots in cities from coast-to-coast. Just two months later, on June 6, Senator Bobby Kennedy, only moments after winning the California Democratic primary and flashing the two-fingered peace sign at his victory speech, was gunned down in a Los Angeles hotel. Anti-war protests at college campuses, along with the grim TV reporting of American boys coming home from Vietnam in body-bags, dominated the news week after week. That summer would also see the brutal "police riot" against anti-war demonstrators at the Democratic Convention in Chicago.

The voting age was still twenty-one, and McGill, like millions of other young men who were subject to the draft, as well as their sisters and girlfriends, had no say in the outcome. The anti-war demonstrations roused what Nixon called the "silent majority," and because the millions of young people most directly affected by the election were precluded from voting, Nixon, who claimed to have a "secret plan to win the war," was re-elected by the narrowest of margins. As another Republican President, Herbert Hoover, once said, "It is old men who make war, but it is youth who must fight and die."

That spring quarter, McGill had finally finished his prerequisites for a degree in Political Science and was free to choose courses in any subject. He signed up for American Diplomatic History and International Law and wanted to find a subject for his term papers that would allow him to research both at the same time.

Vietnam was the perfect topic to kill two birds with one stone, get two A's for the research time of one, and come away with the ammo to shut up any anti-war hippie who disagreed with him.

For Diplomatic History, he set out to prove that America's involvement in Vietnam was in the national interest, and for International Law, that what America was doing was legal. He spent weeks in the library reading everything he could find on Indochina, French colonialism, Vietnam, the battle of Dien Bien Phu, the Geneva Peace accords, anything remotely related to the war. After a couple of weeks he began to feel a sense of dread; there didn't seem to be any evidence at all to support his preconceptions.

The more he read, the worse it got, and when he finally sat down to write the papers he was forced to conclude the opposite of what he had set out to prove. He had experienced intellectual serendipity, having found something he had not intended to find. It was also a moral and political epiphany.

For the Diplomatic History paper, he concluded that the Truman administration had blundered by letting the French back into Indochina after World War II. He argued that the U.S. and the Viet Minh had been allies against the Japanese in World War II, and if the U.S. had recognized Vietnam as a sovereign state in 1946 the two countries could have worked together against Vietnam's ancient enemy, China, and Mao's communists might not have come to power. For the International Law paper, he made the case that the Geneva Accords said that Vietnam was one country, and that the establishment of an independent state in the south violated every premise of international law. Elections were supposed to be held in 1954, but the Eisenhower administration refused to allow a vote because the candidate United States backed, Ngo Dihn Diem, was predicted by the C.I.A. to lose by at least four to one.

The morning after Bobby Kennedy's murder, McGill's Diplomatic History class met for the final exam, and the tearful professor called for a moment of silence. Only weeks before McGill had dismissed Bobby's criticism of American policy in Vietnam. Perhaps if he had taken, say, a film appreciation course instead of Diplomatic History, or an English class on Shakespeare instead of International Law, his Republican rock-ribs would not have turned to sand.

Jenny was devastated by the assassinations of Martin Luther King and Bobby Kennedy. She rode in a chartered bus from Bryn Mawr to Washington to pay her respects to the great civil rights leader as his casket lay in state under the Capitol Dome. Then, just two months later, she returned, this time with her mom and dad and her three older brothers to pay her respects to Bobby Kennedy. As she stood on the sidewalk as Bobby's casket was drawn up Pennsylvania Avenue to Arlington Cemetery, she felt that all her hopes and dreams for America's future were about to be buried with him.

Chapter 6

Draft Night

December 1, 1969

ON THE EVENING OF MONDAY, DECEMBER 1, 1969, PRESIDENT RICHARD Milhous Nixon held a prime-time lottery that riveted America to its television sets. The drawing was not your usual get-rich-quick, jackpot type of lottery, but a roll of the dice to determine which young men would be conscripted to fight, and maybe to die, in the faraway jungles of Vietnam. Nowhere was the sense of foreboding stronger than in the fraternity houses of college communities like "Happy Valley."

There must have been a hundred people gathered in McGill's fraternity for the event. A third were women, the dates and pinmates of brothers and guests as well as TKO's "Little Sisters"—honorary Tokes in *TKΩ–Penn State* sweatshirts. Freshman pledges on bar-duty, wearing mandatory jackets and ties, were filling cups from pitchers from a newly-tapped keg. It was rare to tap a keg on a weeknight, even at a hard-core party house like TKO, but this was to be a night unlike any other in modern American history.

McGill and his old buddy, Frankie Dombrowski, stopped on the landing halfway between the first and second floors, lit cigarettes, and surveyed the crowd below. Frankie was on leave from the Army and had been crashing on McGill's couch since Thursday. He had hitchhiked up with his guitar from Milltowne for a final fling before shipping out to Vietnam. He and McGill had been in a rock 'n' roll band in high school, Frankie and the Dynamos. The girls in Milltowne called Frankie "the Polish Elvis" because of his chiseled good looks, his wavy black hair, and his smooth baritone voice. He'd gone to college at Pitt, and like McGill, he would have been a senior, but last spring he'd flunked French, which dropped his Grade Point Average below 2.0, and the Decatur County draft board nailed his under-achieving ass. With his buzz-cut GI haircut and a U.S. Army field jacket he didn't look much like Elvis any more.

The big window on the landing was swung open for ventilation despite the wintery weather. McGill and Frankie leaned over the wide windowsill to watch the three-way snowball fight in progress between the Tokes, the Alpha Sigs across the street, and the Tekes next door. Guys from all three houses were battling under the street lights, no gloves or jackets, making snowballs barehanded and whooping and yelling like ten-year-olds as TKO's mascot, "Aphie," short for Aphrodite, a gentle giant of a Saint Bernard, romped in the snow barking her low-pitched woof–woof–woofs.

McGill's "little brother," Bob Dawkins, came up the stairs carrying two cups of beer, said, "Here you go, Brother McGill, sir," and handed them the cups. All pledges had to choose a "big brother" when they joined, which obligated them to become the big brother's personal servant. Dawkins had chosen McGill because McGill had a beautiful girlfriend who went to Bryn Mawr and he played guitar, but mostly because they were both from Milltowne and McGill had his own car.

McGill yelled, "What took you so fucking long, pledge?"

Dawkins snapped to rigid attention and yelled, "The keg only pours so fast, Brother McGill, sir!"

"Still the wise-ass, aren't you Dawkins. Drop and give me twenty."

"Yes, *sir*, Brother McGill, *sir*! Thank you, Brother McGill *sir*!"

Dawkins dropped to the floor and began counting out push-ups. It was the second day of Hell Week, and if the pledges made it through they would be "brotherized," becoming full-fledged members of Tau Kappa Omega. The pledges were just at the start of their four-year college deferments, so they weren't too worried what number they pulled under Nixon's new system. But for nineteen-year old males not going to college and for college seniors like McGill, whose four-year deferment ended in June, the lottery could be a matter of life or death.

The pledge-master, Kellner, blew his whistle and shouted, "Clear the living room. Clear the living room. Get your asses out so we can set up."

Dawkins finished his pushups and raced down the stairs to help the other pledges. Everyone who had been in the living room moved into the foyer and the card room and the dining room so the pledges could set up like they did for football games, everyone except Looney Larry. At twenty-four, he was the oldest guy in the house, a super-senior who should have graduated or been drafted two-years ago but had gamed the system into extending his deferment. He just sat and grinned, forcing four pledges to pick up the big leather chair with him on it and move it while he blew smoke rings like the draft-dodging genius that he was.

The pledges arranged the couches and chairs in a wide horseshoe around the color TV, ran the big industrial vacuum, emptied ashtrays, sponged off tables, brought in logs and stoked the fire until it roared. McGill saw a pledge come out of the service kitchen carrying Aphie's scrap dish with the bones and scraps the cook always sent up in the dumbwaiter and hurried down the steps to confront him. "Where do you think you're going, pledge?"

"Uh, I've got Aphie-duty."

"You've got Aphie-duty *what*?"

The pledge snapped to attention and shouted, "I've got Aphie-duty, Brother McGill, *sir*!"

"That's better," McGill said as he took the bowl. "I'll take care of Aphie while you drop for twenty. Consider yourself lucky it isn't fifty."

"Yes *sir*, Brother McGill, *sir*! Thank you, Brother McGill, *sir*!" the pledge yelled as he dropped to the floor.

"Come on, Frankie," McGill said as the pledge started counting out his push-ups. "Let me introduce you."

Frankie followed McGill out to the side porch and McGill called, "Aphie! Come and get it! Aphie!" She ran right over and let him towel the snow off her thick coat and snap the chain on her collar. Frankie gave her a hearty pet and scratched her back. She would be content gnawing on her bones until the pledges let her in later to sleep by the fire, unconcerned who won or lost Nixon's lottery.

The Little Sisters had been busy making twelve narrow posters, one for each month, using magic markers and sheets of butcher paper from the downstairs kitchen. The posters listed the days in a column on the left, and on the right were two columns with blank lines for a name and a number. The pledges put them up all around the living room walls with masking tape, January through December. "Makes the place look like a bookie joint," somebody said when they finished.

When the room was ready, Kellner blew his whistle and yelled, "Listen up! Anybody who's not in the pool yet, see pledge Rhinebecker. Okay. Ready…set," and without saying "Go!" he blew his whistle, setting off a stampede as brothers vaulted over the backs of couches and elbowed each other out of the way to claim the best seats.

Everybody was on edge, but the seniors like McGill were really sweating. He was a political science major with plans to go to law school, but he would be graduating into the teeth of Nixon's new system. A Little Sister came up to him and asked, "Stick, did you send off your applications yet?"

"No, but they're all filled out. If I pull a decent number, I'll write the checks and send them off tomorrow. If I'm screwed, I'll bag it and use the money to go to the Orange Bowl."

He thought his plan made total sense. Penn State had been undefeated for two years in a row, was ranked #2 in the polls, and set to play #5 Missouri in the Orange Bowl on New Years Day. If he was going to die in Vietnam there's no way McGill was going to blow good money on law school applications if he could use it to party in Miami and see his school win a national championship.

A girl in a flowery *Make Love Not War* sweatshirt asked him, "Stick, can't you just get a note from a doctor if you get a bad number?"

Tens of thousands of guys had been getting phony medical "outs" to beat the draft. Trick knees were a favorite because they were hard to disprove. You could also get outs for minor defects like flat feet and curvature of the spine. Doctors for many professional athletes swore their patients' knees or shoulders or backs prevented them from serving in the military, but the defects were somehow not serious enough to keep them from playing professional baseball or football.

For healthy guys who weren't sports stars and didn't have a doctor willing to lie for them, there were various self-inflicted outs, like blowing off your little toe with a gun, inducing high blood-pressure with drugs, pigging out to become overweight, starving yourself and taking drugs to get underweight, and for the really desperate, claiming to be sexually perverted or homosexual. McGill was skinny and klutzy, but neither condition rated an out.

He just shrugged and told her, "Nah, I'm healthy as a horse."

She tried to be upbeat. "Well maybe when you take your physical they'll find something you don't know you have?"

"Ha, now that's a laugh," said Frankie. "Let me tell you what my physical was like."

Everybody nearby came closer to hear what the only person in the room who knew what he was talking about had to say.

"They made us take off our clothes and stand bare-assed with our toes on a yellow line. Then two guys in white coats came along. One said open your mouth and say *aahh*, and the other said bend over and spread your cheeks. Then the first one shined a light down your throat, and the second one shined a light up your asshole. If they didn't see each other, you passed."

Everybody in earshot cracked up, and Frankie said to McGill, "I'm supposed to pick that Annie chick up at her dorm pretty soon. You were going to make me a map to that parking spot."

How Frankie had finagled a date with Annie Chambers, president of Chi Omega sorority and last year's Homecoming Queen, God only knows. He'd just met her that afternoon down at the Lions' Den. McGill couldn't imagine a girl like that going parking on a first date, but ever since seventh grade Frankie always had his way with girls.

It was a strict university rule that women were not permitted above the first floor of frat houses after nine, so McGill drew a map to the duck pond where they could park without being hassled by the cops. "There's blankets in the trunk," McGill said as he gave Frankie his keys. "And don't forget, ladies curfew's at midnight."

"Thanks, Stick," Frankie said, and as he headed out the door he flashed a two-fingered "peace sign" and yelled, "Good luck you guys."

Kellner's pin-mate, Darlene, a sister in Tri-Delt, archrivals of the Chi-O's for best sorority, came up to McGill and asked, "Does your friend really have a date with Chambers?"

"Yeah, why?"

She gave him a sly smile. "You know what they say about Chi-O's and Vietnam, don't you?"

"No, what?"

She was delighted to spread the rumor. "They're all into a Florence Nightingale competition thing. If your friend is going to Vietnam, he'll get a Chi-O mercy fuck."

McGill broke into a laugh and tried to imagine what a Chi-O mercy fuck with a Homecoming Queen might be like. Would the other Chi-O's do a sorority cheer and wave pompoms? "Frankie might get laid, but it won't be out of mercy. Chicks cream their jeans over Dombrowski."

Rhinebecker was walking around carrying a flip-over calendar and a cigar box full of cash—the house pool—while calling out, "Anybody not in the pool better sign up. Only a few minutes to go."

McGill waved Rhinebecker over and said, "How's it work?"

"Everybody puts in a buck," Rhinebecker said. "Third place gets five, second gets ten, the winner gets the jackpot. Ties split."

"Oh, how exciting," Darlene said. "Can I get in too?"

"No chicks allowed," Rhinebecker said with a firm shake of his head.

Her lips turned down in a pout. "You guys have all the fun."

"Oh yeah," McGill said as he handed Rhinebecker a five. "Waiting to see if your life is going down the tubes sure is fun all right."

"When's your birthday, Brother McGill?" Rhinebecker asked as he counted out change.

"March seventeenth."

"Hey, St. Patrick's Day," Rhinebecker said as he flipped the calendar to March and wrote McGill's name in the 17 square. "Luck of the Irish to you, Brother McGill, sir."

McGill gave him a dollar back. "Put this in for Dombrowski. November third."

Rhinebecker furrowed his brow. "But he's already in the Army."

"So?"

Rhinebecker seemed confused. "But the lottery won't affect him."

McGill glowered and said, "Are you arguing with me, pledge?"

Rhinebecker tried to cover his ass and shouted, "No *sir*, Brother McGill, *sir*!" He took the dollar and hurriedly flipped to November and wrote in Frankie's name before McGill dropped him for pushups.

The room was crackling with excitement as Nixon's big show began. Not even during the frenzy over Walt Disney's *Davy Crockett* show had so many "war babies" (who were not yet dubbed "boomers") been glued to the tube at the same time. To one degree or another, the results would impact the majority of healthy guys born between 1944 and 1952. About the only guys who would not be affected were those who were currently serving in uniform, those who had already served in uniform, and the 30,000 or so who had already died in uniform.

The rules for who would be called to serve and who would not had changed over the years as the war dragged on. Between 1964 and 1967, President Johnson eliminated, one by one, the deferments for marriage, children, and graduate school (except for medical, dental, and divinity students). Only the four-year deferment for undergraduates remained. For the past several years, all males between eighteen and twenty-six who were not full-time students with a Grade Point Average of 2.0 were draft bait, with the oldest taken first. The system kept guys at risk for eight long years, and many said it was a major factor fueling the anti-war protests, and there was widespread criticism of it from all quarters.

Nixon was changing the system so that all the American males born between 1944 and 1952 would be assigned random numbers based on their birthdays. Barring a national emergency or a major escalation of the war, males in this pool would be at risk only for the next year—one year instead of eight. New lotteries would be held in succeeding years for boys who had come of draft age that year, and boys in those cohorts who did not receive college deferments would fill future quotas. So the system which previously called "oldest first" would change in succeeding years to calling "youngest and dumbest first."

Critics said the lottery was a devious Nixonian ploy to take the steam out of the anti-war movement. By limiting the risk of being drafted to an unlucky few, and placing the burden of future drafts on younger boys not yet old enough to drive, much less to vote, there would be fewer angry males willing to take to the streets to protest. Nixon wasn't called "Tricky Dick" for nothing.

Before the drawing, the Pentagon had been publicizing the Army's anticipated manpower needs for the coming year so everybody knew what to expect. The official estimate was that the lucky males in the highest third, from about #240 to #366, were relatively safe and could get on with their lives; those in the middle third, from "about" #125 to #240, were in a sort of limbo and would "probably" not be drafted; and all healthy males in the lowest third who had no deferment were goners. The new system was good for freshmen like Dawkins. If he kept a "gentleman's C" for the next year he would be off the hook and not have to worry about the draft unless things got so bad that Viet Cong war canoes came paddling up the Ohio river.

When Nixon's big show began the carpet in front of the TV was packed tight with guys sitting on the rug, beers in hand, like at a rock concert. The crowd behind the horseshoe of couches and chairs stood four and five deep, with guys in back standing up on radiators and tables and chairs brought in from the dining room to get a view of the tube.

The soothing voice of Walter Cronkite, America's most trusted TV newsman, explained how the drawing would work. The camera focused on a clear, cylindrical jar, about three feet high, the same exact one used in the draft lotteries of 1917 and 1940. At the bottom of the jar, were 366 blue plastic capsules, about an inch long, each containing a piece of paper with a different day of the year on it. Cronkite held up a sample, and somebody in back yelled, "What's it look like?"

"Like a fucking horse pill," came an answer from the front.

The capsules would be picked at random, and the order in which your birthday came up was your very own draft number. Unlike most lotteries, the sooner your number came up, the bigger you lost.

When Nixon's face appeared on the screen the house rocked to a cacophony of hisses and boos and shouts of "asshole!" and "motherfucker!" Just then McGill saw Rotsee Ross come in, carrying his white saucer hat in one hand and brushing snow off the shoulders of his navy blue R.O.T.C. overcoat with the other. He grabbed a chair from the dining room and climbed up to be able to see the TV over the crowd in front. When he saw Nixon, he began shaking his white saucer hat at the TV and yelling "motherfucker" louder than anybody.

The lottery began when a dour Republican Congressman nobody had ever heard of stepped up to the jar to pick the first number. The banter stopped, and the house became eerily silent. It must have been like that all across America as millions of guys and their girlfriends and families gulped and held their collective breaths. The Congressman seemed to be enjoying himself as he bent over and shoved his arm into the three-foot deep jar, right up to his shoulder, to get his hand all the way to the bottom. He fished around for a few seconds, then pulled out a capsule and handed it to an official seated at a table. The official opened the capsule, removed the paper, read it, showed it to other officials sitting around and said, "September fourteenth."

"September fourteenth," Cronkite repeated in his most stentorian, anchorman tone. "September fourteenth is number one."

Everybody looked around to see who would claim the first-place money, but no one did. Rhinebecker checked the calendar in case the winner wasn't present, shook his head and said, "Nobody's got it."

A Little Sister wrote "1" next to 14 on the September poster with a marker and put a line through the space where a name would have gone.

After the first pick, instead of an official doing the picking, the remaining numbers were chosen by 365 young men of draft age from every state in the union who had been flown in to do the dirty work. A tall, cheery-faced boy with thick Buddy Holly glasses jumped up and stuck his arm in the jar, picked a capsule, and handed it to the official who announced, "April twenty-fourth," followed by Cronkite who intoned, "Number two is April twenty-fourth."

"Hey that's me!" said somebody's date, but girls didn't count.

Rhinebecker checked his calendar. "Nobody's got it."

A Little Sister with a black marker wrote "2" next to 24 on the April poster, and another Little Sister used a pink marker to write in the name of the girl who didn't count.

On the third pull the official said, "December thirtieth—"

A plaintive "*NOOO*!" wailed out, and up from a couch jumped Baker, a ladies' man who always seemed to have a different girl on his arm, just about the last guy you'd expect to see carrying a rifle. Like McGill, Baker was a senior and out of options. He hopped around, shaking his head, tugging at his blonde, Beatlesque hair and screaming, "NOOO! FUCKING *NOOOOO*!"

The brotherhood offered him its sincerest condolences.

"*Die*, Baker, *die*!"

"Your ass is grass, Baker!"

"Dead meat, Baker!"

Somebody sang out, "Bake, Bake, Baker man, go to Nam, fast as you can," and everybody joined in, chanting, "Bake, Bake, Baker man, go to Nam, fast as you can!"

A Little Sister using a red marker put a "3" next to 30 on the December poster, wrote in Baker's name, drew a fat circle around it and put a big red star next to it.

Rhinebecker took out a ten and a five to cover the second and third place "winners" and handed Baker the cigar box stuffed with cash. "Congratulations, Brother Baker, *sir*!"

Baker opened the lid, peered in, then shaking his head in disbelief, slumped down in his seat on the couch and made a goofy show out of counting his winnings, one bill at a time, but his wide-eyed, shit-eating grin betrayed his utter despair.

With the big money out of the way, everybody relaxed, and the race was on for second. For a while it seemed nobody would take it until the official said, "September twenty-sixth—"

"Holy shit!"

It was a freshman pledge, Sharrock. "Pledge Sharrock takes second," Rhinebecker announced, and handed him the $10 prize. McGill thought it unfair for a freshman to be in the money, since if he kept a 2.0 average for a year he would be safe unless Nixon changed the rules again.

On the twenty-seventh pick, the official said, "July twenty-first—"

"Jesus fucking tits!"

It was Zovis, a junior whose GPA hovered dangerously close to 2.0, putting him at high risk if he got less than a "C" in any course. Already overweight from his job as a fry cook at the Char-Pit, he often joked about eating his way into a medical out. He wasted no time, taking his $5 prize and yelling, "Sharrock, call Marino's for a large pepperoni with mushrooms and extra cheese."

Next up was fourth place, just out of the prize money, the biggest loser of all—the douchebag of the day. A few numbers went by and the official said, "March seventeenth," followed by Cronkite intoning, "Saint Patrick's Day is number thirty-three."

McGill was standing in the back, a cigarette in one hand, a beer in the other, totally dazed, an empty chill already sweeping through him as Rhinebecker yelled, "That's Brother McGill!" and everybody rubbed it in, hooting, "DOOOOSSHH! DOOOOSSHH! DOOOOSSHH!"

The numbers rolled on, with more guys going down. At sixty-seven, Nixon nailed Stugall, a super-senior who was graduating that term. He held his cup up high and shouted, "Fuck this shit! *Tales*!"

An echoing roar of "Tales!" went up, and the guys with bad numbers charged downstairs to the Red Room for what would become a historic session of every fraternity's favorite drinking game—Wales Tales. The Red Room had been TKO's party haven for over fifty years. You could smell it when you opened the door at the top of the basement stairs as the sour aroma of five decades of beer parties wafted up and punched you in the nose. It was about fifty feet long and twenty feet wide, and had a masculine, hunting lodge-meets-rathskeller ambiance. Built into the walls all around the room, were bench seats of cushioned red vinyl. There were six highly-varnished oak picnic tables and benches. The walls were dark maroon with oak trim, with a pair of Old West-style saloon doors leading to the dance room. It was the heart and soul of a party house like TKO, and pledges waxed and buffed its hardwood floors to a glistening shine after every event.

As the lottery moved past #125, where the Pentagon said the cut-off for losers would "probably" be, guys whose birthdays hadn't come up yet got to feeling better and came trickling down to get into the games. When a birthday of a brother was drawn, Rhinebecker rushed down to announce it. When he came down and yelled, "Brother Nichols is two-forty-eight," Nichols stood up, held his beer cup high and shouted, "Here's to Richard fucking Nixon! I'm fucking *out*!"

McGill gave him the finger. "Fuck you, asshole."

The keg kicked about eleven, but the losers insisted on tapping the emergency keg to keep things going. About twelve-thirty, Frankie showed up to the roaring din of six simultaneous Tales games. He came over to McGill's table and handed him the car keys. "How'd you do, Stick?"

"Thirty-fucking-three."

Frankie shook his head. "Damn, that's a bummer."

"Know what you'd have been, asshole?"

Frankie grinned a wide, satisfied smile. "Nah, I was getting to know Annie. She's a very friendly girl."

"Three-forty-eight. You'd be home free if you hadn't flunked French, and now you're gonna get your ass blown away for nothing. Fucking nothing. You really piss me off, Dombrowski."

Draft Night voided all the rules. For the losers, like Baker, McGill and Stugall, it was a night out of the Rubaiyat, a night to forget how screwed you were—*eat, drink, and be merry, for tomorrow we may die*! For the winners like Nichols with high numbers, it was a night to celebrate the biggest victory of their lives. For the guys in the middle, it turned into an emotional, fuck-it-all bull session. Guys argued for and against the war, the winners ragging the losers and everybody wondering just what they were going to do with the rest of their lives.

For the first time in TKO history, the long-haired, semi-hippie "heads" rolled joints out in the open and passed them around like it was Woodstock. Even the most tight-assed "straights" kept their mouths shut, and several straights even turned on for the first time. The Tales games went on like a Roman Saturnalia; if you were feeling sick from too much beer, you went outside, stuck your finger down your throat, blew lunch in a snowbank, and came back for more.

They took occasional breaks from the games and got into the bawdy drinking songs the older alumni loved to sing when they came back for Homecoming. One verse in particular summed up the lifestyle:

> We toast the girls who do
> We toast the girls who don't
> We toast the girls who say they will
> And then they say they won't
> But the girls we toast
> From the break o' day
> Until the late o' night
> Are the girls who say they never have

But just for you they might.
Say I-I-I think
We need another drink
Say I-I-I think
We need another drink
Say I-I-I think
We need another drink
To the brotherhood
Of Tee-Kay-*OOOhh.*

Frankie sat at McGill's table and joined the Tales game, and somebody asked him, "How'd they get you? You went to Pitt, right?"

A sheepish look came over Frankie's face. "I was in a new band and gigging a lot and I didn't put much time into French, so—"

"Oh, bullshit, Dombrowski," McGill said and belched a long, beery *buurrrppp.* "You got your ass drafted because you think you're fucking Elvis. But they drafted Elvis, douchebag, like in *Bye-Bye Birdie.* So now it's bye-bye Frankie, and you're gonna get your ass blown away for nothing. Fucking nothing. What an asshole you are."

"That's how they got Johnny Zimmer," somebody said. "He flunks chemistry and the next thing you know he's beating the bush in some place called Phu Bai."

"Have you thought about going to Canada?" somebody asked.

"I hear Toronto's okay," Frankie said, "but I don't—"

"Screw Toronto!" McGill shouted. "Hump your dumb ass up to Montreal where you can *parlez-vouz* some French and maybe get your fucking grades up."

Frankie grinned and gave McGill the finger, then reached for his wallet and pulled out a piece of paper and began unfolding it. "Talking about being drafted, ever see one of these?"

"What is it?" somebody asked.

"A greeting from Uncle Sam," and he passed his induction notice around the table for everyone to see. When it got to McGill he held it up and read it out loud:

"SELECTIVE SERVICE SYSTEM
ORDER TO REPORT FOR INDUCTION

From: The President of the United States

To: Francis James Dombrowski
184 West Seneca Street
Milltowne, Pennsylvania 16555

GREETING:

You are hereby ordered for induction into the Armed Forces of the United States, and to report at the Federal Office Building, 1000 Liberty Ave., Pittsburgh, Pennsylvania 15222, on 12 July 1969 at 6:45 AM for forwarding to an Armed Forces Induction Station.

Signed Edward T. Blaatz
Clerk of local board #758
For Brig. General John S. Hershey
Commander, Selective Service System"

McGill folded it up and started to put it in his own wallet.

"Hey, what the fuck you think you're doing?" Frankie said.

"I'll hang on to it for you so you don't lose it in a rice paddy, asshole. When you get back, I'll buy you a beer and we'll burn the sucker."

Frankie grinned and said, "You're on."

McGill and Frankie and the other losers stayed up bullshitting and playing Tales until just before dawn. The next day, McGill cut all his classes and he and Frankie crashed until late afternoon, totally hungover. When they got up they showered and drove to the State Store for a bottle of Jack Daniels for Frankie's last night. After dinner, they settled on a couch in the living room, which still had the feel of a bookie joint with Nixon's lottery-results posted on the walls. McGill brought his stack of law school applications down and set them on the coffee table, and drinking and laughing, they meticulously folded the pages into paper airplanes, one at a time, and sailed them into the fireplace.

Dawkins was on door-duty at the small desk just inside the entrance when the pay phone in the coat-closet rang. He answered, came out and said, "Phone call for Frankie Dombrowski."

"Who is it?" Frankie asked.

"Annie Chambers."

Frankie jumped up and closed the closet door, and a minute later came out and said to McGill, "Annie's already snuck out of the dorm. Think I can borrow you car and some money for a motel?"

She was taking a big risk, and could be expelled for violating the university's strict *in loco parentis* rules. McGill gave Frankie his car keys and his last twenty and told Dawkins, "Call the Holiday Inn and book a room for Mr. and Mrs. Francis Dombrowski."

Around eleven the next morning, Frankie brought Annie to the TKO house and introduced her to McGill and Dawkins. Annie's silky blonde hair was in a ponytail, and her complexion so perfect she could have stepped off a Hollywood movie poster, but her eyes were red and puffy, like she'd been crying.

They loaded Frankie's duffel bag and guitar case into the trunk. Dawkins rode shotgun, McGill drove, and Annie clung to Frankie in the back seat as they took her to her dorm. McGill tried not to listen as she sobbed like a kindergartner and Frankie promised over and over that he'd be careful and would write as soon as he could. Frankie gave her a long kiss in the parking lot, and as Frankie climbed into the car McGill watched Annie standing in the snow wiping tears from her eyes and looking like she was the one who needed mercy.

"Man," Frankie said, "chicks are so strange."

On the way to the hitchhiking spot, McGill offered to drive Frankie to Canada. "Niagara Falls isn't far, and if we leave now we can have you across the border before dark. And I've got a couple hundred in the bank I was saving for applications you can have to get started."

Frankie shook his head. "Thanks, Stick, but I'm no deserter. So what are you gonna do now that you know your number?"

"Damn if I know," McGill said. "I graduate in June, so I've got a few months to figure something out."

Dawkins took the duffle bag and guitar out of the trunk as Frankie and McGill shook hands, strong, John Wayne handshakes, followed by a long hippie peace clasp—thumbs interlocked, fingers wrapping around the back of the other's hand—and gave each other hearty slaps on the back.

"Nice knowing you, Bob," Frankie said, giving him a handshake and a peace clasp.

"Same here," Dawkins said. "Be careful over there."

McGill and Dawkins waited in the car watching Frankie, standing in the snow, in jeans, combat boots, Army field jacket, a Steelers stocking cap, and holding the cardboard sign Dawkins made with PITT on one side and MILLTOWNE on the other. Right away a VW bus with a *Peace*

Now bumper-sticker stopped. The side door rolled open, and Frankie handed in his guitar and duffel bag. Then he turned, flashed a peace sign, and climbed into the van for the first leg of his journey to Vietnam.

After Draft Night, things got back to normal for everybody except the big losers like McGill. Dawkins made it through finals and Hell Week and got brotherized, but McGill didn't even bother studying. With a healthy body, a bad draft number, and an expiring deferment, grades didn't matter. Instead, he read the *Hobbit* and all three volumes of *Lord of the Rings* and organized the TKO expedition to the Orange Bowl.

The plan was for a dozen guys to drive down in three cars, meeting up at the Miami TKO house. He borrowed a Chevy station wagon off the McGill Motors used car lot and the day after Christmas picked up Dawkins at his house at five AM. They took the turnpike to Philadelphia, picked up Baker and Nichols, then headed south, taking turns driving and sleeping stretched out with the station wagon's backseat folded down. The Miami TKO house was not locked, and the only guys there were some Tokes from Missouri who had the same ideas about fraternal visitation privileges that the Penn State Tokes did. It was as if the Miami Tokes had purposely left the house open; they were probably used to brothers from other chapters crashing at the Orange Bowl every year. They moved right in, and didn't do any damage McGill knew of, though he was sure the Miami Tokes weren't too happy when they came back and found the mess they'd left.

Penn State's defense dominated the game and won easily, but the team ranked #1 in the polls, Texas, won its game in the Cotton Bowl. Penn State had played the higher-ranked team, and had been undefeated for two straight years. McGill was hopeful that if the sports writers voted for the best team, Penn State would be #1.

But President Nixon, in keeping with his "Southern strategy," killed any chance of that by calling the Texas coach on national TV and proclaiming them the national champions. He didn't even have the decency to mention Penn State's claim to the title, which should tell you all you need to know about the character of Richard Milhous Nixon.

They slept in late, then headed north, stopping at Daytona Beach to spend the night and check out the action. They lazed around on the chilly January beach all the next day, and about eight that evening climbed into the car for the long drive home. They dropped Baker and Nichols off in Philly about ten in the morning just as a freezing rain began to fall. McGill got on the turnpike and pulled into a Howard Johnson's service plaza to clean up and eat breakfast before the final push across Pennsylvania to Milltowne. They had been gone ten days.

There were no lines at the pumps, so they gassed up first, then used the men's room. McGill stayed to brush his teeth and shave while Dawkins went to wait in line for a booth in the crowded restaurant, figuring to clean up after they ate. Dawkins bought a *Pittsburgh Post-Gazette* in the gift shop, got a table, and ordered two coffees. He was leafing through the paper when a headline caught his eye: "Services Today For Local Singer." An icy despair shuddered through him when he looked at the photo and saw Frankie's face looking back at him.

The paper said U.S. Army Private-First-Class Francis James Dombrowski, twenty-one years old, a popular singer from Milltowne, had been killed by multiple fragmentation wounds the day after Christmas while on patrol in Phuoc Long province. He had been in Vietnam for only two weeks. Services were this afternoon at Stigwood's Funeral Home in Milltowne.

McGill slid into the booth and said, "What's new?"

Dawkins was totally numb, hardly able to breathe. It was all he could do to just push the paper across the table. He sat in the bright orange booth and watched as McGill read about Frankie. McGill looked up in wide-eyed disbelief. Tears were streaming down his face as he read it for a second time, then McGill calmly folded the paper and said, "We gotta go."

It was not until he was in the Army himself that McGill came to understand what might have happened: Frankie was the "FNG"—the fucking-new-guy—and FNGs were always screwing up and getting killed. Maybe his platoon came across a village of "doubtfuls," grunt slang for peasants whose loyalty was impossible to determine. Frankie's sergeant might have ordered him to check out a hooch, and in his inexperience, Frankie tripped a booby trap. Chances were high he never knew what hit him.

McGill raced across the sleet-covered turnpike, through the tunnels and past mountain after dismal mountain of naked black trees in the dead January landscape. He kept his foot to the floor, ninety, ninety-five, a hundred-and-five, weaving in and out of traffic, chain-smoking cigarettes, blaring the horn and flashing the lights and yelling, "Get the fuck out of the way!"

They somehow made it to the funeral home alive before the procession left for the cemetery. Dawkins had only known Frankie for a few days, and wasn't sure he even deserved to be there. There were hundreds of somber people, heads hung low, all in their Sunday best. Dawkins felt like a Slobovian jerk in jeans and a sweatshirt, with two-days of stubble on his face. He hadn't even brushed his teeth.

An organist was playing music that made it seem ten times worse. A group of old friends saw McGill and came over, the girls crying and hugging, the guys speaking in whispers. Frankie's two little brothers, Jeff and Jerry, about seven and eight years old, saw McGill and raced up yelling, "Mom, Dad, Stick's here, Stick's here!"

McGill bent down and wrapped them in his arms, and Dawkins followed him to where Frankie's mom and dad were accepting condolences. Frankie's dad was wearing medals on his suitcoat, showing that he too had served his country. Frankie's mom wore was a single Gold Star, pinned on her black dress, which was awarded to mothers whose sons were killed in the line of duty.

The casket was covered with an American flag, and it was closed, so Frankie must have been torn up pretty bad. Flowers were everywhere, and there were pictures of him around the room: at four, in a cowboy hat; at seven, in a Superman cape, pretending to fly; at ten, in a Little League uniform with a baseball bat over his shoulder; at twelve, with his first guitar; at sixteen, in a tuxedo for the junior prom; at eighteen, with his Fender Stratocaster slung low to his waist and belting out a song under a *Frankie and the Dynamos* banner.

It struck Dawkins that Annie Chambers probably didn't know what had happened, and he had a sharp pang of guilt, thankful it would be McGill, Frankie's close friend, who would have to be the one to tell her.

McGill talked to Frankie's mom and dad for a few minutes, then introduced Dawkins. "This is Bob Dawkins. He met Frankie when he came up to see me right before he shipped out."

Dawkins had no idea what to say to the parents of a guy he barely knew who had just been killed in the war. "I...I only knew Frankie for a few days, but I really liked him."

Frankie's dad seemed to understand how awkward it was for him, and curling the corners of his mouth up in a sad smile, said, "That's how Frankie was, son. Everybody liked him."

Others were waiting in line to offer condolences, and as they moved away McGill said, "Bob, stay here. I need to have a talk with Frankie."

McGill saw Frankie's two favorite electric guitars, his Stratocaster and his Les Paul, both with flaming sunburst finishes, sitting on guitar stands next to each other at the head of the casket, a musical island in the sea of flowers. It was as if Frankie was between sets, just taking a break, and he would stroll up any minute, strap one on, and launch into his gritty version of "Susie Q."

Frankie never could decide which guitar he liked better. McGill picked up the Les Paul and strummed a chord. It was in tune. Then he picked up the Strat and strummed a chord. It was out, so he knelt down, rested the guitar on his knee, and meticulously tuned each string. When it was right, he played a few chords, and carefully placed it on the stand.

The casket was draped in an American flag and guarded by two soldiers with ceremonial rifles. A big photo of Frankie, with his wavy black hair and his Elvis Presley good looks, smiled out from a gold frame at the head of the casket.

McGill put his hands on top of the flag covering the casket, and just like he always did, said, "Hey, Frankie, what's happening?"

He was silent for a long minute. Then he picked up Frankie's photo and began talking to it and shaking his fist as he reamed Frankie out for flunking French and getting his ass blown away for nothing.

After a while he put it down, thumped his fist on the casket with a dramatic *WHAM*! and shouted, "*Attention*! I need your attention. And cut the organ. Frankie hated that crap."

The music stopped instantly as everybody froze, their eyes fixated on McGill. There wasn't a sound as he took out his wallet, removed a piece of paper, carefully unfolded it, and held it above his head.

"Frankie came up to see me right before he shipped out, and he gave me this for safe keeping. It's his induction notice from the draft board. I promised I'd buy him a beer and we'd burn it together as soon as he got back. I'm pissed I can't buy him a beer."

McGill held Uncle Sam's "Greeting" in front of Frankie's photo, making sure Frankie could watch. He sparked his Zippo, touching the fire to the lowest corner. The crinkled paper burned slowly at first, then flamed-up in a bright orange *WHOOSH* before dying out in a puff of white smoke and a flutter of gray ashes that came peacefully to rest on the Stars-and-Stripes draped over Frankie's coffin.

Chapter 7

Out *Now*!

JENNY AND MCGILL GRADUATED IN JUNE OF 1970, THE CAMBODIAN SPRING, when anti-war demonstrations engulfed campuses all across the nation after it came out that Nixon had secretly widened the war by sending in troops and bombing the fuck out of Cambodia. The protests led to the tragedy at Kent State University on May 4, 1970, when four college kids were gunned down by the Ohio National Guard. Huge demonstrations erupted at campuses from coast-to-coast, and boycotts shut down universities all over the country. College administrators didn't know what to do, and seniors like McGill didn't know if they would have the credits to graduate if classes were canceled.

McGill hung out playing cards, winning at hearts and bridge but losing at poker. After weeks of uncertainty, administrators reached a consensus that academic progress should not suffer. Many schools, including Penn State, gave PASS/FAIL rather than letter grades so the university system would not crash.

At all-women's Bryn Mawr, there were posters and meetings and teach-ins, but classes went on as usual. Jenny graduated Phi Beta Kappa and was accepted by Yale Law School for the fall semester.

McGill's four-year military deferment was up, and his bad number meant he would be drafted before the end of the summer. Law school was no longer an option.

McGill had reversed his position on the war even before Frankie was killed, but at heart he was still a conservative, convinced America had to stand up to the Soviets. He didn't object to doing his part by serving in the military, just to fighting in an illegal and immoral war.

Since his freshman year, McGill had assumed that the war would be over long before he had to deal with it and now his options were few: he could claim he was a "conscientious objector" on religious grounds, but then he would have to serve two years mopping floors in a hospital; he could go into exile in Sweden or Canada and possibly never return; he could wait to be drafted for two years and risk being sent to Vietnam; he could refuse induction and go to jail; he could enlist in the Navy, Air Force or Coast Guard for four years or in the Army for only three.

He wanted to do his time and get out as soon as possible without going to Vietnam, so the Army was the answer. The recruiting sergeant could not promise what kind of duty he might pull in return for serving an extra year, but he guaranteed in writing that McGill would not be sent to Vietnam. It was right there in the enlistment contract in black and white, a firm deal between McGill and Uncle Sam. The official Army classification for "volunteers" like McGill was that he was a "draft induced enlistment," or a DIE in Army acronymics.

There was no sense waiting, so he requested immediate induction. A month after graduation from college, he began eight weeks of "basic" (Basic Combat Training) at Fort Dix, New Jersey. Then the Army in its wisdom decided that he would make a good cop, and orders came down sending him to Fort Gordon, Georgia, for eight weeks of AIT (Advanced Individual Training) at Military Police School. When he finished, he was promoted to Private First Class and given an MOS (Military Occupational Specialty) of 95 Bravo. He was now a Military Policeman and authorized to carry a sidearm and wear the brass "crossed pistols" MP insignia on his uniform.

He got extra-lucky when the Army assigned him to the MP company at Fort Myer, Virginia, right next to Arlington National Cemetery and the Pentagon and a stone's throw from the vibrant nightlife of Georgetown. It was the Army's most prestigious post, home of the 3rd Infantry Regiment—The Old Guard—the spit-and-polish unit in charge of ceremonial duties at Arlington National Cemetery.

The MP company was tasked with normal police duties, including traffic control at the cemetery as well as at Fort Myer and the Pentagon. McGill was tall, which made him easy to see, so PFC McGill found himself assigned to the traffic detail. With an MP brassard on his upper arm, a Sam Browne belt with a .45 pistol in the holster, a white MP saucer hat, white gloves and a silver whistle, he was on track to spend two-and-a-half easy years directing traffic at the Pentagon. Most guys his rank would have killed for his piece-of-cake job.

His pay was only about $90 a month, so he couldn't afford to live off-post, but he had a car, a burgundy '65 Buick Skylark convertible that his dad let him take off the McGill Motors lot. Every couple of months he saved up enough to either drive up to New Haven to see Jenny or buy her a ticket to come down on the train. It cost him half a month's pay for a cheap motel, but it was worth every penny.

Early in 1971 McGill found himself in trouble with his company commander, Captain Strack, a by-the-book fanatic only a couple years older than he was. Everybody under him thought Strack was a strutting Mickey-Mouse officer with a broomstick up his ass.

One Friday evening as Strack looked out his office window over the parking lot he saw PFC McGill sitting in a convertible with the top down with a beautiful girl right next to him. Strack could not stand to see a low-life enlisted worm with the kind of woman whose affections he, Gunther Stuyvesant Strack, an honors graduate of the Citadel, was being cheated out of because the fucking hippies had turned career military officers into social pariahs.

Strack announced over the PA system, "Attention, all personnel. This is Captain Strack. It has been brought to my attention that morale has not been up to our historic high standards. So, to enhance unit cohesion and esprit de corps, there will be a full inspection tomorrow at zero seven hundred hours. Strack out."

The entire company groaned a collective FUCK! It took hours of polishing and spit-shining to prepare for a white-glove inspection, and it killed any hope of having fun that Friday night. It reminded McGill of the famous warning, variously attributed to a Japanese submarine commander and a drill instructor in the U.S. Marines: "The beatings will continue until morale improves."

McGill thought it was just bad luck; if he had left a minute earlier he would not have been there to hear the order and would have been free until 0700 on Monday. Now, if he were to spend the night with Jenny, he would have to be up at 0500 to get back.

Jenny had never heard military orders except in the movies. The voice over the loudspeakers saying that an inspection would boost morale sounded Orwellian to her.

McGill, cursing Strack with every step, went back to get his Class-A khaki uniform, shoe shining kit, both pairs of combat boots, dress shoes and a can of Brasso. He took her to dinner, but instead of going to the famous Cellar Door to listen to folk music, he took her back to the motel.

He sat on the bed, spit-shining his shoes and two pairs of boots and polishing his brass as the sickly-sweet smell of Brasso filled the room. Finally he said, "That's the best I can do."

They made love and watched *The Tonight Show* with Johnny Carson until McGill said, "Jen, I've got to get some sleep for tomorrow. I'll try to be quiet in the morning. You just sleep in."

"When will you be back?"

"Noon at the latest. Inspections usually take a couple of hours."

McGill arrived at the barracks at 0600 and made up his bunk, tight. He arranged his personal effects in his locker and his footlocker, his socks and underwear in their prescribed places and folded just so. Then he pitched in and did his part, washing windows and depubing toilets. He was confident he would pass; he had never failed an inspection.

The barracks was comprised of three floors of four-man rooms that were inspected room-by-room by the commanding officer—the CO. The first-sergeant came in, called, "TenHUT," and McGill and his bunkmates came to attention next to their bunks as Strack strode in.

Strack gave the bunks a close inspection, opened their footlockers, checking to see that everything was where it was supposed to be. When he came to McGill he rooted around in his footlocker for what seemed like an extra long time, then he opened McGill's metal locker and wiped his white glove around the back of the shelves. Strack seemed disappointed when the glove came out clean. Strack noticed the photo of Jenny and McGill on the back of the locker door, the one from the instant-photo booth at Wildwood. Strack's bulbous nose turned a deeper shade of pink, and he reached down to the bottom of the locker and picked up one of McGill's boots and examined it closely.

"What the fuck is this?" Strack said, holding the boot in his hand.

"*Sir*, it's a combat boot, *sir*," McGill said, wondering what was wrong.

"No, asshole, THIS," and he pointed to a slight gash in the boot.

"*Sir*, it's a scuff mark, Captain Strack, *sir*."

"What's it doing there, private?"

"I got it in Basic under the barbed wire, *sir*. It won't come out, *sir*."

"It won't come out?" Strack said, his voice heavy with sarcasm. "Do you know why it won't come out, Private McGill?"

"Yes, *sir*, because it's too deep, *sir*."

"No, Private McGill. It won't come off because you're too fucking fond of fucking *pussy*."

"Sir, I…I don't understand, sir."

"Pussy. You understand what pussy is, don't you, private?"

"Uh, yes, sir, but—"

"You didn't do you footgear properly because you were more concerned with getting your no good fucking dick wet than you were in preparing for this inspection. Is that not true, private?"

"No, *sir*, Captain Strack, *sir*. My girlfriend came down to visit, *sir*, but I spent the whole evening preparing for inspection, *sir*."

"The whole evening? I doubt that very much. Tell me, private, does your girlfriend have a pussy?"

"Uh, sir, I don't understand, sir."

"It is a simple question. Let me repeat it for you. Does your girlfriend have a fucking pussy?"

McGill was seething; what made him drag Jenny into it?

"*Sir*, all girls have pussies, *sir*."

"Are you sure about that? Have you personally inspected each and every female on this planet to make sure they all have pussies?"

"No, *sir*, I have not, *sir*."

"Have you inspected your girlfriend to make sure she has a pussy, Private McGill?"

Any hint of defiance could get him into real trouble, but he couldn't help it. "*Sir*, with all due respect, that is a personal question, *sir*."

"A personal question? What makes you think you have anything fucking personal in this man's army? You are a fucking GI, government fucking issue. The only thing you have that's personal are your personal problems, private, and you know how much the U.S. Army cares about your personal fucking problems. When a member of my command is derelict in his duty because his mind is on his girlfriend's pussy and not on his military duty then his girlfriend's pussy is no longer just his personal fucking problem because the asshole has made it my fucking problem. Do you understand, Private McGill?"

McGill screamed, loud, like drill sergeants taught in Basic, "*SIR*, with all due respect, *SIR*, my girlfriend's anatomy is none of your business, *SIR*, and I believe your comments amount to conduct unbecoming an officer, *SIR*!" It was all McGill could do to remain at military attention and restrain from punching Strack's lights out.

Strack shouted, "Conduct unbecoming an officer? Why you skinny fucking turd. Come on, assfuckinghole!" He stuck out his chin and pointed at it. "Take your best shot. Come on, you know you'd give anything to come at me right now, wouldn't you, private? Well, come on. What's wrong? You a chickenshit as well as a fucking asshole?"

"*SIR*, that would be assaulting an officer, *SIR*. I am not that stupid, *SIR*, no matter how much you deserve it, *SIR*."

"Not that stupid? Too bad, because I'd love to kick your ass," Strack said as he stuck his face right in McGill's, close enough for McGill to smell his Listerine breath.

"Being a member of the Military Police unit at the U.S. Army's most prestigious post is the highest honor this country can bestow on a no-good piece of shit like you. Every day you are privileged to salute more generals than the average enlisted man sees in a lifetime. It's a goddamn fucking honor, and those of us who serve here are proud of our uniforms, and by God, anyone under my command will adhere to the highest standards of military excellence. Your footgear is not up to those standards. You have failed this inspection, and you are on restriction and KP for a week. Now get your sorry ass down to the mess hall on the fucking double."

Strack strode out the door and the first-sergeant called, "At ease." McGill just stood, not moving, shell-shocked.

"What the fuck was that about" a bunkmate asked.

"I don't have a fucking clue."

And he didn't. He had kept a low profile since arriving at Fort Myer, kept his nose clean and stayed out of trouble. What the hell had he done to bring Strack down on him like that? Could it have been about Jenny?

He called Jenny from the pay phone to tell her he was on report because his boots weren't properly shined.

"But Arty, I watched you work on them. They were perfect."

"I know, Jen. I don't know what I did to piss him off."

He explained he couldn't leave the barracks, and apologized for leaving her alone in the motel. He was careful to leave out what Strack had to say about her pussy, as he didn't want her to think that she had been in any way responsible.

"It's okay, Arty, it's not your fault. I'll be fine, but I'll miss you."

"Well, at least we had one night."

After hanging up he changed into his fatigue uniform and headed to the mess hall to peel potatoes, wash pots, and mop floors.

After a week on KP, McGill was back to directing traffic at the Pentagon, with two days off twice a month. A huge anti-war protest was set for

Saturday, April 24, 1971. What some were calling the "Out Now!" demonstration was expected to be the biggest ever against the war. In the week leading up to it, anti-war events had been going on all over Washington, many organized by the Vietnam Veterans Against the War. Hundreds of these vets threw their ribbons and medals over a makeshift barrier onto the Capitol steps. Several of them testified before a Senate committee, and a highly-decorated U.S. Navy lieutenant named Kerry summed it up by asking the committee, "How do you ask a man to be the last man to die for a mistake?"

Jenny was one of the organizers of the Yale contingent and took the train down on Wednesday night with a dozen others to prepare. She told McGill she couldn't stay with him and would be at the Arlington Marriott across the bridge from Georgetown.

He went to see her Thursday evening after his shift, pilfering her a bouquet of roses that he picked from the gardens of the mansions along Generals' Row. When the hotel door opened he was crestfallen to see a room full of people and a pile of sleeping bags in the corner.

They kissed hello just as the phone rang and someone yelled, "Jennifer." She was on the phone, off the phone, on the phone, in charge.

He watched her in action feeling proud that she was his. Well, sort of his. They had never made a commitment, and the way the Yalie guys were glaring at him, McGill could tell they didn't think anybody with an Army haircut was right for her. When he first arrived at Fort Myer, he soon discovered that his haircut made him an outcast in the Georgetown college bars, like a neon sign flashing: THIS ASSHOLE'S IN THE ARMY! THIS ASSHOLE'S IN THE ARMY!

Finally, Jenny had a break, and a Yalie whispered in her ear and pointed in McGill's direction. Jenny shook her head and said, "No!" and then she came over and gave McGill a huge hug and announced, "Now listen, everyone. This is Arty. I've known him for years. He's not a spy, he's not a baby killer. He just had a bad draft number."

She introduced him to one of her girlfriends. "Arty, this is my good friend, Catherine DeWolfe. We met four years ago when my swim team competed against Vassar, and we went on that tour of Europe together. Remember? Now we're classmates and housemates."

McGill said, "Glad to know you," wondering if she was one of "the" DeWolfes, an heiress to one of America's greatest fortunes. She was cute and glowed in a healthy, athletic kind of way. She was almost as tall as he was and wore her long, auburn hair in a braided ponytail that reached to the small of her back. The word that came to mind was "statuesque," like illustrations in mythology books of Diana, Goddess of the Hunt.

"Hello," she said in a soft, husky voice, and gave him a firm handshake. "Jenny says you're an MP in the Army. Will you be on the other side tomorrow?"

"I sure hope not. Last we heard we were sticking to our normal shifts."

The room was abuzz with comings and goings, pizza and beer and pot. McGill kept quiet as they planned and strategized how to make the Yale contingent heard at the demonstration. At midnight, he could see it was futile to hope for time alone with her, so he kissed her goodnight, went back to the barracks and whacked off in the shower to thoughts of the wonderful whimpering sounds Jenny made when making love.

One of the guys in McGill's unit was selling T-shirts with a peace sign and a dove above the slogan: GRUNTS AGAINST THE WAR. McGill bought one, thinking it was perfect for the demonstration.

As Washington began to fill up with protesters, the Fort Myer MPs were worried that they would be put on alert and confined to post. The first-sergeant called assembly as McGill's day-shift came off-duty on Friday and announced, "Infantry troops are being bussed in to handle any threats to the Pentagon. So until further notice, we will maintain our regular schedule."

That meant McGill had the weekend off. He packed his gym bag for an overnight stay, changed into jeans, tennis shoes and a polo shirt, not daring to wear an anti-war T-shirt on base. He was about to leave when a shout came from down the hall, "McGill, is McGill still here?"

"Yo!" he called back. "What is it?"

"Phone call at the duty sergeant's desk."

McGill never got calls at the barracks. He hurried down, worried it was Jenny with bad news. "Hello."

"Hey, Stick. It's Mulligan."

"Mulligan? The fucking Mulligan Man! Your dad told me you were cruising the Mediterranean."

"That ended last month. I've been home on leave. Your mom said you were an MP at the Pentagon and gave me this number. I'm here for a couple days so I had to look you up. How you doing?"

"I'm okay. You just caught me. I was headed out and don't have to be back till Monday. This is great. Jenny's down here for the demonstration. You'll finally get to meet her. Where are you staying?"

"The BOQ at Fort McNair."

"That's practically next door. Want me to pick you up?"

"Can't tonight. I'm meeting some guys from Annapolis. Sunday or Monday are possibilities, but tomorrow night would be best."

"Tomorrow is going to be nuts. Jenny's a coordinator and I'm going along to help. Why don't you come with us?"

"I've got meetings most of the day. And I've got orders for Vietnam. I fly out Tuesday from Andrews."

"You're going to fucking *Nam*? But you're Navy, you're supposed to be floating around the middle of the ocean, not in the fucking jungles. So what kind of assignment you pull?"

"I won't know till I get there."

"We gotta get together. Let's meet up after the protest and have drinks and dinner. You've just got to meet Jenny."

"Sure. When and where?"

"Let me think. I know they plan to end at six so the crowds can get out of town before dark, and we're supposed to ride a chartered bus into the city in the morning and back after that, so I won't have my car."

"McNair's not far from the Mall," Mulligan said. "How about we meet at the Washington Monument and we'll grab a cab somewhere."

"Great. We'll go to dinner in Georgetown, do it up right. Let's say eight o'clock, the northwest corner."

McGill dashed off to Jenny's hotel, stopping at a deli for sandwiches, potato salad, slices of cherry cheesecake and a bottle of white wine. Her room was full of Yalies, and Jenny was on the phone. When she got off he kissed her and said, "Jenny, great news! I just had a call from Mulligan. He's in town and we're going to see him tomorrow after everything's over. You'll finally get to meet him."

"Wow, that's terrific, Arty. What a nice surprise."

"So let's get out of here for a couple of hours. You need a break, and I need some time with you. We won't have a chance to be alone for the rest of the weekend, I just know it."

"Oh, Arty, I can't, there's so much to do."

"Look, Jen, it's a beautiful evening, and I picked up some wine and sandwiches and cheesecake for a picnic. Just a couple of hours. Please."

Catherine was listening and said, "Go ahead, Jennifer. Everything's under control. You need to relax a little so you'll be at your best."

She was hungry, and Arty was right; tomorrow would be crazy, and she and Catherine were catching the early train back to New Haven on Sunday morning.

"Okay, but only for a couple of hours. This is too important."

"I agree, Jen. Nobody wants the war stopped more than me."

As McGill pulled onto the George Washington Parkway she asked, "Where are we going, Arty?"

"Mount Vernon."

"You mean George Washington's estate?"

"It's not far. Ever been there?"

"No, but I'd like to see it."

As they cruised along Jenny watched the Washington Monument as it came closer, then the Lincoln Memorial came into view across the Potomac. Everywhere was history.

Twenty minutes later they parked in the Mount Vernon lot. He took an Army blanket out of the trunk, and seeing the NO ALCOHOLIC BEVERAGES sign at the head of the path, he used the blanket to cover the wine bottle. They walked around the side of the mansion, stopping for a moment when they came to the breathtaking view of the wide Potomac River and the rolling Maryland hills on the other side.

"It's spectacular, Arty. I had no idea."

They walked down the sloping, tree-studded hillside toward the river. He spread the blanket over the grass in a spot next to some bushes, where they would be partly hidden from other tourists by the trunk of a huge oak. He used the corkscrew on his Swiss Army knife and pulled the cork—skree*POP*—and poured the cool wine into paper cups.

"Here's to us, Jenny," he said, and she blushed as he tapped his cup against hers to seal the toast and leaned over and softly kissed her.

It was pleasant under the trees watching sailboats gliding on the river and clouds changing hues as the sun sank in the west. Jenny did most of the talking, telling him about her problems with the speakers and the scheduling conflicts. There were a few other tourists further down, closer to the river, and young kids playing hide-and-seek. So when they finished the cheesecake they lay on the blanket and just kissed and lightly hugged.

When the first lightning bugs came out, flickering on and off amid the bushes, a guard came around announcing, "The park closes in ten minutes...the park closes in ten minutes."

McGill and Jenny had a low profile on the blanket in the early dusk; it wasn't like they were trying to hide, but the guard flat out missed seeing them. As the guard ushered what he thought were the last of the tourists up the hill Jenny whispered, "Arty, do you think George and Martha ever made love down here."

He was surprised, as he had always been the initiator. "Oh, yes, absolutely. All the time!"

"Do you think it would be disrespectful if we, you know..."

"Oh, no! They'd be pissed if we didn't. I'll bet we'll be the first since they made it a National Monument."

Much later, back at the hotel, Jenny and Catherine shared a bed while McGill crashed on the floor under his sleeping bag next to six other guys. In the morning, McGill and Jenny took their turns in the shower together then went to the hotel's coffee shop for a working breakfast with several other coordinators. A small bus took them to the Capitol steps, where a stage and sound equipment were being erected.

The forecast was for a gorgeous day, with temperatures in the low eighties. Everyone in Jenny's leadership group received a brown paper bag with a sandwich, a packet of peanut butter crackers and a banana to get them through the day.

The Park Service estimated half a million people were there, setting a record for attendance. The District of Columbia police and U.S. Park police, who many feared might get crazy-violent like the Chicago police had done at the 1968 Democratic Convention, instead stood on alert and watched as the protesters marched to the Mall.

Their ID badges got them through security and backstage, behind the phalanx of police. Looking out from the Capitol steps, it seemed like everyone in America was there. But McGill sensed it was all in vain, because the only person who could stop the war, Nixon, had skipped town to his beach house in California.

A man with a silver mustache called out, "Miss Abruzzi, thank goodness you're here! They need you in the tent."

"Professor Hazlett," Jenny said, "this is my friend, Arty. He's in the Army, but he's against the war. Professor Hazlett teaches contracts."

"Glad to know you," McGill said. "I'd like to help in any way I can. I know a little about sound equipment."

"I'm sure they can use a hand. Tell the emcee I sent you," and he took Jenny by the arm and hurried her off.

McGill worked as a roadie for the musicians waiting to play, which put him at the center of everything. There were many anti-war politicians on hand, like Senators J. William Fulbright and Teddy Kennedy, and activists including Abbie Hoffman and Daniel Berrigan, and celebrities like movie star Jane Fonda, and musicians like John Denver and McGill's favorites, Peter, Paul & Mary. But the most poignant moment came when a group of Vietnam Veterans Against the War took the stage in fatigues. These guys had seen combat, and several were in their wheelchairs. When they spoke, everyone in the crowd listened up.

As the vets were leaving the stage the emcee said, "Those guys are back from the war and free to tell the truth, but I'd like to bring up someone who is still under the thumb of the military," and he pointed right at McGill. "*You*! Come on up here. We need your perspective."

McGill was in the back by the loudspeakers. "M…m…*me*?"

"Yes, you. Come on," and before he knew it two burly guys in SECURITY T-shirts were escorting him and then there he was standing in front of the microphone with 500,000 faces staring up at him.

"Tell us your name, son," the emcee said.

"Uh, I'd better not."

"Why is that, son? This is a free country, and even soldiers have the right to speak their mind as long as they're not in uniform. Are you afraid of being punished for speaking your mind?"

"Free speech doesn't matter," McGill said. "The Army can do anything it wants and there's nothing you can do about it."

"So you're in the Army. What is your rank?"

McGill realized he'd already said too much. "I'm just a grunt."

"Have you been in Vietnam?"

"No."

"Where are you stationed?"

"I…I'd better not say."

"Can you tell us what the men in your unit think about the war?"

"Sure, that's easy. Like that Navy officer told that Senate committee last week, nobody wants to be the last guy to die for a mistake."

"Is there anything you'd like to get off your chest?"

McGill hesitated for a moment, but he did have an insight he had never heard anyone else ever discuss. He couldn't help himself. "Yes. Yes I think I do."

The emcee handed him the microphone and McGill took a deep breath. "I'd like to talk about something that at first glance might not seem to have anything to do with Vietnam. It's about a movie everybody knows, *Casablanca*, starring Humphrey Bogart and Ingrid Bergman. It was made in 1941, a year before the Japanese bombed Pearl Harbor and we got into the war. The Nazis had defeated France, Hitler had paraded through Paris, and the Germans were pulling the strings of a French puppet government that controlled the colony of Morocco and its capital, Casablanca.

"Well, it was the same in the French colony of Vietnam, except that there it was the Japanese who were pulling the strings. They ordered the French officials to confiscate Vietnam's rice crop to feed the Japanese army, not just in Vietnam, but their armies in China, Burma, Indonesia and the Philippines as well. The result was a famine, and almost two million Vietnamese starved to death to feed the Japanese war machine.

"Okay, back to *Casablanca*. Do you remember the stirring scene in Rick's Café, the one where the evil Colonel Strasser and some of his officers are singing a German drinking song. The leader of the resistance movement gets up and starts singing the French national anthem and all the other customers leap to their feet and join in, drowning out the hated Nazis. Strasser is furious, and orders Louie, the charmingly corrupt French chief of police, to shut down the bar on any pretext. In one of the greatest movie scenes of all time, Louie blows his whistle and says that he is 'Shocked—*shocked*!' to learn that gambling is going on just as a waiter rushes up and hands him his winnings.

"To me *Casablanca* is instructive, not for what it says about the Nazis, but for what is says about colonialism. The thing about that scene that nobody ever talks about is that there is not a single Arab, not one, singing for the greater glory of France. In fact, the only Arabs with speaking parts in the whole movie are a beggar, a street vendor, and the shady proprietor of the Blue Parrot Café. There is no mention at all about whether the people of Casablanca preferred having the Germans or the French as their masters, or perhaps having no masters at all.

"Now at the end of World War II the new government of France was determined to retake all of France's former colonies. In Vietnam, there were still two-hundred thousand Japanese troops in the country that now came under the command of French military officers. General Douglas MacArthur, then the military governor of Japan, could only watch from Tokyo as the French used the Japanese troops to put down the Vietnamese nationalists who were trying to throw out both the French and the Japanese and gain their independence."

McGill was shouting now, like a fire-and-brimstone preacher winding up a sermon. "MacArthur said, and I quote: 'If there is anything that makes my blood boil it is to see our allies in Indochina deploying Japanese troops to reconquer the little people we promised to liberate. It is the most ignoble kind of betrayal.'

"I say MacArthur was right. It was indeed the most ignoble kind of betrayal, not only of the Vietnamese who had fought on our side, but a complete and utter betrayal of our history and our ideals. We let the French try to take back Indochina after World War II and secretly gave them all the weapons they wanted. If we had not supported French colonialism, Americans would not be dying in the jungles today. I say stop the war and stop it now! Out *NOW*!"

"OUT *NOW*! OUT *NOW*!" came the chant from the crowd.

McGill said, "Thank you for listening," and flashed a two-fingered peace sign as he headed off.

Jenny was staring at him with an awestruck, dumbfounded look when he came backstage. She gave him a hug and said. "Arty, what were you doing out there?"

"I was just standing in the back listening to the speeches when he pointed at me, and before I knew it two guards were hustling me out front. And then I couldn't shut up. Fuck! What an idiot I am. I just stepped on my dick, Jen, big time. If any of my officers or sergeants saw me, I'm dead meat."

Chapter 8

The Ugly Side of Peace

April 24, 1971

THE DEMONSTRATION HAD BEEN PEACEFUL AND ORDERLY ALL DAY. THE cops had kept their distance, and Jenny and the other coordinators were thrilled at how smoothly everything had gone. The last speaker finished about five-thirty and the emcee asked the massive crowd to peacefully disperse. McGill helped pack up sound equipment, and at seven he said, "We should go, Jen. We're supposed to meet Mulligan at eight and it's a bit of a hike."

"Can Catherine come with us, Arty? We're the only women in the room and she doesn't want to go back without me."

"Sure, it'll be like a blind date. They can argue whose hair is redder."

The scattered clouds were turning from light pink to sunset orange. McGill and Jenny put on their sweaters, Catherine put on a jacket from her backpack, and the three of them headed into the milling crowd toward the Washington Monument, a mile and a half away.

McGill guessed there were thirty thousand people still on the Mall, way down from the half million who had been there earlier in the day. It had been the largest turnout for any demonstration ever against the war. But the complexion of the crowd had changed; there were now maybe fifteen guys for every woman instead of the previous four or five.

As they walked he became more and more uneasy as he recognized that they were among the crazies, the drunks, the dregs aching for some kind of action. McGill stepped between Jenny and Catherine, took both of their hands in his, and said, "You two stay close."

After half a mile Catherine said, "This is really strange. There aren't any cops."

Since leaving the Capitol steps they had not seen even a single cop. McGill had been through MP school, had drilled for riot and crowd control, and it was obvious to him it would not have taken much of a show of force to keep the drunken, leaderless hooligans under control. This was no longer an organized anti-war crowd; these were horny guys being rowdy assholes because they couldn't get laid.

McGill said, "This reminds me of the spring-break party riots in

Lauderdale. These guys just want to tear things down for the hell of it."

The further they went, the worse it got. Cars and motorcycles were driving all over the lawn, peeling out, doing wheelies and trying to do as much damage as possible.

Night was coming, and the hooligans began setting bonfires. Anything combustible was fair game; the wooden benches along the sidewalks were the first to go, and cars knocked down small trees to feed the fires. Men climbed bigger trees like packs of wild monkeys and tried to break off branches by bouncing in unison.

"It's like right out a horror movie," Jenny said.

Catherine said, "How did we let this get so out of control so fast? This was not supposed to happen."

"It's as if the cops abandoned the Mall on purpose," McGill said. "Almost like they're deliberately egging on the assholes to trash it."

None of them had ever been in the middle of anything so terrifying. The organizers had not given any hint that there might be a problem brewing. A different, more radical group called the "May Day Tribe" had been planning a separate demonstration the next weekend for months. After years of demonstrations, the war was still on, with over 50,000 American dead. Nothing had worked, so now they planned to use urban guerrilla tactics to end the war by shutting down the government. The action was to start next Saturday, on May 1. They intended to block freeways, bridges, and intersections the following Monday to create massive traffic jams and shut down the government. But they were dedicated activists with a plan, and that plan meant doing everything possible so as to not to be perceived as being destructive. Disruptive yes, destructive no. They had given their word that they would not be disruptive today. That was next week—not today. The hooligans who were trashing the Mall were not anybody's idea of good public relations.

Halfway to the Washington Monument, they came across a pickup truck hitched to a camping trailer that was parked in the middle of the lawn. On top of the trailer a guy was carnival-barking like he was selling snow cones: "Angel dust joints, five bucks. Angel dust joints, five bucks." Several rowdies stood in line drinking beer, waiting their turns.

The biggest fires were at the Washington Monument, where dozens of whooping and shouting vandals were tearing the benches apart with their bare hands to feed the bonfires. Back in 1961, when he was in seventh grade, McGill and forty others in Troop 38 of the Milltowne

Boy Scouts sat in full uniform on these very benches. They were waiting their turns to take the elevator to a tiny room at the top, where a Park Ranger allowed every scout, one at a time, ten seconds to look out of each of the four small windows in the pyramid at the top.

For the first time since the air-raid blackouts in World War II, the capital's most distinctive landmark had gone dark, its spotlights smashed to fragments. Flickers from the bonfires lit the lower portion of the obelisk and left the top towering in the shadows. McGill desperately wanted to do something. Maybe he could convince them that tearing up the Mall played right into Nixon's hands? No, they'd take one look at his haircut and label him a "baby-killer" and maybe come after him. He would do nothing to put Jenny and Catherine in danger. He was as powerless to stop the madness as he was powerless to stop the war.

Jenny was in tears as she watched the anarchistic stupidity. "This can't be happening! How could our people do this? I don't understand."

"You're too nice to understand, Jen," McGill said, "but the world is filled with assholes. At least ten percent of all the people on the planet are assholes, no matter what side they're on."

"But this is only a tiny minority of everybody who came today," Jenny said. "How could we let them ruin it?"

McGill said, "You guys were too trusting, Jen, and the cops gave you all the rope you needed to hang yourselves. You get a crowd that size and the assholes come out of the woodwork after the good guys have gone home. It's totally predictable. You have to be prepared to deal with assholes, because if you're not, the assholes will do you in, every time. Nixon knows that. Ten to one Nixon planned the whole thing, told the cops to stay out of sight. The TV news tomorrow will negate everything good that went down here today. Score one for the Trickster."

Wiping her eyes, Jenny said, "No one could be that diabolical."

"This is Tricky Dick we're talking about here, Jen. Think about it. What plans did you have for security?"

"I don't know, I was just helping to coordinate the speakers."

Catherine jumped in. "I was on a pacification team. We all took a training course on how to talk people out of confronting the police."

"But what if there weren't any police," McGill said, "and everybody on your team headed for home…then what?"

"It was never mentioned," Catherine said. "There's always police."

"Ah-ha, see what I mean about the Trickster?" McGill said. "The son-of-a-bitch knows the black side of human nature from the inside out. When to have police, when not to have police. From the Pumpkin Papers to the Checkers speech to his 'secret plan to win the war,' Nixon knew exactly what he was doing. He'll waste as many guys like Frankie Dombrowski as it takes to get reelected. I'd bet Nixon himself ordered the cops to sit on their asses today. He knows this is what be on the news for weeks and what the country will remember."

Jenny put her arm around his waist and pulled up close. "It makes me sick, Arty."

They waited for Mulligan while the mob fed the bonfires, which would have been great at a pep rally for a homecoming game at Milltowne High, but this was the National Mall. The Suffragettes held rallies here to win women the right to vote. When Martin Luther King gave his "I Have A Dream" speech there had been no destruction.

As she pointed up at the obelisk, which seemed to sway with the shadows and flickers of the bonfires, Jenny said, "Arty, you're the history buff. What's the story behind the different colors of the stone?"

Even in firelight it was easy to pick out the tones of the marble, which changed to a slightly darker hue about a third of the way up. He had heard the story from a Park Ranger when he was there with the Boy Scouts '61.

"I don't remember the details," he told them, "but it had to do with the Know-Nothing Party. They thought if it was ever finished the Pope would rule over America, or some such shit. They somehow took over the committee in charge of construction and stopped work for decades. By the time the Know-Nothings had been laughed out of history, the quarry where the original marble came from was played out, so they had to get the upper part from a different quarry."

Jenny was dumbfounded. "You mean they stopped because they thought the Pope was behind it?"

"Jenny, honey," McGill said as gently as he could, "you have to remember—this is America. The different shades of stone testify to the way America works things out. Everything takes decades."

As they watched the shadows dancing up the sides of the monument, Catherine said, "You know, the judges at the Salem witch trials were not condemned in their time—they were applauded. So were the defenders of slavery, and of genocide against the Indians. They all had public support."

"Yeah, the only good Indian is a dead Indian and all that," McGill said. "It was the same with the Robber Barons. What did they care what history would say? They'd got theirs. The bastards who lied us into Vietnam won't be called to justice in our lifetimes either. It sucks, but that's how it is."

Mulligan had spent the morning at a promotion ceremony with a score of fellow officers. He and three classmates from Annapolis moved up in rank from ensign, a "butter bar" in military jargon because of the single brass bar denoting the O-1 rank. He would still wear a single bar, but as an O-2, a lieutenant, junior grade, the bar would be silver.

He spent the afternoon celebrating over drinks at Fort McNair's posh Officers' Club. He and some others commiserated at their bad luck at getting orders for Vietnam instead of sea-duty. From time to time, he glanced at the TV above the bar and watched as hundreds of thousands of protesters listened to speakers railing against the war.

He saw Peter, Paul & Mary come on stage and sing "Blowin' in the Wind," with Mary messing up the lyrics and having to repeat a verse. The song had been a huge hit in the summer of '63, between his ninth and tenth grades, and it was now the anthem at every anti-war rally.

Mulligan sat at a big table with junior officers from every branch of the military and debated all aspects of the war, especially what effects the combat veterans who had just testified to Congress and who had thrown away their medals would have on the morale of men who would soon be under their command. Nobody had an answer to the question of how to ask a man to be the last man to die for a mistake.

There were maybe sixty officers in the room; about half were Army, with the other half split between the Air Force and Navy along with a couple of Marines and Coasties. Epithets like—"Fucking hippies!" "Commies!" and "Draft dodgers!"—had been shouted at the TV all afternoon. When he went to the bar for another beer, he glanced up at the TV and there was McGill—*making a speech*! Mulligan could have crapped his pants.

"That asshole's on active duty!" somebody yelled.

Somebody else said, "What's it say on his fucking shirt?"

The bartender got up close to see. "I think it says, uh, 'Grunts against the war.'"

Mulligan tried to hear what McGill was saying, something about *Casablanca* and Humphrey Bogart and Vietnam, but all the cussing made it impossible to hear the TV. An Army lieutenant-general, with three silver stars on each shoulder and a chestful of ribbons, came up to the bar and demanded, "Let me have the phone."

The bartender took a phone from under the bar and set it down in front of the general, who dialed and said, "This is General Slocum. There's an asshole up on the hippie stage who claims he's a grunt but doesn't know what it means. Yeah, he's Army all right. I don't care how you do it, but get a copy of that tape and send photos of the dirtbag to every company commander east of the Mississippi. I want his ass."

Later, Mulligan changed into jeans, and hoping to look like a civilian, turned his NAVY sweatshirt inside-out. He put on his Pirates' baseball cap, carried a jacket, and headed out wondering how to tell McGill he was on the shit-list of a three-star general.

It was eerie walking toward the darkened Washington Monument. He had been to the nation's capital many times, and it was always gleaming high above everything. Tonight, it was unlit, a silent testimony to the rancor over the war. As he got closer all the streetlights and traffic lights were out, and the massive government buildings were totally dark. Was it a power outage? As he came to Independence Boulevard packs of young males were casually wandering up and down the middle of the normally busy boulevard with beers and flasks. The only sign of electric light came from headlights of an occasional car picking its way through.

As he came up to the Washington Monument he was shocked to see hooligans ripping apart benches to feed bonfires. He found McGill with his arms around two women, all three of them looking toward the top of the obelisk. He came up from behind, tapped McGill on the shoulder, and said, "Hey, Stick."

McGill jumped, startled, turned around and said, "Damn it, Mulligan, don't sneak up like that. Not with all this crazy shit going down. How the hell you doing?"

They shook hands, tight, and slapped each other firmly on the back.

McGill said, "This is Jenny, and this is her friend, Catherine. They're both in law school at Yale. Ladies—meet the Mulligan Man."

Mulligan could tell Jenny had been crying. She wiped her eyes and held out her hand. "It's great to meet you. I've heard a lot of stories."

He shook her hand and said, "It's great to meet you too. I just wish the circumstances were better."

He extended his hand to the other woman who smiled and asked, "Do you have a first name?"

McGill quipped, "Naw, he lost it in seventh grade," and in the nasally voice of the Culligan lady he ragged out, "Hey, Mulligan Man."

Mulligan sighed, having long ago given up any hope of stomping out the nickname. "It's Mike, but Mulligan's okay. What's yours again?"

"Catherine."

"Pleased to meet you."

Just then a half-dozen rowdies, whooping and carrying a big tree branch, charged past them and used the branch as a battering ram on the Monunent's small iron door trying to break in: BOOM—BOOM—BOOM, like they were in a swashbuckler movie trying to capture a castle. But the door held, and before long they got bored and tossed the branch onto a bonfire.

Catherine said, "I can't stay here and watch this."

Jenny said, "Where should we go, Arty?"

McGill said, "The plan was to grab a cab to Georgetown for dinner."

Mulligan said, "I just walked up here and the power is out for blocks. There are no street lights, no traffic, and no cabs."

"How far is Georgetown if we walk," Jenny asked.

"Maybe three miles, depending," Mulligan said.

Catherine said, "If anybody's hungry, I still have some sandwiches and a couple of bananas in my backpack to tide us over."

"I could use something," McGill said. "Let's go over to the Lincoln. We can sit on the steps and figure things out."

As they began the mile-long walk Catherine asked, "How long since you two have seen each other?"

"Just a couple of times since high school," McGill answered. "Mulligan went to the Naval Academy and then they wouldn't let him out.'

"We got out more than you think," Mulligan said.

"Yeah, but we never saw you," McGill said. "When was the last time? It must have been when you were home at Christmas three years ago and we got together with Frankie...."

McGill's voice trailed off, and there was an awkward silence until Mulligan said, "Yeah, Stick, that was it."

"You know Frankie came up to see me right before he went over," McGill said. "He was there the night I got my shitty number. I told him I'd drive him to Canada, but he wouldn't do it. Said he wasn't a deserter. The asshole would have been three-forty-eight and home free if he hadn't flunked French."

They walked in silence, Mulligan chilling in goosebumps as he remembered Frankie and tried to take it all in. After a while he asked, "Why'd Frankie get drafted, Stick? I thought he was still at Pitt when my mom sent the article that said he'd been killed."

"He flunked French and his average dropped below 2.0," McGill said. "The dumb shit really pissed me off. At least he got laid right before he went. I was the one who had to tell Annie Chambers he'd been killed. Man, did that ever suck. Worst day of my life."

They walked to the other end of the Mall and up the steps of the Lincoln Memorial. It was still twilight, and since there were no wooden benches to burn, the fires were not as big as at the Washington Monument. People were milling around, and as they walked into the chamber they saw a guy up on Lincoln's seated statue, standing on Lincoln's leg, and pissing on Lincoln's lap. Nothing they were witnessing had anything to do with stopping the war and everything to do with drunken anarchy.

They found a spot on the steps. Catherine opened her backpack and pulled out two squashed turkey sandwiches, two over-ripe bananas, and two packets of crumbled peanut butter crackers and passed them around.

When they polished off the last of the cracker crumbs McGill lit a cigarette and said to Mulligan, "So you're really going to Nam?"

"Yeah. I leave Tuesday."

"So what are you doing tomorrow and Monday?"

"Nothing definite. But first things first. What are we doing tonight?"

McGill thought for a moment. "Well, we're here, and we've seen the bullshit at the Washington and the Lincoln. That's two out of three, so I say let's go over to the Jefferson and see how bad it is there. We owe it to, hell, I don't know who or what we owe it to, maybe our grandkids, but we owe it to somebody. We're witnesses to history, fucked as it is."

Catherine took a map out of her backpack. McGill lit his Zippo lighter so she could read it.

"It's about a mile," she said, "but Georgetown's the other way."

Mulligan inched closer, pretending he needed to see the map when he knew exactly where he was. Catherine didn't flinch, or shy away, so he got even closer, thrilling at the contact as he brushed against her and peered at the map. "It's about half-way to Fort McNair, where the power was on when I left. So if we go to the Jefferson then to McNair for a cab we'll save a mile over hiking to Georgetown."

"And we don't have to go to a fancy place in Georgetown," McGill said. "I don't care if we go to McDonalds as long as we can hang out."

It was fully dark now and everybody but Mulligan was bushed and wanted to walk as little as possible. When they crossed Independence Boulevard only a single car was moving, very slowly, with five people hitching a ride on its hood and trunk.

They took the path along the Tidal Basin to the Jefferson Memorial. It would have been magnificent in daylight, but tonight it was black as printers' ink except for the glow of a cigarette or a joint from those going in the other direction. They held hands so as to stay together along the walkway.

The Jefferson's dome was dark. There were no benches to burn and no big bonfires; a light was flickering inside.

"Feels kind of spooky," McGill said, "like a haunted house."

They walked up the steps, still firmly holding hands. Inside only one small fire barely illuminated the interior, like in a cave. There were maybe twenty people, far fewer than at the Lincoln. Most of them were sitting on the floor propped up against the walls, taking shelter, but five or six rowdies were hurling beer bottles and smashing them against the bronze statue of Thomas Jefferson.

Suddenly Mulligan felt Catherine's hand slip out of his. She went up to a guy about to throw a beer bottle and said, "Stop it! What do you think you're doing?"

The guy glanced at her, said, "Fuck you, bitch!" and cocked his arm. Catherine's hand shot out, grabbed his wrist, gave it a twist—"OWWW!"—and just like that took the bottle from him.

"I said stop it and I meant it!"

He lunged at her, but she sidestepped, stuck out her leg, put a hand on his shoulder, and—FLIP—spun him upside down in the air, landing him flat on his back with a heavy THUD.

Mulligan raced up, bent over, grabbed the guy by the shirt, pulled his head up and shook his fist in front of the guy's nose. "You make one more move and I'll break your face!"

Two guys jumped out of the shadows and tackled Mulligan. McGill pulled one off and wrestled him to the ground. Two others were circling Catherine, wary after seeing what she could do. Jenny grabbed an empty beer bottle, snuck up and smashed one of them on the back of the head, sending him to his knees, which allowed Catherine to take the other guy to the ground in an armlock. Mulligan decked his opponent with a right-cross as McGill and his opponent punched furiously at each others' faces.

The guy Catherine flipped struggled to his feet and said, "Let's get the fuck out of here."

The rowdies backed off, picked up the guy Mulligan had decked, and slunk away. The rotunda echoed with claps and cheers from others who'd seen the fight. From start to finish, it had taken less than a minute.

They went outside and sat on the stairs overlooking the Tidal Basin. McGill lit a cigarette and said to Catherine, "You were really something in there. Remind me never to mess with you."

"She has a black belt in judo," Jenny said.

Mulligan said, "Is anybody hurt?"

"I'm fine," Catherine said. "How about you, Jen?"

"Nobody touched me. What about you, Arty?"

"Nothing serious. Probably have a shiner in the morning."

Catherine said, "You took the worst of it, Mike. How are you?"

"Nothing a band-aid can't fix," Mulligan said. He moved his left arm from side to side, then up and down. "And I got a kink in my shoulder from an old football injury. Must have happened when they tackled me. It'll be okay in a day or two."

"Well if nothing else, it was invigorating," McGill said. "I haven't been in a real fight since tenth grade when I got into it with Roger Bishop over Cindy Seymour. So what are we going to call it?"

"What do you mean?" Jenny asked.

"Well, it was a battle, and battles always get names, right?" McGill said. "How about The Battle of the Jefferson? The good guys defeated the bad guys. The Good Guys Law won out."

Catherine said, "The Good Guys Law? What the heck is that?"

McGill said, "You want to be a lawyer and don't know about the Good Guys Law?"

"Never heard of it," Catherine said.

"Me neither," said Jenny.

McGill said, "That's because you're girls. I bet you never played Cowboys-and-Indians or Army when you were kids. Mulligan, you remember The Good Guys Law, right?"

"Not really."

"Where the hell have you been? When I was in kindergarten we'd run around dressed up as cowboys and Indians going bang-bang-gotcha. And there always had to be more Indians than cowboys, like in the movies. When it seemed the cowboys were about to lose, the last cowboy would shout, 'Bad guys have more men, but good guys always win!' and presto, the Indians had to start falling like flies, and the cowboys who'd been shot and scalped came to life to shoot Indians. The good guys had to win in the end. That was the law."

Jenny asked, "So where did it come from?"

"Who knows," McGill said. "Probably from Saturday morning TV and the singing cowboys—Roy Rogers and Gene Autry. It's part of the American psyche."

They were exhausted and knew it. "My feet are killing me, "Jenny said. "And I think we should get some sleep. This is not a night for dinner and drinks."

"I agree," Catherine said.

Mulligan said, "Let's find a good spot."

Catherine said, "Aren't you going back to your fort?"

Mulligan grinned and said, "You're not getting rid of me that easily."

"Our best bet is under trees on the Mall," McGill said, "away from the streets and the paths."

They headed back toward the Mall, passing groups of people leaning up against trees or sprawled on the grass hoping to sleep. At the Lincoln, they sat at the top of the steps overlooking the Mall to take a breather and scope out sleeping spots. Bonfires were still burning at the Washington Monument.

Mulligan said, "It doesn't look too crowded over by those trees."

Jenny said, "It would be good if we had something to cover up in."

McGill stood up and said, "Mulligan, you stay with the ladies so no scumbags get any ideas and I'll see what I can scrounge up."

He walked along the Reflecting Pool looking systematically through the debris: beer cans and bottles, crushed cigarette packs, T-shirts, abandoned OUT NOW! placards, an occasional backpack, beach towels, candy wrappers, umbrellas—all sorts of crap. He lit his Zippo to inspect promising articles, and soon collected a beach towel and three T-shirts he figured they could use as pillows. After a few minutes he found a neatly folded Army blanket exactly like his. Talk about luck! It would be tight, but they should be able to fit under it.

They found a spot under the trees and made friends with the college kids and young adults like themselves at the impromptu campsite. Like Jenny and Catherine, they had come to Washington to stop the war and they were disgusted at the way things were turning out. Somebody passed a joint, but only McGill took a few hits. The four of them lay down close together, McGill and Mulligan on the outside, all of them on their backs. They fluffed up their "pillows" as best they could and stretched out the blanket, but it didn't quite cover them.

"This won't work," Mulligan said. "The taught us in survival school to sleep on our sides and get close, like spoons in a drawer. Our combined body heat will help keep us warm."

They restretched the blanket, then curled up tight against each other and tried to get comfortable; McGill's back to Jenny's front, Jenny's back to Catherine's front, and Catherine's back to Mulligan's front. Everybody but Mulligan fell asleep right way. He lay awake as long as he could savoring Catherine's long, athletic body tight against his. He was a done duck, a cooked goose. What a woman!

In the morning, they used the port-a-potties and drank instant coffee out of Styrofoam cups offered by some campmates who had a Coleman stove. They said good-bye to their new friends and walked along the Reflecting Pool to see how bad The Mall looked in daylight.

Wisps of smoke rose from the ashes of the bonfires. There were still thousands of people crashed everywhere—protesters, rioters, partyers, stragglers. The TV news crews were out in force. Police ringed the Capitol and other government buildings, but on the grass of the Mall itself there was still not a cop anywhere in sight. Along the way, they heard exhortations by May Day organizers who were going from campsite to campsite imploring people to help shut down the government next week.

The worst damage was at the Washington Monument, where the rows of benches, stripped naked of wood, stood guard like concrete sentinels in military formation. In the coming weeks the desecrated benches would become Nixon's favorite propaganda tool for discrediting the demonstrators. Every other day, on one TV network or another, a reporter was at the Mall to do a story with the trashed benches in the background.

Finally, fed up with the infighting among those they call the "English," a column of horse-drawn buggies carrying men, women, children, lumber, and tools, set out from the Pennsylvania Dutch country around Lancaster and clippity-clopped along the back roads of Pennsylvania and Maryland down to Washington for a good, old-fashioned bench-raising. If your neighbor's barn burns down, the Amish get together and help him raise a new one. To the Amish, the benches destroyed by the crazy "English" were no different.

TV and newspapers followed the story of the only Americans who seemed to know exactly what needed to be done and had the know-how to do it. With their horses tethered beside the quaint square-topped buggies with big-spoked wheels, the denim-clad, bearded Amish men and teenage boys in straw hats with big round brims went to work.

The Amish have a place in the American dream quite different from the mainstream. Being strict pacifists, they have never fought in any war. Even more oddly, they refuse to use modern conveniences, such as automobiles and refrigerators, or, for the job at hand, power tools—no Black & Decker electric drills, no Skillsaws.

The camera-shy Amish, who believe that a photograph is a "graven image" forbidden by the Second Commandment, refused to mug it up for the cameras and instead rolled up their sleeves, took their hammers and saws into their heavily-callused hands, and fixed everything up in a couple of days. When they were finished, they climbed into their buggies and, like true frontier heroes, giddyapped into the sunset. It was a great story, a poignant story, but the politicians, editorial writers, and TV pundits could not quite figure out just what lesson America was supposed to learn from it all.

Chapter 9

Good Guys Always Win

THEY WERE GRUBBY AND THEY WERE HUNGRY. CATHERINE WAS LOOKING AT the map when Jenny said, "We should find a cab and get back to clean up and get our things. We can still make the afternoon train."

"No!" McGill said. "You can't go back today. This may be the only chance you'll ever get to hang with the Mulligan Man. He's headed to Vietnam. You can miss some classes. We may never see him again."

There was long, ominous silence, then Catherine folded her map and said, "I have a better idea. Follow me."

"Where are we going?" Jenny asked.

"You'll see. It's not far."

She led them across Constitution Avenue, where the traffic lights were still not working and there were still no cabs, and still no cops. They walked for a while up 15th Street, where at some point the traffic lights started working and cops were everywhere. When they reached Pennsylvania Avenue, Catherine turned into the driveway of the famous Willard Hotel, just two blocks from the White House.

"That's the fanciest hotel in Washington," McGill said. "We can't afford this."

Catherine said, "Let me worry about it."

They looked like what they were—scraggly remnants of the protest not fit to enter the five-star establishment that liked to call itself "America's Hotel." A black-and-white police car with two uniformed cops was parked in the driveway. Both cops watched them intently as they walked to the entrance. An elegant Negro doorman in an elaborate red uniform stopped them and said, "Sorry, the rest rooms are only for our guests."

"Listen," Catherine said, "I know you're only doing your job, but we always stay here when we're in town, and my father stays here several times a year on business. Now, are you going to let us register, or do I have to call the manager?"

The doorman flashed a concerned look. "Who is your father?"

"Edward DeWolfe."

Now the doorman looked worried. "Yes, I know Mr. DeWolfe.

Uh...can I see some identification?"

Catherine took out a wallet and showed him her Michigan driver's license. He looked at it closely and said, "Thank you, Miss DeWolfe."

"It's not Miss, it's *Ms.*," she said.

He opened the door. "I apologize. Thank you, Ms. DeWolfe."

"That's quite all right, just don't let it happen again," and his eyes bugged out as she handed him a twenty.

"Yes, ma'am...I mean, Ms. DeWolfe. Thank you, Ms. DeWolfe."

She led the way through the lobby to the front desk as Mulligan asked Jenny, "What the hell is going on?"

"Catherine's family's loaded," Jenny said. "But I've never seen her throw it around. She always shops in Goodwill and Salvation Army stores. She's usually very down-to-earth."

"Wow. So she is one of *the* DeWolfes," McGill said. "You know, Mulligan, the big timber company that owns half of Michigan? They're zillionaires."

They stood behind her as she said to the clerk, "Let's make this easy. You don't have the authority to do what I need, so please get your manager."

The clerk walked behind a partition and brought out an older man in a blue blazer with the Willard Hotel logo on the pocket.

She showed her ID and said, "We don't have reservations, but I prefer the Oval Suite if it's available. We like it because of the view of the Capitol. If it is not available, we'll take one of the other suites. I assume our account is in order."

The flustered manager looked at her ID, eyeing them all with suspicion, and said, "We have several DeWolfes with accounts here at the Willard."

"My father is Edward."

"Yes, of course, I see the resemblance, Miss DeWolfe, and—"

"It's *Ms.* DeWolfe."

"Yes, of course, Ms. DeWolfe. I do believe the Oval Suite is available. I'll have your luggage sent up."

"There's no need, we're traveling light. Please send coffee and champagne right away and your Sunday brunch buffet for four in half an hour...no make that an hour and a half, so we have time to freshen up. But send the coffee and champagne and orange juice right away."

"Yes, of course, Miss DeWolfe."

"That's *Ms.* DeWolfe."

"Yes, Ms. DeWolfe."

A bellhop escorted them to a suite filled with antiques, oriental rugs, a baby-grand piano and a commanding view of the Capitol Building and Pennsylvania Avenue.

"Thank you," Catherine said as she handed the bellhop a twenty. Just then a waiter with a serving cart was at the door. "Put it by the big couch," Catherine said, and handed him a twenty on his way out.

"Catherine, are you sure this is all right?" Jenny said. "I've never seen you like this before. It feels, I don't know…*odd*."

"Don't worry," Catherine said, "I can handle my father. Look, we've all just had one of the most depressing nights of our lives and Mike's on his way to Vietnam. If I'm able to make things just a little bit better for a day or two, I'm going to do it."

McGill popped a champagne cork, poured four glasses, passed them around and said, "This sure beats sleeping on the floor and sharing a bathroom with those dorks from Yale. Cheers!"

They clinked glasses, and Catherine said to Jenny, "You and Art take the small bedroom and we'll take the master suite. I want to give Mike's shoulder a massage in the Jacuzzi to get that kink out."

Mulligan was speechless as she took his hand and said, "Come on, Mike. Let's get you fixed up."

Catherine closed the door and set her glass down on a dresser. Mulligan put his glass down, looked into her hazel eyes and said, "Am I dreaming? Is this really happening?"

She took his hands in hers and said, "Look, Mike, I'll never forget what happened last night. You were terrific, and waking up this morning with you snuggled up around me was like something out of a fairy tale. I know we hardly know each other, and I don't care if you have somebody else or if anything ever comes of it, but right now all I want is to make love to you. But I don't want you to do anything you don't want to."

He shook his head in amazement and said, "I think I've died and gone to heaven."

He drew her close, gave her a long, dreamy kiss, cupped her firm, athletic buns in his palms, and maneuvered her onto the canopied bed. He nibbled her ear, kissing down her neck. He slipped his hand under her blouse and massaged a breast. She reached behind and undid her bra and tossed it on the floor. He pulled her blouse up over her head, exposing two perfectly proportioned breasts, nipples hard, rosettes flushed. He kissed and licked and gently nipped the tips of her nipples, then massaged one breast as he gratefully sucked on the other. He felt her hand reach down and feel him from outside his pants. He leaned back, thrilling as he watched her undo his belt, unzip his fly, and gasp when his hard-on popped out. She pulled his underwear down, then gave a little laugh and said, "Your hair is even redder than mine."

He chuckled and said, "You're really something," and slipped out of his pants and underwear as she unzipped her jeans.

"Help me get them off, Mike, they're on tight."

He got off the bed, took her jeans at the cuffs, and slowly pulled them off, leaving her naked except for her black silk panties. What a sight! "I can't believe how beautiful you are."

He kissed his way along the right side of her body, from her toes to her ankle, up her calf, along the inside of her thigh, over and around her belly button, then turned south, slipping her panties down to her knees and onto the floor.

"You're right," he said. "My hair is a little redder."

She laughed as he got on his knees and began exploring. She whimpered, "Oh Mike, Mike, yes there, right there!" Mulligan kept at it, and soon she gave a little squeal—"Aaahhh—and scrunched lower, took him in both hands, and guided him home.

After Catherine had closed the bedroom door, McGill said to Jenny, "A thousand to one says Mulligan gets more than his shoulder massaged."

They showered before getting under the luxurious sheets for a leisurely round of lovemaking. Later, they put on the plush Willard Hotel bathrobes and went into the main room. McGill poured champagne and Jenny said, "You should put ice on that black eye. It will help keep the swelling down."

She took some ice from the champagne bucket, wrapped it in the waiter's towel, and said, "Lie down on the couch and hold this on it."

McGill sprawled out with the ice towel on his face while Jenny sat at the baby-grand piano and began playing a Mozart piece.

McGill said, "I don't think I've ever heard you play."

They had known each other for four years, but had only been

together on weekend dates, never more than a few days in a row. Neither had been to the other's home or met the other's family. He had played guitar and they had sung folk songs together a few times, but he had never heard her play the piano.

"I'm really rusty," she said. "I don't think I've played since I started law school."

"Why don't you sing something?"

"Okay…what?"

"Whatever you like."

She thought for a moment. "How about 'Que Sera, Sera.'"

"That corny Doris Day song— whatever will be will be?"

"It's not so corny. It won an Oscar for Best Song. I had just started piano lessons and my mother loved it. She bought the sheet music so she could sing along."

Jenny sang a verse and came to the chorus, "Que sera, sera—"

They both laughed and McGill said, "Seems appropriate considering all the shit that's coming down."

Catherine and Mulligan came out from the master suite and McGill said, "How's the shoulder, Mulligan Man? Get that kink worked out?"

Catherine's cheeks blushed pink as Mulligan smiled and said, "It's much better. How's that shiner?"

"I've had worse."

"Talk about black eyes," Jenny said. "In junior high I had the worst black eye ever. The whole side of my face turned purple. It took over a month to clear up."

"What happened?" Catherine said. "I can't imagine you in a fight."

"No, it wasn't a fight. I was at a baseball game and got hit by a foul ball. Mickey Mantle hit it. I could have been killed."

McGill jumped up from the couch and said, "What did you say?"

"I got hit by a foul ball—"

"And Mickey Mantle hit it?"

"Yes, why?"

McGill glanced at Mulligan. "Hear that, Mulligan? It's *her*!"

"I'm who?" Jenny said.

"Tell us the whole story, Jen, just to be sure," McGill said as he paced back and forth. "Everything. Don't leave anything out."

"Well, it was the World Series—"

"Pirates and Yankees, right?" McGill said.

"Uh...yes."

McGill was bursting with excitement. "Go on! Go on!"

"A boy got his glove on it just as it hit me and—"

"My God. *You're the girl with the secret nose-job*!"

Jenny was incredulous.

McGill was pacing back-and-forth and waving his arms like a madman. "Right before the game started Bob Hope and Bing Crosby came up the steps and my dad stopped them and said hello because he'd known them in the war. Your dad took our picture with my grandfather's Polaroid. Then your dad introduced all of you and Hope made a joke about your father's and your brothers' noses being as big as his and how lucky you were to take after your mother. Then one of your brothers yelled out you'd just had a secret nose-job, and you started crying, and Crosby sang va-va-va-vooom to you. My grandfather took a picture of you and Crosby and gave it to you, remember? And then in the first inning, Mantle hit a foul ball and I stuck my glove up to catch it and you got knocked out. Remember? And after the game I gave you the ball. We have a picture of the girl with an ice-towel on her face. That was *you*! Wasn't it? *Tell me*!"

Jenny was too astounded to speak. McGill sat next to her, wrapped his arm around her and said, "Can you believe it, Jen? I mean, talk about karma."

"Is it true, Jennifer?" Catherine asked. "Did it really happen?"

Jenny felt dizzy, like she might faint. She nodded and in a weak voice said, "Yes."

Catherine was gushing with enthusiasm. "That's just so romantic!"

Mulligan said, "Nobody ever believed Stick's story about catching a Mickey Mantle foul ball and giving it away to some girl. We ragged him for years about the girl with the secret nose-job."

McGill said, "Do you still have the ball, Jen?

She was barely able to speak. "Yes. It's in our trophy case. My dad got Mickey Mantle and Vernon Law to sign it."

"You know what this means?" Catherine said with great authority. "It means beyond any doubt that you two are soul-mates who have found each other. Do you have any idea how lucky you are?"

Jenny was still trembling, remembering her father telling her after the game that the boy might have saved her life.

Catherine opened another bottle of champagne, filled their glasses, and said, "To soul-mates!"

Catherine was into the coming Age of Aquarius—astrology, numerology, yoga, eastern religions and the like—much more than Jenny. Jenny half-heartedly clinked her glass, thinking—but what if we're not soul-mates? It could be total coincidence, couldn't it? And why did Arty have to mention her nose? She wasn't sure how mad to be.

There had never been any "going steady," like in high school, no being a "pinmate" and wearing his college fraternity pin, no engagement or discussions about marriage or talk of exclusivity. Arty and Jenny were unofficially "boyfriend" and "girlfriend." Theirs was an open relationship. When they were not together, which was most of the time because their colleges were far apart, they dated others. Arty often told her he was crazy about her, but he had never said he *loved* her. She found him interesting and funny and great company and an insatiable lover, but...soul-mates? She was sure Father Zyhowski, Sister Mary Grace, and the Pope would all strongly disapprove of the notion of soul-mates.

The waiters brought a sumptuous Sunday brunch on serving carts and a maid took their clothes to the laundry service. While they waited for their laundry to return, they watched the noon news and flipped the dial between stations to catch reports on yesterday's events. In every report, the cameras kept returning to the destruction around the Washington Monument as if nothing else had been of any significance.

"So what now?" Jenny said when their clothes came back.

"Let's forget the fucking war," McGill said. "Mulligan, what time do you leave on Tuesday?"

"I catch a shuttle from McNair at zero-six-hundred."

McGill said, "Jen, you and Catherine aren't going back till after Mulligan leaves, right?"

Without consulting Jenny, Catherine said, "We're both staying."

"So, let's go get my car and see some sights and have dinner," McGill said. "I don't have to be on duty until tomorrow. If I stay tonight, I'll have to be up at five to get back, and Mulligan can ride along and then take the car so you'll have wheels to go sightseeing. Then you pick me up after my shift and we'll have another night. I'll drop Mulligan at McNair on Tuesday and you two take a cab to catch the train."

They took a cab to the Marriott to get their bags and McGill's convertible. It was a gorgeous afternoon, so McGill put the top down and took them for a drive along the Potomac to the Maryland side of

Great Falls National Park, just fifteen miles away.

As Catherine took out her top-of-the-line Nikon camera out of its case, Jenny said, "Cate's a serious photographer."

Catherine went on a photographic binge, snap-snap-snapping away. She asked a tourist to take a few photos of the four of them with the Great Falls rapids in the background. Not a word was said about Vietnam. For one day, the war was a million miles away.

At 0510 Monday morning, McGill kissed Jenny goodbye and said, "I'll see you tonight." Later, after she and Catherine and Mulligan finished breakfast and decided which museums to visit, Jenny said, "Let's go watch Arty at work first."

Mulligan put down the convertible top and drove to the Pentagon, with Catherine in the middle with her arm around him and Jenny riding shotgun. In spite of how Jenny felt about the military and the war, she was terribly proud of Arty, so handsome in his khaki uniform, even with his black eye, with his MP brassard on his upper arm and his white saucer hat and the accouterment she knew he hated more than any other—the white gloves.

He always had a lot of nervous energy, and she was surprised at how he was able to put it to such good use, blowing his whistle, wheeling and pivoting and waving orders to cars and busses with a rapid windmill motion. She had never paid much attention to traffic cops, but Arty was the most animated, interesting and effective traffic cop she had ever seen. She knew he was always getting into trouble for not adhering to the by-the-book hand-motions a U.S. Army MP was required to use, but he said that whenever he did it their way traffic always got snarled.

They drove past him a few times, honking and waving and Catherine snapping away with her camera. He grinned but kept traffic flowing, in total command of his busy intersection.

After seeing Arty at work, they visited the Smithsonian Air and Space Museum, then the National Gallery of Art. Jenny felt like she was tagging along, the odd-girl-out as Catherine and Mulligan, holding hands like in a corny Disney movie, billed and cooed their way through the museums, barely seeing the exhibits.

Jenny felt privileged to watch them. They were both big, strong, and redheaded. She tried to imagine their offspring, and said a prayer that they would work out as a couple.

They picked Arty up after his shift and went back to the hotel. They ordered dinner from room service and the two couples had one last glorious night together. At 0515 Tuesday morning, Arty kissed Jenny as Mulligan kissed Catherine.

"Be careful, Mike," Catherine said, gave him a tight hug, and handed him a Willard Hotel envelope with addresses and phone numbers written all over the outside.

"Please write, Mike. I'll be at school for another month and with my parents in Michigan all summer. You can call collect any time."

He gave her another kiss and said, "I'll write. I promise."

The instant the door closed Jenny wrapped her arms around her friend as Catherine broke down sobbing.

Chapter 10

Mayday!

IT WAS STILL DARK WHEN MCGILL PULLED THE CAR OUT OF THE HOTEL AND headed toward Fort McNair to drop off Mulligan. They had not said a word about the war for over a day.

"I can't believe your going to Nam," McGill said. "Nixon's supposed to be winding things down. Vietnamization and all that."

"We still have over two hundred thousand in-country," Mulligan said. "Listen, Stick, I didn't want to say anything in front of Jenny and get her worried, but there's a three-star general named Slocum after your ass."

"What?"

"I was in the O Club bar when I saw your speech and—"

"You mean…it was on TV?"

"Yeah. He came up to the bar while you were still talking and used the phone. He gave somebody an order to get the tape and send your picture around to track you down."

"What did you say his name was again?'

"Slocum."

"I've seen him. He's got one of the fanciest mansions on Generals' Row. He won't have to look far to find me. Fuck!"

"Just stay cool if any shit comes down. Don't be the wise-ass you think you are. It's not junior high with McCracken and Pugliano and a wooden paddle. Suck it up and grovel. Anything else, they'll fuck you even worse. I know how they think and it is *not* how you think."

McGill shrugged it off, Army style. "Don't mean nuthin'. What's the worst they can do—send me to Vietnam?"

"Yeah. Exactly."

The early-morning drive to Fort McNair took less than ten minutes. McGill pulled up outside the gate. "You take care of yourself, Mulligan Man. Don't be a hero. We already lost Dombrowski."

"You watch your ass back here, Stick," Mulligan said as they shook hands. "Don't mouth off like you always do and end up doing time in Leavenworth."

McGill stood his regular duty rotation and watched the news every night. The organizers of the May Day protest deliberately chose the first day of May because of its close association with revolution, rebellion, and the struggle for workers' rights. It was also the international distress call repeated three times: Mayday! Mayday! Mayday! It came from a French phrase meaning "come help me"—*venez m'aider.* It meant you were in serious trouble. It

By Friday 30,000 to 40,000 protesters were in West Potomac Park near the Washington Monument for the demonstration on Sunday. These were the hard-core activists dedicated to ending the war, veterans of many demonstrations. On the other side, federal troops, including 4,000 from the 82nd Airborne Division, were arriving at local military installations, a reported total of 10,000 to back up the 7,000 police and 2,000 National Guard troops.

Fort Myer, home of the top generals in the U.S. Army, was small as Army bases go, with maybe 6,000 troops on post. Suddenly, here comes the 82nd, who bunked in the old WWI barracks scheduled for demolition, turned every open space into a bivouac area, and overwhelmed the mess halls, showers, and latrines.

The scuttlebutt in McGill's barracks was that civilian government workers would be told to stay home to minimize problems if protests tied up the streets. It sounded great to the Fort Myer MPs, as it would make traffic-control much easier than dealing with massive tie-ups.

But Nixon, who was still safely out of town in his California beach house, would not give an inch, and ordered all federal workers to report to their jobs as usual. A collective groan went up in the barracks when they heard the news. The shit was about to hit the fan, and they would have to be the ones to clean it up.

Strack ordered a company assembly for 0630, and at the appointed time the first-sergeant called out, "Fall-*IN*!"

McGill and the rest of the Fort Myer Miliary Police company formed up and came to proper military attention.

Strack, in sunglasses and carrying a riding-crop like a South American dictator, strode to the front of the formation. He nodded to the first-sergeant who called out, "Parade—*REST*."

Every soldier in the unit smartly spread his feet and clasped his hands behind his back at the parade-rest position.

"President Nixon is taking this shut-down-shit seriously," Strack told them, "so until further notice, all leaves and passes are cancelled and no soldier is to leave this post without permission. The uniform-of-the-day is fatigues and helmets, no soft caps. Be ready for anything."

That was ominous. At this time of year, Army MPs assigned to the Military District of Washington, unless they were on KP or garbage detail, wore Class A summer khaki uniforms. And in all the months he had been at Fort Myer, he had never once worn a "steel-pot" to direct traffic or stand guard at the gate.

"Our orders," Stack continued, "include preparation for riot suppression and crowd control. Now I know this was not taught until just last year, so those of you who graduated from MP School at Fort Gordon since last October—front and center."

Morale in the U.S. Army in 1971 was arguably at its lowest point since the winter at Valley Forge in 1778. It had been seven years since Lyndon Johnson won the '64 election by running as a peace candidate. Then, just weeks after the election, he sent the first of 500,000 troops to Vietnam.

As the war dragged on year after bloody year, officers and NCOs had become the targets of their own troops. The most infamous method was "fragging," or tossing a fragmentation grenade into a hooch or a tent. Riots and rebellions by soldiers at Army bases had forced a change in the curriculum at the Army's Military Police School. The courses now included riot and crowd-control training with gas masks and shields to subdue, not civilians, but their fellow GIs. McGill's was the first MP class to have taken the new training.

He took a spot at attention in front of Strack. Strack looked them over, nodded to the first-sergeant who said, "Count—*OFF*!"

They counted off, in proper military fashion—one to twenty-three. Enough bodies for two squads, half a platoon. "I wish we had more of you," Strack said, "so we could really kick some ass. You are relieved of other duties and are to report at zero-seven-hundred for a refresher course by an instructor they're sending up from Gordon. Men, I want any peacenik that tries to violate the real estate you're defending to pay the price. Do us proud."

The instructor, an E-7 master sergeant, divided them into two squads. Even though McGill was only an E-3, Private First Class, he was senior to the others in the squad and therefore the squad leader. After a day of training in the use of shields and batons, the sergeant ordered them not to return their .45s to the armory so they would be ready to move out at a moment's notice. A bus was on stand-by outside the barracks to take them wherever they might be needed.

On Saturday the MPs were confined to the barracks and on full alert, awaiting deployment. McGill got into a poker game and everybody listened to the reports on the radio of how the authorities had dispatched a helicopter to hover low over the demonstrators in order to disrupt the rock concert and their strategy sessions. But that plan was foiled when the protesters launched helium balloons on wire cables that could have caught up in the helicopter's rotors and brought it crashing down. That *really* pissed off the authorities, so the Interior Department revoked the permit and ordered the protesters to leave.

"How'd they get a fucking permit in the first place?" somebody asked. Nobody in the barracks had an answer.

Sunday, at the break of dawn, the local police joined with the U.S. Park police into an assault force of over 7,000. They formed up behind shields and marched through the encampments like Roman legionnaires driving the protesters in front of them and knocking down their tents.

Soon helicopters landed at the Washington Monument, where they off-loaded more police and outflanked the protesters from two sides. The protesters scattered; many gave up and left town, some sought refuge in churches; some at the campuses of Georgetown, American, and George Washington universities. Police stormed through the entrance to Georgetown behind a wall of tear gas, and by the end of the day thousands of protesters had been arrested. Most would be held for days behind a chain-link fence in the parking lot of RFK Stadium without adequate food or water or sanitation. At McGill's barracks, the MPs waited for a call to join the action, but none came.

Monday was the real test. If the protesters could clog intersections, off-ramps, and bridges, even a few thousand could shut down the government. There were only maybe 10,000 organized protesters who had not been driven out of town or arrested the day before, but they had been planning their moves for months. Breaking off into small groups of twenty to fifty, they used classic guerrilla tactics to avoid the massed presence of government forces and attempted to disrupt traffic.

Two groups of protesters somehow got across the Potomac and behind the police lines and were advancing on a major intersection just outside the Pentagon. Even though there were federal combat troops available, they were the last line of defense, for to use combat troops on American civilians was unheard of in modern times. It hadn't happened since 1932, when Herbert Hoover ordered the Army to clear 40,000 "Bonus Marchers" out of Washington. General Douglas MacArthur personally led the cavalry and infantry charge supported by six tanks, driving the Marchers in front of them and burning their tents.

But combat troops were only to be used as a last resort, and Army MPs were technically support troops, not combat troops, and this was their turf. The call came at 0940. They clambered onto the bus in full gear along with the new sergeant and Captain Strack. The bus took them to a freeway off-ramp, where thirty or so protesters were sitting in the middle of the road. The protesters would link arms and go limp whenever the cops tried to cuff them and haul them away to the paddy wagons. A TV crew was filming everything.

There were an equal number of protesters on the side of the road shouting, "PIGS!" Whenever the cops would handcuff a protester and take him away, another would run down to take his place.

Strack and the new sergeant conferred with the civilian cops, and Strack gave the order, "Men our job is to push these assholes back and keep them off the road. Form *UP*."

The two squads got in formation, shoulder to shoulder. Everybody was scared. McGill held his shield in his left hand, and with his right clutched the "MP's best friend," what in MP nomenclature is a "baton" but what everybody else on the planet called a "nightstick" or a "billy club." In MP school they learned the baton was designed to break at the handle if it struck an object with greater than forty pounds of force, a blow deemed by U.S. Army specifications to be sufficient to subdue a miscreant but not enough to do permanent damage.

The sergeant ordered, "Forward," and they advanced on the protesters, herding them off the road and away from the group sitting in the road. "Hold 'em, hold 'em. Keep your shields up, move 'em back."

Just then a dozen new protesters climbed over the fence along the road and charged at them, crashing into their shields and forcing the MPs back a few steps. From behind Strack called out, "Gas! Put 'em on!"

They grabbed their gas masks and removed their helmets to slip them on. McGill heard muffled pops as Strack, using an M79 grenade launcher, shot tear gas canisters into the ranks of the demonstrators.

Plumes of choking vapor hissed in the air, forcing the protesters to run. Vapors leaked through his mask, making his eyes burn, but taking the mask off would make it much worse.

The protesters regrouped a quarter-mile away, and a dozen or so made a dash for the bus parking area on the far right flank a hundred yards away behind another chain link fence. The sergeant ordered McGill's squad, "Keep them off those busses!"

McGill double-timed his squad and got in position just ahead of the demonstrators and blocked their way. McGill was in the middle yelling, "Move up, move up." They advanced in tight formation. "Hold off with the batons," he yelled to his men. He tried to reason with the demonstrators, shouting, "We don't want to get anybody hurt. Back off." Several protesters charged the line and two broke through. McGill ordered his men, "Get 'em and cuff 'em."

The skirmish lasted fifteen minutes until the MPs and Virginia cops had arrested enough protesters to make it clear they would not be permitted to block the intersection.

McGill felt pretty good about how he handled himself. He had been scared, but he hadn't panicked. He had done his job, he hadn't hurt anybody, and he may have prevented some injuries.

Over 12,000 had been arrested, the largest mass-arrest in American history. Most would be held at the outdoor detention area for days, with little food, water, shelter, or bathroom facilities. The civil liberties violations would later cause the government to pay out millions in restitution. Only seventy-nine were convicted of anything, all misdemeanors.

Life at the barracks was soon back to normal, and after three weeks, since nobody had said anything about his speech, McGill figured he was off the hook. Then one day Strack gave orders for the company to assemble in front of the barracks the next morning at 0930.

McGill was annoyed because it meant he had to put on a uniform even though it was his day off. As they stood around waiting everybody was speculating as to what it was all about. When the first-sergeant appeared and yelled, "Fall IN*!*" they formed up in ranks, squad-by-squad, platoon-by-platoon. When they were all at attention, the first-sergeant said, "Men, we're going to see a show. Right, *face*"

They marched to the auditorium and took seats in good military order. There was a big movie screen in the back of the stage, a long table with several chairs off to one side, and a podium off to the other.

"Atten*SHUN*!" somebody yelled, and the company jumped to attention as down the aisle came Strack, a full-bird colonel, a major and two lieutenants. Something big was up. A moment later, McGill's stomach churned as a general with three stars walked down and took the center seat at the table on the stage. The first-sergeant stood behind Strack at the podium. When the general was seated, the first-sergeant said, "At ease, men, and take your seats."

After things got quiet Strack said, "Men, we have recently been through a crisis, and for the most part this unit acquitted itself well. However, recent events have served to point out some problems.

"But first I would like to welcome General Slocum, U.S. Army Chief of Staff for Personnel. General...."

The general came to the podium. "Men, you did a fine job during the recent engagement. I personally observed your actions repelling the enemy from my office in the Pentagon. Captain Strack, you and your men have earned a unit citation for meritorious service in a civil disturbance."

The general smiled and handed Strack a document. Strack beamed. "And for all you men who earned this citation, never forget that in the United States Army we're all individuals because each of us has his own number."

"What the fuck does that mean?" whispered the guy next to McGill.

"Don't mean nuthin'," said somebody in back.

Strack was beaming and said, "Thank you, General Slocum," as the general returned to his seat. "We'll start with a short piece of film."

The lights went down and the countdown on the film-leader wound through, then footage showing the crowds at the U.S. Capitol during the Out Now rally. The camera zoomed in on the stage, and McGill sat in horror as he watched himself being whisked by the security guards from back-stage and up to the emcee. Loud murmurs of, "It's McGill" and "That's McGill" filled the room as everyone turned to look at him. He was in deep, deep shit.

"Freeze it there!" Strack ordered, walked to the screen, and said in his loudest command-voice, "Private McGill, come to attention."

McGill leaped up and came to rigid attention.

Strack, while tapping on the image of McGill's face on the movie screen with a rubber-tipped wooden pointer said, "Is that you, Private

McGill?"

"Uh, yes, sir," he said, trembling so hard he could barely be heard.

"And what is that you're wearing?" Strack said. He tapped the pointer on the image of the same GRUNTS AGAINST THE WAR T-shirt that McGIll and several guys in the unit were wearing under their uniforms at that very moment.

He answered in a feeble voice, "It's a T-shirt, sir.

"Indeed it is. Does it reflect your feelings about the war, Private McGill?"

"Uh...that's complicated, sir."

"Are you wearing it now, Private McGill?"

"Uh...yes, sir."

"A non-regulation T-shirt would make you out-of-uniform, would it not?"

"Uh, it's not visible so, I don't think—"

"Let's see it, Private McGill," said Strack.

"Uh—"

"Unbutton your fucking shirt!" shouted the first-sergeant.

McGill tugged the shirttail out of his trousers and unbuttoned, exposing his T-shirt front. "Turn around and show everybody," said the first-sergeant. McGill rotated 360 degrees.

"Very well, roll the film," Strack ordered, and for the next few minutes McGill stood frozen in fear as he watched himself speaking to the crowd on the Mall. There would be no bullshitting his way out of this one. Life as he knew it was over.

The film ended with him flashing the peace sign as he left the stage. When the lights came up Strack said, "It does not appear that your opinion of the career military personnel you called 'lifers,' is very high, is it, Private McGill?"

What was left to lose? "Sir, it is my opinion about the war which is not very high. And with all due respect, sir, 'lifer' is a term used by everyone in the Army."

"Very true, Private McGill, very true, but for me it means a lifetime of duty, while you denigrate that dedication. So, Private McGill, did you enjoy yourself up there on stage disparaging not only your fellow service members but the United States of America?"

"Sir, the Uniform Code of Military Justice does not prohibit military personnel from exercising our First Amendment right of free speech as long as we're not in uniform. I was not in uniform, and with all due respect, I was not disparaging America. I love my country, which is why I was trying to convey the truth about the war."

The general spoke up, "Just a moment, Captain Strack. Private, uh...McGill is it?"

"Yes, sir."

"I was watching on TV when you gave your anti-American speech. Did you prepare your remarks while on duty?"

"No, sir, I had not prepared anything, and it was not an anti-American. It was like I was drafted, sir. I was just schlepping sound equipment for the musicians, and then there I was in front of all those people. But once I was up there, I knew I had a perspective nobody ever talks about, and that made it my duty to try to keep any more of us from dying for lies."

"We all understand about duty, Private McGill," said the general. "But if you were so interested in exercising your constitutional rights by deprecating America before the world, why were you so reluctant to tell anyone your name?"

"Sir, I was not deprecating America, I was telling the truth. And yes, I was afraid I'd be punished. And it looks like I was right, sir."

Strack interjected, "Oh, but you are wrong, Private McGill. You are not going to be punished, you are going to be rewarded."

General Slocum said, "Not just yet, captain. I have a question for the history professor here about his T-shirt and his high opinion of himself. Tell me, private, what makes you think you qualify for the honor of calling yourself a grunt?"

That threw McGill off. "I...uh, excuse me, sir. I don't understand."

"The grunts I commanded in Vietnam," said the general, "have a term for anyone who is not a grunt. Do you know what that term is, Private McGill?"

"Uh...I think so, sir."

"And just what is it?"

"'REMF.' It stands for 'rear echelon mother fucker.' I think."

"And just who is a REMF?" asked the general.

"I...uh, it's, it's somebody with cake duty who's not in combat?"

"Good guess," said Slocum. "And by those terms, what is a grunt? Think logically. They tell me you're a college boy."

McGill had heard that the term came from the grunting sound an enlisted man made when he hoisted a sixty-pound pack on his back; he had always assumed he qualified as a grunt. Was he wrong?

"Uh...uh, I think it's somebody who's not a REMF, sir."

"That's a start," said the general dryly. "Now, you're stationed here at Ft. Myer. Does that make you a REMF, or a grunt?"

"I...I never thought about it like that, sir. I guess I'm not a grunt."

"No, Private McGill, you are not. You have dishonored the true grunts by claiming an honor you have not earned. But the Army has seen fit to give you the chance to earn that privilege. You'll be glad to know your little speech resulted in a priority requisition for your services by a unit in dire need of peacenik skills. You'll be going to the one Military Police unit in the world with combat and reconnaissance duties. You may yet get a chance to earn your stripes as a true grunt."

"But sir, I—"

"Captain Strack," said the general, "please continue...."

Strack nodded at the first-sergeant who said, "Private McGill, front and center."

The first-sergeant came down the steps and stood in front of the stage as McGill made his way out of his row and up the aisle and came to attention. "Private McGill, reporting as ordered."

The first-sergeant handed him a packet of papers.

"Go ahead, read it out loud," Strack ordered from the podium, "so we all know where you're going."

McGill read aloud the orders transferring him to PERP, the Prisoner Escort and Re-education Project in the Republic of Vietnam. "But Captain Strack, sir," McGill said, "I was guaranteed I wouldn't be sent to Vietnam. I've got it in writing."

"Oh, you have a contract, do you?" Strack said, oozing with sarcasm. "Well, of course you'll have the right to file a complaint through the proper channels once you have reported to your new duty station."

"But sir, I—"

Strack yelled, "You will speak when you are spoken to, Private McGill. Your peacenik skills are required at the prisoner compound at Camp Kiley, which those of you who have seen duty in Vietnam know as Dam Luc. You have a slot on the next flight out of Andrews. It leaves at sixteen-thirty. The duty sergeant will insure that you don't miss it."

"But, sir, I have—"

"You have your assignment, Private McGill, that's what you have,"

Strack said. "Peacenik MPs are in great demand in the Republic of Vietnam. Your particular talents could be critical to winning hearts and minds. Who knows, perhaps others may wish to follow in your footsteps. The PERP unit needs sensitive MPs with proven people-skills. There are billets for any others who would like to accompany Private McGill."

Strack looked around the room, making eye contact here and there, relishing the moment. "Anyone?"

The room was graveyard silent as the officers on the stage chuckled and smirked.

"No takers?" said Strack. "Very well. Thank you, General Slocum, for your time and your insights." Strack nodded at the first-sergeant who called out, "Company, ten*hut*!!"

Everybody jumped to their feet as the general's party and Strack started for the exit. After the officers had left the room the first-sergeant said, "Private McGill, remain at attention. Company, dismissed!"

When the room cleared the first-sergeant told him, "Sgt. Reynolds and his driver will assist you in packing your things and escort you to your flight."

"But what about my car, and—"

"Your car will be put in storage until you return or can arrange to have it picked up. Fill out the form at HQ and leave the keys when you sign out. The quartermaster will ship whatever you can't take with you wherever you designate."

McGill called Jenny from the pay phone in the barracks, but a housemate said she was in class. He was allowed to pack whatever fit into his duffel bag and nothing more. His escorts helped him box up the rest of his stuff and his prized Guild guitar and drove him to the quartermaster to drop it off for shipment to his parents' house in Milltowne. Just before signing out at company headquarters, he was allowed to call his parents from the duty-sergeant's phone. His mom started crying when he told her he was going to Vietnam.

"Don't worry, Mom, it's a good assignment," he said, lying to keep her from knowing he was heading into the worst duty a U.S. Army MP could possibly pull—escorting POWs down the Mekong from a hellhole called Dam Luc. His dad told him to keep his head down and he would send a car jockey to pick up the Skylark and drive it back.

McGill finally got through to Jenny the next day during a layover in

Hawaii. He could hear her crying as she said into the phone, "Oh, Arty, what happened? Was it your speech?"

"Yeah. There was no way I could talk my way out of it. Andy Warhol says we'll all be famous for fifteen minutes, which is maybe half of what I had last week. I think I'll be anonymous after this. Fame is too dangerous."

"Oh, Arty, it's all my fault. If I hadn't brought you backstage—"

"Jen, that's nuts. It has nothing to do with you."

"But...but, Arty, what can you do? What can I do?"

"I don't know, Jen. It's either go to Nam or go to prison or desert to Canada and never come back. They've got me by the short hairs. And I'll be too far out in the boonies to do much of anything to fight it except file paperwork claiming breech-of-contract, which won't mean shit. My dad's got my enlistment contract. I told him to send you copies, and I'll send you copies of my new orders. Maybe you can file a motion or a petition or find a loophole or something."

"I'll get you out, Arty, I swear I will."

In all the years they had been dating the words "I love you" had never passed their lips. They had skipped around it, believing in "free love" and keeping your options open.

"Jen, I know we've never really talked about getting serious. But I'm gonna think about you all the time."

"Oh, Arty, I...I...be careful, please, please, please, be careful."

Chapter 11

Dam Luc

McGILL LANDED AT SAIGON'S TAN SON NHUT AIR BASE IN THE BELLY OF A C-5A cargo plane on June 6, 1971, at 0830, Vietnam time. On that same day, in 1944, his father had been an observer flying reconnaissance in the Army Air Corps during the invasion of Normandy. Also on that very day, in 1918, his grandfather had seen action in the Battle of Belleau Wood, the first major battle in which Americans fought against the armies of the Kaiser. And now, here he was in Vietnam, on his own personal D-Day, scared shitless and about to be in a war that he was certain was illegal and immoral.

The MP's wore brassards with CUSTOMS embroidered in medium sized letters above the big white MP letters. When one of them saw the crossed-pistol brass insignia on McGill's uniform, identifying him as a fellow MP, he pulled him aside and gave him the preferential treatment that MP's always give to their own.

The hundred other "newbies" on his flight were bussed to the reception barracks for processing, but McGill, the only MP of the flight, was given a bunk with the Customs MPs in the cleaner, safer, Air Force barracks. These MP's were unusual—an Army detachment stationed on an Air Force base—and for that they were truly grateful, and not only because the Air Force was famous for having better chow than the Army. Even better, there were far fewer Army officers around to get on their case and Mickey Mouse them over the length of their hair or the shine on their shoes. It was not the job of the U.S. Air Force to enforce discipline in the U.S. Army.

The unit clerk told him to come back for his paperwork after a trip to supply. He was issued a soft jungle "boonie" hat, a steel pot helmet, a flak jacket, a rain poncho and two pairs of lightweight jungle combat boots with mesh insteps that let water drain out. The Air Force supply sergeant impressed on him the necessity of taking malaria pills every Sunday when they were handed out in the chow line if he didn't want to get malaria and live with it for the rest of his life.

When he reported back the clerk said, "You're assigned to Echo Company at Camp Kiley. Now, go get some chow before they shut down the line and come right back. The top wants to see you at thirteen-hundred sharp."

McGill asked everybody at his table in the mess hall what they knew about his new duty station at Camp Kiley.

"Nobody calls it Kiley," one guy told him. "It's Dam fucking Luc, the worst hell hole in the delta."

McGill said, "What's Dam Luc means in Vietnamese?"

One guy said, "It just sounds like it's gook. It's like Chu Lai. It don't mean a goddamn thing."

After chow, McGill reported to the first-sergeant.

"Troublemaker, are ya?" said the top as he looked over McGill's file.

"No, top, I swear, it's all a mistake. I'm not supposed to be here. It's in my contract. I need to talk to the JAG office."

"You want a lawyer to file a complaint, do ya? Well, you'll just have to wait till you're at your duty station. Now, I don't know what you did and I don't want to know. You're somebody else's problem, not mine. But you better keep your nose clean and your head out of your ass. Now, no matter what they sent you here for, they sent you here to be an MP, and an MP is what you will be. Do I make myself clear?"

"Yes, top, very clear."

"Good, now as an MP, your life is in danger every time you turn around and not just from Charlie, but from our guys as well. Maybe more so. There's been a lot of racial bullshit over here between whites and blacks, and MPs take it from both ends. And if you ever have to break up a bar fight, the only guys on your side are your fellow MPs. Now, I've been looking over your record, and it says you outscored everybody in marksmanship in Basic and MP school. Is that right?"

"I'm from Pennsylvania, top. Hunting's big back there."

The top chuckled and said, "You better hope you never have to find out how good you really are. Take this requisition and pick up your weapons from the armory. Test your weapons on the range before you leave. You'll be required to demonstrate you can disassemble, clean, and reassemble both weapons before you can sign them out. And I need not remind you, do I, Private McGill, that only officers and MP's are authorized to carry sidearms outside of a combat zone. Don't ever abuse that privilege."

"No, top, I won't. But top, a friend of mine who went to Annapolis just got to Nam a couple of weeks ago. How do I find him?"

"The Navy's been pulling out and turning their bases over. There's only a few thousand Navy still in-country. Chances are he's up at Cam Ranh. You'll have to check with them."

He put on his new poncho to keep out the driving monsoon rain and ran across the sprawling base to the armory. He chose what he thought was the best .45 pistol and M16 rifle, and spent an hour on the indoor shooting range sighting in the M16 and getting the feel of the pistol. He had not fired an M16 since Basic Training. Sighting it in reminded him of Wildwood when he won Jenny the big pink teddy bear at the .22 booth. He disassembled and reassembled both weapons as an Air Force sergeant watched and signed him out.

He had nothing else to do, so he hung out with the customs MPs as they worked the flights. They seemed to compete with each other to see who could hurry up the line the fastest, asking in rapid fire staccato: "Do-you-have-any-alcohol-tobacco-medication-drugs-of-any-sort-pornographic-literature-or-any-kind-of-weapon-okay-move-along," over and over and over.

Spec-5 Houseman, a dog-handler with a perfectly-trained German shepherd named General, put McGill to work as a jeep driver. Houseman's regular driver was down with the clap from too many nights with the boom-boom girls.

They went outside and dashed through the monsoon rain to an MP jeep with a canvas cover. Houseman said, "You drive," and McGill followed directions to the Household Goods holding area, where the personal effects of officers and high-ranking civilians were waiting to be checked through customs. McGill followed along as Houseman and General walked through the luggage and boxes and crates as the dog sniffed for drugs.

He and Houseman hit it off right away. Houseman had grown up on a farm and gone to the University of Indiana for a couple of years studying to be a veterinarian but dropped out because he couldn't afford it. When his draft notice came, he signed up to be a dog handler, a military occupational specialty that might prove useful when he went back to school on the GI Bill.

McGill drove where he was told, ending up back at the customs line. The MPs had just finished working a flight and the next one was not due for hours. Houseman asked, "Want to smoke one?"

McGill said, "Fuckin' A!"

Houseman dropped off the dog at the kennel, then told McGill to drive to the barracks, where they picked up two other MPs, and the four of them drove through the monsoon to a collection of Quonset huts behind the motor pool and parked the jeep where it couldn't be seen.

"So you just got here?" one of the new guys said.

McGill said, "Yeah. A couple hours ago."

"Well look at the bright side—you've only got three hundred sixty five and a wake-up to go."

"How about you?" McGill asked.

"I'm getting short. Be a two-digit-midget next week," by which he meant he would be a "short timer" with fewer than a hundred days left to go on the countdown of his one-year, in-country tour of duty. "Then I'll be hopping a Freedom Bird back to the fucking *World*, man."

"Only good thing about this fuckin' job is the grass is free," the other new guy said as he fired up a joint and passed it to McGill.

"Free?" McGill said as he held in a toke. "I don't get it."

"From the amnesty box," Houseman said. "Good grass is cheap on the streets, better than anything back home, but why pay for it if you don't have to? We'll fix you up before you head out. You're gonna need it where you're going."

McGill had never heard of an amnesty box. When he and Houseman went back to HQ Houseman said to a staff-sergeant reading an *Incredible Hulk* comic book, "Gonna do the box, sarge. Got the keys?"

"Who's checking you?"

It was SOP—military jargon for Standard Operating Procedure—that any time the amnesty box was emptied at least two MPs had to be present to insure everything was accounted for.

"Renton," Houseman said.

"Just make sure nothing's missing," said the sergeant as he handed over a set of keys.

"Nothing's ever missing when I do the box," said Houseman.

"Yeah, right. Just be sure to give the captain what he wants."

"You got it, sarge."

They found Renton in the PX cafeteria and Houseman told McGill, "Chow down good while you're here. You'll lose ten pounds your first month in the boonies."

McGill still lived up to his nickname of "Stick" for being skinny, so he had a burger, fries and a chocolate shake even though he'd had lunch in the mess hall just a couple of hours earlier. They went to the departures lobby where every day hundreds of GIs, NCOs, officers and civilians boarded the "Freedom Birds" that would take them back to "The World."

Just outside entrance was a blue metal box made out of quarter inch steel. It looked like the blue mail boxes with the rounded tops found on street corners all over the United States, but it was taller, at least twice as deep and four times as wide. Above it was a sign in giant red letters:

AMNESTY BOX
DEPOSIT CONTRABAND HERE
NO QUESTIONS ASKED
DON'T BE STUPID
THIS IS YOUR LAST CHANCE

Renton fetched two big cardboard boxes and a luggage cart from a storage closet as Houseman opened the padlock on the door at the bottom of the amnesty box.

"Stand back," Houseman said. "You never know what's in there."

He shined the flashlight inside and peeked in, then crawled halfway in and used his baton and flashlight to poke around and inspect the contents. Deciding it was okay, he stood up and ordered Renton to scoop everything into the boxes.

They wheeled the cart to a small room that contained a single table and a tall steel safe and began sorting the contents. McGill was amazed at the take: Four switchblade knives, nine porno magazines, one hand grenade, two bayonets, three American passports, two military ID cards, one claymore mine, two syringes, one set of brass knuckles, three balloons containing the residue of some kind of white powder, a Marlboro box full of machine-rolled joints, a Saturday Night Special, an empty fifth of Beefeater gin, seven dope pipes, one set of dog tags, five baggies with varying amounts of pot, and an AK-47 with a fully-loaded banana-clip.

"Not bad," Houseman said. "I've seen better, but not bad." He took a baggie and a porno magazine for himself, gave a baggie and a magazine to Renton, and handed the box of joints to McGill. "We gotta split with the other guys and turn enough in to make it look good, but this ought to hold you for awhile."

"Wow, man, thanks," McGill said. "How often do you clean it out?"

"Depends. Sometimes twice a day. Anything else you want?"

McGill looked over the rest of the haul, but he had never been into hard-core porn and he had no need for brass knuckles, switchblades, or syringes. He did take a small wooden pipe that fit easily in his pocket. Then, what the hell, he copped a porno magazine, maybe to trade for something.

On the drive back Houseman gave McGill a steady stream of advice. "You're gonna be way the fuck out in the boonies. Get yourself a mama-san to clean your hooch and shine your boots. And if you don't want your dick to fall off, don't do any boom-boom girls without a rubber. And never, under any fucking circumstances, touch any white powders no matter how bad it gets. 'China white' will waste you're ass if Charlie doesn't waste it first. In the delta the monsoon goes till the end of October. The dry season is when Charlie's gonna fuck with you, so keep your shit together and don't get too comfortable in those fancy sandbagged bunkers."

McGill asked, "So why does everybody call them 'Charlie?'"

"It comes from the radio call signs for the Viet Cong: V-C," Houseman said, "V is for Victor and C is for Charlie. Victor Charlie."

They passed a pair of South Vietnamese police in spiffy uniforms—white shirts, sky-blue pants, white saucer hats, and shiny white patent-leather holsters for their .45s.

"And another thing," Houseman said. "Watch out for the White Mice and the QC."

"White mice and QC?"

Houseman pointed at the two Vietnamese. "The white mice are the National Police, the most corrupt mothers in the whole fucking country. They've got a real attitude. The QC are the ARVN MPs and have QC on their helmets like we have MP. They're not as bad, but they're just as incompetent, and with Vietnamization you'll be working with them everywhere you go. And because you're an MP, they'll figure you think like they do, which ain't like you think at all. Be careful around 'em."

McGill asked, "What the hell is ARVN anyway?"

"Ha," laughed Houseman. "You really are a newbie. It's short for the Army of the Republic of Vietnam, A-R-V-N. They're on our side. Or they're supposed to be."

In the morning, McGill and six others boarded a helicopter, his first chopper ride ever. It was the first of three choppers and two boats he would take on his two-day journey to Dam Luc, in the heart of the Mekong delta, just twenty klicks from the Cambodian border.

There were very few places in the densely-populated delta suitable for a modern army's needs, so the Army Corps of Engineers created a flat, 100 acre base by pumping sand from the river into some rice paddies like they'd done at Dong Tam, the more famous 600 acre base on the My Tho branch of the Mekong river. Both bases were built for the Mobile Riverine Force—the MRF—a combined Army-Navy command. It was the first "brown water navy" operation since the Civil War, when the Navy had a fleet of boats on the Mississippi river. The Riverine Force operated throughout the delta's maze of 1,500 miles of rivers and 2,500 miles of canals conducting ambush and search-and-destroy operations. The force was being phased out and its mission handed over to the ARVN as American troops drew down. But with Nixon taking the war into Cambodia, Dam Luc was still an important staging area and a POW holding compound.

A double row of ten-foot high razor-wire surrounded a compound for POWs. Teams of Army linguists trained in Vietnamese and ARVN officers who spoke fractured English did the interrogations. Then the Viet Cong POWs were shipped down-river to whatever the ARVN had in store for them. Another compound held civilian refugees in the "pacification" program, all under the watchful eyes of MPs and QCs.

Dam Luc was also home to two floating barges used as artillery platforms. There were also Army PBRs (patrol boats, riverine) which were assigned the futile task of policing the thousands of junks and sampans that plied the myriad of waterways every day. There were also Tango boats, like the boats in WWII that landed troops on the beaches of Normandy and Iwo Jima. A Tango could ferry forty soldiers at a time, and they often moved in convoys of four to six boats on missions designed to provoke Charlie into a firefight to up the body-counts. We lose three, they lose a hundred. It seemed fair to the generals.

In the previous two years, Nixon's policy of Vietnamization had pulled most of the Navy out of the delta, leaving riverine operations to the Army and the ARVN. Dam Luc was still under U.S. control, and it had first dibs on USO movies before other units in the area. The field hospital was said to be okay, the PX was usually stocked with cigarettes and low-power three-two beer, and the ice machine in the EM club usually worked.

Every month or so, a troop of mostly-female USO performers came through to put on a show. Accompanying them were a few Red Cross "donut dollies," female volunteers in light-blue uniforms who were all recent college graduates who had volunteered for a year overseas. The Red Cross training manual mandated that they must strive to be "nonsexual symbols of purity and goodness" who reminded the troops of girls back home. The infantry grunts on search-and-destroy and ambush patrols considered the MPs at Dam Luc to be rear-echelon-mother-fuckers for their sandbagged hooches and USO shows with round-eyed women.

Like everybody else at Dam Luc, McGill was miserable. As the fucking-new-guy he was tasked with the worst details, and nobody made friends with an FNG because they were always the first to get their asses blown away and nobody wanted to care too much.

His first weeks were uneventful; only the occasional mortar attack disrupted the routine. He was grateful his main task was to escort prisoners to and from the interrogation huts, his .45 in his holster, his M16 locked and loaded, and to take his turn in a watchtower. He bitched about the heat and the mosquitoes, smoked "Buddha grass" like the other guys who bunked in his hooch, read comic books and month-old newspapers and anything else he could find. He saw some vague references in the military newspaper, *Stars and Stripes,* about something called the *Pentagon Papers* that apparently told the secret history of the war, but there was no TV and the only radio was the Armed Forces Network which broadcast two hours of rock and two hours of country every day as well as a weekly baseball game. His only thrills came at mail-call when he got a letter from Jenny and hearing scores on the radio as the Pirates kept on winning.

Then he got lucky, hearing that one of the cooks, a short-timer with two days left in-country, had a guitar he was trying to sell. McGill went to the guy's hooch to check it out. It was a Gibson J-45, a mid-range model called "The Workhorse" that was played by people like Bob Dylan. It was identical to the one the Mulligan Man had when the two of them and Dombrowski thought they'd be the next Kingston Trio until the coaches convinced Mulligan to give up music for sports. It had a gorgeous inlaid Peace Sign in the upper bout, and it showed a lot of wear; it had been around.

McGill played a few chords. The tone was great, so he checked the action and said, "A buddy of mine from junior high had one just like this. Who did the inlay?"

"No idea. I got at a pawn shop in Bangkok when I was on R&R. It's supposed to be genuine Cambodian ivory."

"So how come you're selling it?"

"I bought a ton of stereo stuff and don't have room to ship it back. And I've got three guitars back home, so I don't really need it."

McGill bought the guitar and six sets of strings for $20, practically stole the thing, and soon found himself the most popular guy in Dam Luc's EM Club; everybody wanted to buy him beers if he would sing their favorite songs. When he wasn't standing guard duty, he was the life of the party who could get everybody singing along to homesick songs like "California Dreaming," "Carolina in My Mind," and everybody's favorite, "Leaving on a Jet Plane."

The fact that "Jet Plane" was about a guy who *doesn't* want to leave where he happens to be didn't matter. Nobody cared about the details of the lyrics. Singing out, "I'm leaving on a jet plane" as loud as you could conjured up the feeling of being on a Freedom Bird heading back to The World.

McGill stayed out of trouble and was soon promoted to Specialist, 4th class, a "spec-4," pay-grade E-4. The promotion was routine, a function of his time-in-grade (military jargon for the amount of time spent at a specific rank).

Specialists were "soft stripes," as they did not wear V-shaped "hard-stripe" chevrons on their sleeves like corporals and sergeants. Instead, specialists wore a patch resembling a shield with an eagle in the center. For command purposes, soft-stripes came under the authority of hard-stripes of the same pay-grade, so a spec-4 would take orders from a corporal even though they were both the same E-4 pay-grade. The difference had mostly to do with job classifications. Hard stripes were trained for combat duties, like armor and infantry, whereas specialists were trained in support duties, like typing and communications. In addition, the chevrons made corporals non-commissioned officers with drinking privileges at NCO Clubs, while soft-stripes of the same E-4 pay-grade could only drink in the lowly EM Clubs until they achieved the rank of spec-5.

Being promoted to spec-4 was no great honor, as it was the most common rank in the Army. The promotion did mean an extra $13 dollars a month, but the biggest benefit was getting out of the shit-burning detail. Now the newest newbie took over his job on the weekly ritual of mixing gasoline and diesel fuel and burning the human excrement collected in fifty-five gallon drums underneath the outhouse latrines. Rank did indeed have its privileges.

It seemed to him that the Mekong delta smelled like fish, day in and day out. There were few roads, just endless canals and tributaries that acted like interstate highways for thousands of junks and sampans. At night, the areas outside the "villes" were "free-fire zones," and anything moving after curfew on the land or on the water was assumed to be Charlie and subject to being "offed," no questions asked.

He was thankful to bunk in a hooch within the base perimeter instead of being one of the true infantry grunts who went out into "Indian country" on ambush missions and slept on the open ground or in foxholes. He had heard grunts joking about going out on "shambush," and only pretending to be trying to goad Charlie into a fire-fight and instead doing everything possible to avoid one. No sense dying just to make some officer at HQ look good.

"*There it is*!" was the sardonic catch-phrase for the daily bullshit.

"Fuckin' *A*!" was the philosophical rejoinder.

McGill hired a mama-san who was maybe thirty but looked seventy to shine his boots and launder his fatigues, just two hundred piasters and a carton of Salems a week (for some reason the Vietnamese loved menthols). Despite the ragging he got from the other guys, it had been a matter of intense pride that he would never, ever, pay for pussy. His pride had so far kept his dick in his pants when the water-borne boom-boom girls floated in on sampans to ply their trade. But time was taking its toll, and it wasn't long before he grew tired of the buxomly, round-eyed girls in the porno rags he got from the amnesty box that he had come to know so well. They just weren't as hot as they used to be.

Chapter 12

In-Country

MULLIGAN ARRIVED AT THE NAVAL SUPPORT FACILITY AT CAM RANH BAY on a Navy cargo plane four months later than he had expected. The Navy had changed his orders when he was in Hawaii, and instead of Vietnam, they sent him to the huge base at Subic Bay in the Philippines for additional training with a group of junior officers in an intensive language course designed to give them the communication skills they would need to train Vietnamese in maintenance and repair. In the mornings they studied the language with Vietnamese instructors, and in the afternoons they learned to fix all types of equipment while learning the Vietnamese names for parts and procedures.

The base commander, Rear Admiral Bodean, was blunt. "Gentlemen, you're here in Cam Ranh because I requested engineering officers to help round up equipment and get whatever we don't hand over to the Viets repaired and shipped stateside in good working order. We're supposed to be out of here by this time next year, and there's a shitload to do. In addition, you'll be training the locals to operate and maintain the equipment we're leaving. It's a thankless job and it won't earn you any medals. Now I know you are all hot to trot to see some real action. I know I was at your age. But Cam Ranh is more secure than any place in this whole godforsaken country. The VC don't fuck with us here very much, and the only action you're likely to see is in the bordellos. And I'll tell you what I've told every officer in this unit—you damn well better use a rubber because any officer under my command who comes down with the clap *will* face a court martial. Underfuckingstood?"

The five of them answered, "Aye, aye, sir."

Mulligan knew that military mail often played catch-up with anyone transferring between bases. Still, he was worried he had not heard from Catherine. He couldn't get her out of his head, and was mystified as to what she was really like. He had sent her a postcard when he landed in Honolulu. He had given her Cam Ranh's FPO ZIP Code, but instead of going directly to Vietnam he found himself in the Philippines. He wrote her a letter from Subic telling her about the change, but since his time at Subic was indeterminate he told her anything she sent should be addressed to Cam Ranh and they would forward it to him. When he checked with the post office at Cam Ranh, they told him that a batch of mail had just been forwarded to him at Subic. It could take weeks to get back.

The Navy issued him a photocopied manual to communicate the details of repairing and maintaining equipment in his rudimentary Vietnamese. His assignment was like being a high-school shop teacher. It took just two days to realize he hated it. His training was being wasted. He had not spent four years at Annapolis just to become a shop teacher.

One Friday night he was in a poker game in the O Club when two journalists joined the game. One was English and the other was French. They had just arrived on a State Department press junket for European journalists.

"So how's the war going?" asked the Englishman to nobody in particular as Mulligan raked in the pot he had just won and collected the cards for his turn to deal. No one said a word; all officers knew to never say anything of significance to a journalist.

The Englishman tried again. "Blimey, mates, come on, now, how's it going? How about you, lieutenant?" he said to Mulligan. "Do you have an opinion?"

Mulligan ducked, saying, "I've only been here a few weeks."

The Englishman sighed in frustration and asked, "So how many of you have read *The Pentagon Papers*?"

Again, nobody said a word.

"I see you're all tongue-tied," he said with a laugh. "I've got a copy I'll leave with you," He took a paperback out of his side pocket and laid it on the table. "I just finished it. Let me know what you think when I come back through."

The officers stared at America's newest *New York Times* #1 best-selling paperback, which purportedly told the true story of the Vietnam War and was written by a team of Pentagon insiders. The report was only supposed to be for the edification of high-level officials as to how their predecessors had lied to the public and dragged the country into the war. It was never meant for publication.

Mulligan had kept up with the controversy, cutting out and saving every serialized installment in the three-day-old *New York Times* that he bought first thing every morning in the off-post newsstand when he was at Subic. But few of the other officers at Cam Ranh knew much about it, because the *Times* had mysteriously vanished from the newsstand racks in the Cam Ranh PX once the story broke.

Mulligan shuffled the deck a couple of times and said, "Ante up," and began to deal. Regardless of what was in *The Pentagon Papers*, true or untrue, the entire subject was career-killing Kryptonite for any officer in any branch of the service who expressed an honest opinion.

The journalists added a unique flavor to the conversation, and kibitzers listening in surrounded the poker table. It was a rare opportunity for Americans to ask British and French journalists about everything and anything, from their attitudes toward the war to European colonialism to what it was like to lose a money-making colony that supplied much of the world's rubber. Eventually the discussion turned to the French defeat at Dien Bien Phu.

"How did it feel to lose like that?" somebody asked.

The French journalist answered, "I was eighteen, right out of what you Americans call boot camp. We were waiting to ship out when news about Dien Bien Phu came over zee radio."

"Damn," somebody said, "that must have been tough, being a soldier and hearing about the defeat of your own army."

The Frenchman laughed and said, " Oh, no, no, not at all. Everybody was jumping around and cheering. We were—how you say—*threelled*."

Mulligan asked, "So why were you cheering for the defeat of your own army. I don't get it."

"Because we thought it meant zee end of zee war, and none of us wanted to die for Michelin Rubber."

The next morning, Mulligan was at breakfast in the officers' mess discussing the start of the World Series: the Pirates against the Orioles. The eleven-hour time difference meant the broadcast would begin at midnight. There would be very few Americans in Vietnam who did not stay up to hear at least the beginning of the game. The Orioles had won two World Series in a row and were favored. He had a really good feeling the Pirates would win the Series, remembering 1960 and beating the Yankees in seven games, so he bet more than he could afford on the outcome of the Series: he put $20 into the pool and made another $50 in side bets at good odds—three-to-five.

That afternoon, he was on the wharf taking inventory on a shipment when a jeep pulled up and a sailor told him he was to come with him to HQ to see the admiral. Mulligan walked into the office, where the admiral and a chief petty officer were going over some papers. Mulligan saluted and said, "Lt. Mulligan reporting, sir."

The admiral returned the salute and said, "At ease, lieutenant, and shake hands with Chief Dungy. The Navy has a special assignment for the two of you. Take a look at this." He held up a photograph. "Know what this is, lieutenant?"

"Aye, sir. It's called a 'pacvee,' a 'patrol air-cushioned vehicle.' It's the fastest and loudest boat in the Navy. We saw a film on them at Annapolis. But I thought they'd shipped them all home when we started drawing down?"

"That's the official story we cooked up for Charlie," said the admiral. "There were only six ever deployed in-country, three of the Navy's and three of the Army's. The last Navy PACV has been locked up in a bunker for two years. It took some damage after the support ship pulled out, so they dry-docked it. Now you're going in to get it."

"Why me, sir? I've never even been on one."

"None of the other officers here have either. Now the monsoon will be over in a few weeks and we want to get her out before the dry season. This may be our last chance before we pull all the way out next year. Here's the report from her last commander. Chief Dungy was engineer's mate on a PACV and knows them inside out. Your job is to patch her up and bring her in if you can. She cost Uncle Sam a million bucks and he wants her back. If you can't, cut her up and scuttle her."

"Aye, sir. I understand. But there's only two of us and a PACV has a complement of four or five."

The admiral said, "You will have the authority to requisition a crew and all the support you need from whatever Army units are there."

"Aye sir," Mulligan said. "Where is she, and when do we leave?"

"It's at a hotspot up the Mekong across from Cambodia. It's officially Camp Kiley, but everybody calls it Dam Luc. You leave first thing in the morning."

"Chief," said the admiral to Mulligan's new partner, "it's your job not only to work with Lt. Mulligan on the boat but use your experience to help him deal with the fucking Army. You'll be on an Army post, and it's a whole different world, fucked up with insubordination and race riots and draftees who don't want to be there, nothing like the Navy."

"I've dealt with the Army plenty of times, sir," said Dungy.

"Well, that's about it," the admiral said as he handed Mulligan an envelope. "Here are your orders and authorizations. We'll have a chopper ready for you at zero-six-hundred."

The orders came from the Military Assistance Command, Vietnam, written MACV and called "macvee" and known as the "Pentagon East." The orders commanded that all personnel give him anything he needed. He had to be up before dawn to catch the chopper, so instead of enjoying the game over drinks and poker at the O Club, he sat on his bunk studying reports and blueprints of the hovercraft while listening on the radio as the Pirates lost to the Orioles, five to three.

The helicopter, a Bell UH-1, affectionately known as a "Huey," skimmed the treetops at 125 miles per hour across the valleys, plains, jungles and rubber plantations in the heartland of South Vietnam. Looking out the chopper's open door, everything was a sea of green, every shade of green as far as the eye could see. Too green.

"So what do you think, chief," Mulligan shouted to Dungy over the noise of the chopper. "Will we be able to get her going?"

"Hard to say, sir," Dungy shouted back. "They were always a pain in the ass, breaking down all the time. They needed as much maintenance as a helicopter, maybe more. When they worked they were a thing of beauty, a great boat, and they were super in the swamps and marshes because they could go faster than hell where no other boats could even think of going. But there was always something breaking down. I think that's why they pulled them out. But they scared Charlie shitless. They called 'em 'quai vat,' Vietnamese for 'monster.'"

From the touches of gray on Dungy's temples, Mulligan sized him up as being in his late thirties, a "lifer" who probably joined the Navy right out of high school. As a chief petty officer, pay-grade E-7, he must be close to having twenty years in service and was looking forward to retirement and a life of leisure at half-pay. He wore no wedding ring. Mulligan didn't ask about wives or kids, and neither did Dungy.

"So what's this place like?" Mulligan said.

"It's everything you heard about the boonies and worse—hotter than hell, wet, swampy, with swarms of mosquitoes. And leeches, snakes, and fire ants. There's even tigers, and elephants, though I never saw any. Alligators, though, I saw plenty of them. And bats. And at dusk there's millions of bats, but they don't fuck with you. I did a year's tour on a PACV back in sixty-seven. We worked out of Moc Hoa on the Plain of Reeds, but we put in at Dam Luc a few times. The admiral called it a shithole, and he's right as the monsoon rain."

They landed at the air base at Bien Hoa and took a two-hour break for refueling, maintenance, and lunch.

"Chow down while you can, lieutenant," Dungy said. "We won't see anything halfway decent till we get back."

Rather than eat for free in the mess hall, Mulligan joined the pilot and co-pilot for lunch in the O Club. Like most chopper pilots, they were warrant officers, ranks W-3 and W-4, hovering between NCOs and commissioned officers but eligible to enter officers' clubs. Dungy and the chopper's crew-chief, an E-6 petty officer, headed for the NCO Club while the gunner, an E-3 seaman, quickly chowed down for free in the mess hall then hustled over to the EM Club for a beer.

They touched down at Dam Luc at 1530. The chopper crew did not want to spend a single minute longer than necessary at Dam Luc, and were determined to get back to the much safer base at Bien Hoa before nightfall. Mulligan and Dungy thanked the crew and shook hands good-bye, and a corporal driving a jeep took them to see the base commander, a lieutenant-colonel named Lombard.

Mulligan saluted. "Lieutenant Mulligan, reporting, sir."

Lombard was bulldog-stocky with a shiny baldpate and a grey fringe. He returned the salute and said, "We don't see much of the Navy in these parts any more. Let's see why you're here."

Mulligan handed him the envelope; Lombard read the orders and said, "So you're here to fetch the Navy's air-boat?"

"Aye, sir, if we can."

"Well, it's been locked up since before I took over here. I've never even seen it myself and don't know what shape it's in. Let's go take a look."

The driver took them to a Quonset hut. "Nobody's been in here for over a year," the colonel said as he opened the door and flicked on the light. The boat, almost forty feet long, was covered in camouflage tarps. Mulligan and Dungy pulled the tarps off and walked around the boat.

"She doesn't look too shot up, sir," Dungy said. "The rubber skirts seem okay, but I can't really tell until we inflate to see if they'll hold. Let me try to start her."

He hopped up on the bow and went into the cabin and soon said, "Deader than dead. We should charge her up overnight, lieutenant, then tomorrow we can see what we've got."

"You'll have the enthusiastic support of our shop for anything you need," said the colonel. "They'll love the challenge and the change of pace. It'll be great for morale."

"Colonel," said Mulligan, "Naval Intelligence is worried about security because of South Vietnamese mixed in with all our units everywhere. There's a lot of intel about infiltrators. They're worried if the enemy learns there's a PACV here in Dam Luc, Dam Luc could become a target."

"Yes, uh, yes," said the colonel. "I see what you're saying. So how can we help?"

"Give me a repair crew that doesn't include Vietnamese. Anybody in helicopter maintenance could be useful. And this boat is *loud*. Is there a building near a landing zone where we could camouflage the noise when we test by coinciding with chopper activity? If there are any VC operatives on the base, maybe we can fool 'em."

"A good idea, lieutenant," said the colonel. "I'll see what I can do."

Dam Luc's Bachelor Officers' Quarters was in a sandbagged Quonset hut. His berth was a cubicle with unpainted plywood walls lit by a bare overhead bulb with a pull chain and furnished with a cot, a folding chair, and a one-drawer desk with no lamp. Thankfully, it was only twenty yards from the outhouse latrine. It reminded him of the ramshackle quarters in the movie *M*A*S*H*. He set his alarm for 0530, and hit the rack worrying and wondering about Catherine.

Chapter 13

The Home Front

CATHERINE HAD RECEIVED A POSTCARD MIKE SENT FROM HAWAII, SAYING he hoped to see her again and gave his address as San Francisco, FPO and a Zip Code. It could have been anywhere. Who could tell? She wrote right back, telling him that Art got into trouble because of his speech and had been sent to Vietnam but she had no address for him, to please be careful, and that she'd had a super-exceptionally wonderful time and hoped to see him again.

Then her period was late. And later. And then even later. As the days went by with nothing happening, the more frightened she became. She had been on "the pill" for years and never had a problem before. Had she skipped a day? No, her pill dispenser showed she had been diligent, except when she'd left it in her backpack at the Marriott hotel during the demonstration and ended up sleeping on the Mall and making love to Mike in the Willard in the morning. She only took it a few hours late. Could it really make such a difference?

She didn't tell anybody, not even Jenny. After the last final exam, she and Jenny went apartment hunting and put a deposit on a student flat to share in the fall. They hugged good-bye for the summer, and she left in her ice-blue '62 Corvette convertible for the twelve-hundred mile drive to the DeWolfe estate in Grosse Point.

Her first day home, she had an attack of nausea after breakfast. None of the servants seemed to notice. Is this what morning-sickness was like?

She knew that the "rabbit test" for pregnancy required a sample of her very first morning urination, so that night she cleaned out the last of a jar of grape jelly, carefully washed it out with soap and bleach, set the alarm for six, got up and peed into it. Then she drove fifty miles to a Planned Parenthood clinic in Ann Arbor hoping that enough time had passed that she wouldn't be recognized from her days in the Detroit newspapers' sports sections as a state swim champion and in the society sections as a debutante from the second richest family in Michigan. She told the receptionist she was a student and gave a phony name and a campus address. So far, no problem.

She went back three days later for the results. "Congratulations," the doctor said, "the rabbit died."

"What exactly does that mean, doctor?" She hoped she was wrong about what it meant but knew that she wasn't.

"It means you're going to be a mother."

Terrified at whatever the next answer might be, she asked, "But...but what if I'm not ready?"

"Abortion is not legal in Michigan."

She was breathing heavily now, scared. "But what if I need one?"

The doctor took her hand and said, "I see you have no wedding ring. Does the father know? Would you like to talk about it?"

She wanted to scream and shout and cry YES–NO–YES—NO—YES! She took a deep breath and said, "It was something of a one-night stand. We'd just met, and now he's in Vietnam."

"I see," said the doctor. "That is difficult. Would you like to talk to a counselor? We have some very fine people?"

There was no way she was going to talk to the shrink her father paid to spy on her, let alone some stranger and risk exposing herself. She could see the headline in the *Detroit Free Press*: DeWolfe Heiress Knocked Up! Her mother would kill her.

"No, thank you, doctor. I'm a big girl. So what are my options?"

"New York is probably the closest state where abortion is legal, and it's legal in Canada. But you should make a decision before the end of your first trimester. After that, the procedures are much more dangerous. And you can't even consider it after your second trimester. You're due in January, around the twenty-fifth, give or take a few days."

She wrote a long letter to Mike saying how sorry she was to put him through this, and that she would do whatever he wanted, and that he was under no obligation to her. Weeks went by until finally—a letter!

She ripped it open, but he said nothing at all about a baby, only that he had been diverted from his original destination and didn't know for how long. Their letters must have crossed in the mail, and with all his moving around he probably had not even received hers yet. The trimester was almost up, and she shuddered to think of the possibility that Mike might never come back from the war and never have an heir.

Having no instructions or any way to discuss it with him, she consulted the astrology books hidden in her closet that she had not opened since high school. She knew Mike's birthday, May 18, so he was a Taurus, an Earth Sign. She was a Cancer, a Water Sign, so they should be compatible at a basic level. Though she considered herself to be a feminist, Cancer was a mothering sign, almost antifeminist. There was no getting around the fact that she loved young children, their enthusiasm, their innocence. She had always been the favorite aunt of her nieces and nephews and young cousins and enjoyed babysitting. She was sure she wanted the experience of being a mother. If nothing else, to do a better job of it than her own mother had done it with her.

She decided to go with her feelings. It felt totally karmic to go with the flow. She would keep it from her parents. If they found out, they would demand she have a quiet abortion. Her mother would be furious if her grandchild were to be born out of wedlock.

She was confident she could get through the summer keeping the secret from her parents and the servants. For years she had worn hippie-style "Earth Mother" dresses just to piss her mother off, so her new condition would be easy to hide when she started showing. She would return to law school in the fall, make an excuse for missing Christmas—sailing in the Bahamas, perhaps—and have the baby in New Haven. She could give it up for adoption without her parents ever knowing.

Jenny was about to leave for a paid summer internship in the legal department of Mellon Bank and needed a copy of Arty's enlistment contract to file a lawsuit to try to get him out. She had never met or spoken to his parents, but when she called his mom seemed to know all about her. His father got on the phone and said, "Arthur said you'd be calling. I've already made copies of his contract. So are you the girl Arthur's always talking about?"

Thank God they couldn't see her blushing. "I…can't really say. We're both dating other people. We don't have a commitment."

"It's you all right. So, is there anything else I can do?"

"Nothing that will help get him out, but…but there is something."

"So what is it, young lady?"

"Well, Arty said you had photographs from the World Series in 1960. I was wondering if you could make copies and send them. Arty was going to, but they sent him away before he had the chance."

"Yes, I'm sure we have them. But…why?"

"Well, Mr. McGill," she said, feeling totally awkward, "I was at that game and got hit with a foul ball and—"

"Holy moley!" his dad yelled. "You're the girl he gave the baseball to. You're the girl with the secret nose-job!"

She flushed again, thankful she was on the phone. "We think so, but we only just figured it out and we want to be sure. My mom has a Polaroid of me and Bing Crosby and Arty thinks his grandfather took it. I'll make a copy and send it to you when I get home."

When the envelope with the contract and the photos came, she was shocked to see herself a dozen years younger, and Arty, gawky and even skinnier than he is now. She showed the photos to Catherine who said, "It's karma, Jennifer. You are soul mates. Accept it. It's a magnificent gift."

She gave a copy of Arty's contract to Professor Hazlett, who filed a lawsuit demanding Arty be sent home due to breach-of-contract and for retaliatory violations of his civil rights.

Hazlett, Yale's expert in contracts, expected the Army to concede because the evidence was so straightforward—the contract stated that he would not be sent to Vietnam, but there he was in Vietnam. Jenny prepared the brief, Catherine helped with editing, and Hazlett assured her there was no reason for the Army to retain a low-ranking soldier like Arty in uniform. It made no legal, political, or military sense.

Late in August, Hazlett called. "I'm sorry Ms. Abruzzi, but somebody high-up wants to screw your friend. Now they're saying his skill sets are so vital to national security that 'military necessity' prevails. The judge took it under advisement and set a date in November for a hearing. I think they're trying to stretch it out until his one-year tour-of-duty is up and the issue becomes moot."

She didn't have the heart to tell Arty. Instead, she lied and wrote that there was no news on the lawsuit.

She returned to New Haven for her second year and moved into the new apartment with Catherine. Right away she noticed something was very different. Catherine was not her usual fiery self. She had been a champion swimmer, a black-belt in judo and an exercise fanatic who never showed even a hint of fat, but here she was with her face puffing out. After dinner that first evening in the new apartment, they were having coffee and brandy when Jenny gingerly asked, "Have you gained a little weight, Cate?"

"Uh...I haven't checked in a while," Catherine said, flushing pink.

Jenny's BS detector rang out like a fire alarm: CLANG-CLANG-CLANG. She'd always been good at telling if males were lying, or hiding something. It was a little harder with females, but not with Catherine.

"Cate, you're a terrible liar and you know it. What's going on?"

In early October McGill had enough time in-country to qualify for his first "rest and relaxation" leave, R&R, a pass to any approved destination he could get to and back from in six days. He didn't have the cash to fly to Tokyo or Bangkok or Manila or Hong Kong or Australia. That meant he had the choice of the only two approved in-country R&R locations: China Beach up north, or Vung Tau near the mouth of the delta. Vung Tau was closer, and what sealed the deal was an article from an old *Argosy* magazine on the EM Club bulletin board: "Vung Tau, Vietnam, Pleasure Capital of the World."

He and two other guys he barely knew traveled together for a day of chopper, ferry, and bus rides.

With over a hundred bars and strip joints, Vung Tau was the most scenic and militarily safe area in the entire country. Located about eighty miles south of Saigon at the tip of a small peninsula on the South China Sea, Vung Tau was a stand-in for Waikiki, Wildwood, Ft. Lauderdale and Laguna Beach right there in a war zone.

The war seldom bothered Vung Tau. Word was it was because Charlie liked to take his R&R at Vung Tau too and didn't want to screw it up.

The day before he left, a month-old letter from Jenny arrived at mail-call. He read it lying in his bunk, and when he came to the part that there was nothing new on the lawsuit, he shouted, "FUCK!" at the top of his lungs.

"There it is!" one guy said. Others commiserated, "Fuckin' A!"

The letter said Jenny was heading back to Yale law school where she and Catherine would be roommates. She hadn't heard from Catherine all summer. She asked him if he'd heard from Mike, and gave him her and Catherine's new address and phone number.

He was determined to talk to her, and he knew that the USO Club at Vung Tau had a short-wave radio phone patch that troops could use to call home. But there was a long waiting list for the free five-minute call. He would sign up the first chance he got.

Their bus arrived in Vung Tau at 2210. They found a cheap hotel, took three separate rooms, and headed to the bars. It was nearly midnight, but the bars were packed with GIs waiting for the start of the first game of the World Series at midnight. Signs written in Pidgin English like Happy All Game Hour! and Here Series Here! were in every bar window.

McGill wanted to hear the whole game but his buddies' teams weren't in it so they didn't care too much and left after the third inning to hit the rack. McGill stayed on drinking beer at the bar to the bitter end, and when the Pirates lost he chugged a double Jack Daniels and stumbled back to the hotel.

He woke up with a hangover about 0930 and immediately went to the USO to sign up for the call to Jenny. The earliest phone-call slot he could get was 1830 the next day, which in New Haven would be five-thirty in the morning. Jenny would still be in bed.

In the early afternoon he found his new buddies drinking beer on the beach. Around 1600 they left the beach and made the rounds of the bars, and by dusk they were all three-sheets-to-the-wind. They stumbled into a joint called the Dream Away Club and sat at a table as a Filipino rock band played "Sunshine of Your Love." Three bar girls came right over, and one gave him the sweetest smile, saying, "You numbah one cute, GI," and before he could speak she sat on his lap and put her arm on his shoulder. "You buy me drink, cute GI, yes?"

He had been shooing bar girls away, but this one was almost as beautiful as Jenny, with long, silky-black hair just like Jenny's, and smooth olive skin, almost like Jenny when her Italian complexion had its late-summer tan. She was perfectly proportioned, like Jenny, but with smaller, perkier breasts, and Oriental eyes, not at all like Jenny's.

The band was loud, so he cupped his hand to her ear and said, "You remind me of a girl back home."

"Numbah one!" she squealed, all smiles and giggles. "She boo-koo pretty like me, yes?"

"Oh yes."

"What her name?"

"Jenny."

"Oooh," she cooed, soft, like a kitten, and squirmed in closer. "My name Jenny too, cute GI. Tonight, I be you Jenny. You like Vung Tau Jenny. Numbah one boom-boom!"

McGill's resolution to never, ever, under any circumstances pay for pussy totally broke down that night at the Dream Away Club in Vung Tau, The Pleasure Capital of the World. In the morning he felt guilty, but just a little. He and Jenny had never agreed not to date others, so it wasn't like he was cheating, though he suspected that his Jenny would not agree that a boom-boom girl who called herself Jenny for fifteen dollars a night qualified as a true "date."

But hell, Jenny could be screwing half the guys at Yale for all he knew. And he was in an honest-to-god, no-shit, real fucking war-zone. It was only luck that he hadn't killed anybody yet, or even fired his weapon, but he had dived into bunkers under mortar attacks and loaded body-bags onto choppers. That should be reason enough to make it more or less okay to justify getting laid once in a while.

It wasn't like he was alone. A famous drinking toast from World War I went: "To our wives and sweethearts—may they never meet!"

In many areas of Vietnam, bordellos were sanctioned by the military and the women who worked there were issued "entertainer" cards and given regular venereal checkups by Army doctors. Secretary of Defense Robert McNamara was reported to have said in 1965 that, "[The] main idea was to keep troops contented and satisfied. Ice cream, movies, swimming pools, pizza, hot dogs, laundry service and women."

Almost a third of American troops contracted VD during their tours. Everybody got a physical exam prior to out-processing, and nobody with any symptoms was allowed on a plane. The best strategy to avoid venereal detention was to lay off the boom-boom girls before your PCOD, or "pussy cut-off date." This precaution allowed short-timers a few weeks to clear up symptoms. Of course there were always guys who pushed PCOD to FPCOD, then to AFPCOD, and even to AAFPCOD, with the F standing for final, the AF for absolute final, and the AAF for absolute-absolute final. The timing was imprecise due to the different incubation periods of the various maladies.

McGill hated the routine of the fucking rubber as much as he hated the routine of the fucking war, but he used one because of the fear of catching some super-strong strain of VD that laughed at penicillin and made your dick turn purple and fall off like a scab. He had a girl he hoped to come home to, and if he brought back some exotic oriental VD the real Jenny would dump him down the drain faster than a foul-smelling carton of rancid milk.

McGill was to meet Vung Tau Jenny at the Dream Away Club at 1930. The plan was for her to take him to a local place and show him what great Vietnamese food was like. He was sick of GI bars and just wanted to go to dinner, go back to his room, jump in the sack with her for an hour, and then listen to the second game of the World Series.

He bought a cheap transistor radio from a street vendor. He figured she would go to sleep soon after it started while he stayed awake. It should be over in about three hours, so he could get a few hours sleep and have time for a quickie before breakfast and catching a bus to Saigon.

He and his buddies spent the day at the beach. The waves in the bath-water warm ocean were wimpier than New Jersey's so they mostly just sat on blankets under an umbrella trying not to get sunburned.

He went to the USO building an hour early to make his call. He had been there yesterday, but just to sign up, and he didn't know much about the USO. This particular club was supposed to have great T-bone steaks, probably from local water buffalo.

He chatted with the cute receptionist. He asked where was she from, what she was doing in Vietnam, all the usual pick-up lines, all of which she effortlessly parried.

"You must get hit on a lot?" he said.

She just gave him a coy smile. "It's the job of a USO volunteer to politely say no without hurting any feelings."

McGill had hung out in USO lounges at airports between flights, but this was his first USO Club. All he knew about it was that his father had been a captain in WWII whose job as a morale officer had him flying all over England and France setting up logistics for USO shows with stars like Bob Hope and Bing Crosby.

"So what's USO stand for? United States…*what*?"

"No," she said, "everybody gets that wrong. It's for United Service Organizations." She informed him that the USO was an association of non-profits, including the YMCA, YWCA, and the Salvation Army. Its mission was to keep up the morale of troops overseas. She told him, "Our motto is 'A Home Away From Home.'"

McGill asked, "So how'd you get into it?"

"They recruit college seniors with theatrical experience or who majored in things like recreation and broadcasting. You have to be outgoing and personable. They don't take just anybody. I majored in music and dance. We write and produce a lot of the shows ourselves."

He had seen two USO shows at Dam Luc, different troupes of six USO women who flew in on Hueys to entertain the base for a night. The performances had been pretty good, and just seeing real American girls got guys pumped up.

"And it's not just doing shows," she said. "Guys come in here all the time looking for somebody to be their mother."

"Their mother?"

"Yeah, for things like sewing. It's amazing how many guys can't use a needle and thread. We sew on lots of buttons and patches and stripes."

McGill asked, "So is there a USO uniform?"

"No, not like Red Cross Donut Dollies. But we're to always wear perfume and a skirt, and never slacks or jeans."

"Really? No jeans?"

"It's all about being feminine. The USO commander gives the same speech to everybody on our first day. 'Your job in Vietnam is to be happy. Never let the men see you cry.'"

When his turn came, another cheery USO volunteer took him to a small cubicle with a telephone while somebody in another room used the crackly short-wave radio to connect him to Jenny's number.

"Remember, just five minutes from the time they answer," she said. "Then they cut you off."

"What if nobody answers? Or they're asleep, and can't get to it?"

"You get twenty rings. Then you'll have to wait your turn all over again. There's dozens of guys behind you."

Jenny woke up on the fourth or fifth ring, she couldn't be sure. She started to get up but heard Catherine, who in her prenatal condition had not been sleeping well, shuffle from her bedroom to answer. "Hello.... Yes, operator.... No, this is his her roommate."

Then came a shriek: "Jennifer! It's Art! From Vietnam! Hurry!"

In the twenty seconds it took to find the light, scramble out of bed, and slip on her robe she listened to Catherine talking to Arty, "She's coming. Are you okay?... That's wonderful. Have you seen Mike? Is he okay?.... Dammit! If you see him have him call right away.... I know, but if you do please, please have him call. Promise you'll have him call... Yes.... Me? Upset? No. Why would I be upset?... Yes, really, I swear....

Here's Jennifer. Stay safe, Art."

Catherine handed her the phone, saying, "I'll leave you two alone," and closed her bedroom door.

"Arty, is it really you?"

"It's me. We only have a few minutes. How's law school?"

"Everything's fine. We're still working on getting you out, but they're…they're dragging their feet. There's no real news."

"Don't worry about it, Jen," he said, though she could hear his sigh of disappointment. "I'm getting shorter every day."

They chatted for a stop-and-go-it's-your-turn minute about what his base was like, how her parents were, all small talk while saying not much of anything. There was an awkward pause for a few precious seconds until Jenny said, "Did you watch the Pirates' game?"

"No, but I heard it in a bar and couldn't help thinking about you."

"Me too," she said, laughing. "Oh, your dad sent copies of the photos your grandfather took. It is definitely us, Arty."

"It's kind of spooky," he said.

"No kidding. Will you be able to hear the rest of the Series?"

"Tonight for sure, then I've got to get back. It depends."

"I'll pretend we're at every one together," she said.

"Just don't get beaned again," he said with a laugh and then turned serious. "Jen…what's with Catherine? She seemed all worked up about talking to Mulligan. She was out of it."

"Uh…she hasn't been feeling well."

"No, she was really out there just now, Jen. Kind of nuts. A guy here had a girl go mental on him when she found out she was knocked up. It felt kind of like that."

"I…uh—"

"So she is knocked up, isn't she? I knew it. So, say I do run into Mulligan? Do I tell him, or what?"

Jenny couldn't guess how he figured it out. Maybe he was bluffing and didn't know anything. Arty was good at that. But it felt like the cat was out of the bag, the horse was out of the barn, and the chickens had flown the coop. It would do no good to lie. "No, Arty, it's not a good idea. She wrote him weeks ago but she hasn't heard back. If you do see him, and he hasn't seen her letter, have him call, but don't tell him anything. Just say you talked to me and it's very important. She really should be the one to tell him."

"And if he has seen the letter?"

"Then tell him he's an asshole if he doesn't call."

"So what's she going to do?"

"She has a couple weeks before she's too far gone. She's dying to talk to him but doesn't know how to reach him."

"So Mulligan's going to be a father?"

"I can't be sure what she'll do. Cate's unpredictable, and I've never seen her so unsure of herself. She may end it, or have it and give it away just to keep it from her parents. It depends on what Mike wants."

The short-wave operator cut in, "You have ten seconds—"

"It was really good to talk to you, Arty. You be careful, promise?"

"I swear, Jen, I'll be extra-careful."

That night McGill was extra-careful not to fall for Vung Tau Jenny's manipulations. Her fancy restaurant cost a bundle. After paying her for their "dates" he would barely have enough cash to get back.

He bought a quart of "33" beer on the way to the hotel. They undressed and she took a pipe from her purse and stuffed it with grass. They had a few tokes, and after making love she fell asleep when the ballgame started, curled up next to him, kittenishly beautiful, his own Jenny's equal in every physical sense. He liked her, and she did everything imaginable to please him. She could even make him laugh, but they had nothing to talk about.

He peeled off the damned rubber to take a leak, turned the radio down low so she could sleep, and took occasional tokes off her pipe and listened as the Pirates got their asses kicked, eleven to three. They were down two games to none in a seven game series. It didn't look good.

In the morning, Vung Tau Jenny gave him an enthusiastic quickie, free of charge, then he took her to the USO club for an American style T-bone steak-and-eggs breakfast. They went back to the hotel and he talked over plans with his new buddies. They wanted to stay another day, but he wanted to see the nightlife on Saigon's famous To Do Street. She walked him to the bus stop, wrote out her address, told him he was, "Numbah one GI," and hugged and kissed him like she meant it.

In Saigon, he signed in for a bunk at the Army transient barracks, ate in the mess hall, then hit Tu Do Street at dusk. He could only afford a couple of beers, and went back early, tired and bored. He found a *Stars and Stripes* in the lounge, propped himself up on his bunk to read it, and turned the radio on low so he'd know when the game started.

Suddenly "Reveille" was blaring over the loudspeaker, bugling the barracks to GET THE FUCK UP! He jerked straight up and knocked the radio to the floor. As he picked it up the DJ said, "Gooood morning, Viet*NAM*!" He had slept through the whole game, which the DJ reported the Pirates had won, five to three. He was thrilled that his team had won the game but pissed at himself that he'd missed it.

He ate in the mess, then went to the cafeteria and bought a roast beef sandwich to go, a bag of chips, two Hershey bars, and a Seven-Up. He took a bus to a ferry, which took him to another bus. He hitched a last ride on a Medevac Huey, called a "dust off," that was heading to Dam Luc to extract wounded from the field hospital.

They approached Dam Luc at dusk, but for no good reason he could see the pilot kept circling above the zillions of bats that were in a mosquito-feeding frenzy over the landing zone. McGill yelled to the pilot, "Don't worry about the bats. They'll move their asses."

"It's not that," the pilot yelled back. "They want to clear us to land on their signal and not before. And then they want us to keep the engine revved up until they tell us to shut her down. Some kind of security thing."

McGill had never seen Dam Luc from the air before, and he was astonished at the extent of the defoliated perimeter around the base, a dead zone at least a hundred yards wide holding the jungle at bay. He knew what it looked like from inside the razor-wire on the ground and had asked his sergeant, "What happened to the jungle?"

"They wanted it cleared so we could see Charlie coming. Sprayed the shit out of it from choppers."

"Spayed it with what?"

"Something called 'Agent Orange.'"

"What's that?"

"I don't know, but it works," the sergeant had said, but it took seeing it from the air to realize just how totally dead the jungle was all around the base.

When they were allowed to land McGill gazed out the open door into the misty Mekong dusk as the chopper descended through clouds of swarming bats. He was surprised to a see a new Quonset hut next to the landing zone that had not been there when he left six days ago.

He showered and wrote a short letter to Jenny, barely mentioning his R&R except to say his five minutes on the phone with her had been the best part of the whole trip. Before he crashed, he put spare batteries into the radio to be ready for his morning shift and the fourth game of the Series. For the first time in baseball history, a World Series game was to be played at night, with the broadcast starting at seven, Pittsburgh time. That made it 0600 in Vietnam, and his shift started at 0700. He didn't want to miss a single inning, but whoever heard of baseball at breakfast?

His radio fit easily into a baggy pocket of his fatigue pants. With luck it would be a morning of quiet guard duty at the stockade. He should be able to patrol with the radio on and hear most of the game without too much hassle from the lifers. Or from Charlie.

Chapter 14

Up the River

MULLIGAN WAS HAVING COFFEE AND DONUTS IN LOMBARD'S OFFICE AS they discussed the engine test. The monsoon was rapping on the corrugated roof like an orchestra of snare drums. In the next room, a sergeant had the game on the radio, barely loud enough to hear through the door. It was the second inning, and the Bucs were already down three to nothing and had pulled their starting pitcher. It didn't look good.

"Well, lieutenant," said Lombard, "got any skin in the game?"

"Aye, sir. I'm from Pittsburgh. Beat 'em Bucs."

"They're getting their clocks cleaned, lieutenant."

Mulligan said, "Like Yogi Berra says, 'It ain't over till it's over.'"

The colonel chuckled and said, "So what's the story on that flying boat of yours? Can you get her going?"

"Aye, sir, we think so. The only problem is one of the blades on a lift-fan is shot to hell. Probably from one of their coconut mines. The engine is fine, but that blade makes her unbalanced. Chief Dungy says we won't get far before it shakes all the joints apart."

"Can you fabricate one?"

"No sir, we've talked to the machine shop. We need to get a spare if we're going to take her out under her own power."

"So can you get one?"

"Maybe. We turned over the base at Cat Lo in April. I've got a manifest of everything we left behind and there's two fan blades on it. With any luck the Viets haven't sold them for scrap yet. If we can get one we can have her ready in a couple of hours. I've sent a message to Admiral Bodean. We should know soon."

"So say you get the part, what then?"

"She has a cruising range of about a hundred-sixty miles, so we should be able to get her to the support ship offshore with fuel to spare. We'll need to borrow a second officer and a gunner's mate for the trip."

"We have a Coast Guard ensign about to finish up a training stint who's going to need a ride out of here. Carver, I think it is. Will he do?"

"If he's any good. But what's the Coast Guard doing here?"

"They come over a couple times a year to train our boys in harbor operations. Coasties are the experts. As far as a gunner, I don't want to break up a boat crew, but the newbies are scheduled for weapons-training this week. I'll give you whoever does best."

"Sounds good, sir."

"Now you'll need a call sign," said the colonel as he slid a three page, typewritten sheet across the table. "You can have anything that isn't taken."

Military call-signs are designed to confuse the enemy as to which units were which and who was talking to whom. Mulligan picked up the list and read some random call-signs: Ladder Echo; Farmdale; Bull Puckey. He asked, "What's Dam Luc's, sir?"

"Centerfold," said the colonel.

Just then they heard the radio through the door as the crowd began yelling "Arriba! Arriba!" after Roberto Clemente beat out a grounder for a base hit. In idiomatic Spanish "Arriba!" was a command, a direct order meaning "Get up!" or "Hurry up!" or "Come on!" or "Get your ass in gear!" In baseball it was the nickname of the Pirates' super-star right-fielder, bestowed on him by the fans for always hustling no matter what the score. For over a decade, the stands in Pittsburgh erupted in chants every time Clemente got a hit, stole a base, made a diving catch or nailed a runner at the plate from deep right field with his javelin-champion's throwing arm. Many baseball experts said that Clemente, in addition to his four National League batting titles, was the best defensive right fielder to ever play the game.

"How about Arriba, colonel?" Mulligan said. "The fastest boat on the Mekong."

"Fine with me," said the colonel. "Anything else, lieutenant?"

"Yes, sir. I've never been on the river. Is there a chance I could tag along on a patrol to get a feel for what I'm getting into?"

"I'll have Carver take you out tomorrow. I think it's his last training. Report here at zero-seven-hundred."

McGill was trying to keep dry as he walked patrol in the monsoon with his poncho over his helmet, his shoulders hunched, slopping in the mud between the rows of chain-link fence topped with razor-wire. His M16 was slung stock-up over his shoulder to keep water out of the barrel, so if he had to use it the damned thing wouldn't blow up in his face.

He was much too far away to hear the radios in the hooches, and the asshole colonel wouldn't let the game be played over the loudspeakers. But it didn't matter, because with his new radio in his baggy pocket he could hear every play. Between innings, he glanced in the doorways of the thatched huts on stilts which housed the detainees in their black pajamas. And he kept a watchful eye out for sergeants and officers who would put him back on the shit-burning detail if they caught him listening to the game while on guard duty.

The Pirates came from behind to win—five to three—tying the Series at two games each. The fifth game started at midnight tomorrow, so he should be able to listen to it in the hooch without lifers hassling him. All was right with The World, even if just barely okay in The Nam.

At lunch he was in line with his tray on the sliding rack waiting for the cooks to scoop him up a piece of gravy-soaked mystery-meat when a spec-5 came up and said, "You McGill?"

"Yeah. Why?"

"Weapons training," he said as he looked at his clipboard. "You go out tomorrow. Be at the docks at zero-seven-hundred."

"Go out where?"

"Up river to the firing range."

"In the monsoon?"

"The colonel says it makes it more of a challenge."

This was good, a change of pace. It would be the first break in his routine in weeks, and a chance to go out in one of the patrol boats.

He finished his shift at 1800 and went straight to the mess hall before they ran out of everything edible, then to the PX for a carton of smokes, Marlboros in a box if they had 'em, and a six-pack of the only beer available, low-power Black Label. Warm three-two beer was better than no beer at all.

He waited at the shower-tent for his two-minute turn in the luke-cold water, and at he 2130 dropped out of the poker game and asked his bunkmates to keep it down and wake him just before the ballgame started. He'd have to be up at 0500, so he wanted to get a couple hours sleep before the game. He took a final hit on the communal bong, crawled into his rack, pulled his flimsy pillow over his head and pressed it tight over his ears and eyes to try to shut out The Nam.

Mulligan had been waiting all day for word on the fan blade, but nothing had come. He'd gone to the mess hall at 1700 and seen a sign on the bulletin board and knew where he'd be catching the game:

World Series Poker Game Tonight
BOQ lounge • 2400 sharp • Officers Only

Tomorrow, Dungy would get the boat ship-shape and await the delivery of the lift-fan blade, if it existed, while he went out on a PBR to get a sense the Mekong. After chow, he went to his cubical and studied the maps of the rivers, tributaries, and canals between Dam Luc and the coast. Taking the PACV downriver to a support ship offshore should be a piece of cake. Everything hinged on the fan blade.

At 2130 he set his alarm for 2350 hoping to get a little sleep and zonked out thinking about Catherine. When the alarm went off, he brushed his teeth and shaved so he'd be alert for some serious poker.

The BOQ lounge was a twenty-by-twenty cubical with plywood walls in a sandbagged Quonset hut. It had a couch of patched yellow vinyl and two matching chairs that would have been rejected by Goodwill. Two card tables were set up in the center of the room. Other amenities included a clock radio, a table with a hot plate and a percolator, a bookshelf with old copies of *Time, Newsweek, Argosy, Popular Mechanics*, and *Stars and Stripes*, and a stack of folding chairs for card games, usually poker but sometimes bridge, hearts, gin, blackjack, and cribbage.

Mulligan took a seat across from an Army captain wearing an Orioles cap who asked if anybody had the balls to bet against Baltimore. Mulligan bet him $10, even odds, and chipped in on three fifths of Johnny Walker Black. Poker had been huge when he was growing up in gambling-crazed Milltowne, and he seldom lost. He remembered the stories about Dwight Eisenhower, who as a cadet at West Point and later as an up-and-coming Army officer, routinely cleaned out his fellow officers' wallets in poker games. The story went that Ike had to give up playing poker because his constant winning was causing resentment among his peers and hurting his career. Mulligan wondered if he would have to give it up, too, but if he ever did, it would not be today. Winning at poker at a table of Army officers would not hurt his Navy career, and it was a lot of fun taking their money while sipping decent scotch.

The fifth game was a two-hit shutout that ended with the Pirates winning, four to nothing. The $10 from the bet plus $163 from his poker winnings made it a banner night. It was too bad the sixth game was two days away; he could get rich this way.

In the morning, there was still no message from the admiral about the fan blade. He was late to the mess hall, and the powdered scrambled eggs, all the bacon and sausages and even the hot oatmeal were gone. He had a bowl of Wheaties with warm powdered milk, a piece of cold toast, a glass of warm grape Kool-Aid, and a mug of what passed as coffee. He would not make the mistake of being late for chow here again.

He went to see the colonel, who asked, "Any word on that part you need, Lt. Mulligan?"

"No sir, not yet."

The intercom buzzed and a voice said, "Sir, Ensign Carver is here."

"Send him in." The colonel flicked off the intercom: "You're going out with Carver. If at the end of the day you want him, he's yours. If not, I'll get you one of my people."

"Aye, sir. Understood."

The colonel made the introductions then said, "Carver, I see you're here for a few more days. What's left on your schedule?"

"Just training the last two of your crews this morning."

"Good. I want you to take the lieutenant here with you and show him the territory. He's new to the delta."

Carver was five-nine, medium build, with dark, wavy hair, a bulbous nose and square jaw that added up to a ruggedly handsome face. He looked like he was in his late twenties, old for an ensign, which made Mulligan worry that he was a doofus who couldn't get promoted. But as he got to know "Hank" it turned out that he had served six years in the enlisted ranks before being accepted to Officer Candidate School. Still, Mulligan was cautious, as this was Carver's first assignment since receiving his commission and his first time in Vietnam.

They walked to the dock, where two PBR boats were idling their diesel engines. "Pick a boat, lieutenant," said Carver.

One had *Proud Mary* on her stern, the other, *Susie Q*, which sent a chill through Mulligan as he remembered Frankie up on stage singing "Susie Q," and he wondered for the hundredth time just how Frankie had died.

"Lieutenant, you okay?" said Carver.

"Yeah. I was just thinking about an old friend who had a band, Frankie Dombrowski. He was drafted and killed over here a couple years ago. I never did find out what happened. 'Susie Q' was his killer dance song. Let's take it first."

PBRs often patrolled in pairs to cover each other in a fight. Statistics showed that one out of three members of PBR crews were killed or wounded during their tours. At this late stage of the war, each boat had a four-man American crew plus an ARVN sergeant who was training to be a skipper and a civilian Vietnamese interpreter. Two flags, American and South Vietnamese, signifying joint operations, flew on the sterns.

Ten minutes upriver there was a floating marketplace, where dozens of vendors in small sampans were selling all kinds of fish and fruit and rice and meat. It was like the Middle Eastern bazaar in *Casablanca*, but all the shops were afloat. He was astounded at the intensity of life on the waterways of the delta, hundreds of times more activity than he'd ever seen on the Allegheny or the Ohio. The delta wasn't just a corridor for tugs hauling barges laden with iron ore, limestone, coal and steel like the rivers he knew. The waterways of the Mekong were home for millions who lived their entire lives in the floating villages throughout the delta.

As he surveyed the river with binoculars, he noticed that painted on the bow of every boat was a fierce face with black pupils staring from white eyeballs, all of them with red cheeks, red noses, and scowling red foreheads, as if they were wearing red Lone Ranger masks.

"What's with the faces, sergeant?" he asked the skipper, a coal-black Army staff sergeant about thirty years old who was totally in command of his PBR despite the presence of Navy and Coast Guard officers.

"They're superstitious as hell, sir. They think the faces ward off evil spirits, see in the dark, and bring good luck. Me, I think radar works better."

Carver's job was to instruct the PBR crews in Coast Guard interception, boarding and inspection techniques. The two PBR boats worked in tandem, checking for weapons and contraband, especially drugs. Stopping the flow of heroin coming down river from the remote areas of Burma, Laos and Cambodia known as the "Golden Triangle" had become a high priority. Over the course of the day, they randomly boarded and searched about three dozen small, one and two-person flat-bottomed sampans that were propelled by men, women and sometimes children using poles and oars and wearing the conical straw hats the British called "coolie hats." They also boarded a dozen larger junks, with their distinctive battened sails, some with crews of three or four. No obvious Viet Cong or weapons were found, and no drugs.

They docked after a long day amidst the fetid smells of the delta. As they came down the dock, the harbormaster handed Mulligan a handwritten note from Dungy: "Shipment arrived. Testing at 1700."

This was great. If it worked they could take the PACV out for trial run in the morning. If all went well, they could leave and make it to the rendezvous with the supply ship off of Vung Tau by dusk. Carver had shown he knew boats and would be a good second in command. "Hank," Mulligan said, "I have an interesting job for you."

McGill and four other newbies spent a day on the PBR *Fortunate Son* learning the basics of every job on the boat in case somebody was wounded or killed and they had to fill in. They took turns steering, and learning the radar and the radios. But the best part was shooting at buoys and shore targets from various angles, distances, and speeds while a sergeant made notes on a clipboard. McGill had always been a crack shot, but he had never been on a boat speeding across the water at thirty miles an hour while machine gunning targets like a Hollywood cowboy on horseback.

Blasting away with the .50 caliber heavy machine-gun was a total gas. The famous Browning M2, nicknamed "Ma Deuce" by Army troops in WWII, was also used in fighter aircraft for blowing enemy planes out of the sky. It had a range of up to four miles and could rip apart trucks and concrete walls and even cut down trees.

The weapons-training also gave them turns on the M60 light machine gun and the MK18 grenade launcher. For McGill, it triggered memories: of winning Jenny the pink Teddy Bear at the .22 booth in Wildwood; of deer season at the hunting camp with his dad's Winchester .30-30 and cases of beer in the snow for the poker games; of plunking ground hogs with his very own single-shot .22 when they popped their heads up in his grandfather's cornfield when he was ten years old. That in turn reminded him of the Amish family up the road that was always happy to take them for groundhog stew, and *that* triggered the memory of the Amish bench-raising after the anti-war demonstration. What the hell was he doing here?

When they docked the sergeant said, "McGill, you did pretty good out there. Report to HQ tomorrow at zero-seven-hundred. Full gear."

This was not good. "Why, what's up?"

"No idea. Top just said send to him whoever did best."

Shit. Had he stepped on his dick? What had he been thinking? Guarding prisoners and refugees sucked, but except for the occasional mortar attacks, Dam Luc was relatively safe. He should have played the doofus and missed every target on purpose instead of kicking ass. What an asshole he was. Were they going to put him on a night patrol, silently floating, hugging the shore, stalking Charlie and hoping for a firefight. Last month a PBR on night patrol didn't come back. He had no desire for medals. He was against the fucking war.

In the morning, McGill ate in the mess and reported to HQ with a full pack, his .45 holstered at his side and carrying his M16 and his flak jacket. A corporal took a folder from a cabinet and ushered him into the top's office. He stood at attention as First Sgt. Birkman, a beanpole everybody called "Gobbler" because his long, skinny neck and huge Adam's apple made him look like a turkey when he walked. He glanced at McGill, opened the file, took the breach-of-contract complaint out and said, "So you're the pain in the ass the Pentagon sent me?"

"I'm not supposed to be here, top. It's in my contract."

"Don't mean shit to me, soldier."

"I can't kill anybody, top. I'm telling you right now, I won't do it."

"Do I look like some kind of fucking shrink or something? You got personal problems, talk to the chaplain."

"But top—"

"Shut up!" he snarled, scowling as he leafed through the file. "You did better than the other assholes did yesterday, and your scores in Basic tell me you are exactly what this man's Army needs behind a machine gun—a gunner who can hit what he shoots at."

"But top, I can't kill any—"

"Bitch on your own time, soldier. You are a GI, government-fucking-issued, and you have qualified as a machine gunner. Congratulations. As of now, you are temporarily assigned to the U.S. Navy for a mission. Now get your ass out of here and report to Pier Three ASAP. Dismissed."

"But top—"

"Disfucking*SMISSED*."

McGill was making his way to the pier while reading his orders and wondering what kind of assignment he'd pulled with the Navy when a loud roaring caught everybody's attention. The roll-up front door on the new Quonset next to the LZ was open and something that sounded like a helicopter but looked like a cross between a boat and a blimp emerged, floating effortlessly over the muddy ground like an air-hockey puck. A big propeller on the back revved up, blowing a stream of air between two airplane-like tail rudders, and the strange vessel glided over the ground spraying a brown mist of water and splatters of mud that dirtied everything for twenty feet on either side. On the tail-fin was an American flag above US NAVY and a big "3." It headed to the marshland next to the piers, slowing as it slipped onto the water while blowing up clouds of spray like in a car wash. Then the engine growled even louder, and the propeller on the stern shifted into high and the boat sped over the grassy marshes like it was dancing on air and zoomed onto the open water leaving a path of flattened grasses in its wake.

McGill found an ensign at the end of the pier, watching as the strange air-boat sped up and down the river. The ensign's name-badge said "Carver," and he had a seabag next to him, like he was in-transit, changing duty stations.

"Specialist McGill, reporting as ordered, sir," he said as he came to attention and saluted, surprised that the insignia on the engisn's uniform was Coast Guard, not Navy.

"At ease, soldier. Looks like we're both in for an interesting ride."

"What's it all about, sir?"

The ensign pointed to the boat, or whatever it was, that was zooming around on the river. "That's a PACV, the last one in Vietnam. She's one-third helicopter, one-third airplane, and one-third boat. She can hit sixty-five miles an hour, the fastest combat boat in history. She's been drydocked for a couple of years and they just got her running. Our job is to get her back to the States."

"I…I don't understand, sir."

"We're taking her to a support ship off Vung Tau. It should be a milk run. Wow, look at that?" he shouted as the boat made a hairpin turn like an Olympic skier on slalom course. "I can't believe I'm getting the chance to actually serve on one. With luck we'll be there this afternoon, spend a night in Vung Tau, then tomorrow I'm out of this hell hole."

"Where are you going, sir?"

"Back to Key West to bust drug smugglers. Two weeks temporary duty here is two weeks too long."

Carver's enthusiasm for the hovercraft was infectious, and the possibility of a night with Vung Tau Jenny overcame any worries McGill had about getting killed. This could be a good assignment.

When the PACV pulled up McGill saw the same fierce eyes that were on the bows of most Mekong boats; just above the waterline was a menacing mouth of red-white-and-yellow shark's teeth painted around the black, rubberized skirt. With the engine roaring and blowing spray an approaching PACV looked and sounded like a fat, fire-breathing dragon billowing clouds of wet smoke who was coming to eat you.

As the engine throttled down its skirt slowly deflated and the boat settled onto the water, like a circus elephant kneeling down. The front window opened upward like a hatch door, and Col. Lombard and a Navy chief came through it and on stood on the deck as two Army soldiers tied the boat to the pier while the engine idled. The colonel called down into the cabin, "You have a safe trip, lieutenant."

The colonel said something to the chief, shook his hand, then came down the gangplank, walked up to Carver, returned Carver's salute and said, "The boat checks out A-OK, so you're on your way, ensign. Good luck. As for you," the colonel said to McGill, "you're aboard to make sure this boat kicks ass if there's trouble. When you've delivered her, report to the nearest MP unit and arrange for transportation back here."

Carver shouldered his seabag and McGill followed onto the boat. As he came aboard the Navy chief, equivalent to an Army master sergeant, eyed McGill's shaggy, non-regulation haircut which everybody in the boonies had and said, "I'm Chief Dungy. And you are—?"

"Specialist McGill."

"You're in the gun tub, McGill. Make sure everything is in order. Put on the headset so we can communicate. And put on the goggles. You'll have wind and bugs in your face for hours."

McGill climbed up to the .50 caliber M2 in the gun tub perched atop the cabin, in front of and below the radar array. It reminded him of a dorsal fin on a dolphin. He took off his pack and his M16, inspected the M2 and checked its ammo supply as the chief cast off lines from the pier. The chief yelled into the cabin, "All clear, lieutenant. Take her slow."

The lift-fan engaged and the rubberized skirt inflated like an inner tube, lifting the boat, awkwardly, as if it were getting out of bed one kink at a time. Once the skirt inflated and the boat was hovering inches above the water, the big aft propeller revved up and they moved away from the pier and headed toward the main channel.

McGill heard someone in the cabin yell from below, "Hang on!" Then the engine roared and the boat breezed over the river on a cushion of compressed air, faster and faster gaining speed and momentum. He put on the goggles and the headset as Dungy and Carver slipped down into the cabin and closed the hatch, leaving him alone up top with the wind in his face. How fast could this thing go? He had a few joints in his Marlboro box. Was it safe to toke up with everybody else below?

"Gunner," came a voice in the earphone, "this is Chief Dungy. Can you hear me?"

"Yes, chief. Loud and clear."

"Keep alert, keep your head down, and enjoy the ride."

"I'll do my best, chief."

Chapter 15

Reunion

Mulligan listened as Dungy, sitting at the helm, gave him and Carver a lesson in piloting a hovercraft. Unlike other boats, it was steered not with a wheel, but with a joystick, like a helicopter. And it was loud. Inside the cabin with the roar of the engine you had to get up close and almost shout to be heard. "As long as you've got lift," shouted Dungy, "she'll do almost anything you want if what's under you is flat. Rivers, swamps, marshes, paddies, even dry land. She can go over any obstacle less than three feet high, so with all the paddies flooded she can go pretty much anywhere. But be careful of the elephant grass. You can go where you want, but you can't see where you're going."

Carver took a turn at the helm as Mulligan opened the map. As it flowed out of Cambodia and into Vietnam, the mighty Mekong split into branches and subbranchs and branches of subbranchs, a labyrinth of natural waterways and man-made canals and the most productive rice-growing region in the world. The terrain was flat and green, no landmarks of any kind above the thick, dense, jungle canopy.

"You sure about the course, chief?" Mulligan said as once again he reread the teletype from MACV and worried about the specifics of their route. If you didn't know exactly which branch of the subbranch you were on you were screwed because everything looked the same.

"Done it a couple times in '67, from Cat Lo to The Plain of Reeds and back," Dungy said. "We'll take the My Tho where it splits off all the way to ocean then scoot up the coast. No shortcuts, not here. If we get lost we're fucked up royal. And if you're driving the boat, weave down the middle of the channel so we don't give snipers a good shot. They can hear us coming. Whoever bags us gets a big promotion."

Carver asked, "What was a typical day on a PACV like, chief?"

"We did a lot of things," Dungy said. "A lot of insertions and extractions of Special Forces, you know, the Green Beanies. They liked to ride on deck where they could use their own weapons. With them on board, we could bring a lot of firepower real quick. And we worked with choppers a lot. They'd scout for sampans, anything that looked like VC, and we'd go in and check it out when nobody else could. Pissed me off when the dumb fucks at MACV disbanded the Riverine Force. It was working."

"Ever lose anybody on your boat, chief?" Mulligan said.

"I don't want to talk about it if you don't mind, sir."

Nobody spoke for a while until Carver said, "Smell that?"

The side windows were open, sucking in diesel fumes along with the swampy Mekong miasma and a whiff of…marijuana.

"It's the hippie gunner," Dungy said with a shake of his head. "He's fucking Army. They're all druggies and peaceniks any more."

Because of the nature of the mission in Vietnam, it was the U.S. Army that bore the brunt of the war in terms of numbers who served and casualties incurred. The Navy and Air Force did not have any draftees, and while the Marines did have about a thousand, their numbers paled compared to the Army's seven hundred thousand. Over four out of five U.S. military personnel who served in Vietnam were in the Army. The scuttlebutt in the U.S. Navy in 1971 was that morale throughout the U.S. Army was at its lowest point since before there even was a U.S. Navy.

How different it was from his and McGill's and Dombrowski's senior year at Milltowne High, when "The Ballad of the Green Berets," by Staff Sergeant Barry Sandler, was Number One for five weeks straight and the Number One song for all of 1966. Polls at that time showed that eighty percent of the public supported America's role in Vietnam, and everybody he knew in Milltowne was gung-ho for what they were sure would be a short, John Wayne kind of war once American boys got over there to kick commie ass. Five years later, heroin, race riots, desertions, AWOLs, fraggings, anti-war protests, and over 50,000 dead and dozens more still dying every month had eroded the Army's morale, especially among the Army troops still in Vietnam. And the Navy knew it.

Mulligan said, "You know, at Subic they gave us a lecture on how to handle druggies. But we don't need to. He's the Army's problem, not ours. We just need to get through the day. I'll go up top and put a good scare in him."

"No, don't let him know we're on to him," Carver said. "Drug interdiction is my job, and an MP could have major connections. If he's doing dope up there now, he has more for later. They always do. Who knows what he knows or who he knows or how he fits into the smuggling rings. The heroin coming out of here is one of the biggest problems we've got. If we catch him with drugs on him it gives us leverage to make him cooperate, maybe turn him into an informant. I'm going to order him to empty his pockets and search his pack as soon as we dock. Ten to one he's holding, and if he is, his ass is mine."

A few minutes later the radio crackled with Dam Luc's call-sign. "Centerfold to Arriba. Over. Centerfold to Arriba. Over."

Mulligan answered, "Arriba here. Over."

"Intel picked up radio chatter that a 'monster' is headed down river. Charlie knows who you are lieutenant. All VC units in the delta are on alert with orders to take you out if you come their way."

Mulligan signed off and Dungy said, "They want our ass bad, and with good reason. We'd be a real trophy."

"Gunner," Mulligan said into the intercom, "we just got word the enemy is gunning for us, so stay alert."

"Yes, sir."

With Dungy at the helm and Carver at the radar screen, Mulligan said, "I'm going topside to check it out and talk to the gunner."

"Why talk to him?" asked Carver.

"This is my first command, Hank, and I've never been in combat. If we're going to see action I'd like to know who I'm responsible for."

"Just don't let him know we're on to him," Carver said.

"Watch your footing up there, sir," Dungy said. "The deck is sloped and the slipstream's pretty strong and there's not much to hang on to. We don't want to have to fish you out."

Mulligan climbed up and onto the bow as Carver closed the hatch behind him. Outside the cabin, the roar was even louder. He stood up carefully and felt the swampy delta in his face as they cruised at the optimal speed for fuel efficiency while zigzagging irregularly. Dungy knew how to do it.

Mulligan turned and glanced up at the gunner, who was seated in the gun-tub atop the cabin, ten feet away and three feet higher. The gunner was facing starboard pretending to scan the shoreline while doing what enlisted personnel always tried to do around an officer: look busy, avoid eye-contact, and hope they don't get noticed. He was acutely aware that the gunner was the first EM under his direct command.

He didn't speak and instead went to the stern, getting a feel for the boat as she zoomed over swirling brown water like an ice skater. She was the fastest boat he'd ever been on and she wasn't even trying.

He thought about Catherine, wondered what she would be doing in New Haven, where it was eleven hours earlier. Probably sleeping. He thought about the game tonight; the rendezvous ship should have it on the radio; the Pirates were up three games to two and could put it away with a win. There would be a poker game to fatten his wallet even more.

After a minute he walked to the gun-tub, reached up high and tapped the gunner on the back of his flak jacket; the gunner turned around and looked down at him. His helmet, with a big, white MP on the front, completely covered his forehead, and with a headset-earphone over one ear, a microphone in front of his mouth and dark aviator glasses over his eyes, he looked like a faceless alien right out of *Star Trek*.

Mulligan looked for the soldier's name, but his name-tag was covered by his flak-jacket. He said as loud as he could without shouting, "What's your name, soldier?"

The gunner gave no response. Maybe he hadn't heard? Mulligan cupped his hand to his mouth and yelled, "I said, what's your name?"

"Hey, Mulligan Man. Is that really you?"

"*Stick*?"

The gunner whipped off his helmet, headset and goggles, revealing a familiar shit-eating grin, and stretched out his hand, saying, "Far fucking out. I mean, is this karma, or what?"

"What...what are you doing here?"

"That general screwed me just like you said. How did you get here?"

"They needed somebody to bring this boat in and I was there."

"So you're my commanding officer...right? Wow. Is that weird, or what? So do I have to call you 'sir' and salute and all that military shit?"

"Damn right you do."

"Then here you go," McGill said as he stood up, came to attention and said, "Lieutenant Mulligan Man, *SIR*!" and gave a snappy Nazi salute and broke out laughing.

"Don't be a wise-ass, Stick. I won't tolerate insubordination."

McGill was guffawing like it was a kindergarten fart joke. "So...so what...what...what are you gonna do to me, Lieutenant Mulligan Man, sir? Send me to Vietnam, Lieutenant Mulligan Man, sir?"

"How about Long Binh jail for insubordination and smoking dope on duty. Now, you will come to attention, soldier. That's an order."

"Long Binh jail—"

"I said atten*SHUN*! I will not have my authority undermined and I don't care how long I've known you."

"You really mean it, don't you?"

"Goddamn right and I won't say it again. Atten*SHUN*!"

McGill came to attention, "But—"

"Shut up until I give you permission to speak. Just what the fuck were you thinking doing dope on duty? You want to get us all killed?"

"But—"

"I said shut up. If you think we couldn't smell it you're even dumber than when Pugliano caught you with cigarettes in your underwear. And you better get rid of anything else you got because Carver's going to bust your ass as soon as we dock. He thinks an MP doper has to be involved in heroin smuggling and—"

"Heroin? But—"

"I said shut the fuck up. If he catches you with anything he can blackmail you into doing whatever he wants."

"But—"

"Shut up! I'm responsible for this boat and its crew and out of the blue I've got the biggest wise-ass on the planet manning our primary means of defense. Now put on your gear and man your station and pretend we don't know each other."

"Pretend we don't know each other...why?"

"Because, asshole, I would not be warning anybody I didn't know he was about to be busted for dope and if anybody suspects we're both fucked. Toss it, right now."

"But—"

"I want to see you toss whatever could get your dumb ass busted right fucking now, soldier!"

McGill reached into his breast pocket, took some joints out of a Marlboro box and pitched them high where the vortex sucked them through the aft propeller. "You do know you can be a real fucking asshole, Lt. Mulligan Man, sir?"

"Goddam right I can and don't you forget it. And you are to remain at attention when I'm speaking to you. Understood?"

McGill snapped back to attention. "Yes *sir*, Lt. Mulligan Man, *sir*!"

"Now listen up, asshole, and listen up good—you are not to touch any dope while you are under my command or I'll bust you myself. That is a direct order. Is that understood, Specialist McGill?"

McGill clicked his heels together and gave a straight-armed Nazi salute. "*Jawohl, Lieutenant Mulligan Man, SIR*! *Perfectly understood, Lieutenant Mulligan Man, SIR!*"

"Quit the wise-ass bullshit, Stick. I've got a job to do, and so do you. I hope we have time to catch up when we get where we're going if Carver doesn't haul your ass off to Long Binh jail first. Until then, do your job."

"What about the game tonight? I got a little radio in my pack or are you gonna give me the ossifers-can't-fraternize-with-enlisted crap?"

"I have no idea what to expect when we get to the rendezvous, so I don't know. I hope we can get together."

"Oh, before you go, this is really fucking important, so listen up, Lt. Mulligan Man, sir—have you heard from Catherine?"

"No," he said with a sigh. "I wrote a couple times but haven't heard back. But my mail's all screwed up. Have you heard from Jenny?"

"Then you don't know?"

"Don't know what?"

"I talked to them last week. You gotta call, right away."

"You talked to Catherine?"

"I was on R&R in Vung Tau and got a short-wave connection to Jenny and Catherine answered. She was freaked. You gotta call her, right away. I got the number in my wallet."

"What do you mean she was freaked?"

"I...uh, I asked what was wrong, but she said it was nothing."

"What is it, Stick? Don't fuck with me."

McGill squirmed. What to do? Mulligan had not received her letters, so he didn't know he'd knocked her up. Jenny said that the news should come from Catherine, but that was last week and time was running out. Mulligan might not have another chance.

"I'm not supposed to be the one to tell you, but Catherine's pregnant, and you're it. From what I can tell she's only got a week to decide what to do."

"But...she's on the pill?"

"I guess it didn't work. She was like some kind of psycho begging me to get you to call if I ran into you. She wouldn't say why, but I guessed and Jenny came clean. Catherine's freaked about having it, not having it, telling her parents, wondering what you want, worrying you'll get blown away and this would be your only heir."

"She...she said that?"

"That's what Jenny told me. Lots of crazy shit goes through chicks' heads over baby-making crap that we never think about. They're all fucked up that way. You gotta call and tell her what you want or it'll be too late for you to have any say one way or the other. Got something to write on?"

Mulligan felt like he'd grabbed an electrified fence and couldn't let go. He could barely pull out the Vietnamese-English dictionary in his back pocket and hand it to McGill, choking up as he watched him write on the inside cover and hand it back.

"So what are you gonna say to her?" McGill said.

Mulligan could barely shake his head. "No idea. Thanks, Stick. I gotta think. I hope we can check out the game together. If not, I'll write as soon as I can now that I know you're at Dam Luc."

"Wait! One more thing. I've been thinking about it for a week. It's a no-brainer. You gotta get her to marry you. Period. She's hot and she's rich and you're both oversized carrot-tops. With all due respect, what's there to think about, Lt. fucking Mulligan Man, sir?" McGill said "Ja wohl," and gave yet another snappy Nazi salute.

Mulligan shook his head and gave McGill the finger. He needed to think. He went below and told Dungy, "Let me take the helm for a while, chief." Maybe driving the boat would help distract him, center him?

Carver asked, "How'd it go with the gunner?"

"I just told him to keep alert," he said as calmly as he could with his mind racing trying to take it all in. Pregnant? Catherine was pregnant? Could that be right? They hardly knew each other. How soon could he call? How would he call? Maybe a telegram? Would the support ship have a way to connect? What would he say? What did he want? Was he really the father? Oversized carrot-tops?

"You okay, lieutenant?" Dungy asked after a few minutes. "You seem distracted or something."

"Just thinking about home, that's all, chief."

They were on a narrow channel, just a hundred yards wide with thick jungle on either side when they heard a series of dull thud-thud-thuds on the hull of the boat. Dungy growled, "Snipers."

McGill's voice shouted over the intercom, "We're under fire!"

Mulligan gunned the engine full throttle as more thuds hit.

Dungy yelled, "Gunner, can you see where it's coming from?"

"Negative. It's all jungle."

Mulligan said into the intercom, "Gunner, is it coming from port or starboard?"

"I'm not in the fucking Navy! They're on the fucking right!"

Dungy jumped to the starboard M60, the light thirty-caliber machine gun. Carver opened the window as Mulligan muttered, "Fucking asshole," and steered sharply to port.

"Gunner," Dungy yelled as he set up the M60, "rake the riverbank above the waterline. They dig bunkers behind the reeds and the sound of the guns will keep their heads down no matter where they are."

"I don't want to kill anybody!" blared McGill's voice over the speaker.

Multiple thud-thud-thuds hit the boat and a bullet shattered the window in the rear of the cabin spraying the cabin with shards of glass.

Mulligan screamed, "Blow the fuck out of the mother-fucking riverbank and that's a fucking order!"

McGill's .50 caliber M2 roared like a vengeful dragon, popping up spurts of dirt and vegetation all along the riverbank. Dungy got the M60 into the fight but aimed for the canopy of the jungle hoping to get lucky and hit a sniper in a tree. After a few seconds McGill yelled over the intercom, "Smoke! *RPG! RPG! GET DOWN!*" then opened up with the fifty caliber at the origin of the smoke.

They all ducked low, arms curled over their heads. The shell looped over and went off harmlessly in the water; a Soviet RPG, a shoulder-fired "rocket-propelled-grenade," could easily take them out. A direct hit from an RPG could destroy concrete bunkers as well as any vehicle up to and including the most heavily armored tank.

"HERE COMES ANOTHER!"

Mulligan saw the trail of the rocket and instinctively veered the joystick hard to starboard. The RPG blew off in the air, thirty yards away.

Dungy gave a little laugh as he raked the treetops with the M60 and shouted, "Keep up the zigzags, lieutenant,"

McGill's M2 was still roaring as a loud BOOM came over the water from the spot where his rounds had been hitting. The side of the riverbank at least twenty feet wide coughed up debris into the air in a fog of smoke.

"Must have hit an ammo cache, or maybe gasoline," Dungy said into the intercom. "Nice shooting, gunner."

"Everybody okay?" Mulligan said.

"Got the adrenaline up is all," said Carver. "Nobody's ever shot at me before."

"Me neither," Mulligan said, then into the intercom, "You okay up there, gunner?"

The shouted reply oozed with sarcasm. "Not a scratch on my enlisted fucking ass, Lieutenant. Mulligan, *SIR*!"

"Keep alert, soldier," Mulligan said and cut the connection.

"That insubordinate fucking jerk," said Carver. "I really want to bust his ass."

"He's just another Army hippie," said Dungy. "They're all like that over here now...Peace Signs on their helmets, hippie hair, smoking dope, disrespectful. They know we're pulling out, and they don't want to die. You can't really blame 'em. If I may say so, sir, cut him a break. I've seen a lot worse, and he's real handy with the M2."

"You sound like a peacenik, chief," Carver said.

"No, sir," said Dungy, "It's just that after three tours I've seen too many body-bags going out of here to buy into the bullshit any more."

Chapter 16

Arriba!

McGILL SCRUNCHED LOW AND TOOK HIS RIGHT HAND OFF THE BACK OF his upper left arm to see how bad it was. Blood was everywhere, but he felt no pain. Could he be in shock? The sniper's bullet or shrapnel or whatever it was had somehow ricocheted around the gun-tub and hit him from the opposite direction from where the attack had come. Or from where he thought it had come. All he knew was that he'd been hit.

He removed his flak jacket, which was supposed to protect his chest and internal body parts, stripped off his fatigue shirt, tied a sleeve around his upper arm and twisted it into a tourniquet to stanch the bleeding like he was taught in Basic Training. It wasn't too bad, just a "flesh wound." He'd been "winged." Marshall Dillon on *Gunsmoke* and Paladin on *Have Gun Will Travel* took worse all the time; John Wayne would have laughed it off. He lit a cigarette and slumped down on the gun-tub floor.

Now there was PAIN. He managed to get the first-aid kit out of his backpack and tape a bandage to the wound. Was the bullet or shrapnel or whatever it was still in there? He couldn't tell. He cursed Mulligan for making him throw all his joints overboard as he could really fucking use one right fucking now.

He lit another cigarette, still shaking and sweating like a race-horse at the finish line. What the fuck had just happened? He'd gone crazy with the machine gun not because Mulligan ordered him to but because he'd been hit and it scared him shitless. Charlie had been trying to kill him, and that had really pissed him off. Had he killed any of them? He'd certainly been trying, and whatever he'd blown up back there must have fucked somebody up good. He'd never seen any faces, or even human figures. Just reeds on a riverbank and little puffs of debris before it went BOOM. He was grateful he had not seen any faces. He was just shooting up a fucking river bank. Like B-52 crews who dropped their "Arc Light" carpet-bombing clusters from 30,000 feet, or artillery shelling map coordinates ten miles away. Never see their faces. If you had to kill somebody, that was the way to do it, not like being a grunt staring eyeball-to-eyeball with Charlie in a rice paddy. What the fuck was he doing here?

If he told Mulligan he'd been hit he'd call for a dustoff to medevac him to Saigon or Long Binh. That would slow them down by hours, they'd miss the rendezvous, and the boat would be a sitting duck. He felt an overpowering need to complete the mission. What the fuck was wrong with him? Had that chief's pat on the back about "good shooting" made him gung-ho? No. But he was pretty sure his shooting had made a difference. Maybe saved their lives. Then again, probably not. Was it because Mulligan was his CO? No! It didn't matter; he was the gunner and he would do his job and get the boat and everybody on it wherever the hell they were supposed to go. Charlie better not fuck with them again. He would not hesitate again. Fuck that! They would not fail because of him. No one would die because he didn't do his job. If he fucked up Mulligan would never let him hear the end of it.

He stood up, wincing at the pain, but still able to use both hands and function okay. He checked the M2, inserting a new ammo belt and thinking "be prepared," like in the Boy Scouts. If Charlie came at them again, he was ready.

A sudden rain-shower reminded him he wasn't wearing anything above the waist except his dog tags and the half-assed bandaging job he'd done on his own arm. He had to hide it from Mulligan and the others. He put his flak jacket back on over his bare upper torso and his rain poncho over that, completely concealing his arm. He put on his helmet and goggles and wiped the blood off his hands with his bloody fatigue shirt and stuck it in his pack so none of them would see it. No big deal. He'd let them know he'd been hit when they got where they were going. Who knows, maybe he had the proverbial "million dollar wound" grunts were always praying for, that lucky nick not serious enough to fuck you up too much but bad enough to get you a ticket to The World instead of back to the boonies for more fun and games with Charlie. But he doubted it. He'd seen guys who took hits way worse than his little scratch come back after a couple of weeks in a field hospital showing off their new Purple Hearts after being deemed "fit for duty." It only took three Purple Hearts without being KIA, or "killed in action," to hit the jackpot and win a ride on a Freedom Bird no matter how long you'd been in-country. He laughed and yelled over the roar of the engine, "One down, only two to go. There it is—*FUCKIN' A!*"

Mulligan radioed Dam Luc to report the enemy contact. They in turn would report to Delta Control at Vung Tau, which would in turn send word up both the Naval chain-of-command to the rendezvous ship and the Army chain-of-command to Army HQ at Long Binh, which would dispatch ARVN troops to the site of the fight, estimate the size of the enemy force, and determine the official body-count for the press. He also reported the various checkpoints as they passed; the huge base that the Army Engineers and the Navy Seabees had claimed from the river at Dong Tam, and the city of My Tho, "Gateway to the Delta" and its waterborne bazaar of sampans and junks.

Dungy said, "At top speed we're half an hour from open water and less than an hour from the rendezvous if the monsoon don't get worse. But it don't look good, lieutenant. You can see it coming."

Mulligan turned over the pilot's seat to Dungy and said, "Crank it up while you can, chief. The sooner we're into open water, the better."

He glanced over Carver's shoulder at the radar screen without really seeing it. "Should be easy from here on, Hank. Hand me that map."

He sat in a spare seat while staring vacantly at the map, thinking about Catherine: How could he contact her? What would he say? He thought about the firefight. How would he report it? They had been attacked. It was his first combat action. Had his performance been acceptable? What was he going to do about McGill? Should he come clean with Dungy and Carver? Was he really going to be a father?

They were just twenty klicks from the South China Sea when the monsoon swept in. Dungy slowed down and Carver monitored the radar, directing them around the dozens of barely visible sampans, junks and freighters. Then the radio came to life. "Arriba, this is Chain Link. Can you read me? Over. Arriba, this is Chain Link. Over."

Dungy consulted the call-sign list and said, "That's Delta Command. This ain't good."

"Chain Link, this is Arriba," Mulligan answered. "We read you loud and clear. Over."

"Arriba, we have a problem. There's a Broken Arrow in your AO...."

The emergency distress call from a unit about to be wiped out was "Broken Arrow." A Huey was down in the monsoon outside a village named Song Tai with a big-shot general among the survivors. Delta Command had been monitoring their progress and knew they were fifteen minutes away from the crash if they really could fly over the flooded rice paddies where no other boat could possibly go. Could they do it? Nobody working that shift at Delta Command had any experience with what a PACV could really do, but choppers would take at least half an hour even in perfect weather, and Charlie was closing in. Could they get them out or hold the enemy off until more help could arrive?

"What do you think, chief?" Mulligan asked as they studied the map. "It's at least five klicks inland."

"Yes, sir," Dungy said, "but it's all rice paddies flooded by the monsoon. It's just what these boats were made for."

Mulligan said into the radio, "We're on our way, Chain Link." He and Dungy and Carver huddled to assess the situation in detail: distance, weather, armaments, fuel, morale.

"I gotta say something," Mulligan said. "Maybe I should have told you earlier, but I didn't think it would matter. You've both been down on the gunner, but when I went up top to I about shit when he took off his goggles. His name's McGill. Art McGill. Everybody calls him 'Stick."

"What? You *know* him?" said Carver.

"Yeah, since junior high. He can be an asshole, no doubt about it. I don't know how he got here—Lombard said he'd give us whoever scored best in weapons-training. It's a one in a million the two of us are here. But I can't think of anyone I'd rather have as a gunner. Hunting is huge where we're from and he always got his limit. And he's not shooting heroin. Or smuggling it. Trust me."

"Yeah, okay," Carver said uneasily. "If you say so."

"I do say so, but he is a fucking pothead. I told him to keep his mouth shut about us knowing each other or I'd beat the fuck out of him when we got home." He looked at Carver, "And I told him you were going to send him to Long Binh jail so he better throw anything he had overboard. I think he did."

Carver didn't seem pleased. "And if you hadn't recognized him first and I did catch him with dope, what would you have done when you saw who he was?"

"I don't know, Hank, probably killed my Navy career by sticking up for his dumb ass. Now don't tell him I told you until we're out of this. And if we get through the rest of the day, I want you to join us for tonight's game. The last time Pittsburgh won a World Series, McGill and I were both on sitting on the detention bench waiting to get swats when Mazeroski hit the home run to win it. Regulations be damned. I'm buying and taking all bets. Beat 'em Bucs!"

Carver and Dungy looked at each other and nodded. Dungy said, "You want to tell your friend what we're getting into, lieutenant?"

"No. It shouldn't come from me. He'll respond better if it comes down the chain-of-command."

McGill slouched with his back against the gun tub wall and punched his bayonet through the top of the OD-green can labeled: "Peaches, Canned." He'd taken it from one of the two boxes in his pack of "Charlie-rats," the in-country term derived from World War II "C-rations," slang for "Rations, Combat," that was printed on the cans.

He pried back the top with the bayonet and sipped the glorious juice, wasting not a precious drop but nicking his lip on the ragged edge of the can. He scooped the fruit chunks out with his fingers and slurped them down. With Charlie-rats it was always desert first. He polished off the stale biscuit and the crumbled cheese crackers, but he'd had the bad luck to pull the worst of the four Charlie-rat entrées, lima beans and ham, universally reviled as "ham and motherfuckers." So he saved it for a last-ditch emergency when there was nothing else to keep him alive.

He was surprised when the boat suddenly lurched in a sharp ninety-degree turn, slamming his body against the side of the gun-tub and sending his arm pounding in pain. He stood up to see what was happening and felt the sting of the monsoon in his face at sixty miles per hour. They were heading straight for shore, with flooded terrain as far as he could see beyond that.

Then came a new sound as a U.S. Navy F-4 Phantom jet screamed overhead, loud even over the roar of the PACV's own powerful engine. Half a minute later he saw a fiery flash followed by an explosion in the direction they were heading. Napalm. Only a few klicks away.

"Gunner, this is Chief Dungy," said the voice on the intercom. "We've had a Broken Arrow call and are going in to help. Be prepared for anything. Are you locked and loaded?"

"Yes, sarge…er, chief. Yes chief."

"You did good last time. Keep it up."

McGill was shaking and sweating under his rubberized poncho as he gripped the handles of the M2 heavy machine gun preparing to blow Charlie out of the water. The boat slowed down as it approached a dike and slipped over it on its air-cushion like it wasn't even there. They zoomed over marshes and swamps and paddies toward the thick black smoke as the F-4 Phantom circled for another bombing run.

McGill needed a cigarette. He ducked out of the wind to light up, then grabbed the binoculars to see how bad it was. There was a Huey, maybe a klick away, crashed on its side in the swamp. Two hundred yards further thick smoke from the blazing fires of the sticky-jelly napalm, which was clinging to anything it touched and burning at a couple thousand degrees Fahrenheit. He saw an armada of sampans, spread wide in a semi-circle tightening around their quarry like a noose as two-man teams of VC poled like Venetian gondoliers to be first through the thick swamp-grass to claim the honor of capturing or killing the survivors. He watched as the F-4 came in for another run and the torpedo-shaped canister detached and tumbled like a graceful acrobat before exploding in flames and plumes of hellish black smoke on top of some of Charlie's sampans. McGill felt the shock wave and a sudden burst of napalm-heat on his face as they raced to join the battle.

In the cabin below, Dungy said, "What do you think, sir?" as Mulligan surveyed the battlefield with binoculars.

Battle-swamp was more accurate. The F-4 pilot was reporting that at least two dozen sampans converging on the downed Huey. There was no radio contact, but survivors were waving from atop the wreck. The F-4's napalm had slowed Charlie's' advance, but Charlie was so numerous that two cannisters of napalm had not been enough. The pilot was making strafing runs with his machine guns, but one plane could only do so much, and he was taking heavy fire.

Mulligan opened the intercom and said, "Gunner, this is the skipper. We're going to run right over their lead boats like we're bowling while you take out as many as you can. Then we double back and hit 'em again then haul ass to get our people out before they can regroup. Be ready to evacuate survivors."

"Yes, sir," McGill said as he smoked the cigarette right down to the filter, wondering if it was his last. Fucking Mulligan had the nerve to call himself "skipper." Who did he think he was? He was only a fucking lieutenant. Maybe it was some kind of bullshit protocol thing, like whoever was in charge on a boat was always a "captain" regardless of his actual rank. And he'd actually answered "sir" to Mulligan. *What was wrong with him? What was he doing here? How many had he killed today?*

They were closing fast on the sampans. How many? Twenty? Thirty? More? Bad guys have more men, but good guys always win. It was the law, right, from Cowboys and Indians. But this was Gooks and Grunts. He selected a target, sighted in, and shot a burst; the sampan tipped over as two figures splashed into the water.

Dungy's voice was in McGill's headphone, "Nice shooting! If you see an RPG cylinder on somebody's shoulder, blow that fucker away before he gets us. I'll take the boats closest in and you take the next ones out. When we make our turn and come back from inside you get the ones I missed and I'll get the ones you missed and Carver'll take the other side. Don't waste ammo on any one boat. Harass as many as you can to buy us time to get our people out. Got it?"

Was the chief was messing with his head, playing nice? Maybe Dungy wasn't such an asshole after all.

The sampans were scrambling to scatter as the PACV roared closer. McGill took short bursts at this sampan or that, figuring that even if he didn't hit anything he'd scare the enemy into jumping ship and take them out of action, which was almost as good as killing them.

He tensed up as they approached the lead sampan at full-speed. The VC jumped out at the last instant as the PACV rushed over the sampan with barely a *thump*, as if it were a small pothole on a country road.

The PACV whomped three more sampans while McGill kept up a steady fire. Then the PACV did a sharp U-turn, and came ripping back around through the middle of the pack of sampans, with McGill on the .50 caliber M2 and Dungy and Carver on the port and starboard M60s, all of them trying to buy enough time to make the rescue and get out before getting killed.

Mulligan yelled, "We'll go around back and use it as a shield." He steered the joystick into a sharp ninety-degree turn and dashed for the downed chopper as AK47 rounds thudded against the hull. He steered behind it, putting the wreck between them and the enemy. He disengaged the lift-fan and the PACV settled onto the swamp thirty feet from the crashed Huey, where three GIs were crouched low and firing their M16s at Charlie.

Dungy opened the hatch and raced on deck, crouching low as he yelled to a soldier in the door the chopper, "What's your status?"

"The pilot's gone," shouted the soldier. "Three okay, two wounded, including me."

"Have your men keep up your cover fire," Dungy yelled. "We'll get you out."

Without being ordered, McGill tore off his poncho and flak jacket, jumped into the swamp, and parting the grasses with his arms in the hip-deep muck, he waded toward the chopper.

A corporal passed a wounded man down. "Be careful, it's a fucking general," said the corporal, a huge black guy who reminded McGill of Big George Trent, the first guy from Milltowne to die in the war over five years ago, all the way back in 1966.

"How many more?" McGill yelled.

"Just me and the pilot. I'm shot up pretty bad, but he's gone."

McGill yelled, "Get him to the door. I'll be back."

He hoisted the wounded general on his back like he was taught in Basic and carried him to the PACV as the others on the chopper crew kept up the cover fire. When he got him to the boat, Dungy and Carver took the general by the shoulders and pulled him up.

McGill slogged back to the chopper and the corporal passed the pilot's body out the door; McGill laid it on the swamp-grass. It was a warrant officer; his name-tag read: "Winters."

"You're next," McGill said to the corporal. "I'll come back for the pilot."

The corporal slipped out of the door, crying out in pain as he collapsed into the swampgrass, unable to walk. McGill put his shoulders under the corporal's arms, and carried him to the PACV and Dungy and Carver pulled him up.

McGill started back for the pilot as the crack-crack-cracks of Charlies' AK47s grew louder as the others in the chopper crew backed their way to the boat while keeping up cover fire.

Not worried about the pilot crying out in agony or exacerbating his wounds, McGill grabbed the body by the arms and was pulling him toward the boat when an RPG blew up twenty feet away and knocked him face down into the muck and right on top of the dead pilot. He stumbled up and dragged the body to the boat and passed it up, but when he tried to climb up himself his hands wouldn't grip the rope and he fell backwards into the swamp.

Dungy jumped down, lifted McGIll by the armpits, passed him up and climbed aboard shouting, "*GO* lieutenant! *GO-GO-GO*!"

Chapter 17

Dustoff

MULLIGAN REVVED-UP THE LIFT FAN, INFLATING THE RUBBER SKIRT AND raising the boat up off the swamp, engaged the aft propeller and gunned the engine, and as they sped away from Charlie's sampans on a cushion of air he radioed for a dustoff. Carver, bleeding from small wounds in his arm and face, came down into the cabin.

"You okay to take the helm, Hank?" Mulligan asked.

Carver said, "I'm from the Bronx. This is nothing."

Carver took the pilot's seat and Mulligan went on deck. A soldier from the chopper was in the gun-tub fireing the .50 caliber. Dungy was carrying a shoulder-fired rocket called a LAW, a light-antitank-weapon, and climbing up to the radar antenna, the highest spot on the boat, to try for a clean shot high over their own propeller and dual-rudders.

"Keep her straight and steady, Hank," Mulligan yelled down the hatch. "The chief's gonna take a shot."

"Aim for the fuel tanks," yelled the wounded corporal as Dungy, wrapping his legs around the antenna's pole to brace himself, took aim. As the first sampan reached the downed chopper Dungy's rocket roared out of the tube in a smoky *vooosh* and two seconds later turned the chopper into a fireball, leaving Charlie nothing to scavenge.

"Nice shooting, chief," Mulligan yelled, then he carefully made his way around the port side of the cabin, where a soldier was lying with one arm around the general and his other arm around the dead pilot, still with his headgear on. The curved deck of the PACV made riding on deck an adventure, and the soldier was doing his best to keep the two limp bodies, one still alive, one very dead, from rolling into the swamp.

"You okay?" Mulligan asked the soldier.

"Yes, sir. Doc said Winters was gone and he gave the general something to knock him out and said not to let them fall off the fucking boat. He's taking care of your guy now."

Mulligan went to starboard and saw McGill, shirtless, covered in mud lying slumped on the deck as a medic was bandaging him up. Balancing on the curved deck of the speeding boat and trying not to lose his footing, Mulligan asked the medic, "How bad is he?"

"He took some shrapnel but it doesn't look too bad. And he was already patched up," the medic said, pointing to the bloody bandage on McGill's arm. "Looks like he put it on himself."

"He told us he hadn't been hit," Mulligan said.

"No...I didn't, asshole," McGill said, opening his eyes and trying to rise, then wincing in pain and slumping down. "Oh fuck, that sucks."

"Take it easy," said the medic. "Don't move or try to talk."

McGill moaned and said, "Fuck that. I said didn't have a scratch on my enlisted fucking ass, Lt. fucking Mulligan Man, sir. I didn't say shit about any other body part, Lt. fucking Mulligan Man, sir."

McGill still had his sense of humor, a good sign. Mulligan said, "So why didn't you tell us you'd been hit? We'd have called for a dustoff."

"No way you're kicking me off this boat ride. It's like that time up at Lake Erie in your dad's outboard with those chicks from Ohio State. Remember?"

"He really should calm down, sir," said the medic.

Mulligan said, "Yeah, Stick, I remember. You did real good out there today. Now you just take it easy."

McGill said, "How's everybody else?"

"Carver took some shrapnel, nothing serious. The chief and I are fine. We rescued five. You'll be on the dustoff going out."

"Fuck that! We're gonna get this fucking boat where it's going."

The medic said, "He's getting too excited, lieutenant. I'm gonna calm him down."

"No, Doc, wait!" McGill yelled as he felt the medic stick a syringe in his leg. "Mulligan, what about Catherine? I'm gonna write Jenny soon as I can and tell her what happened and that I told you. What do I tell her you want to do about Catherine and the baby?"

"I...uh, let me do it."

"Fuck that, you may not make it. This is the fucking *Nam*, asshole. I gotta tell her something even if you don't. She's out of time."

"Tell her...tell her I'll do anything she wants and support her whatever she decides."

"But what about *her*, douchebag? Chicks care what you feel, not what you fucking think. Do you want her to keep the baby? You gonna marry her or not? What'll I say?"

"Tell her I think she's terrific, and—"

"That fucking sucks and you know it," McGill said as he struggled to stay alert. "If I make it I'm gonna tell her you'll marry her if she'll have your asshole ossifer ass whether you like it or not. But if I don't make it, I got a nice Gibson back at Dam Luc, just like your old one before you gave it up and became a full-time jock. Plays great. It's yours. You can write her a love song."

"You'll make it, Stick. The world needs assholes like you."

"Yeah, me and Dom...Dombrowski," McGill said slurring, getting whoozy. "We're on for the g...game, tonight, right?"

"Damn straight, Stick. Beat 'em Bucs!"

McGill tried to sit up, groaned, and lay back in pain. He was in a bed, bandaged like a mummy, strapped down and stuck with needles and tubes.

"This guy's waking up," a nearby voice yelled. McGill turned his head to see a black guy in a bed also with needles and tubes in his arms, and his leg suspended from a hanger. He looked vaguely familiar.

"Where are we?" McGill asked the guy.

"Queen Tonic," the guy said. "ICU."

"Huh?"

"Intensive Care Unit, 24th Evac Hospital, Long Binh, call-sign 'Queen Tonic.' Everyone knows Queen Tonic is where to go to save your ass. You McGill? That's what they been callin' ya, but ya never know."

"Yeah, I'm McGill. You?"

"Stanton, but it don't matter. Thanks for pulling me out, but I ain't gonna make it. You will, though. I heard 'em talkin'. But watch out. They'll put you in for a medal and send you back to the boonies to get blown away again in no time."

"I don't want a fucking medal. Why won't you make it? You seem okay."

"Some serious shit. I heard 'em talkin'."

"Don't believe everything you hear," McGill said in a feeble attempt to cheer the guy up. "Know what I'm sayin'?"

"Fuckin' A," Stanton said, and coughed and coughed and coughed.

An Army nurse in fatigues came to McGill's bed and picked up his chart. "Hello, there, uh, Specialist McGill is it? How are you feeling?"

"I've been better. What about the others?"

From the next bed Stanton called out, "They won't tell us shit."

"I have no idea," said the nurse, "but there's someone who came in with you who wants to know when you wake up." She called to another nurse, "Would you tell Ensign Carver his friend's awake."

"How long have I been here?"

She checked the chart. "You and Corporal Stanton and Ensign Carver and General Brewer came in yesterday at sixteen-thirty-nine."

"Yesterday?" McGill said. "You mean I missed it?"

"You missed what?" said the nurse.

"The World Series. Who won?"

"The Birds won three to two," said Stanton, with more coughing. "Seventh game's tonight."

"You sound like you like Baltimore?" McGill said.

"Damn straight," said Stanton. "Go Birds!"

McGill said, "Five bucks says Baltimore loses and you're gonna live to pay me off. Take it or leave it."

Stanton laughed and said, "Fuckin' A. You're on."

"So what's the story?" McGill asked the nurse. "Will I make it?"

"You have multiple shrapnel wounds, a bullet wound and a slightly fractured humerus," said the nurse, "but you will definitely make it."

Hoping he had that magical million-dollar wound, he asked, "Does this mean I'm going home?"

"That's not for me to say," and she took his wrist to check his pulse.

Carver walked up to the bed, his left arm in a sling and several small bandages taped on his face. "How you doing, gunner?"

"Okay. You?"

"I've cut myself worse shaving. They want to keep me another day, but there's no way I'm missing my flight tonight."

"So does that mean you're not gonna bust me for getting high?"

Carver laughed. "No, I was wrong about you. I don't know if the Army will listen to a Coastie, but I recommended you for a medal. "

"I just want out of here. What happened out there? The fucking medic knocked me out."

"A dustoff took you, me, General Brewer and the other survivors and the dead pilot out of there, and Mulligan and the chief headed for the rendezvous. I wanted to stay, but Mulligan said they were just fifteen-minutes from the ocean and wouldn't listen."

"Did they make it?"

"I don't know. They won't tell me fucking thing. It's classified."

"So you don't know if…er, if the lieutenant talked to his…uh—"

"You don't have to pretend, gunner. Mulligan told us you're old friends who grew up together. Don't worry, I won't say anything."

"Great, that means you can be a big help. You catching a Freedom Bird tonight, right, so you can call her when you land. The number's in my wallet. See, Mulligan knocked up this rich chick and…."

The Yale professor cut short his Torts and Courts lecture so the class could catch the most significant event in American sports—the seventh game of the World Series. Since the first World Series, in 1903, only thirteen times had the contest "gone the distance." The Pirates had won three seventh-games, in 1909, 1925, and 1960. Games one through six would never have cancelled a Yale Law class, but a seventh only came around every five years or so. The seventh game was extra-special.

Jenny and Catherine went to a Yalie bar filled with fans wearing Pirates and Orioles T-shirts, jackets, and caps. They shared a booth with friends and pitchers of beer and baskets of peanuts and pretzels. Everybody could see that Catherine, drinking only sodas, had a cake baking in the oven. Not even her loose-fitting Earth Mother dresses could hide it any more, so guys had completely stopped hitting on her. Rumors of who it was and when it happened and whether or not her parents knew had been flying all over campus.

Jenny, who just wanted to follow the game, was trying not to attract her usual crowd of Casanovas. She tucked herself into the corner of the booth next to Catherine so guys couldn't easily come up spewing pick-up lines. She had been on many dates since Arty went to Vietnam, and she was on the pill, but she had been watching Catherine, who had also been on the pill, dealing with a surprise pregnancy. It wasn't like she was saving herself for Arty, she just hadn't been tempted to sleep with anyone. Law school was demanding enough.

The game was a scoreless pitchers' duel until the top of the fourth, when Roberto Clemente smashed a tape-measure home run to give the Pirates a one to nothing lead. Jenny leaped up and joined the half of the bar-crowd rooting for Pittsburgh in shouts of, "Arriba! Arriba!"

Catherine asked, "What's the Arriba thing about?"

"It's Clemente's nickname," Jenny told her. "If Arty and Mike are listening, they're yelling too."

"Arriba! Arriba!" Catherine shouted. She was happy for Jenny, and for Art, and especially for Mike, wherever he was. And though she didn't care much for baseball, when the Pirates got the last out and won not just the game, two to one, but the whole World Series, she joined Jenny and the other Pittsburgh fans yelling, "Beat 'em Bucs! Beat 'em Bucs!"

The next afternoon Catherine was alone in the apartment writing a brief for her turn in moot court. For months she had vacillated between having the baby and having an abortion, procrastinating until it was too late to have it safely. She felt extremely good at how it was working out. She wasn't sure if she would give it up for adoption, tell her parents, or Mike's parents if something happened to him or he didn't want to be a father. But that could wait. The baby should come in late January, conveniently between semesters. And if it came on time it would be a Capricorn, very compatible with her Cancer and Mike's Taurus. She put her hand on her belly and was feeling little karate kicks inside and thinking it is definitely a boy when the phone rang. "Hello."

"Is this the number for Catherine and Jenny?"

"Yes...who's calling?"

"Uh, hi. I'm Ensign Hank Carver, I just got back from Vietnam. Who am I talking to?"

"I'm Catherine!" she gasped. "What's happened?"

"Oh, good. It's you I need to talk to. Before I say anything, have you talked with Mike Mulligan in the last couple of days?"

"No...why?"

"He's going to try to phone you, but it's almost impossible from Vietnam, which is why I'm calling. I'm in the San Francisco airport. Mike and his friend McGill were on a boat with me and McGill made me promise to call you as soon as I landed and tell you that Mike told him that he hadn't received any of your letters. So he told Mike about your condition and said to tell you Mike said he thinks about you all the time and will do whatever you want and supports any decision you make."

"Mike...Mike...Mike said that? Did I hear you right?"

"No, McGill told me to tell you that that's what Mike said."

Catherine said, "I'm sorry, but I don't understand."

"Well, McGill and I were wounded, and—"

"WOUNDED!"

"Don't worry. We were evaced out on a dustoff. He thought it would be faster if I called when I got back than to wait for Mike to find a way to call. He said you needed to know ASAP because of the baby. I wish I could tell you more, ma'am, but I only knew Mike for a couple days, and McGill only for a few hours."

"Is Mike okay? And you say Art was wounded but is okay?"

"McGill's in a field hospital but he's not hurt too bad. The docs say he'll be fine in a few weeks. Mike was good last time I saw him. We were taking a boat down the delta from Dam Luc when we got diverted on a rescue mission. We saved five of our guys, but we got hit and McGill and me and some of the guys we'd rescued were evaced out. But Mike was fine. The boat took some hits, but not bad, so they went on."

"Went on to where?"

"A support ship off the coast. I tried to find out if they made it, but it's classified and they wouldn't tell me anything and now I'm back here so I can't follow up."

"How…how did they end up together? Isn't that unusual?"

"Oh yes, ma'am, unusual as hell. Neither of them knew the other was on the boat when we set out. I mean, there were only four of us for what we thought was a half-day milk run. They were blown away when Mike went up on deck and saw McGill in the gun-tub. It was just the luck of the draw. The military can be like that. I was still at the hospital in Long Binh when McGill woke up and dictated a letter to you. I hope you can read it. My handwriting's not the best, and he was talking fast. I brought it with me and just put it in the mail."

"You mean he couldn't write it himself?"

"He was all bandaged up and couldn't use his arm. I've…I've got to go, ma'am, my flight's about to board, but there's one last thing I promised him I'd do. I'm supposed to read this, word for word. It's a little strange, but here goes: 'Catherine, you and Mulligan are oversized carrot-tops and if you don't get married I'll come back and kick both your freckled asses.'"

Chapter 18

Missing

McGill listened to the seventh-game flat on his back in the ICU at Long Binh along with Stanton. It was a bummer not having any beer, and the nurses only let them listen on his tiny radio after he and Stanton teamed up and cursed and bitched and swore that they would raise holy fucking hell all night fucking long if they couldn't hear the goddamn fucking game. The nurses gave in, but only after they vowed to keep the volume low and talk in whispers.

"Us grunts gotta stick together," Stanton said.

"Fuckin' A," McGill said, feeling a surge of pride that he was no longer just a lowly rear-echelon-mother-fucker, but that he had been accepted as a true grunt. He'd been there. He'd done it. He qualified.

When the Pirates got the final out and took the World Series four games to three, McGill yelled in a whisper, "Beat 'em Bucs!" and Stanton muttered, "We took the last two, but you can't win 'em all. I owe you."

The nurses confiscated the radio to make sure they went to sleep; when McGill woke in the morning somebody new was in the next bed.

"Where's Stanton?" McGill asked. "Is he okay?"

"They medevaced him out," a nurse said.

"But what about me? We came in together. I should be with him."

"You're not that serious. They're moving you to the general ward."

He felt he had done all he could to help with Mulligan's baby-making mess by enlisting Carver to call Catherine. The timing was pure luck, and if Carver did as he promised at least Catherine would know that Mulligan knew. It wasn't much, but it was something.

He asked every day if the PACV had made it, but nobody would tell him anything. He figured he should get a Purple Heart and he asked about how to recommend medals for the others. But he was Army and they were Navy and Coast Guard, each with their own ponderous bureaucracies, and nobody was asking his opinion.

A cute USO volunteer came around every day and took dictation for letters to Jenny, Catherine, Mulligan, his parents and Mulligan's parents. On Nov. 6, Jenny's twenty-third birthday, they removed the splint on his arm and issued him a new uniform. In a ceremony in the hospital lounge, a major pinned a Purple Heart on him and then surprised him with a Bronze Star with a V-device for valor.

He knew the Army gave out bronze stars like candy to the desk jockeys at MACV, but his had a V-device, which meant he'd earned his in combat. It wasn't a Silver Star, or the Distinguished Service Cross, or the Congressional Medal of Honor, but it wasn't too shabby. A master sergeant read his citation detailing what he'd done during the rescue action at Song Tai as attested to by both Ensign Carver and a major general named Brewer whom he'd carried on his back.

But his wounds were not million-dollar bad, and the Army doctors sent him back to Dam Luc for thirty days of "light duty," enough time to completely heal. The rescue action at Song Tai was now embellished and exaggerated beyond recognition in Dam Luc's EM Club and he was treated as a celebrity. Everybody wanted to see his scars, like in junior-high when he and Mulligan got swats from Whackin' McCracken. Everybody asked how many Viet Cong he'd killed, but he refused to guess and tried not to think about it. The Army had authorized him weapons, but the Army had not authorized him a conscience.

Light duty meant that he had the day-shift and didn't have to do guard duty in the monsoon. He reported to the top sergeant every morning, who had him filling in as radio operator, typing reports, doing various headquarters desk jobs, supervising squads on small projects, and of course, gofering.

He crossed off the days on his *Playboy* calendar and counted down to his DEROS, or Date-Eligible-for-Return-from-Overseas, his "three-sixty-five and a wake-up."

One day at mail-call he got several letters:

— Jenny thanked God he was alive, was ecstatic he'd seen Mulligan, but she still had no news about the lawsuit. She begged him to be careful and wished he was home and signed it "Love, Jenny."

—His mom wrote that his dad and his brother and grandparents and everyone at McGill Motors were thrilled that he was alive and begged him to be careful and wished he was home.

—Catherine thanked him for everything he'd done, announced that she was having the baby in January, and begged him to be careful. But she still hadn't heard from Mike. Was there anything he could do?

—Mulligan's parents thanked him for the news about Mike and asked if he knew where Mike was and why he hadn't written and begged him to be careful.

On December 7, a ceremony honoring the anniversary of the Japanese attack on Pearl Harbor culminated with the playing of "Taps" for the fallen. By chance, it was the same day he came off light duty, but instead of pulling guard duty at the POW compound as he expected, he was ordered to report to Col. Lombard's office.

"At ease, specialist," said the colonel after they finished the salutes. "Do you know why you're here?"

"My case was approved! I'm going home, right?"

"No, that's not it. You're halfway through your tour...correct?"

"Yes, sir. My DEROS is June sixth, but if my case goes through I'll be out long before then."

"I've looked into it, and somebody at the Pentagon wants you here. You're not going anywhere."

"But—"

"Give it up, soldier" said the colonel. "For the next six months, they've got you by the balls. So here's the deal: we just got word Nixon's sending another seventy thousand troops back by March, and the rest of us by the end of August."

This was very strange. "So...so why are you telling me, sir? Nobody in the Army has ever consulted me about anything."

"Because I need to use all of my resources to make sure this unit stands down in good order with minimal loss of life. I'm not looking to up any body-counts. I don't need a fucking promotion. I need men I can trust to help me get our asses out of here in one piece."

"I...I don't understand, sir."

"You were sent here for mouthing off, but you have shown bravery in combat and you get things done around here most everybody else screws up. You're not the fucking-new-guy any more, and you know the routine. I'm told most of the men like you for your singing, and now that you have a couple of medals, even the ones who think you're a total asshole, and I'm told there a few of those, respect you. I need leaders under me who have earned the respect of the men and can help me get all of us out of here alive,. You have and you can."

"I...uh—"

"Now Lt. Tuller rotates back this week, and any butter-bar just out of ROTC they send me won't know shit from shinola. Since you're going to be here anyway, and I have been assured that you will finish your tour in-county, I'm going to let you help this unit no matter who I piss off. I'm retiring and don't have to play games. We are under battlefield conditions. The dry season's coming up, and MACV's telling us Charlie's on the move. It's quiet now, but something big is coming."

McGill listened, bewildered. This wasn't making any sense.

"So," said the colonel, "because of your recent gallantry and our imminent danger, I am using my authority as your commanding officer to jump you in rank. Congratulations, Staff Sergeant McGill."

McGill just stood there, dumbstruck and dumbfounded as the colonel shook his hand and gave him a set of staff-sergeant's stripes. Was the colonel really promoting him from a soft-stripe Specialist Fourth Class, E-4, to a hard-stripe E-6 with command responsibilities?

"I…I don't know about this, colonel."

"You want to get out of here alive as much as I do," said the colonel, "and I have the duty to utilize any man under my command who can help me do it. I don't want to potty-train a fucking-new-guy when we're bugging out of here in a few months. You are the best man I've got for the job. I need you, and this company needs you. Running a platoon does not require an officer, just the right sergeant. Your fellow soldiers need you."

"I…uh…but sir, I'm against the war, and—"

"So fucking what?" said the colonel, his face reddening. "I'm against the fucking thing too. I'm putting you in a position of authority, and if you do your job as well as I think you can do it, you will help to insure that you make it back and maybe some others make it back who wouldn't have if somebody other than you was doing the job I need you to do. Do you understand? You're going to be here either way."

This was too strange. With a sprinkling of military fairy dust, *poof*, the colonel was making him an NCO in charge of a platoon. Could he do the job? Would some butter-bar lieutenant do it better? No, he was sure of that. But he had to know about Mulligan.

"Uh…before I say anything, I need to know what happened to the PACV and the crew."

The colonel said, "Sorry, that's classified."

"Sir, it's personal. Lt. Mulligan and I grew up together."

"*What*?"

"Yes, sir. Neither of us knew we were both on the boat when we left. He had no idea I was at Dam Luc, and I was only there because I did okay in weapons training."

"Yes, you had the best scores, so I assigned you myself, but I'd have never done it if I was aware you two knew each other."

"Sir, it's even more complicated than that. Mulligan knocked up this girl but didn't know about it until I told him. I wrote to her when I was in the hospital and told her that I'd seen him and he was going to try to call. But she hasn't heard anything and she's begging me for answers and all I can tell her is I don't know. Sir, with all due respect, just what happened to Lt. Mulligan?"

Lombard walked around to the back of his desk, opened a drawer, and pulled out a file. He flipped through it for a few seconds, then opened a different file that was on his desk and flipped through it.

"So you're both from the same hometown," Lombard said with a shake of his head. "Milltowne. I should have caught that before I assigned you."

"Yes, sir. We sat next to each other in home-room all through junior high."

"I'm very, very sorry. I liked Lt. Mulligan. He reported their position when they started out after your dustoff and there hasn't been a word since. We've searched all along the routes they would have taken and found nothing. In cases like this, he and Chief Dungy will probably be listed as MIA."

"You mean, nobody knows what happened?"

"These things take time to determine. They don't want to worry the families unnecessarily. One thing we do know is that if Charlie had captured or destroyed the PACV it would be a helluva propaganda victory and he'd be bragging from the rooftops. But he isn't."

"So…so what can I tell the mother?"

"Until he shows up, or we find a body, or he's officially declared missing and his next of kin notified, you can't say anything."

"But his parents are his next of kin and they don't know anything about the baby or the mother, so who will notify her?"

Lombard shook his head, sighed and said, "Fuck this war. I don't know the answer. I'll see if there's anything I can do to speed up the notification process, but I doubt it. In the meantime, not a word to anybody. Classified means classified. Understood, sergeant?"

"Yes, sir."

"And get a haircut before you put on those stripes. You have to set an example."

"Yes, sir."

McGill wandered back to the hooch in a total fog, thinking "Mulligan Man's MIA and probably dead and I'm a sergeant taking over a platoon."

His hoochmates were not impressed with his new position. One guy laughed and said, "You're replacing Tuller? Ha! Gimme a break. What are we supposed to call you, Sergeant Bong?"

"You're gonna be a fucking lifer, McGill," said another. "You hate takin' orders, but you're gonna love givin' 'em."

"Bullshit," McGill said. "I'm gonna try to get us out of here without anybody getting killed. That's all I care about. But you better do every fucking thing I tell you. I can be a real asshole if I have to be."

He lost all interest in Buddha-grass and boom-boom girls. Getting his men back to The World alive was all that mattered.

McGill only learned that Mulligan was officially missing when he opened a letter from his mom to find clippings from the January 21, 1972, edition of the *Milltowne Gazette* and saw the headline: "MULLIGAN MAN" MIA. The article said that the Navy had told the family that Lt. Michael Patrick Mulligan was missing in action in operations in the Mekong delta, but gave no further details.

The second clipping was an editorial, with the Annapolis graduation photo of Mulligan in his spiffy white Navy uniform next to the photo everyone in Milltowne knew—his leaping end-zone catch against Hempfield. The editorial extolled Mulligan's football and basketball exploits and joined with the family in praying for his safe return. It also informed readers that Lt. Mulligan was Decatur County's first MIA. Listed in a sidebar were the twenty-nine local boys who had already been killed in action—starting with the first to die, Private First Class George Edward Trent, "Big George," who had starred on the same teams with Mulligan six years earlier. The *Gazette* asked readers to pray that the Mulligan Man would not join Big George on Decatur County's KIA roster, then went on to praise President Nixon's bold and wise policy of Vietnamization and urged his re-election in November.

Catherine was on the couch cleaning up Little Mike's chin after a breast-feeding. His flaming red hair and emerald-green eyes made him the cutest baby ever. She heard the mailman in the lobby, late as always, and called out excitedly to Jenny, "Mail's here."

"I'll get it," Jenny said.

Michael Patrick Mulligan, Jr., now twenty-three days old, had been born on January 17. Catherine thought it an auspicious day for a birthday, sharing it with Benjamin Franklin as well as with heavyweight boxing champ and anti-war hero Muhammad Ali, though she wasn't sure what she thought about his also sharing it with gangster Al Capone.

Her plan to keep the baby a secret from her parents had worked so far. She had been sailing her own thirty-foot sloop, the *Athena*, on Lake Michigan since she was twelve years old, so it was easy convincing them that she and some friends would be sailing the Caribbean over the holidays.

If only she had a clue what Mike wanted. Yes, it was difficult to call from Vietnam, but why didn't he write? Thanks to Art, she knew Mike had not received her letters, but Art had told him all about the baby. Why didn't he write? What had Mike meant when he told Art he "thought about her all the time" and he "supported whatever decision she made" and would "do whatever she wanted?" What did he really mean? Why didn't he write?

She read and reread Art's letters about what happened. She was sick with frustration, and there were so many decisions. Should she give the baby up for adoption without telling anybody? Should the baby be called Mike, or Michael, or maybe Pat or Patrick? If he wanted the baby, would it be odd having two Mikes in the house? How about Mickey? Should he be circumcised? Baptized? She and Mike had never talked one word about religion in their few days together.

Jenny came in with the mail and said in an ominous quaver, "Here's...here's something for you. From Art."

A shudder rippled through her at the sight of the large envelope.

"Trade you," Jenny said, taking the baby.

"I'm scared to open it, Jen."

"Want me to do it?"

"No."

She used a nail file to slit the end and emptied the contents on the coffee table. There were two letters, one to her, one to Jenny, and two articles paper-clipped together, and when she unfolded them and they both saw the headline—"MULLIGAN MAN" MISSING—she and

Jenny and the baby all burst into tears.

The news that Mike was missing changed everything. After crying most of the night, by morning she knew exactly what to do. Mike's parents had to be told.

She took her bright-orange mountaineering backpack out of the closet and packed her camera, all the relevant photos and letters, a few of her essential things and every possible baby thing; she removed the sleeping bag and jammed the stuff-sack full of diapers. Jenny drove them to La Guardia airport, where with the jumbo pack on her back and Little Mike in her arms, she booked the noon flight to Pittsburgh. When she arrived, she changed the baby and breast fed him in the ladies' room, then bought a *Cities of Pennsylvania* guide with maps of every town in the state. She rented a car with a baby seat, and after plotting the route to 326 Beaver St. in Milltowne, she drove with the heater on full blast to keep the baby warm.

Maybe it would have been better to call ahead? She couldn't say. Just showing up at the door seemed the best idea, and not even Jenny had tried to talk her out of it, so it must have made sense.

Dusk was falling and it was lightly snowing, making it difficult to read the house numbers from the car. It was an older, lower middle class neighborhood of tidy wood-framed houses. She drove slowly past what she thought was Mike's house. She circled twice around the block, double-checking, gathering her courage, collecting her thoughts, while constantly glancing back to watch Little Mike sucking on his pacifier.

She parked just as the street lights lit up. She left the baby in the car and rang the bell. A porch light blinked on and a tall, middle-aged man with graying hair who looked something like Mike opened the door and said, "Hello."

"Excuse me, are you Mr. Mulligan?" she asked as fragrant cooking odors wafted out and an attractive woman in an apron with hair redder than Lucille Ball's came down the hall and stood behind him.

"Yes," said the man.

"Are you Mike's father?"

"Yes."

"I...I...my name's Catherine, and yesterday I heard Mike was...was missing. I knew him...uh, but only for a little while. Is there any more news? Anything at all?"

"No," said the woman, stepping forward, her voice fearful. "We've heard nothing more. I'm his mother. Do you know anything that we don't?"

"No, no, not…not really. Well, actually, yes. I, uh…would…would, would you like to meet your grandson?"

The dry season meant that Charlie would be stepping up his mortar attacks. A squad of VC would sneak in a few hundred yards away, shoot off five rounds in under a minute at no specific target, and then melt back into the jungle. The mortars had limited accuracy, did little damage, and had not killed anyone in over a year, but the damn things disrupted sleep and everyone grabbed their helmets and flak jackets and scrambled to a mortar pit to hunker down. Charlie never let you forget a war was on.

He'd always thought that his birthday, St. Patrick's Day, was the best possible day of the year for a birthday because there was always a party. He got packages of homemade cookies from his mom and his grandmother and a box fudge from Jenny. It had only been a few weeks since he had gone from being one of the guys to leading the platoon, but now they all called him "sarge." Everybody recognized that he was on their side. He gave his second in command, Cpl. Lewis, $20 in scrip to buy four cases of the only beer available at Dam Luc, warm 3.2 Black Label, and threw his platoon a Saint Paddy's party, but with a three-beer limit in case Charlie decided to fuck with them that night.

He had become an old-timer in a unit where the average age was twenty. He couldn't help thinking about his draft number, thirty-three, the same mystical –33– on the back of Rolling Rock beer bottles, the history of which nobody could explain. It was also the name of the best beer made in Vietnam, "33." Contemplating the mysteries of beer bottles made more sense than wondering where he'd be if he'd been born a day earlier or later with a different draft number. At least halfway through law school, he was sure about that.

Jenny wrote that law school was going well and she loved helping Catherine and having the baby in the apartment. She said Catherine had been to Milltowne and stayed with the Mulligans for a few days, sleeping with the baby in Mike's own bed. It was the first good news in months. He was not surprised that there was no news on his lawsuit. In his own letters, he had not mentioned the bronze star or his promotion to sergeant in charge of a platoon to either Jenny or to his parents. It was bad enough that Catherine had told everybody that he'd been wounded.

A few days later, he got a letter from Catherine and dozens of photos. While she been in Milltowne with Mulligan's parents she had phoned his own parents, explained who she was, and driven across town to show them Mike's baby and to give them copies of photos she'd taken of him directing traffic at the Pentagon and of the four of them at Great Falls. She had gone bonkers photographing the baby and Mulligan's parents as well as his own mom and dad and his brother Tommy.

She had made copies of the Polaroids from the World Series in the McGill family photo album and she included copies of those as well. McGill was amazed how much Jenny looked today like she did back then whereas he, with his NIXON button and a gaudy Madras shirt, had looked like a total douche. He was relieved that none of the Polaroids showed his red suede loafers.

Catherine wrote and told him how grateful Mike's parents were that he'd had the chance to tell Mike about the baby. But if he read her letter correctly, she still had not told her own parents about the baby, and she begged him not to tell anyone about her being a DeWolfe.

"I told them my name was 'Wolfe' and my parents were deceased," she wrote. "I don't want money to be any part of this." McGill figured it was some kind of rich-chick-heiress-psycho thing.

Now that he was responsible for a platoon, he resigned to staying until they turned Dam Luc over to the ARVN, even if it meant extending his tour past his DEROS date in June. Nixon said all combat troops would be out by September, but they'd had no word from MACV, and everybody worried the base's status as a prisoner-processing center made it uniquely important for Military Intelligence, so it was possible that the troops at Dam Luc would be among the last to leave. As much as McGill wanted to get back alive without killing anybody else, he knew he would instantly blow away anyone trying to hurt any of his men.

On March 28, they had good news: they would officially hand Dam Luc over to the government of the Republic of Vietnam on Monday, April 18, just three weeks away.

But on March 30, the shit hit the fan as North Vietnam launched what historians would call the "Easter Offensive." At least 20,000 troops of the Peoples Army of Vietnam, the "NVA," with 200 tanks and heavy artillery, swarmed over the Demilitarized Zone (the DMZ) and routed the ARVN forces defending the border. Then came an assault opening up a second front out of Cambodia in a drive toward the city of Hue which, if successful, would cut South Vietnam in half. Then they opened a third front, also out of Cambodia but further south, not quite to the delta, threatening Saigon itself. North Vietnam had committed almost its entire army to the offensive, totally surprising MACV, Saigon, the Pentagon, and the White House at the intensity of the offensive. The commies were throwing everything they had at it. They weren't fucking around.

Now Charlie's mortar attacks at Dam Luc sometimes came twice a night. Everybody was tired, angry, grubby, on edge. Morale was the shits in his platoon and even worse for war-weary grunts with "thousand yard stares" who had seen too much for too long. Trying to be wise and fair but tough as a platoon sergeant was the hardest thing McGill had ever done. He just wanted his tour to end before somebody under him got killed and he had to write to the guy's parents.

Every morning at the daily briefing, Lt. Col. Lombard used his rubber-tipped pointer to update the staff on the situation, with First Sgt. Birkman at his side and Captain Paletonio sticking colored pins in the big wall map to denote the movements of the ARVN and NVA units as they set up to square off against each other. As McGill sat with the other NCOs, he felt like he was in a World War II movie with Jimmy Stewart and Henry Fonda and Spencer Tracy and John Wayne and wishing he was on the *Enterprise* with Kirk, Spock, Scotty and McCoy.

Ten days into the offensive the action was in the three northern military zones. The southernmost zone, their zone, was not expected to be involved in the heaviest fighting as it seemed to be outside the strategic objective of the offensive, which was thought to be to split South Vietnam in half. But there was sure to be trouble beyond the routine mortar attacks. Charlie never let the dry season pass, and this year he was certain to join in the fun with his NVA comrades up north.

There were few confirmed NVA units this far south and it was unlikely that Dam Luc, in the swampy delta, would experience a tank assault. They were just facing good ol' Charlie, highly motivated in sandals and black pajamas and carrying AK47s, machine guns, rocket-propelled grenades, mortars and 122mm rockets.

South Vietnamese forces were moving north from the delta to the battlefront to join the fight to stop the enemy advances. Intel said that

Charlie would try to tie them up, slow them down, confuse and divert the ARVN units from the enemy's real objective.

Preparations for the turnover proceeded on schedule. ARVN troops now manned the PBRs and patrolled the perimeter. Anyone scheduled for DEROS got a Huey ride out and was not replaced. Their unit was being broken up piecemeal and sent back in ones and twos.

McGill was getting short, just six weeks to go. Col. Lombard handed him orders for Long Binh, home of the infamous Long Binh jail, not-so-lovingly nicknamed "LBJ" after the president who sent America into Vietnam. "I wish I could help you, Art," the colonel said, using McGill's first name for the first time. "But all I can really do is give you the highest possible evaluation and hope it helps down the line."

"Thank you, colonel. But what about after I get back, sir? What happens then? Does the promotion change anything about my breach-of-contract?"

"I'm not a lawyer, but they're trying to shrink the Army as fast as they can and looking for reasons to let people out." The colonel chuckled and said, "It's unlikely they'll try to keep somebody like you once your tour's over, which is too bad, because you're damn good at your job and damn good with the men. Just be sure to keep your nose clean and cover your ass. Somebody high-up wants to screw you."

Charlie hit that night with a barrage of mortars, and sappers somehow snuck in and blew holes in the first two lines of barbed wire. When the call came in that the VC had breached the perimeter in Sector 3, the colonel ordered McGill to take his platoon's two remaining squads and back-up the ARVN. McGill grabbed his M16 and his .45 and strapped on his web-gear hung with grenades. When they reached the fighting he looked out across the barren, dioxin-defoliated perimeter, which was lit up like a football stadium by a dozen flares floating to the ground in tiny parachutes. Scores of VC were pushing closer as the outnumbered ARVN soldiers were backing up, retreating but not fleeing before the assault. McGill could press his men forward to defend the first line of bunkers and hope for the best, but made a snap decision to take a stand here while his unit was intact. He yelled, "Take cover!" and yelled out the order to put weapons on full automatic, "Rock and Roll!"

McGill kneeled behind sandbags and fired his M16 in mortal combat for the first time. Everything was in *s-l-o-w*-motion as he compared the M16 to the .50 caliber M2, which spread huge volumes of heavy lead in a general direction with minimal accuracy. The M16 was like shooting groundhogs on his grandfather's farm. Instead of wasting his ammo, he did his deadeye best to save his men by firing single shots at the silhouettes under the glow of the flares, like he was plunking fast-moving metallic ducks in a .22 booth to win a pink teddy bear.

As in trench-warfare in World War I, the D-Day beaches, and battles like Gettysburg, the attackers usually took the worst of it. A rule of thumb was that two attackers to each defender made the odds of a successful assault fifty-fifty. Charlie's sappers had opened a hole in the barbed wire and seemed to know where the mines were, like someone had drawn them a map as they stepped around them in the flarelight.

When his M16 was out of ammo, he heaved his grenades about ten seconds apart and took his .45 out of its holster and prepared to aim for the whites of Charlies' eyes. Suddenly, a platoon of ARVN reinforcements joined the fight and drove the enemy back. When Charlie stopped shooting and began dragging his wounded and fallen the ARVN stopped too, observing an unstated truce to retrieve casualties.

McGill ordered, "Cease fire!" Two of his men were slightly wounded, mere scratches that were bandaged up in minutes, but worthy of Purple Hearts. The ARVN suffered four KIA and many wounded.

When MI debriefed him the next day, he said he couldn't guess at the numbers of KIA or wounded in the fight. When they told him an ARVN in a guard tower counted forty-three bodies, he just said, "He had a better view." When asked how many he had personally killed, he said quietly, "None that I can be sure of," refusing to put a number on his personal body count.

The next day, Charlie, despite losing dozens of KIA the night before, was back to his mortaring routine as if yesterday had been just another day at the office. Charlie never seemed to learn.

McGill's last days at Dam Luc dragged on worse than algebra in summer school. By the night before the turnover, all operations had been delegated to the ARVN. The only Americans remaining were Col. Lombard, his staff, and the two remaining squads of McGill's platoon serving as a security contingent. Several Hueys were coming to extract them in the morning and Charlie, knowing they were leaving, bid them a not-so-fond farewell with the heaviest mortar barrage Dam Luc had ever seen. Nobody slept, but nobody was hurt.

At morning formation, both national anthems played over the loudspeakers as the Stars and Stripes was lowered and the flag of the Republic of Vietnam, with three red stripes on a yellow background, was hoisted up. Lombard saluted the ARVN general, who saluted back, and that was that.

McGill handed up his duffel bag and guitar, and with his M16 slung across his shoulder, he climbed aboard the last Huey out. A surprise passenger was a cheerful reporter from *Stars and Stripes* who was writing an article hailing the successful Vietnamization of one of the last American bases in the delta.

"How's it feel to be leaving, sergeant?" the reporter asked.

"Some of us are staying," was all McGill said, turning his gaze away so the asshole reporter would shut the fuck up.

He felt he had done all he could; no one had died under his command. As the Huey lifted off, he thought about Mulligan and Dungy—MIA. And Frankie—over two years KIA. And the pilot he'd pulled out of the downed chopper, whose face he would never forget—Winters—KIA. And what about Stanton, the Orioles' fan he'd carried from the chopper who still owed him five bucks from the World Series?

Long Binh was still the biggest American base in Vietnam. At its peak, in 1969, it was home to 60,000 military and civilian personnel, more than one out of every ten Americans in-country. By late April, 1972, it was down to 5,000 or so, still about one out of ten, and by grunt standards, every single one were rear-echelon-mother-fuckers, REMFs, with showers and bunks and bowling alleys, movies, and fancy restaurants with cold beer and burgers and pizza. Officers even had a golf course and a steam bath.

"Looks like you're something of a special case, Sgt. McGill," said the CO of the MP company, a major, as he read through McGill's file. "They send a PFC up the river to the shittiest MP post anywhere for being an anti-war asshole and he comes out a staff sergeant with a Purple Heart and a bronze star."

"I'm nothing special, sir." McGill said, no longer giving a shit if he sounded insolent or insubordinate or wise-assed. Fuck that. What could they do—send him to Vietnam?

"Well, the Pentagon's got your number, and they want me to find you something to do that will make you miserable. Any suggestions?"

"No, sir. It would be damn hard to make me more miserable than I was at Dam Luc, sir."

The major chuckled and said, "How short are you?"

"Thirty-eight and a wake-up, sir."

"Frankly, I don't know what to do with you. The last thing I need is some asshole the Pentagon wants me to horse-whip. But I don't give a shit what they want. Everybody wants out of here. We turn the whole damn base over in November. Lights out. You know what I'm saying?"

"Yes sir. I don't want to cause anybody any grief. I just want out."

"So what do I do with you?"

"Give me five weeks leave, sir. You'll never even know I was here."

"Ha, you really are a smart-ass. No wonder they want me to fuck you up. Well, let's see what the top thinks. Check in and report here tomorrow at zero-seven-hundred."

They gave him a job patrolling the twenty-five square mile base in a jeep from dusk to dawn checking guard posts while watching the B-52 "Arc Light" bombings light up the night as they pulverized NVA tanks on the front lines of the battle just twenty miles away. He knew he was lucky not to be in the boonies. The fighting was the most intense of the entire war, but the U.S. Army's combat role was greatly diminished as Vietnamization now pitted the ARVN on the ground along with American Air Force and Naval air support bombing the shit out of Charlie and the NVA. McGill was grateful to once again be a REMF.

McGill still had zero interest in Buddha grass, not since Mulligan ordered him to toss his stash overboard, or in boom-boom girls, who were everywhere. He did have a couple of beers at breakfast in the NCO Club every morning after his shift, then slept most of the day, the shades of his small, private room closed tight. When not eating or sleeping or on duty, he sat on his bunk and worked on songs, chain-smoking Marlboros like Humphrey Bogart in *Casablanca* as he counted down the days like a four-year old agonizing for Santa to come.

June 7, 1972 was his "wake-up." His year in-country was up; his tour-of-duty was over. He had survived.

He put on his Class-A short-sleeved summer khaki uniform, which was newly-bedecked with his combat ribbons and a set of staff-sergeant's stripes that had been sewn on by a cute volunteer at the Long Binh USO club. He put on the flat, soft-cloth headgear officially called a "garrison cap" but which, because of the way it unfolded when it opened, was universally known as a "cunt cap." He looked in the mirror and said, "You look like a goddamn lifer, Sergeant fucking McGill."

He picked up his personnel file at HQ and was surprised by new orders to attend a hearing on his breach-of-contract complaint at the Presidio of San Francisco. Finally.

A Huey flew him and five others to Tan Son Nhut to catch a Freedom Bird back to The World. When he saw the blue amnesty box he worried they'd screw with him, maybe plant drugs in his duffle bag when he went to take the piss test. He also wanted to thank Houseman for what he had done for him a year ago, and who could maybe help if they fucked with him.

He showed his paperwork at the ticket counter and got a boarding pass, but there was a long line at the customs station as guys waited for their turn to piss for "Operation Golden Flow," which was designed to catch drug users before they returned to the States. All enlisted personnel and officers up to the rank of major were required to pee in a bottle under the watchful eye of an MP to make sure they didn't cheat. If you were shooting or smoking smack, a test strip dipped into your bottle would change colors, from blue to red. If it even turned a soft shade of pink you weren't catching your Freedom Bird. The military was deliberately unclear as to whether the test also caught marijuana, speed or other contraband drugs. And if for any reason you couldn't piss on demand, you didn't get on the plane. Sorry about that.

His flight wasn't for nearly two hours, so he walked with his duffel bag and guitar case to the snack bar where he saw a spec-4 with a Customs MP brassard taking a break and drinking coffee. He walked up to his table and asked, "Is Sgt. Houseman around? He's a dog-handler. Has a bushy mustache. He showed me the ropes when I first got here."

"Oh, you mean Dogface," the guy said. "Nah, he caught his Freedom Bird months ago." Then he noticed McGill's crossed-pistols insignia and said, "Hey, another MP. Where you been, sarge?"

"Dam Luc, way up the Mekong."

"Shit, man. I hear that's tough duty. They shut it down, didn't they?"

"Yeah, a couple months ago," McGill said. "

"Looks like you ain't been through customs yet," the guy said as he pointed to McGill's duffel bag.

"Nah, the line for the piss test was too long and I wanted to look up Houseman."

"Well, you still gotta piss in a bottle, but being as you're one of us, you won't have to stand in line and we won't have to watch. Bring your stuff and follow me."

Bypassing the customs inspection procedure completely, he led McGill to a room where Vietnamese women wearing aprons and white rubber gloves were processing urine samples. He handed him a small bottle with wide mouth, directed him to a bathroom and said, "Bring it back here to me when you're done and we'll get your stuff checked through." Being an MP did have its advantages.

Aboard the Pan American jet, a Boeing 707, guys were catcalling and whistling at the round-eyed stewardesses in their mini-skirts, the first American girls most of them had seen in months. But some guys were wary—the ones with the thousand-yard-stares—who kept watch out the windows for tracer fire or the exhaust from an RPG.

As everyone was buckling up, McGill's seatmate, a spec-5, said, "This is as fucking short as a short-timer can get," cupped his hands to his mouth in a megaphone and yelled, "Fuckin' A! *SHORT*!" and the plane erupted in joyous chants of, "SHORT! SHORT! SHORT!"

The plane just sat there on the runway, way too long. They were a sitting duck, and more that a few guys started getting antsy.

When at last the engines roared and they began to move somebody began stomping his feet, and as they picked up speed everybody joined in until the stomping was as loud as the roar of the revving engines, almost like they were trying to add their energy to help get the plane up to speed and off the ground, everybody STOMPING-STOMPING-STOMPING! until the instant they were airborne when the stomping stopped as if on a "Cease-fire!" command. They'd done it. They were leavin' on a jet plane.

McGill looked out at the endless green of Vietnam receding beneath him for what he hoped would be the last time. He thought about Mulligan and Frankie and began tearing up. As the plane climbed toward the clouds everyone was quiet, holding his breath—

Charlie could still bring them down.

When they banked over the South China Sea, safely out of range, the cabin erupted in whooping and cheering and grinning and laughing like everybody's home team had just won the World Series, though a few guys just sat in their seats and cried.

Chapter 19

Welcome Home

THE SAN FRANCISCO AIRPORT WAS A MENAGERIE OF FAMILIES WITH KIDS, college students on summer break, hippies in tie-dyed T-shirts, businessmen in suits and ties, Japanese tourists and Hare Krishna chanters in flowing robes shaking tambourines. For most guys, it was the first time they had set foot on American soil in a year and it seemed like nobody they saw had anything to say. Nobody said, "Hello," nobody said, "Thanks," nobody said, "How you doin'?" Nothing. People either stared at them like they were freaks or avoided eye contact.

As they approached the Army busses outside the terminal, a handful of anti-war protesters with placards were yelling, "Baby killers!" under the watchful eye of the local police. Everybody had heard rumors about protesters tossing rotten eggs and tomatoes, and sometimes even spitting on returning troops, but McGill didn't see anything like that.

Four buses took most of the EM and NCOs to the sprawling Oakland Army Base for processing. But because McGill was to receive a hearing at the Presidio, he rode in a separate bus with the officers to Fort Winfield Scott which was at the western edge of the Presidio overlooking the Pacific. Located at the tip of the Golden Gate, the Presidio had been a military base since 1776, when Spain ruled California. "Presidio" means "garrison" in Spanish, hence, "Garrison of San Francisco," and the U.S. Army had kept the traditional name. McGill was impressed with the elegance of the historic buildings. Many thought the historic architecture, combined with its location, made it the most beautiful military installation anywhere in the world.

It had been a long flight, over forty hours, with a refueling stop in Tokyo and two weather delays in Honolulu. Coming from tropical Southeast Asia, they were all dressed in short-sleeved summer khaki uniforms. The sergeant who signed them in said, "I tells everybody to break out your field jackets A-S-A-P. This ain't the fucking Nam. And if you ain't got one, talk to supply before you goes anywhere. This is fog fucking city. It gets cold at night. But don't take it from me," and he pointed to a sign above the counter which read:

The coldest winter I ever spent was a summer in San Francisco.
Mark Twain

It was early afternoon when McGill sat down at the bar of the NCO Club for a burger and a beer. He asked the bartender and everyone at the bar where to go for nightlife and wrote down a list of suggestions. Then he walked to the shoreline under the old artillery fortifications beneath the Golden Gate Bridge and listened to the long, rhythmic bellowing of the foghorns as ships came and went.

He walked to the huge PX and bought a new guitar case and civilian clothes—jeans, sneakers, and a Pirates World Champions 1971 sweatshirt from the discount rack for last year's styles—then went to his bunk to get a few hours sleep before a big night on the town.

Since the early Sixties, the Bay Area had been Ground Zero for the counterculture and a hotbed of anti-war activism. It had a reputation as being a hippie heaven thanks to the student protests in Berkeley, the Summer of Love in the Haight-Ashbury district, and for being home-base for many of the most famous bands in rock'n'roll: the Jefferson Airplane, the Grateful Dead, Creedence Clearwater Revival, Santana, and many others. McGill was eager to take in as much of it as he could.

After a four-hour nap he showered, put his field jacket on over his sweatshirt, took his guitar case to the main gate and hailed a cab. He told the cabbie, "Take me where there's an open mic. Are there any good ones in Haight-Ashbury?"

"The Haight hasn't been about music or Flower Power for years," said the cabbie. "Not since the junkies took over. But there's a bar right over the bridge and you never know who'll you bump into. Maybe Carlos or Jerry or Grace. They all hang out there when they're in town."

The cabbie dropped him off at a bar in Mill Valley called the Sweetwater and he signed up for the open mic, number fourteen, next to last. "You go on about midnight and get ten minutes," said the bartender. "You can stash your guitar in the back."

McGill ordered a draft; he had to watch his drinking, as this was "real" beer, not the low-power crap you got in Nam. Tomorrow was big. He didn't know what to expect at the hearing except that he would be making his case in front of a review board. He must not get fucked up.

He took off his field jacket, draped it over the bar stool, and headed to the back while scoping out the women. It was early, not yet nine, but the tables were full. He was horny as hell but he wasn't sure how to talk to an American girl. The first thing he would be asked about was Vietnam, and he didn't want to get into it.

He wasn't sure why he'd held off on the boom-boom girls—he had simply lost interest after being wounded and Mulligan went missing. Now, his interest in women was back with a vengeance, but it felt like they were all glaring at him, his field jacket, and his short Army haircut.

The emcee stepped to the microphone. "Welcome to the open-mic competition at the Sweetwater. The best act as judged by yours truly gets two hours of studio time at Belltone Studios right here in Mill Valley."

The acts were a mixed bag of singers with guitars, two stand-up comics, even a barbershop quartet. McGill just sat at the bar slowly drinking beer and waiting his turn. He did not engage anyone in conversation until a guy in a fatigue shirt with a spec-4 patch came up and asked, "When'd you get back, brother?"

"Just today. This is my first night out."

"Welcome home. Where were you?"

"Mostly in the delta, at Dam Luc. You?"

"Pleiku, sixty-eight."

"Glad you made it," McGill said.

"Same to you," and they shook hands in a hippie peace-clasp.

As his turn got close, he went to the back room to tune up. A beautiful woman with curly blonde hair in a blue-and-gold Cal T-shirt was tuning up her guitar. "Hi," he said. "You up next?"

"Yeah."

"Good luck."

"Thanks," she said, turned her back, finished tuning, and left.

So much for breaking the ice.

He went into the hallway to be ready for his turn and watched her sing Joni Mitchell's "Both Sides Now" and the Beatles' "Here Comes the Sun" in a sweet, bluesy style. The crowd loved her.

"Next up," said the emcee, "is Art McGill."

"Boy," he said as he stood in front of the mic, "talk about a tough act to follow. Well, I…I just got back this very afternoon from a year in Vietnam, and when we weren't killing babies or burning down villages I wrote some songs."

The bar went silent. His casual comment about killing babies and burning villages had grabbed their attention.

"Before I start, let's clear something up. There's a lot of confusion about whether it's pronounced Viet*nam*, rhyming with 'damn' and 'ma'am,' or whether it's Viet*nom* rhyming with 'bomb' and 'mom.'

"Now I love Country Joe's 'Vietnam Rag,' but he gets it wrong. He sings, 'Don't ask me I don't give a damn, next stop is Vietnam.' But the correct pronunciation rhymes not with damn or ma'am, but with bomb and mom. And I can prove it.

"Now, the final arbiters of such matters are the drill sergeants of the United States Army whose primary job is to instill discipline in the troops. Whatever they say goes. There is no argument. Like Drill Sgt. Watson used to say, 'There's three things you don't do. You don't piss against the wind, you don't shit standing up, and you don't fuck with Sgt. Watson.'

"The most common method for instilling discipline is the cadence call, and every drill sergeant has his favorite. Sgt. Watson marched us around the sands of Fort Dix, New Jersey, singing this one."

He turned his guitar sideways and put the neck up to his shoulder as if the guitar were a rifle, said, "Ten-*hut*!" snapped to rigid military attention then began marching in place and singing:

"I'm gonna go to Vietnam
Honey, honey
I'm gonna go to Vietnam
Babe, babe
I'm gonna go to Vietnam
I'm gonna kill the Charlie Cong
Honey oh baby mine
Gimee your left your right your left
Gimee your left your right your left.

"So you see what I mean," he said as he slipped the guitar strap around his shoulder and into playing position. "It has to be Viet*nom* in order to kind of rhyme with Charlie *Cong*.

"Now when I was in junior high me and a couple of friends wanted to be famous folk singers like the Kingston Trio, and I recognized Sgt. Watson's cadence call from an old Woodie Guthrie album. It's called 'The Crawdad Song,' and it goes like this."

He played a few bars in Woodie's up-tempo style and sang,

"You get a line and I'll get a pole
Honey, honey
You get a line and I'll get a pole
Babe, babe

You get a line and I'll get a pole
We'll go down to that crawdad hole
Honey oh baby mine.

"Now one time when we were hanging out in our sandbagged hooch waiting for the next mortar attack I came up with some new lyrics, kind of merging Watson's cadence call with Woodie's folk song. I call it 'Gotta Save Pittsburgh.' Now, there are two real people in the song, Frank and George, both of whom graduated with me in 1966 from Milltowne High back in Pennsylvania. This song is dedicated to them. He began to play and sang:

"I'm gonna go to Vietnam
Honey, honey
I'm gonna go to Vietnam
Babe, babe
I'm gonna go to Vietnam
I'm gonna kill the Charlie Cong
Honey, oh baa-aa-by mine.

Gotta save Pittsburgh from the Charlie Cong
Honey, honey
Gotta save Pittsburgh from the Charlie Cong
Babe, babe
They say if Nam goes down like a domino
They'll be paddlin' up the O-hi-o-oooo
Honey, oh baa-aa-by mine.

We're gonna win their hearts and minds
Honey, honey
Teach 'em to wear suits and ties
Babe, babe
We're gonna win their hearts and minds
Bomb 'em 'till they're civilized
Honey, oh baa-aa-by mine.
Gimme your left your right your left
Gimme your left your right your left.

Big George could really run the ball
Honey, honey

With a better defense we'd 'a won it all
        Babe, babe
George could dunk and George could shoot
He was perfect for killin' commies too
        Honey, oh baa-aa-by mine.

Frank wrote songs and played guitar
        Honey, honey
The girls all said he'd be a star
        Babe, babe
They got drafted over to The Nam
Played shoot to kill with the Charlie Cong
        Honey, oh baa-aa-by mine.

Frank and George ain't here no more
        Honey, honey
Frank and George ain't here no more
        Babe, babe
George never got to be a big pro star
And Frank's mom still shines up his old guitar
        Honey, oh baa-aa-by mine
            Gimme your left your right your left
            Gimme your left your right your left.

Get a room with twenty Democrats in it
        Honey, honey
Make 'em talk about nuthin' but Vietnam
        Babe, babe
Get such a room with twenty Democrats in it
They'll wring their hands and fight and bitch
        Honey, oh baa-aa-by mine.

Get a room with twenty Republicans in it
        Honey, honey
Make 'em talk about nothin' but Vietnam
        Babe, babe
Get such a room with twenty Republicans in it
You'll hear the same old lies and the same old shit
        Honey, oh baa-aa-by mine.
            Don't gimme no left no right no left

Don't gimme no left no right no left.
Fifty-five thousand already died
Honey, honey
Fifty-five thousand American guys
Babe, babe
Fifty-five thousand American guys
Are dead and gone because of those lies
Honey, oh baa-aa-by mine.

They tried to save Pittsburgh from the Charlie Cong
Honey, honey
Died to save Pittsburgh from the Charlie Cong
Babe, babe
Fifty-five thousand American guys
Are dead and gone because of those lies
Honey, oh baa-aa-by mine.
Gimme your left your right your left
Gimme your left your right your left.

Gotta save Pittsburgh from the Charlie Cong
Honey, honey
Gotta save Pittsburgh from the Charlie Cong
Babe, babe
They say if Nam goes down like a domino
They'll be paddlin' up the O-hi-o-oooo
Honey, oh baa-aa-by mine.
Honey, oh baa-aa-by mine.
Honey, oh baa-aa-by mine." *

He let the guitar droop from his shoulder, wiped back a few tears, and looked out at the crowd, which he could barely see because of the spotlights. There was total silence. They'd hated it. It was too ironic, too satirical, too cynical, too historical, too personal, too political.

"Thanks for listening," he said. "I really needed to get that out of my system."

He started to walk off when the applause began, then increased with cheering and whistles and bravos. As he came off the stage and looked out again everybody in the bar was on their feet in a standing ovation.

He was in the back room putting his guitar in the case when the

*see Author's Notes, p. 323

woman in the Cal T-shirt came in, picked up her guitar and said, "You were terrific up there. Very powerful. Everybody was stunned."

"Thanks. You were great too. I love your voice."

"Thanks, but it's the song that counts. Everybody loved your song."

"I just wish I could have written it and got it out there seven years ago. Who knows, maybe it could have stopped the war."

"I don't think anything could have stopped the war."

"You're probably right."

"Anyhow, if you win it's a really nice studio. I'd be happy to help out."

"If I do win I probably won't be able to use the time."

"Oh…why?"

"I find out in the morning what the Army wants to do with me. With any luck, by this time tomorrow I'll be a civilian on a flight back home."

"So you really did just get back?"

"Oh yeah. Except for the cashier at the PX, you're the first girl I've talked to. I'm a little rusty."

Her cheeks blushed as she looked down at the floor in embarrassment. "I'm sorry I was rude, I—"

"Don't worry about it. Guys are used to getting shot down. It's part of the job. If you want to make up for it, let me buy you a drink."

He joined her at a table with her friends. Her name was Maggie, raised in Chicago until her family moved to San Jose when she was in high school. She had a room on a houseboat, a degree in English from Cal, sang in bars and coffeehouses—sometimes solo, sometimes with a band—worked as a waitress and was thinking about graduate school. When the emcee announced, "Tonight's winner, hands down, is Art McGill. Come on up here, Art."

Maggie said, "See, I told you."

The emcee handed him a certificate for two hours of studio-time as the crowd applauded.

"Thank you," McGill said into the mic. "You know, when I was in Vietnam I came across an old Chinese proverb. It went: 'It's not those who write the laws who run the country, it's those who write the songs.' I'm hoping that it's true."

He returned to congratulations all around. "It's been fun," he said as he showed Maggie the certificate. "Give me your number and address. If

I can use this, I'll call, and if I can't, I'll mail it so you can use it."

"You're leaving?" she said, a hint of disappointment in her voice.

"I've got a big day tomorrow. Where can I catch a cab?"

"Where are you going?"

"The Presidio."

"It's close. I'll drive you."

"I don't want to impose."

"You're not. I really want to. But on one condition. No cigarettes."

"I think I can do that."

They put their guitars in the back of her pale-yellow VW Squareback, which had a single DayGlo daisy painted on the hatch. "Let's go to my place for a nightcap," she said as they settled into their seats. "It's right on the way, and my roommate is up in Tahoe, so we won't keep her up if we work on your song. I have a good tape recorder so we can see how we sound."

McGill suddenly remembered the rumor about Chi Omega mercy-fucks for guys headed to Nam. Could he be about to get a mercy-fuck for making it back? He *really* needed a cigarette.

Maggie drove to the houseboat community along the Sausalito waterfront and parked with dozens of other cars in an unpaved lot in front of a long pier jutting over the mudflats. The Gater Five area was a ramshackle collection of houseboats and live-in "anchor-outs" floating on the bay. Along the shoreline were wrecks of sailboats and barges and a decrepit paddlewheel ferry amidst the concrete remains of the massive World War II shipyard which once employed 20,000 workers on that very site making fuel tankers and "Liberty Ships." Now it was known as the home of artists and musicians and writers and famous for the high-powered, counter-culture conclaves of "hippie elders" hosted by the Zen philosopher Alan Watts where poets like Alan Ginsberg and Gary Snyder and LSD guru Timothy Leary discussed the fate of the universe while Jerry Garcia played guitar in the corner.

McGill carried their guitars as they walked almost to the end of the long pier. It was low-tide, and all the boats were flat-bottomed and resting on the mud. Some were expensive marvels that had gained fame in photo spreads in *Architectural Digest* for their flamboyant design and in *Rolling Stone* for their hippie eccentricity, while others were derelicts that looked like they should be towed out to sea and sunk.

They walked down the gangplank of the *Northern Light*, a well-kept but ordinary houseboat, halfway between flamboyant and decrepit. "What's it like living on a houseboat?" McGill asked.

"I've been here six months and it's great. I love the birds and the water, rising and falling with the tide. We're just renting, but I want my own. Make yourself at home," she said, motioning to the couch as she turned on a light. "Beer or wine?"

"I'm easy," he said as he set the guitar cases down.

He settled in on the couch while she used a corkscrew to open a bottle of white wine from the refrigerator. She poured two glasses, set a large candle on the coffee table, lit it, turned off the other lights, sat right next to him and toasted, "Here's to music."

"I can drink to that," he said as they clinked.

"I have some nice Columbian Gold if you'd like to smoke some."

"No, not tonight," he said, thinking of Mulligan ordering him to throw his stash overboard and not to do anything illegal. He knew it was irrational, even superstitious, to think that Mulligan would come back if he followed orders to the letter no matter what, so he just said, "The Army could still make me pee in a bottle, and I just want to get out."

"So…so do you have a girlfriend back in Pittsburgh?"

"I…uh, not exactly. It's complicated."

"It always is. What's she like?"

McGill took out his wallet and showed her a new photo of him and Jenny that Catherine had taken when they were at Great Falls. "Her name's Jenny."

"She's beautiful," Maggie said.

"Yes, and smart," McGill said. "She's in law school at Yale. And she plays piano and sings. I'd love to get you two in a band together."

"Are you in love?"

"We've never made a commitment, but I never got a 'Dear John' letter either. It's hard to say what it will be like after a year in Nam."

He told her about the foul ball at the World Series and how they'd dated off and on for years without knowing about the connection until he got a black eye at the anti-war protest and they'd figured it out.

"Sounds to me like you're soul-mates," Maggie said.

"That's what her friend Catherine is always saying, but she's into all that New Age stuff. How about you? Got anybody special?"

"The real Mr. Right hasn't shown up yet. I thought I'd found him once, but he didn't work out."

"A girl as gorgeous as you must have guys beating down your door with jackhammers."

She turned away, embarrassed. "It can be a problem. So you…you were in the jungles, right?"

"Yeah, more or less."

"So how long…" she said, pausing as she leaned in even closer, her braless nipples popping out the fabric of her T-shirt, "…how long since you've been with someone?"

"With anybody I could talk to, months and months," he said as calmly as he could with his heart pounding and his skin on fire and his pecker hard as hard could be.

She smiled and said, "Well, you know how the Stephen Stills' song goes: 'If you can't be with the one you love, love the one you're with.'"

She put her fingers on his chin, drew close and kissed him ever-so-tenderly on the lips, pulled slightly away and said, "Is it okay if we skip playing music?"

Chapter 20

Hometown Blues

WHAT FINALLY GOT MCGILL OUT WAS NOT HIS LAWSUIT BUT A Congressionally-mandated reduction in forces, a "rif." Congress ordered the Army to shed 50,000 troops by the end of the fiscal year, and it was playing havoc with the Pentagon's personnel system as the Army tried to shovel troops out the door as fast as it could.

"Why keep me in when you've got this deadline coming up in just a couple of weeks?" McGill said as he made his pitch before the review board. "I'm certain to win once it gets to court no matter how much some bigshot general wants to screw me."

Three days later, the Army gave him a Dept. of Defense Document 214, his "DD-214," stating that he had been honorably discharged from the U.S. Army as a sergeant with the rank of E-6. He had served about the same amount of time he would have served if he had been drafted.

The sun was setting as the 727 circled low over downtown Pittsburgh. The new Three Rivers Stadium, which he had never seen, was lit up and filled with people. The Pirates must be playing.

Had he made a mistake? Lots of guys were discharged in California and never left. It was traditional. The Hells Angels motorcycle gang was founded by World War II vets who were discharged in The Golden State and stayed rather than going back to Kansas or Ohio or wherever.

Just what was he coming back to? He was no longer interested in law school or anything to do with the "Establishment." And he was absolutely certain he didn't want to waste his life selling cars in Milltowne.

What was here was Jenny. She would be home for the summer, but in September she would leave for her final year of law school. What then? How would she feel about him? How did he feel about her? Who had she been seeing? Who had she been fucking? Was he really in love?

And what would he tell her about Maggie? Would he play Jenny the tapes of Maggie & McGill? Yes, they were too good not to. Would he show her the photos of him and Maggie in the studio? Maybe. Would he show her the photos Maggie's roommate took of the two of them sunning themselves on the houseboat deck, him in his underwear and

Maggie topless? Definitely not.

After four days of playing music, recording, and screwing he was confused and conflicted. Maggie had told him, "I like you, Art, I like you a lot, but I'm not ready for a live-in boyfriend. If you don't go back you can stay with me until you find your own place, but don't unpack your bags. You can't move in."

He was eligible for unemployment, so he wouldn't have to get a job right away. He also had the GI Bill if he went back to school. It wasn't a lot, a couple hundred a month, much less than the GI Bill benefits that WWII and Korean War vets got, which paid full tuition even if you went to Harvard, but it would help. But that could wait. For now, between his combat pay and his sergeant's salary, he would be discharged with nearly five grand in the bank and have a soft landing wherever it was.

He could have stayed, found a room, dated Maggie, and become a part of the vibrant San Francisco music scene. They had spent most of their time playing and recording on the houseboat, ending up with three of his original songs and three of hers. She took him around to meet her many musical friends and get their feedback. They all agreed their voices sounded great together, so McGill bought a second cassette player and a case of blank tapes at the PX, hooked the two players together, and spent hours making copies. The idea was for her to take the demo tapes to radio stations and music honchos around San Francisco and maybe Hollywood, and he would do the same in New York and maybe Nashville. In music, lightning could strike. Their name was a no-brainer: Maggie & McGill.

They also recorded "Gotta Save Pittsburgh" professionally using his free studio time. It wasn't the kind of song that could ever be a hit, nobody would ever dance to it or want to sing along, but he hoped it could have some effect on somebody, some time, somewhere.

The morning of his flight he showered, put on his uniform for what he hoped would be the very last time, and joined Maggie on the houseboat deck where she was tossing pieces of bread to squawking seagulls that were swooping and diving and catching them in the air. The sun was warm, the sky was blue, the tide was in, and the retreating fog was hovering over the water fifty yards away like a fuzzy white quilt. He took a deep breath, savoring the smell of the crisp salt air.

"Well look at you, Sergeant McGill," Maggie said as she came up close and brushed a piece of lint off his shoulder. "Now I understand why they say women can't resist a man in uniform. But I thought you got your discharge papers?"

"I did, but the airlines let you fly for free if you're in uniform."

Maggie drove him to the airport, and after kissing him good-bye, she said, "I hope it works out with your girlfriend, but be sure to call first if you decide to come back. Don't just show up. You never know—Mr. Right might have come along while you were asleep."

When McGill's flight landed at the Pittsburgh airport his father and his younger brother, Tommy, were waiting at the gate, both of them in suits and ties like they were headed to a wedding. His father, beaming with pride, shook his hand with a firm grip and said, "It's good to have you back, Arthur. Wait," and pointing to McGill's sleeve his father said, "What's this? You made sergeant?"

"Uh, yeah, Dad," and hoping to change the subject, McGill looked up at his not-so-little brother and said, "But who's this giant?"

The two brothers hugged and McGill said, "So how tall are you, Tommy?"

"Six-three. Doctor Pearson says I might still be growing."

"Tommy's the athlete you never were, Arthur," said his father. "Milltowne went to the quarter-finals because of Tommy. And he has a two handicap. He could get a scholarship in basketball or golf."

Tommy said, "So what are all the ribbons for? Which one's the Purple Heart?"

His father reached out and tapped a ribbon on McGill's chest and said, "That one, Tommy. It's the same as it was in my day. And that's the Good Conduct Medal, and...what...is that a Bronze Star...with a V-device for valor! Is that what that is? ...Arthur, answer me."

"Uh, yes, Dad."

"Tommy, your brother's a hero! Why didn't you tell us, Arthur?"

"It didn't seem important. Let's go, Dad. I want to get out of this damned uniform and kick back and have a beer."

His father answered like he hadn't even heard. "We're meeting your mother and grandparents at the club. They're dying to see you."

"I need to change first."

"Nonsense," said his father. "They want to see what a real American hero looks like."

As they waited at the luggage carousel for his duffle bag and guitar case, Tommy eagerly asked, "Did you kill anybody, Art?"

The last thing he wanted to talk about was killing people in Vietnam, so he just said, "I don't want to talk about it. Okay?"

His father, talking loud and proud, said, "What did you do for the Bronze Star, Arthur?" making sure everybody in earshot knew that his son was hero.

McGill said in a loud whisper, "I pulled some asshole general out of a crashed helicopter. There was nothing heroic about it. Now can we please stop talking about the fucking war?"

"Watch your language, Arthur. You're not in the barracks any more."

"Yeah, okay. I'll try. So what's been going on around here?"

"The Pirates are in first place," Tommy said. "Did you get to see the World Series over there, Art?"

McGill thought of Mulligan—they'd hoped to listen together before he got wounded and Mulligan went missing—and Stanton in the ICU with all the tubes in his arm—and Vung Tau Jenny, who didn't understand a thing about baseball….

"Arthur, are you all right?" said his father. "Tommy asked you a question."

"Oh…sorry, Tommy. I'm spacing out. No, I didn't get to watch. There was no TV. But I got to hear a few games on the radio."

As they were leaving the terminal a young woman, maybe eighteen, rushed up and yelled, "Baby killer!"

Tommy shouted, "Hey, that's not fair."

His dad said, "Now listen here, young lady—"

McGill shouted, "Ignore it, Dad! Just keep walking."

It was an awkward hour in the car as they tried to find subjects that didn't touch on the war. His father asked, "Are you serious about that girl with the secret nose-job? She seemed very nice on the phone. What's her name again?"

"Jenny, and it's hard to say, Dad. It's been over a year."

"We liked her friend who brought Mike's baby over," said his father. "We're all really sorry about Mike, Arthur. Is there any news?"

"Thanks, Dad, nothing new."

"Your girlfriend looked really hot in those photos," Tommy said. "When can I meet her?"

"Let's see if she'll even go out with me first. Is that o-fucking-kay?"

"Sheeesh, okay, okay," Tommy said. "Don't get snippy."

"I'm not getting fucking snippy. So what else is going on around here? We didn't get a lot of news over there."

"Every time you open the paper they're closing down another plant," said his father. "Sheet and Tube, in Youngstown—closing. Johnson Bronze and Mesta in New Castle—gone. Even Homestead's down to one shift. The newspapers are starting to call this whole area the 'Rust Belt.' So what about law school, Arthur? Where will you apply? Do you have to take the law boards again?"

"I don't know, Dad. I need some time to figure things out."

"You know with your training and your war record you could walk right into a job with the FBI or the Secret Service and they'd pay for law school."

"I've had more than enough of being a cop. So how's McGill Motors doing?"

"It's a good thing your grandfather bought that building when he did or we'd be on the streets. Anybody leasing right now is eating dust. We could use you on the sales floor, Arthur. Customers like war heroes."

"Dad, you know I was a shitty salesman when I tried it, and I'm not a war hero. Tommy's the one to take over the garage, not me. You know it and I know it and even Grampa knows it. Besides, Tommy's great at golf and I suck. End of story."

"Well you've got to do something, You just can't sit around."

"Maybe I'll be a musician. What do you think, Dad? Get rich and famous and get on *Ed Sullivan*?"

"Don't be ridiculous, Arthur."

The Milltowne Country Club was lit up for a party, with an awning over a stage set up on the terrace and colored lights around the big swimming pool. They could hear a band playing what sounded like "Chattanooga Choo Choo."

"What's going on, Dad?" McGill asked.

"It's the June Invitational. The best event of the year."

"Yeah, for old farts like him and Mom," Tommy said. "I can't believe they're making me go to this thing."

"It's because your brother's home and your grandparents will be here," said his father.

"I agree with Tommy," McGill said. "You know what all us hippies say don't ya: 'Don't trust anybody over thirty.' Well, I've got my own version: 'Don't party with anybody over thirty.' Just take me home."

"Don't be a wet blanket, Arthur," said his father in his do-it-my-way voice. "Your mother and your grandmother are looking forward to dancing with you. You know how women are. It's important to them. I don't know why, but it is. You're going to do it and that's all there is to it."

"Okay, one dance, half with Mom, half with Gramma, then I'm out of there. No schmoozing with your golf buddies. Tommy can drive me home and come back and pick you up."

"That's a good compromise," said his father. "I'll talk to the band and see if they know 'Moon River.' Your mother and grandmother both like it."

The Decatur County Country Club's membership and guests were the crème de la crème of the local White Anglo-Saxon Protestant establishment. The standard joke in the country club's locker room about Milltowne went: "The Jews own it, the Catholics run it, and the Protestants pay for it."

The band went on break just as they walked in. His mom let out a shriek and ran over and hugged him and started to cry. His grandmother came over and McGill hugged her. His grandfather slapped him on the back and admired his ribbons. A reporter for the *Milltowne Gazette* came over, said, "Smile," took his photo and said, "Can I get an interview?"

"I just got back," McGill said. "Thanks anyway."

"How about next week?" said the reporter.

"Probably not."

His father showed him off to his parents' circle of friends and to the bank president, his car-dealer competitors, doctors, lawyers, and especially the mayor, bragging about him. Blah blah blah. His grandfather showed off the Polaroids from the 1960 World Series of him with his NIXON button and told everybody, "He's a real Republican."

The mayor introduced him to a Republican candidate for Congress who was wearing a "Re-elect the President" button on one lapel and "Cameron for Congress" on the other. Cameron shook his hand and said, "You're the kind of veteran I could use on my staff. Come around to my campaign office and we'll talk."

Bronze Star, Purple Heart. Bronze Star, Purple Heart—that's all he heard over and over for twenty solid minutes. He was the only person in a military uniform and nothing he could say or do short of making a really embarrassing scene would make his bragadocious father and grandfather and his gushing mom and grandmother *shut the fuck up.* He downed four quick glasses of champagne as he shook hands like a politician on a rope-line saying, "Thanks, I'm glad to be back. I'm not a hero. I was only slightly wounded. I'd rather not talk about it."

Besides Tommy and himself, the only people there who were under thirty were the waiters. Most of the crowd were of the WWII and Korean War eras, and most of the men had been in the military. There were also a few World War I vets like his grandfather. Without exception, all the veterans of previous wars wanted to shake his hand and hear about his exploits and tell him about theirs.

McGill whispered to Tommy, "I feel like a chimp in a fucking zoo. I gotta get out of here. Get the keys from Dad so you can drive me home as soon I'm done dancing with Mom."

The band came off its break and the bandleader said, "We've had a request from the father of a war hero who is just this minute back from Vietnam," and he held up a napkin and read, "Sgt. Arthur Bolton McGill the third. Give him a hand."

McGill wanted to crawl behind a couch.

"His father," the bandleader continued, "asked us to play 'Moon River' for a homecoming dance with his mother."

McGill loved the playing and the singing parts of music, but being the klutz that he was, not the dancing part. He wanted to make music, not dance to it. He tried extra-hard not to step on his mom's feet. Halfway through the song, he traded partners with his grandfather, Mom for Gramma, and everybody was happy. He had done his duty. He gave them both a good-bye kiss, shook his grandfather's and father's hands, and said to Tommy, "We're outta here."

As they were leaving a waiter about his own age, with a single glass of champagne on a tray, stepped in front of him and shouted, "Fuck you, you ain't no hero!"

McGill stood stone still and said, "You're right about that."

Then the waiter tossed the champagne, not at McGill's face, but at the ribbons on his chest and soaked his uniform. McGill said calmly, "Would you like to spit on me too? Go ahead. Get it out of your system."

"I wouldn't give you the satisfaction!"

Tommy said, "I'll take care of him."

McGill shot out his arm and yelled, "NO, Tommy! No fighting. I am fucking sick of fucking fighting."

Two men came up behind the waiter and grabbed him but McGill said, "Please, everybody, stay back, leave him alone. Nobody's going to get hurt here."

A circle formed to watch the developments. There was not even a whisper in the Milltowne Country Club.

"Sick of fighting?" the waiter shouted. "You don't know what fucking sick of fighting means."

McGill recognized the vacant thousand-yard-stare turned inside-out: the intense two-foot-stare of hate right to the eyeball that primed a soldier to toss a fragmentation grenade into a tent of a superior. This was not a peacenik war protester, this was an embittered combat vet who was hoping to make a few bucks in a shitty job as a banquet waiter until McGill showed up in uniform wearing sergeant's stripes and set him off in a rage.

"Maybe I don't know as much about it as you," McGill said, "but I know enough. So what was your AO?"

The waiter seemed surprised. "Cu Chi, what's it to you?"

"You want to talk about it?"

"Don't try that psycho stuff on me. It won't work. Tell us what you did for the bullshit fucking medal. Nobody comes back from that fucker a hero unless they're a glory-hounding bullshitter. I heard you in there telling everybody you didn't want to talk about it. Well, I think you don't want to talk about it because you got nothing to fucking say."

McGill looked around and thought: I have an audience, maybe the perfect audience. "Okay," he said to the waiter, "let's ask the people whose party we're interrupting if they want to hear it."

He turned to Tommy and said quietly, "Run and get me my guitar on the double."

"But—"

"You're not back yet? *GO!*"

He saw his mom and dad, each with a don't-do-whatever-it-is-you're-thinking-of-doing fear in their eyes, and he thought that if anybody needed to hear this, it was them. He took a breath, and addressed the room like an orator: "Now some of you have been asking me to tell you about Vietnam. It's not something I really want to talk about right now. I mean, I just got back and hour ago. I haven't even had time to change, and my duffle bag is still in the car. But at the request of my fellow Vietnam-vet friend here, maybe this is my chance to get it all out all at once so I never have to do it again. Would you like to hear a personal report from Vietnam, right here, right now? It'll take, oh, maybe ten minutes."

There was murmuring all around the room until the mayor stepped forward and said, "Go ahead, sergeant."

"That okay with you?" McGill said to the waiter, who seemed calmer.

"Fuckin' A," said the waiter. "Do it."

Tommy made his way through the crowd and handed McGill his guitar. McGill stepped up on the band platform and sized up his audience: all white, early middle-aged to very old, prosperous, and ninety percent Republican. Many were country-club regulars who had always been around the swimming pool or the putting green while he was growing up—Mr. and Mrs. This; Doctor and Mrs. That.

"About a year ago I spoke in front of a big crowd on the National Mall," he said as he checked the tuning on the guitar, "and I got my butt sent to a place called Dam Luc because of my big mouth. You'd think I'd learn, but here goes."

He did the schtick he used at the Sweetwater, marching with the guitar to the cadence call and singing a verse of "The Crawdad Song."

"Now this may be difficult for some of you," he said when he got to the song itself, "as my version mentions two guys from right here in Milltowne. You may have known them, or know their families. Frank in the song is my old guitar-playing buddy, Frankie Dombrowski. We had a band back in high school, Frankie and the Dynamos. And Big George is George Trent, our fullback on the team that beat Hempfield for the West Penn championship. We all went to Milltowne High.

"I'd also like to ask for your prayers for U.S. Navy Lt. Mike Mulligan, who everybody calls 'Mulligan Man.' He was the tight end on that same team with Big George and is now missing-in-action in Vietnam. By a quirk right out of *The Twilight Zone*, the Mulligan Man and I served together for half a day on a boat in the Mekong delta. It was last October. I was an Army MP stationed at that hell hole called Dam Luc and was assigned for a day of temporary duty to be a machine gunner on a boat with a Navy crew.

"The boat was a hovercraft, called a PACV, the last one in Vietnam. The Navy crew had come to take it out of drydock to a support ship offshore. I reported as the boat was idling at the pier. I took my station in the gun tub, and off we went on the fastest boat on the delta. After a while the hatch opens and the skipper comes on deck. The odds were a zillion to one, but there in the monsoon, twenty klicks from Cambodia, was Mulligan, both of us on the same four-man boat.

"The Pirates were in the World Series that night, the sixth game. The games came on at midnight over there, and we figured we could have a few beers and listen to it together once we got where we were going. I got up the nerve to tell him about some things back home he didn't know, like the fact that he might soon become a father.

"On the way to the rendezvous the call-sign 'Broken Arrow' came over the radio, which meant a unit was about to be overrun. A chopper was down, and we were the closest unit that might be able to get them out, so we went off the river and into the swamps and paddies. That damn hovercraft could go where no other boat ever thought of going. One of our jets came over and dropped napalm to buy us time and show us to the crash site and we headed for the smoke. A couple dozen of Charlie's sampans were closing in on the crash, but Mulligan slowed them down by running right over their lead boats like in a bowling alley. We got there first and I pulled three guys out and took a little shrapnel in the ass. No big deal. One guy was a general, so I got a medal. If he'd been a private, no way.

"Mulligan got us the hell out of there and called in a dustoff for the wounded. We saved five guys, but lost the pilot. He was gone when I pulled him out. His name was Winters. I'll never forget his face. Then a medic gave me a shot, and the last thing I remember was Mulligan kneeling over me saying, 'Beat 'em Bucs.'

"I woke up in the hospital at Long Binh, and nobody has heard from Mulligan or the boat since. He doesn't know that he's the father of Michael Patrick Mulligan, Junior, born last January 17. Wherever the hell the Mulligan Man is, I should be there with him. So for Frankie, Big George, the Mulligan Man and fifty-five thousand guys I never knew, this is 'Gotta Save Pittsburgh.'"

Chapter 21

Fuckin' A!

JENNY WAS CHECKING THE BOTTLE OF BABY FORMULA THAT WAS WARMING in a pan of water on the stove when the doorbell rang. She looked out the peephole and saw a tall, silver-haired man in an elegant suit who looked kind of familiar.

"Hello, Jennifer," he said when she opened the door. "Remember me? We met six years ago in New York when you and Catherine returned from your summer tour of Europe."

OH MY GOD! "Mis–mis-Mister DeWolfe! Oh yes, yes, I remember, yes, of course." She felt herself trembling and tried to think. "But, but Cate's not here, she—"

"Yes, I know. She's taking her last final and won't be home for at least two hours. It's you I came to see, Jennifer. May I come in?" and he brushed right by her and stepped inside. "I'd like to see the baby."

She stammered, "B…b…baby? What—"

"Please Jennifer, it's bad enough that Catherine's been lying to us. Don't you do it too. Think of it from my perspective. I'm out on the golf course when a business associate comes up and says, 'Congratulations, grampa, where's the cigars?' and I had no idea what he was talking about. How would you feel? And what would you do?"

"I…I—"

"Well I remembered a big hotel bill Catherine charged up last April, and her story about going sailing at Christmas. So I hired a private investigator to tell me what the hell was going on with my daughter. I'm sure she thinks I've been checking up on her all her life, but I haven't, not really, no more than any father would. And I can't tell her mother of course, though it won't be long until somebody congratulates her for being a grandmother at some party or other. You have no idea how horrendous that will be for her, and the hell that it will cause for me. I need to be ready and I need your help to know what's really going on. I can't trust to get the truth from Catherine."

"But how—"

"How did I find out? You can thank the Yale Gossip Society. I went here too you know, and somebody blabbed about a DeWolfe having a child out of wedlock and it made it back to me on the golf course in Palm Beach. Next thing you know, it will be in the *National Enquirer*. Now may I please see the baby?"

He obviously knew; no lie could possibly work. "Okay," she said, "but we have to be quiet. Walk softly. The floors creak."

Jenny opened the door to Catherine's room and they tip-toed in and peered over the crib.

He whispered, "Cute little rascal. He has Catherine's red hair."

"The father's a red-head too," Jenny whispered.

"Tell me about the father," he said. "Who is he, and how could he do this to my daughter? Has he no honor?"

"It's not like you think, Mr. DeWolfe. Let me show you."

They tiptoed out and Jenny closed the door.

"You know," he said, "this is going to be very hard on Catherine's mother. She's, well, let's just say she's very status conscious, and having a grandchild out of wedlock will be humiliating. The Detroit newspapers are merciless. And then there's the Heirs Committee."

"The Heirs Committee?" Jenny said. "What's that?"

"It's not all caviar and yachts in a wealthy family, Jennifer, especially when some have a lot more than others. You see, every legitimate descendant of J.C. DeWolfe automatically inherits the right to an equal share of the proceeds from a trust when they turn twenty-five. It's not a huge amount, I think the endowment is $135 million or thereabouts, so it works out to about a hundred thousand a year for the two dozen or so recipients. I get a share of course, but I donate it to charity, but some of the other heirs actually have to try to live on it."

"So Cate will get it too?" Jenny asked.

"Yes, on her next birthday. And she'll get far more than that when I'm gone if she doesn't force me to disown her first. As for my grandson, any illegitimate child must be approved by a two-thirds majority of the committee."

"That seems very odd, Mr. DeWolfe."

"Perhaps to an outsider, but not to us. Since 1867, DeWolfe has been a forest products company, so over the years there have been a lot of babies with DeWolfe genes born out of wedlock in places like Brazil and Borneo and Montana. Being accepted as a legitimate heir of J.C. DeWolfe is an honor and a privilege, and a child born out of wedlock is not legitimate. Most have been voted out."

Jenny said, "That is so strange."

"Yes, I'm sure outsiders would think many of our family traditions are strange, but the courts have upheld J.C. DeWolfe's will every time."

"I don't think Catherine has given that any thought at all, Mr. DeWolfe. You see—"

"Of course she has. She's studying the law, for heavens sakes. She just hasn't said anything to you about it. Every DeWolfe knows not to talk about it outside the family. So did she marry him? It would make all the difference to her mother and would not involve the committee."

"No, she—"

"Damn. So why didn't she tell us?"

"Because—"

"I'm sure it has something to do with her mother," he said, once again interrupting before she could answer and then going on and on just like Catherine said he always did.

"They have a relationship I just don't understand. Her mother has an obsession with propriety, but it goes far beyond that. I have a psychiatrist friend who tells me that of all family relationships, father to son, father to daughter, brother to brother, sister to sister, brother to sister, mother to son, out of all of them the most difficult is mother to daughter, and it is certainly true with us."

Jenny had a great relationship with her own mother, but she had heard exactly the same thing about mothers and daughters. "It's not like that with me, but—"

"So who is the father?" he said, interrupting again as he pulled a folded sheaf of papers out of his suitcoat pocket. "I have the hotel registration here from when you stayed at the Willard," and he read, "Arthur McGill of Milltowne, Pennsylvania, or Michael Mulligan, also of Milltowne? The birth certificate," he said as he shuffled the pages and read, "is dated January seventeenth, and says the father is Michael Patrick Mulligan, but you can't be sure Catherine told the truth. So, who is he? Some dirty hippie she met while protesting the war?"

"No, Mr. DeWolfe, he's—"

Suddenly cries of, "Whaaaaaa! Whaaaaaa!" came through the door.

"I'd better get him," Jenny said. "He'll fuss until he gets his bottle."

"Is there anything I can do?" he said.

"Yes. You can bring it and dry it off. It's warming on the stove."

Jenny brought the baby into the living room and said, "Mr.

DeWolfe, why don't you give him the bottle while I find some things that will answer most of your questions?"

"Well, I don't know," he said, sounding very uncomfortable. "The last time I fed a baby it was Catherine twenty-four years ago."

"Oh, come on. It's easy. But you should take off your jacket in case he burps up on you. Sit right there on the couch and put the towel over your lap."

He removed his suitcoat and Jenny passed the baby and then handed him the bottle.

"Just don't ask me to change his diapers, Jennifer. I wouldn't know how. I never even did it for Catherine. The maids took care of it."

Jenny went to her room and grabbed the big envelope with all of Arty's letters, then went to the kitchen table and picked up the three-ring binder Catherine had made of everything to do with Mike and the baby: dozens of photos, the newspaper articles, Mike's postcard and letter, the letter to Catherine from Arty, copies of articles and photos Mike's parents gave her, all neatly tucked into and protected by plastic sleeves.

She sat next to him on the couch, opened the binder, and flipped to the page with the clippings from the *Milltowne Gazette* about Mike being MIA and held it up so he could read. "I think you should start here," she said, and pointed to Mike's Annapolis graduation photo. "That's him, Mr. DeWolfe. Lieutenant Mike Mulligan, U.S. Naval Academy, class of 1970."

His eyes bugged open and his jaw dropped in disbelief. "Well I'll be damned. I thought for sure he was a dirty hippie. So he's a naval officer, and he's missing in action?"

"Yes, sir. His nickname is Mulligan Man, like in the Culligan water softener commercials," and in the nasally voice Arty always used Jenny said, "'Hey, Mulligan Man.' I'm certain you'd like him. Let's pray you get the chance to meet him."

Catherine had a glass of wine with some classmates after her last final exam, then walked home, preparing to change and powder the baby. When she opened the door she gasped at the sight of her father with a towel over his shoulder burping Little Mike. "Daddy? *What—*"

"Don't go into one of your fits like your mother does," he said.

"Jennifer here has shown me your album and told me all about it."

Jenny said, oh-so-diplomatically, "Why don't I take the baby for a stroll? He could use some air, and you two need to catch up."

There was an awkward silence as Jenny took the baby, quickly fastened him in the stroller, and bolted out the door saying, "We'll be an hour or so. Bye."

Catherine's father looked at her, opened his arms, and said, "Come here, little girl."

She broke down, sobbing. "Oh Daddy, I didn't know what to do, have it and give it away and not tell anybody, or get an abortion and not tell anybody. I wrote to Mike, but he never got my letters and he didn't know until Art told him the same day he went missing. And I couldn't come home and embarrass Mother."

"Yes, Jennifer filled me in," her father said, patting her on the back to comfort her. "She read me her boyfriend's letter about what happened over there."

"And then the baby came," Catherine said, "and then the newspaper clippings that Mike was missing. After that, I knew I couldn't give him up without telling anybody. I knew I had to tell Mike's mom and dad."

"I can see it has been very difficult for you, Catherine," her father said. "But why didn't you let us know? I don't understand."

"You know how Mother is, Daddy. She'd have insisted I sneak off to Switzerland for an abortion. And then there's all that craziness about who's a real DeWolfe and who isn't. And not knowing if Mike was alive or dead and wondering what he would want me to do. I only knew him for a couple of days. I mean, I just couldn't deal with all that and Mother too."

"Well," he said, "now that I know the father's not a dirty hippie or a money-grubbing gigolo, everything will be all right, at least on our end. Don't you worry about it. Your mother can tell her friends the father was a tragic war hero and that she's a victim deprived of a son-in-law. You know how she is. But what about his parents? Jennifer showed me photos of them, but what kind of people are they?"

"He's some kind of machinist or something and a shop steward for the steelworkers union, but his plant's closing down. He'll be out of a job soon. But I didn't tell them who I really was, Daddy. I told them my name was Wolfe. They think my parents were killed in a car accident."

"Why did you do that?"

"You've always told me everybody would be after me for our money. I often tell people my name is Wolfe. It makes things much easier. And I didn't want it to be a factor. They've offered to help me financially, but I told them that with loans and scholarships I had enough to finish law school."

"But I'm paying for everything."

"Yes, Daddy, I know. But I couldn't tell them that."

"Hmmm? Well, it seems to me getting them on board is the immediate question. We have to deal with this head on, Catherine, before somebody tells your mother she's a grandmother at some hoity-toity tea party. It's only luck I heard about it before she did. I want you to take me to meet his parents, right away. You're the mother, you have custody, there's no question about that. If the father comes back and you two get married, everything is hunky-dory. If he comes back and you don't get married, there's no court in the world that will take the baby from a birth mother unless she's in jail. The real question will be what will happen if he doesn't come back. You say you're on good terms with them?"

"Oh yes, Daddy, we—"

"Good. So if you assure them they'll have all the rights of grandparents and that you'll keep them involved and they can visit whenever they want, I think that will bring them on board. Let's just show up tomorrow and tell them everything. They'll understand why you lied better if they hear from me that your own mother doesn't even know yet. Dealing with them should be the easy part. Your mother will be tougher. God only knows what issues you two have with each other. I certainly don't understand it."

McGill was in his bathrobe eating a bowl of corn flakes at his parents' kitchen table and going over the rental listings in the *Milltowne Gazette*. He'd been home just two days but he already knew he had to get out of the house and away from the fights with his father over the war and the election. One listing in particular looked good: "Secluded cottage on Algonquin Creek."

His father had not been pleased with his musical performance at the country club. "Dammit, Arthur, I know you're opposed to the war, but why did you have to make fun of Republicans like that? That line about the same old lies and the same old shit in front of the entire club probably cost us half a dozen sales, maybe more."

"Dad, the point of the song is not about car sales. It's about stopping the war."

"The hell it is. When I was in the Army, everybody supported the war. Nobody protested."

"Yeah, Dad. And you never saw any action. You were a fucking REMF."

"I was a *what*?"

"A rear-echelon-mother-fucker. I was one too for most of my tour, but I was in the bush long enough and did more than enough to get to call myself a grunt."

"I have no idea what you're talking about, Arthur."

"I'm talking about how you can call McGovern a peacenik when he flew thirty-five missions as a B-25 pilot while Nixon sat on his ass playing poker. Why are you opposing a war hero who was in the Army Air Corps just like you? He won the Distinguished Service Cross for heroism, the next highest to the Medal of Honor. What medal did Nixon ever win?"

"McGovern's a peacenik and Nixon's tough on the commies."

"So you're saying screw their actual war records? Come on, Dad. Are you saying McGovern's thirty-five missions don't mean shit? No big deal? Well, I've lost one close friend and probably two thanks to Nixon, not to mention the guys in the body-bags I helped load onto dustoffs who would all be alive today if Nixon hadn't won the last election. If those like me whose asses were on the line could have voted, Nixon would have lost and Frankie and Mulligan would still be alive. So just stop it, Dad. Please, get your head out of your ass or shut the fuck up."

It had been a tough two days.

McGill registered to collect unemployment and made the rounds of the bars at night. He ran into some guys he knew, but it had been six years since high school and all the girls he'd had the hots for had married or moved away.

Most everybody did a double-take because of his beard. "Stick, is that you?" There were handshakes and how-you-beens and peace clasps and swapping war stories with fellow vets, but none of his good friends were still in town. He phoned his old friends' parents and got the latest numbers and addresses, but nobody was within fifty miles. He thought his "little brother" from TKO, Bob Dawkins, who was two years younger, might be around, but Dawkin's mother said he had just graduated with a BA in Psychology and was on a trip to Europe. With nobody to hang with, there was only the prospect of seeing Jenny.

McGill's plan for bringing her back after finals was to leave tonight around midnight, arrive in New York in the morning, and spend the day dropping off the Maggie & McGill demo tapes at music publishers and record companies. Then he would drive to New Haven, spend the night at Jenny's, and then drive her back to Pittsburgh for the summer.

He was just finishing his cereal when the phone rang. "Hello."

"Arty, it's me."

"Jen, hi. I can't wait to see you. I figure I'll get there about seven or eight tomorrow night."

"Arty, everything's changed. Cate's father showed up last night and he knows all about the baby. He wants Cate to introduce him to Mike's parents to set things right, and for me to come along. He wants you there too."

"Me? I, uh—"

"So can you pick me up at the airport?"

"Sure. What time? What airline? Allegheny?"

"No. We'll be on his private jet. We're at the New Haven airport right now and take off in about an hour. The pilot says it should take an hour and a half gate-to- gate."

"So you mean this afternoon?"

"Yes."

"Uh, wow, okay. Uh, I'll get it together and head out."

"Are you sure you don't mind?"

"Are you kidding? It saves two days of driving and I get to see you a day early."

"They'll rent a car and follow us to Mike's, then you can drive me home. Her father wants to know if you've seen Mike's parents or told them anything."

"No, I've been too busy fighting with my Dad since I got back. And my little brother thinks Nixon's great for ending the draft and lowering the voting age and—"

"Arty, wait, hang on...yes, Mr. DeWolfe. Okay...Arty, Mr. DeWolfe wants to talk to you himself. Here he is."

"Hello, this is Catherine's father. You're Art, correct?"

"Yes, sir."

"Jennifer says you have not talked to your friend parents about Catherine or who she is. Is that correct?"

"Yes, sir, I only just got back and—"

"Good. Can you wait for us and we'll all go there together? I think they'll appreciate you being there since you've been so involved. Does that sound good to you? If it doesn't, I need to know."

"Uh, yes, yes it does, sir. I know his folks really well."

"Good. We'll meet you at the airport at the car rental area. If there are no delays, we should be there about one. The four or us will have lunch somewhere and then we'll follow you and Jennifer."

McGill quickly showered, washed and vacuumed the Skylark, put down the convertible top, told his mom he was looking for a place to rent and not to worry if he didn't come home tonight, and drove to the real-estate office to check out the rental ad for the cottage. The photos showed a pine-panelled cottage with a fireplace and a screened-in porch just fifty yards from Algonquin Creek, which was popular with canoeists and rafters and renowned as a top-notch trout stream. The cottage was ten miles out of town, and the nearest neighbor was half a mile away. It seemed like the kind of place where he could sit outside and play guitar and sing at the top of his lungs and not bother anybody.

McGill asked the real-estate agent, "So what's wrong with it?"

She shook her head and said, "Well, the TV reception is terrible, and it has a two-holer outhouse. Some people have a problem with that."

McGill laughed and said, "In Vietnam we dug our own latrines, and I haven't watched TV in over a year. I'll take it."

He got the keys, but the cottage was in the opposite direction from the airport, so he would not have time to check it out. With luck, he would convince Jenny to spend the night with him there and take her to her parent's house in the morning.

When he saw Jenny on the escalator he shouted out like he was still in the Army, "*YO!* Jenny!"

"Arty!" She rushed up to him and they hugged and kissed. Then he and Catherine, with the baby in her arms, embraced in a bittersweet hug and he shook her father's hand. Then McGill looked at the baby and said, "Hey, little Mulligan Man."

Catherine was trembling as they pulled up and parked behind Art's car. "Now don't worry, little girl," her father said as he placed a comforting hand on her shoulder. "Everything will be all right. I'll make sure of it."

Art and Jenny were waiting, holding hands, while Catherine got Little Mike out of the car seat. When she had him cradled in her arms just right, she finally spoke, her voice unsteady, "I...I guess I'm ready."

"Trust me," Art said. "It's going to be cool. Follow me."

She somehow felt better when Art, instead of knocking at the front door, led them around the side to the small gate and shouted, "Hey, Mr. M! You back there?"

"Stick? Is that you? Come on back."

Art led them to a free-standing garage with a pair of barn-style doors, one of which was swung open, revealing half of a big powerboat on a trailer.

Art said, "Wait here a sec," and went inside. Catherine saw Mike's father hop down from the stern and vigorously shake Art's hand.

"Thank God you made it back, Stick."

Art said, "I don't know what to say about Mike, Mr. M. He's the luckiest guy I know. I'm betting he's coming back."

"We all are, Stick, we all are."

Art said, "Congratulations on being a grandfather. I gotta tell you, the Mulligan Man couldn't have done better if he tried."

Catherine froze when Art pointed right at her and said, "Look who's with me."

"Catherine!" Mike's father said when he saw her. "What a surprise." He rushed out of the garage, gave her a kiss on the cheek, smiled at his grandson and said, "How's he doing."

"Just fine, he's—"

Catherine's father stepped in and stuck out his hand. "Hello, Mr. Mulligan, I'm Edward DeWolfe. My daughter tells me she's been fibbing to you. Her mother and I are very much alive. But don't feel bad, she's been lying to us as well. I'm here to try to set things right. My wife doesn't know she's a grandmother yet, and I'm hoping to enlist your help with that. It's going to take a team effort with her."

Mike's father looked at Catherine's father's outstretched hand and said, "Just a sec." He put the wrench on the workbench, wiped his hands with a rag, and extended his hand. "I'm Jonathan Mulligan, and I think the mother of my grandson is one of the finest people I have ever met.

It's an honor to meet her father."

"Well that went better than anybody could have hoped," Jenny said as she gave a final wave while Arty pulled the Skylark into the street. They had only stayed for half an hour, declining an invitation for dinner because Arty wanted to inspect his new cottage in the daylight. Little Mike's grandfathers were getting along like long-lost shipmates, and Jenny and Arty would just be in the way of their family discussions.

"Yeah," Arty said, "as soon as her father asked about Mr. M's boat and they started talking about the Navy and figured out they were both in the Battle of Leyte, it was over. They'll swap stories forever. I think we played our parts pretty well."

"I was really proud of you, Arty. You made it much easier for all of them. And I think it's great that Mike's mom and dad are going with Cate and her father to help break the news to her mother."

"Yeah, having them there with that album Catherine made with the photos and articles should convince anyone that Mulligan is a class guy."

"What do you think Mike's chances are, Arty? Really."

"He's tough and smart and he's lucky. He always wins at poker, and the Navy gave him a quickie course in Vietnamese, so that might help if he's a prisoner. And in golf, when you screw up a shot and want to do it over, you 'take a mulligan' and hit the ball again. He's got a free shot coming."

"You mean a 'mulligan' is a term for cheating?"

"Depends how you look at it."

They hadn't talked much about themselves in the drive from the airport, it had mostly been about the baby and Cate and what their roles would be. Now they were heading to Arty's new cottage, and Jenny was nervous, not sure what she was feeling or what to expect. "I bought a couple of joints from some guys down the hall before we left in case you wanted some," she said.

"No thanks, Jen. I've been strictly legal since Mulligan ordered me to throw my stash overboard. I can't do anything until he says it's okay."

"I...I don't understand, Arty."

"Me neither. It's like maybe he'll come back if I just follow orders."

"Arty, you're not making sense. You're out of the Army."

"Of course I'm making sense, you just don't know how it was."

After a worried pause she asked, "What do you think happened to him?"

"They must have run into a real surprise not to have had time to use the radio. So we have to hope he's a POW."

"Isn't there a list? I've seen some guys interviewed."

"A list? Not really. The POWs we know about are mostly pilots shot down over the North. What you probably saw were some guys in the Hanoi Hilton. But in the South, POWs don't get reported because Charlie moves them around in the jungle and doesn't tell the Red Cross who they are or how many they have. A guy in intel told me they think Charlie has anywhere from a couple dozen to a couple of hundred POWs, but they're just guessing."

"Damn, Arty," she said. "I really hate this war."

Arty chuckled, then shouted an angry, "FUCKIN' A!"

She furrowed her brow, confused. "I…I don't understand, Arty."

"It's what passes for humor in Vietnam, Jen. It's part of the lingo, know what I mean?"

"No, not really."

"Fuckin' A! kind of either means 'that's great!' or 'I couldn't agree with you more.' It's all in the tone. So when you said you hated the war, I was agreeing with you. Understand?"

"I, uh…I think so."

Arty said, "So what do you say we stop for a pizza and a couple of six-packs and break this place in right."

She started to speak, "I—"

"Now," he said, deliberately interrupting, "if we were in the Nam, Jen, instead of saying 'yes' or 'okay,' you'd say 'Fuckin' A!'"

She laughed. "Ha, okay. Fuckin' A!"

They stopped at a restaurant called Augustino's where Arty bought two six-packs and ordered a large pepperoni and mushroom pizza to go. While the pizza was in the oven, they went across the street to an A&P supermarket for bread, milk, coffee, eggs, juice, and toiletries as well as mosquito repellant, candles, and a flashlight.

"I've only seen photos of this place," he told her as they found the number on the mailbox and drove down the long gravel driveway to the bottom of a steep hill and parked by the garage. It was about seven o'clock on one of the longest days of the year. He flipped on the power at the fuse box while she put the perishables in the refrigerator.

The cottage had the same musty smell as the ones her father rented for two weeks every summer up on Lake Erie or the Jersey Shore. She flipped the light in the main room and yelled, "Arty, there's a piano!"

It was an old upright; she played a few scales and said, "It's even in tune." She opened the door to the front porch. "Oh Arty, the creek is right there."

"I think we're going to like it here, Jen. It's the perfect place to get back into The World."

She tingled at his use of "we," almost like he assumed they were now a couple. She wasn't sure she was ready, though most of her high school friends were already married and had kids, some were even on their second husbands, and she wasn't getting any younger.

"It's a gorgeous evening, Arty. Let's picnic down by the water before the pizza gets cold and the sun goes down."

Arty carried an army blanket, his guitar case and a six-pack while she carried the pizza and the mosquito repellant. He led her down a path to an overlook above the creek ten feet below. A sweet, humid fragrance from the rippling water hung in the air. Fifty yards upstream, a fisherman in chest-waders was fly-casting as songbirds warbled love songs in the trees.

They didn't need the blanket, as four wooden Adirondack chairs and a picnic table were waiting on the overlook in front of a fire pit. It was a perfect perch to view Nature's panorama.

The geology was unique, part of the "end moraine" marking the furthest glacial advance of the last Ice Age. Everywhere there were rocks of all sizes interspersed with boulders weighing tons that had been left behind ten thousand years ago by the receding glacier.

Arty opened two bottles of beer, gave her one, and toasted, "To us." She clinked her bottle on his, and as they were digging into the pizza a Great Blue Heron, with a wingspan of at least six feet, came gliding downstream. The elegant bird cocked its head and seemed to wink at her as it passed, not twenty feet away, before swooping low over the water and disappearing around the bend.

"Wow, Jen, did you see that? I think we're going to *really* like it here." A worried look came over him. "You are going to stay here with me this summer, aren't you?"

Jenny squeezed his hand, and said, ever-so-politely, "Fuckin' A!"

Chapter 22

Playing House

JENNY CREPT OUT OF BED AND MADE HER WAY TO THE OUTHOUSE BY THE light of the moon. Earlier, Arty had made jokes about joining her on the two-holer's second spot, but she refused to even consider it.

"That's how the pioneers did it," he said with a smile.

"Good for them. I'm not a pioneer and don't intend to start now."

He had told her he had some minor wounds, but she was not prepared for the extensive scarring. With his shirt off his back he looked like the photos of slaves after whippings. What worried her more was the way he slept, with the pillow pulled tightly around his eyes and ears, like he was shutting out the universe. They had spent the night together many times, but he had never slept like that before.

Arty had not shaved since he was discharged two weeks ago, saying he was tired of being a "face-scraper." It was the heavy-stubble stage of a new beard, so he looked ragged, even dangerous, but surprisingly sexy. And while it was too early to tell how it might turn out, he was growing a ponytail and vowing that nobody would ever again look at him and think he could possibly be a conservative.

She sat for a long time, thinking, looking out the outhouse door at the moonlit creek rippling and gurgling, a background soundtrack for the happy chirping of the crickets and the desperate croaking of the lovesick bullfrogs. She tried to examine her feelings like a trained attorney, objectively assessing the pros and cons of the case. She felt warm, tender, affectionate, sexually excited—but somehow very scared. Arty had changed. He had a harder edge than the happy-go-lucky Arty she had known, which was the aspect of him that had always appealed to her the most. He wasn't a handsome Prince Charming, though he was cute enough. He did not have a football physique, that was for sure, and he was a bit of a klutz, but he was smart and kind and always interesting.

Since they'd discovered their World Series connection, many of their friends and family had turned, well…weird. The worst were Cate and Mama Antonia who both blurted out "soul-mates" the instant they heard the story. Was it destiny? Karma? Fate? Jenny didn't buy it.

Her mom and dad wanted to meet Arty, his mom and dad wanted

to meet her. It was as if both sets of relatives assumed that because she got beaned with a baseball twelve years ago, then met him in a bar on the Jersey shore, that they were destined to be together for all eternity. She had only talked to him that night in Wildwood because he looked so ridiculous wearing a Goldwater '68 button.

Cate and Mike had a baby together; what did she and Arty have except a Mickey Mantle foul ball? Maybe a summer in a cottage on Algonquin Creek would answer the question.

In the morning, Arty made coffee and she made an omelet. Her parents weren't expecting her until the weekend, and he had told his not to worry if they didn't see him for a few days; they were off the parental radar. They took their plates outside to the overlook to casually dine while watching the canoes and rafts passing every few minutes.

For some reason he seemed anxious, nervous, antsy. He asked, "What would you like to do today, Jen? We've never really done any outdoorsy stuff except for that time we went surfing. There's a canoe and an inflatable raft in the garage and a swimming hole down the path from the stone bar-b-que."

"Maybe later, Arty. Right now, let's just relax and watch the creek flow by. I haven't been in such a peaceful place in years. Get your guitar and we'll sing some songs like we used to do."

He showed off the Gibson with the inlaid ivory peace sign he brought back from Vietnam, set up his portable tape deck, and they sang like they were back in college. When the tape ran out, he rewound and played it. As they listened he said, "We still sound really good together Jen," but there was an odd tone in his voice.

"Are you okay, Arty?"

"Uh…yes. Why?"

"Well, you seem, I don't know…edgy."

"No kidding. I waste a year in Vietnam and come home to my father who wants to make me into some kind of war hero to help sell cars and get into arguments with my kid brother who thinks Nixon's great. Yeah, I'm a little edgy. And then there's you. You've got me worried, Jen. Have you been seeing anybody?"

She didn't dare tell him that yes, she'd been with other guys. For the first few months she hadn't, but the second year of law school was less demanding, and she began accepting dates, and sometimes spent the night. And she was certain that he had been with women in Vietnam. "I don't ask you and you don't ask me, Arty. We agreed on an open relationship long ago."

"Yeah, but I've got to tell you about this girl I met last week when I got back. Do you want to hear?"

She didn't like the sound of this. "Last week?"

"Yeah, Maggie. I met her my first night back. We recorded a demo tape. Everybody said we sounded great together."

"Who's everybody?"

"Well, everybody in the studio and her friends on the houseboats."

"Houseboats?" she said, feeling a sharp pang of jealousy.

"Yeah, in Sausalito. It was really a musical thing between us, Jen. I mean, I just got back, and she felt sorry for me. It was a mercy fuck, know what I mean? And being with her made me realize how much I wanted to be with you."

"A mercy fuck?" she said, trying not to show her fury.

"You went to a girls' school, Jen, you wouldn't understand. Look, the point is, I think she helped me figure things out. Maggie was terrific, but I think I'm in love with you. I had fun with her, and I needed somebody, but she wasn't you. I don't know what the hell that means, but, like we say in Nam...there it is."

They knew that meeting each others' parents would be difficult, but informing them that they would be living together for the entire summer would be a true ordeal. They decided to get it over with all at once. When the technician installed the new phone at the cottage, Arty called his parents and asked if they could come over for lunch so they could meet Jenny, just the four of them, no Tommy, no grandparents. When that was set, she called her mom to say she'd be home for dinner and could she bring Arty, which sent her mom into a tizzy about preparations. "Please Mom, I just want you and Dad there. That's it. Nobody else."

At Arty's house his mother gave her a tour, showing her the bedroom where Arty grew up. When Arty's father arrived he said, "So you're the girl with the secret nose-job. That's really quite a story."

His father went to another room and came back with a photo album and held up the Polaroids next to her face. "Yup, it's you all right. So, young lady. Do you have a job in the city for the summer?"

"Yes. It's an internship in the office of a federal judge."

"It's about an hour's drive in rush hour," said his father. "What kind of car do you have?"

"My dad will find me something."

"No, no, don't go buying anything for crying out loud," said his father. "We'll fix you up. We just got a VW bug in on a trade-in. I think it's a '67. Should get you good mileage. If you want to borrow it for the summer, just let me know. And if you can't drive a stick-shift, we'll find you something else."

"Thank you, Mr. McGill, that's very generous, but—"

"There's no reason to thank me, young lady. It won't cost the company a dime. So, Arthur, have you seen the article about you in yesterday's paper?"

"An article…about *me*?" Arty said.

His father handed him a newspaper. "The publisher called to tell me they were running a story about you coming back from Vietnam and singing anti-American songs. He was there at the club and saw the whole thing. He read it to me over the phone, and I told him if he ran the story like that he would never see another penny's worth of McGill Motors advertising. He had them rewrite it and buried it in the Style section."

The headline read: "Veteran Sings for Peace." There was a photo of Arty in uniform playing the Gibson guitar with the peace sign. The caption read:

> Just back from Vietnam, Sgt. Arthur Bolton McGill III, recipient of a Purple Heart and a Bronze Star, entertained the Milltowne Country Club with a song of peace.

And that was it.

"What bullshit," Arty said.

"But it's a wonderful photograph," said his mother. "You are so handsome in a uniform. And Arthur, please shave. It's disgusting."

"I didn't know you were a sergeant," Jenny said as she looked at the photo and read the caption. "I thought you were a specialist."

"I got a promotion."

"And a Bronze Star for gallantry," said his father as he wagged a finger in her face. "The fourth highest honor in the military. You should be proud of him even if he isn't proud of himself."

Jenny said, "Why…why didn't you tell me, Arty?"

"It didn't seem important."

"Be sure to let your father know he's a hero, young lady," his father advised her on the sly when Arty was in the bathroom. "It will help make up for that damned beard."

At Jenny's parents' house it was more of the same, though her mom and dad were more wary of the mysterious character just back from Vietnam than Arty's parents were of a wholesome Italian girl from Pittsburgh. Things got off to a good start with the banter over the Mickey Mantle foul ball and all the photos, but whenever her father tried to draw him out about the war, Arty got defensive.

As they were sitting down to dinner Jenny took her father aside and whispered, "Dad, he got a Bronze Star and a Purple Heart and he lost his two best friends and he doesn't want to talk about any of it. Please change the subject. Talk about baseball or something."

Not much later her father said, "So, Art, in those photos from the World Series, you're wearing a Nixon button."

"Yes, sir. I was pretty dumb back then."

"That was twelve years ago," said her father. "What do you think of Nixon now? Will you vote for him?"

"No, sir. He's stretching out the war just to get re-elected. I have friends I'll never see again because of him."

"What do you think will happen when we pull all the way out?" her dad said.

"I can't begin to say, sir, but it won't be good."

"I'm a life-long Democrat," her father said, "but I have a problem with McGovern if he wins the nomination. I was with Patton all the way from Normandy to the end of the war. McGovern's ideas concern me. I don't like Nixon one bit, but I may have to vote for him, and I've never voted for a Republican in my life."

"Well for me," Arty said, "it's my first chance to vote at all. If the voting age had been eighteen in '68, everybody I know would have voted against Nixon and my friends Mulligan and Dombrowski would still be alive today."

"Point taken," said her father, who dropped the subject and asked about Arty's plans for his future.

"I just don't know what I'm going to do, Mr. Abruzzi. I've got some money saved and six months of unemployment to cover the rent. If I go back to school, I've got the GI Bill to help out. All I'm sure about is that for the next few months I'm going to do all I can to defeat Nixon."

"How?" her father asked. "Handing out leaflets door-to-door?"

"Maybe a little of that, but I wrote some songs over there, and I've got a demo tape I'm going to try to get on the radio. I plan to sing at every open-mic I can find."

"You mean political songs?" said her father. "Like union songs?"

"These days they're called 'protest songs,' Mr. Abruzzi. Would you like to hear one? I've got my guitar in the car, and I can leave you a tape."

Jenny tensed up. "No, Arty, I don't think that's wise."

"Why not?" her father said. "I'm friends with the mayor and I play poker with the chairman of the Allegheny County Democratic Party. If I like it, I'll pass it along. And if I don't like it, I'll tell you why."

"I appreciate that, Mr. Abruzzi. I'm trying to change the minds of people just like you."

Arty brought in his guitar and began by saying, "First, in case you hate my song, I want to do a song that in Vietnam was everybody's favorite, 'Leavin' on a Jet Plane.' Jenny's going to help out on the chorus."

He began to play, she joined in, and when they finished her parents applauded and her mom said, "You two sing so well together."

Arty said, "I've always told Jenny we should start a band. Now this next one I've got to do alone."

He went into his "Gotta Save Pittsburgh" schtick, standing in front of the TV with her dad and mom sitting in their usual chairs and Jenny on the couch. She was tingling in fear as she watched her parents' reactions, petrified something would go wrong. But nothing did.

When Arty finished, her parents applauded and her father said, "Very well done, Art. The idea of Vietnam attacking Pittsburgh makes the absurdity of the premise for the war very clear. And that line about Democrats fighting and bitching among themselves is just what it's like. I'll pass your tape along. The party will be behind McGovern even if I'm not. I don't agree with everything in it, but your song deserves a hearing."

"Wow. Thank you, Mr. Abruzzi. That means a lot to me."

When her parents raised objections to their living together, Jenny cut them off. "Mom, Dad, listen to me. I'm almost twenty-four. I'm not your innocent little girl any more. I make my own decisions."

When it was time to go she packed up some things from her room and said, "Please come and see us, and bring your fishing stuff, Dad. We're right on the creek."

On the drive back Arty said, "I really like your father. He actually listened to me. Mine's hopeless."

Her new plan, of which she had no clue until three days ago when Arty showed her the cottage, was to stay with him until she began her final year of law school in September. A summer with him in a cottage would be a real test. She was old enough to do whatever she wanted, but young enough to change her mind if she had to.

McGill had never lived with a woman for more than a weekend in a motel, and four years in a college fraternity followed by two years in the United States Army had not prepared him for dealing with the finer points of female sensibilities. His notion of manhood consisted of opening doors, ordering at restaurants, paying the tab and charmingly persisting until he got to first base. He had heard that women could get angry if men didn't put the toilet seat down at night, but since the cottage had an outhouse he didn't have to worry about that.

One of his conceptions of what comprised manhood was the absolute prohibition against ever, under any circumstances, striking a member of the fairer sex. It was okay to restrain a woman in self-defense if she went hysterical on you, sure, but you could never hit a female. It was a universally understood notion of chivalry he had absorbed from the cowboy ethos of TV shows like *Roy Rogers* and *The Lone Ranger* and from the good-guy cowboy movies of John Wayne, Gary Cooper, Gene Autry, and Hopalong Cassidy.

He was confused by the new politics of what everybody called "feminism" that was suddenly everywhere. He learned one lesson the hard way when one evening about a week after they'd moved in he found Jenny lying on the couch. She looked miserable, so he knelt down and took her hand. She told him what was wrong, and he stroked her cheek gently and asked as sweetly as he could, "Is it always like this when you're on the rag?"

"ON THE RAG!" she shouted as she sat bolt upright and shoved him away, "is a male chauvinist pig term that fits right in with the rest of the dominating pig formula!"

He wondered if sitting upright so quickly might have caused an oxygen imbalance in her system, because suddenly her face paled and she stood up, raced outside and blew lunch next to the concrete path. Later, as he was hosing it down, he vowed to himself to never again let on that he noticed any monthly changes. Silence is golden; discretion is the better part of valor. There were many clichés which could have applied.

One night the phone rang. It was Jenny's father. "Art, I played your song at a meeting of the Democratic county committee, and I'm sorry to say, they don't think voters will get the ironic humor of Viet Cong war canoes paddling up the Ohio."

"But Mr. Abruzzi, audiences love it."

"This is an election, Art. I'm sure it goes over at college bars, but it's just too radical to associate with a political campaign. It's over the head of the average voter. If you asked a typical voter around here to define 'irony,' they'd say it has something to do with making steel."

Jenny had kept a diary on-and-off since the fourth grade, and in the languid summer evenings on Algonquin creek she filled the pages up faster than ever. Maybe it was because they had no TV, or maybe because life with Arty gave her so much to write about.

On workdays, she was up at six, on the road at seven, at her desk in the Federal Building in Judge Alford's office by eight-thirty, off at four-thirty and back to the cottage by six-thirty. Arty wasn't much of a chef, but he knew how to use the stone bar-b-que and chop vegetables for a salad. They always had fresh corn-on-the-cob from an Amish roadside stand to go with either burgers, hot dogs, steak, or fish he'd caught that afternoon ready to toss on the grill.

They had no TV reception, but they had a radio for baseball games. One day he went to a music store in Pittsburgh and bought her an electronic keyboard and extension cords so she could jam with him on the overlook above the creek.

She worried about his irregular sleeping, his night-sweats, and his moodiness. She read how his symptoms were like the "shell-shock" of the doughboys of WWI and the "battle fatigue" of GIs, Marines and sailors of WWII. There were stories all over the news about the heroin and cocaine problems of Vietnam veterans, but thank God Arty had given up anything illegal. The cigarettes and the six-packs were bad enough.

Since their very first date, she had known he was a bit of a pot-head. She had let him turn her on a few times, and she believed him when he told her he would never shoot up because he hated needles. He swore he had not done anything more than take a few acid trips, pop Dexedrine to study for finals, and snort coke a few times at parties. But thanks to his promise to Mulligan, Arty had even stopped smoking pot.

"It's like I'm under orders, Jen," Arty had told her more than once. "If I stay straight, Mulligan's coming back."

She thought it was strange, almost loopy, but if Arty had to have a superstition, this one was okay with her, though it did tempt her to call Dr. Westcott, the psychologist they consulted all those years ago about the rhinoplasty, to ask about what was going on in Arty's head. But she was crazy scared of what a psychologist would say, and how Arty would react if he found out, so she put off making the call.

One evening Arty drove into Pittsburgh for a meeting of the Vietnam Veterans Against the War from the tri-state area. He came back dejected. "There were over a hundred guys there, Jen, but there was so much bullshit over rank and medals and who had it worse and nobody could agree on what to do. But they loved 'Gotta Save Pittsburgh,' and I passed out tapes. Maybe they can spread it around. And I made a list of all the open-mics and places to play that anybody knew about."

Arty got maps from AAA, looked up addresses in the phone books in the library, and traced out routes to over twenty bars with open-mics from Wheeling to Pittsburgh to Youngstown. But after only two nights he told her, "This isn't working, Jen. Driving an hour or two each way for ten-minutes in front a few barflies is not going to make a difference."

Radio was his best shot, and he had a radio-ready version of the song with "bitch" and "shit" bleeped out. He went back to the library, plotted out routes to radio stations, and drove all over the area dropping off tapes and following up with phone calls. The answer was always the same; the programmers and DJs all told him it was "Too radical."

He went to the Decatur County Democratic Party's headquarters on "The Diamond," Milltowne's town square, to volunteer and came back bummed out by how desolate the core of the city had become. "I can't believe how many storefronts are vacant, Jen. When I was growing up downtown was busy as hell. Now there's nobody on the sidewalks."

He began wearing a McGovern button everywhere, which really

pissed off his father. He did canvassing in the morning, and in the afternoons went fishing or canoeing, played guitar, and started trying to write, not only songs, but short stories, poetry, political opinion pieces, maybe even the proverbial "Great American Novel." Who knew what might pop out?

One day she came home to Arty's shouts of, "Jen, I got a gig! Jen, I got a gig!"

"A gig?"

"Yeah, a bar where I did an open-mic is auditioning new acts and called to see if I wanted to try out. If I can keep people in their seats on an off-night, they might bring me back on a weekend."

"You mean you'd be getting paid?"

"Five bucks a set plus tips. I try out tomorrow night. It's right downtown, right in the city. Will you come?"

She met him at a new bar called Cicero's, in Market Square, a mile or so from her job. It was a Happy-Hour crowd right off the elevators of the downtown office towers loosening up after a long day.

Arty asked the manager for a small table at the very back of the bar. "I don't want you too close, Jen. You'll distract me. But will you help me out if I call you up for a song?"

"No, Arty. Please. You've got to do this on your own because I won't always be around."

They shared an order of Buffalo wings and garlic fries and a pitcher of Iron City beer. As he filled their glasses she asked, "So are you nervous?"

"No, not really. I did this every night in the EM Club in Dam Luc for months."

Arty was one of three singers trying out. He went on first, at seven. The stage consisted of a small riser, a spotlight, two mics, and an empty beer pitcher with a TIPS sign in it. He asked the audience what they wanted to hear, and when someone called out a song he knew, he would sing it—songs by James Taylor, Bob Dylan, the Beatles, the Kingston Trio, John Denver, Simon and Garfunkel, and Peter, Paul and Mary. His style was perfect for the nachos-and-beer crowd. Jenny had never seen Arty perform in front of an audience, and he was as intimate and fun as anybody could be. His rapport with the audience was terrific.

"I only have time for one more," he told the crowd. "I got back from Vietnam a few weeks ago, and over there the most popular song on the juke box captures everybody's dream of hopping a Freedom Bird back to the World. So I want you to imagine you're not in the most happening bar in Pittsburgh. Instead, imagine you're at a hell-hole called Dam Luc, deep in the Mekong delta just a few miles from Cambodia. You're sweating in the jungle heat and you're sick of the mud and the mosquitoes and the monsoon and the mortar attacks. You're off-duty killing time drinking piss-warm three-two Black Label beer in the Enlisted Mens' club when the bartender yells 'Last call' and 'Leaving on a Jet Plane' comes on the jukebox and everybody sings along as loud as they can. So I want you all to sing along as loud as you can."

By the end of the song most of the crowd was singing, and they applauded and gave him cheers and bravos. As Arty came off the stage Jenny was shocked to see several women rush up and fawn all over him. One stuck what looked like a folded bar napkin in his shirt pocket. She felt a pang as she realized how even an unknown troubadour with a guitar was catnip to groupies. *Groupies*!

Arty made his way back to their table, followed by a waitress carrying the tip-jar as the next performer took the stage. He sat down, took a long swig of his beer, and said, "What did you think, Jen?"

Fighting the urge to reach over and pull the napkin out of his pocket and read it out loud, Jenny said, "You were terrific, Arty."

He was counting his tips when the manager came to the table, handed him a five dollar bill and said, "You were okay up there, McGill. What's your take?"

"Looks like eighteen and change."

"That's better than most," said the manager. "If you want to stick around, you can go on again at ten and we'll see how you do with a late crowd."

"You bet!"

Jenny looked at her watch. "Arty, I have to be up at six." She gave him a kiss, wished him luck, and drove to the cottage, worrying. He had come clean to her about sleeping with whores in Vietnam and the houseboat girl in California. She could accept that because it was the war and they had never made a commitment. But *groupies*?

Thinking about the women who had thrown themselves at him like B-movie harlots kept her awake. If she hadn't been there he could have had his pick. Maybe after she left, he had? She tossed and turned, watching the luminescent dial on the clock. One-thirty; two; two-fifteen; two-thirty. Where was he? With a groupie?

He came in after three, wildly excited. "Jenny, I kept the bar full till last-call and made another forty in tips! They want me to do three sets this Friday, Jen, and if I do as well as I did tonight it could be a steady gig. I might not need a real job!"

She watched him undress and toss his clothes on the chair, and when he went outside to take a final leak, she hopped out of bed and looked in his shirt pocket for the napkin the woman had left, but it was gone. She sniffed his shirt for perfume, but hours in a smokey bar had imbued it with the foul stench of tobacco smoke.

She took the tube of body lotion from her make-up kit and lubricated her labia. When he slipped into bed she snuggled up and said, "You've had a big night. You just lie still be quiet."

"Uh...."

"I said hush up." She cuddled in closer and nipped his ear-lobes and neck. She got on her hands and knees and hovered her torso over his, dangling her breasts in circles, her nipples ever-so-lightly touching his chest and abdomen.

She slipped her hand down, gently massaged his balls, palmed his rapidly engorging cock, and began softly stroking. She licked and kissed her way down around his belly-button and sucked on his hard-on, and when he was primed and ready she straddled him, lowering herself onto his erection. She wriggled him in deep, squeezed her vagina tight, whispered, "Let me do all the work," and proceeded to fuck his eyeballs out because she felt he totally deserved it.

Chapter 23

The Future Lies Ahead

THE NEXT WEEK ARTY'S MOM INVITED THEM FOR SATURDAY DINNER, AND Arty and his father instantly got into a fight. After politely saying hello to her, his father turned to Arty, scowled, pointed at Arty's McGovern button and said, "Do you have to wear that damn thing everywhere you go, Arthur? How many times have I told you, a salesman never talks religion or politics? We're in the business of selling Cadillacs to Republicans and Chevys to Democrats."

"So get Tommy a Nixon button to balance us out. And you can make it an ad campaign in the *Gazette*. Or better yet, a billboard. Here's the headline: Civil war at McGill Motors—brother versus brother. I can see the photo now: There's me in my uniform flashing a peace sign and Tommy in a coat-and-tie waving a flag."

"Dammit, Arthur," said his father, "why do you always have to be such an assenheimer? Now that you're an adult it's *really* annoying."

"Thanks, Dad. That must mean I'm doing something right."

"McGovern's got no chance, Arthur. He's deserves to lose. He's a damned peacenik."

"Dad, listen to me. Nixon stretched out the war on purpose to make sure he wins the election and almost twenty thousand guys my age are dead because of it. Kissinger's peace talks in Paris are a joke. I was in Vietnam, Dad, but you think you're the expert and nobody has ever been able to tell you a goddamn thing. You're Mr. Know-It-All. So what do you say we all shut up about the election and the war so we can get through dinner without killing each other in front of Jenny. Okay?"

There was a pause as they pondered the proposition until Arty said, "So…it's agreed—no war—no election. Good. So how about the Pirates? They're five games up in their division. Can you score us some tickets, Dad? I haven't seen the new stadium yet."

"I haven't seen it either," Jenny said hoping the change of subject would calm his father down.

"For the girl with the secret nose-job," his father said, "anything is possible. Let me see about getting us all a box for a day-game. You can bring your family, Jenny, and we'll make it a reunion."

Talking about baseball made dinner go much better. When they moved to the living room after dinner Arty went upstairs and got the Guild guitar out of his bedroom closet. "I'm taking the Guild out to the cottage, Mom. And can we borrow your typewriter? I'm doing some writing, and Jenny brings a lot of stuff home from work."

"Yes, of course" said his mother, "but I thought you had the guitar you brought back with that peace-sign thing on it out there?"

"You can never have too many guitars, Mom."

Just before eight Tommy said, "It's time," and turned on the TV.

"Time for what?" Arty said. "I haven't seen much TV in a year."

"It's called *All in the Family*," Tommy said. "It's about a guy who doesn't like Jews or blacks or hippies and loves the war. He reminds me of Dad."

"That's enough Tommy," said his mother.

Jenny said, "It takes on controversial topics and makes you laugh. Cate and I watch it every week."

In that episode, the main character, Archie Bunker, opposes a candidate for local office because she's a woman and women "belong in the kitchen," and calls her, "Just another loudmouth liberal who never knows when to shut up."

"You're right, Tommy," Arty said. "He is a lot like Dad. The only difference is Dad drinks martinis and this guy drinks beer."

On the drive back to the cottage Jenny said, "I'm worried about our families getting together."

"No kidding. They'll all expect us to tell them we're engaged or something, and I'm not ready to even think about it, Jen, and you have another year of law school."

There was no correct response, so she said, "You haven't really told me anything about what You are planning to do, Arty. All you've said is I don't know–I don't know–I don't know. It worries me."

"I know now I'd hate being a lawyer, and I'm not the type to kiss-ass up the corporate ladder. Maybe I'll get a masters in creative writing and teach English or go into advertising or journalism or…*something*. I need time to think."

"You'd be a great litigator, Arty. You're really good on your feet."

"I wouldn't be a good liar for something I don't believe in, Jen. It's the biggest part of the job. I used to think all you needed to get over was the proper amount of bullshit. I never thought of it as lying, but ever since Nam I can't put up with anybody's bullshit...even my own."

They were eager to show off the cottage to their families. Arty went first, inviting his parents, grandparents and his brother for a Sunday afternoon Italian feast prepared by Jenny. In all her time dating Arty, she had never had the use of a kitchen; this was her first opportunity to show him and his whole family that she could cook with the best.

For the main course, she made lamb lasagna following the family recipe Mama Antonia brought to America from the rugged province of Abruzzo, which was famous for having the best marinara in all of Italy, and everybody raved. Later, Arty took his mother and grandmother out on the creek, the first time either of them had ever been in a canoe. In the evening, Arty built a fire in the fire pit and she and Arty sang them a few songs. As they were leaving, the McGills took turns hugging her and telling her how much they loved her cooking and her singing. The day could not possibly have gone any better.

The next Saturday, they hosted her mom and dad and two out of three of her brothers and their wives and her three young nephews. She knew Arty got on well with her dad, but he had never met her brothers, and they could be idiots. Except for Thanksgiving and Christmas dinners, she hadn't seen much of them for years, so she wasn't sure how they felt about the war or the election. But there were no scenes, Arty took all the men to a fishing hole, and her nephews had a great time swimming and rafting in the creek. In the evening, Arty grilled the fish they'd caught along with steaks and burgers and hot dogs and corn from the Amish roadside stand. At dusk as they sat by the fire pit, she and Arty performed a few songs and Arty got all of the Abruzzis, even her nephews, singing together on her mom's favorite song, "Que Sera Sera."

Two weeks later, Arty's father got twelve box-seat tickets behind the Pirate dugout for a Sunday afternoon game against Cincinnati, compliments of the Milltowne branch of Mellon Bank: six for the McGills and six for the Abruzzis. All the Abruzzis who had been at the 1960 game were there except her brother, Nicky, who was in the Navy, so she gave his ticket to her eldest nephew, ten-year old Dom.

In addition to Arty's father and grandfather, there was his mother, brother, and grandmother. She and Arty had been worried about how their fathers would get along, but right off the bat they got into war stories about Patton and Eisenhower. To Jenny and Arty's great relief, nobody in either family said anything about marriage.

Jenny wanted the summer to go on and on and on, like when she was a kid at Camp Tioshango. Her only concerns were Arty's episodes of melancholy and brooding. He looked terrific; stronger than in college, still thin, but no longer skinny. His beard was now fully grown; it was light and he kept it neatly trimmed, which made him look like a grad student, and his hair hung over his ears in a shaggy mop-top on its way to becoming a ponytail. All in all, he was a respectable semi-hippie who understood her sense of fun better than any guy she had ever met. Could she actually be in love?

There was no TV reception at the cottage, so their news from Vietnam came from the radio, magazines and newspapers. They followed the peace talks in Paris and he explained the maps in *Time* and *Newsweek* depicting the fighting of the ongoing "Easter Offensive." A minor scandal called "Watergate" was also in the news once in a while.

One evening as she walked in from work he said, "Jen, will you come with me to meet Frankie's family? I can't put it off any longer."

He had mentioned many times how guilty he felt about avoiding them. "I need you there, Jen. I don't know how they'll react. I mean, Frankie and his mom are both in the song. And there's his little brothers. I just don't know how they'll take it."

"But they like you, don't they?"

"Yeah, but it's not like with Mulligan's mom and dad. I've gone on fishing trips with them. I've never really talked politics or the war or anything with Frankie's parents."

Jenny had never met Frankie, though Arty had played her tapes of them jamming in high school and shown her photos of the band; she could see why girls called him "The Polish Elvis." She asked, "What are his parents like? What's his father do?"

"He's a mailman. His mom is just his mom. They're down to earth. His brothers are Jeff and Jerry. They're maybe nine or ten now, something like that. I haven't seen any of them since the funeral."

The Dombrowski's two-story, yellow-brick house was similar to the three-story red-brick house where she grew up, and the neighborhood was much like her own. Arty took her by the hand, peered in through the screen door, and called, "Hello! Anybody home?"

"Who's there?" came a woman's voice.

"Art McGill, Mrs. Dombrowski."

"*Stick*! Oh my!" A woman rushed out and gave Arty a hug. "Thank

God you're safe and well."

"Thank you, Mrs. Dombrowski. This is my good friend, Jenny."

Jenny said, "Glad to know you," and they shook hands.

Arty asked, "How are Jeff and Jerry? They should be, what, fifth grade or so by now?"

"They're at Camp Kon-O-Kwee all week. Jeff will be in fourth-grade and Jerry in fifth. Oh Stick, I'm so glad you're back. Thank God! Do you know anything more about Mike Mulligan? I heard he's a father."

"He's still missing-in-action, but he's going to be okay, I can feel it. Little Mike is his spitting image, another carrot top."

"What's the mother like?" Frankie's mom asked.

"Catherine? Uh...she's a carrot top too, and, uh...."

Jenny came to the rescue. "She's my best friend, Mrs. Dombrowski. No baby could have a better mother."

"That's very comforting. Thank you, Jenny."

Frankie's dad came out and shook Arty's hand. "Stick, it's great to see you. I read in the paper you were back."

"I've been meaning to stop by, but I just wasn't ready. I'm not sure I'm ready now. But I'd like you to meet my very good friend, Jenny Abruzzi."

Frankie's dad gently shook her hand, smiled and said, "In case you haven't figured it out, young lady, Stick here is a bit of a flake, but he's basically okay." Then he turned to Arty. "The paper said you have a Purple Heart and a Bronze Star."

"It was nothing, Mr. Dombrowski, really. I was pulling a general out of a downed chopper and got hit in the ass with some shrapnel. That's all it was. No heroic stuff at all."

Frankie's father said, "Someone told me you've been singing an anti-war song and Frankie's in it.

"Yes, sir. Before anything else, I've got to do it for you. If you hate it and want to kick me out, better sooner than later." He pulled a cassette out of his pocket and handed it to Frankie's mom. "Here's a studio version I'm trying to get on the radio."

"Why should we hate it?" she asked as she accepted the tape.

"Because I'm trying to tell the truth about the war as I see it, and I don't know how you and Mr. Dombrowski see it. But I want to do it for you in person. Let me get my guitar from the car."

Frankie's mom said, "No, Stick, wait. Play one of Frankie's. He'd want you to."

Frankie's dad said, "Let me get us all a beer and I'll meet you down in the rec-room."

The walls of the rec-room were covered with photos of performances and band rehearsals. There was a dart board, a couch, a TV, a bar with three stools, and a ping-pong table.

Frankie's mom opened a sliding door revealing a closet stuffed with guitar cases, amps. microphone stands and boxes of electronics. "Jeff moved into Frankie's room, so now he and Jerry each have their own. All of Frankie's equipment is here, his guitars and everything else."

"Aren't they playing, Mrs. Dombrowski?" Arty asked.

"I've tried to encourage them," Frankie's mom said. "At their age Frankie was copying songs off the radio and practicing like the dickens, but they just want to watch TV and play football. Times were different. Maybe it's too much television, I don't know."

"Frankie put every dime he made into guitars, Jen," Arty said as he pulled out a case. "He had a Strat *and* a Les Paul and he could never decide which one he liked best." He opened the case and held up a guitar for her to see. "This is his main acoustic, a Martin D-38. It's the one he brought when he hitchhiked up to see me the last time we...the last time we played together."

Jenny thought Arty might break into tears as he put the guitar back in the case, but Frankie's dad came down the stairs just in time and handed them all cans of Iron City beer. "Frankie told us he had a great time that weekend. He said he met a girl he really liked."

"Yes, Annie Chambers," Arty said. "She was last year's Homecoming Queen. He only knew her for a couple days. The hardest thing I ever had to do was tell her about Frankie."

Arty opened another case and took out a guitar with a flaming-orange sunburst finish. "Is it okay if I play his Les Paul, Mrs. Dombrowski? It's been years."

"Of course, Stick."

Jenny sat on a bar stool as Frankie's mom and dad settled in on the couch. Arty plugged in an amp and tuned up. He set the volume and gain low. "I've got a little act I do before I get into the song," Arty said. "The audience needs context."

Jenny watched Frankie's parents closely, just as worried as Arty was about how they would react. Frankie's mom teared up, and at the line about shining up his old guitar Frankie's father gripped his wife's hand.

When Arty finished Frankie's mom said, "I think that's the greatest tribute to Frankie that ever could be." She got up and hugged Arty, saying, "Thank you, Stick, thank you. You…you've made it almost make sense somehow."

Frankie's dad said, "Stick, all I can say is keep it up. Frankie would kick my ass if I didn't tell you to keep going."

"Thank you, Mr. Dombrowski, that really means a lot."

Arty started to take the guitar strap off his shoulder until Frankie's mom said, "Wait, Stick, sing something else for us. I don't think we've heard you play since you and Frankie went away to college."

"Uh, sure, okay," Arty said. "What do you want to hear?"

"Something Frankie would have liked," said Frankie's dad.

"In that case, I'll do every grunt's favorite song. I sang it a lot over there in the EM Clubs. Jenny, will you help out?"

She and Arty sang "Leaving on a Jet Plane," and Frankie's mom said, "Oh Stick, that was wonderful. You two are just terrific. Have you been playing in public?"

"No, just for friends and family," Arty said. "Jenny's going back to law school in couple of weeks."

"So what are you going to do, Stick," Frankie's dad asked. "If I recall, you wanted to be a lawyer too."

"Yes sir, but that was before I went to Nam."

"So what are your plans?" his dad asked.

"For now, I just want to get used to being back. I've done some open-mics, and I landed a Friday night gig through Labor Day. The tips are pretty good. Next year will take care of itself."

"Why not start up the Dynamos again?" said Frankie's dad.

Arty looked surprised. "Without Frankie?"

Turning somber, Frankie's mom said, "Life goes on, Stick. You've got to think about the future. You've got your whole life ahead of you. Besides, it was you who came up with the Dynamos name, wasn't it?"

"Yeah, but I just played rhythm and sang back-up. Frankie was the front man. Without him there was no band. He was always on my case about my playing. I was lucky he didn't kick me out."

"Oh Stick, you know it wasn't like that at all," Frankie's mom said with a laugh. "You sang so well together. He just thought you were lazy and should practice more."

Arty chuckled and said, "He was right about that."

"Well," said Frankie's mom, "why don't you take his guitar and do Frankie justice with it. But you have to promise to practice."

Arty seemed confused. "I...I don't understand."

Frankie's dad said, "He always told me that him on lead with his Stratocaster and you playing rhythm on his Les Paul made the sound he wanted. He would have wanted you to have it."

Arty flushed, embarrassed. "No, no, I couldn't...I...what about Jeff and Jerry when—"

Frankie's dad dismissed the objection with a wave of his hand. "They've got his Martin and his Strat and the old Silvertone if they show any interest. You know what his guitars meant to Frankie. Jeff and Jerry were too young to understand."

"Oh, I couldn't...I—"

"Of course you can, Stick," said Frankie's mom. "Frankie would have wanted you to have it. But only if you promise to practice."

Catherine strapped Little Mike into the car-seat as the head butler put her luggage in the trunk of the '67 Mustang that she'd bought just yesterday at a used car lot. Her treasured '62 Corvette, waiting in storage in a New Haven garage, had no back-seat and would not be practical for a single mother with a new baby.

She'd spent all day at car dealerships trying out the new models. She had her criteria: It had to have a back seat for Little Mike's car seat; it had to be fun to drive, with a four or five-speed stick-shift on the floor; it had to be a convertible; and being from Michigan, it had to be American-made. But in recent years American cars, even the new Corvettes, had grown boxy and bloated. A six-year-old '67 Mustang was the only American-made car she could find, new or used, that felt right. She decided that she would drive it in the coming year and let Jenny use the Corvette to make up for the babysitting Jenny was sure to be doing. But she vowed to never give the Corvette away or sell it. It would be Little Mike's surprise present on his sixteenth birthday.

In the morning of the Thursday before Labor Day, Catherine said good-bye to her parents at the estate in Grosse Point, and headed east for the drive to Milltowne. The plan was to stay the weekend at Jenny and Art's cottage and spend quality time with Little Mike's grandparents. On Monday, she and Jenny and the baby would drive to New Haven to reclaim their apartment from the summer subletters. The following week, they would both begin classes. It was all planned out.

Catherine followed Jenny's directions and drove down a long gravel driveway. She saw a bearded guy with shaggy hair in an olive-drab Army shirt waving to her from the door of a nearby cottage. Was that Art? As he walked closer, except for his broad smile and the McGovern button on his shirt, he could have been another of the crazed Vietnam vets who were all over the news. If she had seen him crossing the street while she was stopped at a red-light, she would have rolled up the window and locked the door.

Catherine had talked on the phone to Art about Mike several times, but she had not been able to draw him out about what happened. She had only known Mike and Art for that one weekend, and even though Art's and Jenny's charts said that they were likely soul-mates, she worried that Art was not right for Jenny. Jenny had told her that Art was different since he'd come back from the war, smiling and carefree one day, with black, silent moods the next.

It was very confusing. Catherine had been seeing a new therapist, and had asked him why Art was so reluctant to talk. The therapist told her: "If his friend is missing, he probably feels what's called 'survivor's guilt.' You should be careful what you say to him. On the other hand, if you can get him to talk about it, it could be therapeutic for both of you."

She bought a high-end tape recorder with a shoulder-strap, the kind TV reporters used for interviews. Her plan was to tape a talk with Art face-to-face, so he couldn't put her off like he did on the phone. She would treat him with kid gloves, but she was determined to have a recording for Little Mike about what had happened in case Big Mike didn't come home.

Art gave her a warm hug and said, "It's really great you're here. The guest room is all made up, and I got my old baby crib out of the attic and bought mosquito netting like we used in Nam at the Army-Navy store. You've never seen mosquitoes if you haven't been to Nam."

"What a nice spot," Catherine said, motioning toward the creek. She did not want to talk about Vietnam. Not yet. "Where's Jenny?"

"She usually gets home a little after six."

Little Mike began fussing in his car-seat. "He's getting hungry," she said. "Is there a place we can sit?"

"Let's go out on the overlook. Is there anything I can do?"

"Yes. You can bring the baby bag and the carrier."

She took the baby out of the car-seat and carried him in his blanket as Art led them out to a picnic spot with several chairs, a picnic table, a fire pit and a stone bar-b-que. A portable radio on the table had a baseball game on.

He turned off the radio as she settled into a chair, pulled up her blouse, and nestled the baby close. "I'm trying to train him to want the bottle, but he's stubborn."

"Ha, just like his father," Art said. "Never give up a good thing."

Catherine felt herself blushing. Mike was much too evolved to ever make such an insensitive, sexist comment like that. Wasn't he?

"So have you heard any news?" Art asked.

Catherine shook her head. "Nothing. The Navy keeps telling his mom and dad there's no way to know if the Viet Cong have him until prisoners are repatriated. But the talks just keep dragging on and on."

Art said, "Nixon's gonna have Kissinger make a deal before the election. You wait and see. He'll be home before you know it."

"I don't want to wait, Art!" she half-shouted in a surprise rush of frustration. "I just want the war to be over so Mike can come home."

He seemed taken aback; he hung his head and said, "Yeah, me too."

"I'm sorry, Art, I don't mean to take it out on you," she said, angry with herself for forgetting about his survivor's guilt. "It's just that I get so...so *mad* when I think about the whole stupid politics of it. The war never made any sense, and I don't know if he's ever coming back. I've got to think about the future, for me and for the baby, and until I'm sure about Mike I don't even know how to start."

They were both quiet for over a minute. The only sound was the soft gurgling of the creek.

When Little Mike finished, she wiped his chin and gave him his pacifier. Finally she said, "I love being near the water. Everything smells so fresh."

Art cheered up. "If you leave your window open at night you can hear the creek while you're in bed."

"It sounds very peaceful, Art," she said, glad they were conversing again. "Jenny says you're working for the McGovern campaign."

"Yeah, I've been knocking on doors and playing at a few rallies and arguing with my father."

"Do you really think he has a chance?"

The corners of his mouth turned down and he let out a long sigh. "The polls don't look good, but we can't give up. And if we do get four more years of Nixon, then we deserve him. Say, is it okay if I play you a song? It's about Vietnam."

Perhaps this was the perfect opportunity to get him on tape without making him feel self-conscious? It would be just the two of them and Little Mike until Jenny arrived, and she might not get another chance to be alone with him. After he sang his song she would just let the machine keep running and try to get him talking.

"I'd love to hear it, but let me put the baby down first. He'll sleep for a couple hours if we're quiet. And I need to use the ladies room."

"We only have an outhouse."

"I'm a big girl, Art."

He showed her to the guest room; she tucked the baby into the crib, used the outhouse, and washed up in the kitchen sink while he brought her bags in from the car and opened two bottles of Rolling Rock beer. She put a roll of film in her camera, and as she was removing the tape recorder Art said, "There's no need for that. I have a good studio version."

"But this will be my version," she said as she put in a new ninety-minute cassette.

He brought a guitar case and an amplifier out to the overlook, she snapped photos as he plugged into an extension cord and tuned up. "This is a Les Paul," he told her. "It belonged to our good buddy, Frankie Dombrowski. His folks gave it to me last month on the condition that I promise to practice. I talk about Frankie in the song."

"So have you been practicing, Art?"

"Yeah, quite a bit."

Art went into a presentation of a song about Pittsburgh, and before he was halfway through she found herself in tears. "Thank you, Art," she said when he finished. "You've made me sad and you've made me furious. Did Mike ever hear it?"

"No, I wrote it later," he said as he put the guitar back in the case. "And I didn't put him in it because he's coming back. He's the Mulligan Man."

"So, Art, you've never really told me much about what happened. I mean, just how did you to meet up over there? What did he actually say?

Jenny says you've quit smoking pot because Mike gave you an order. Is that true?"

"Yeah, he was reaming me out for smoking a joint on duty. Man, was he ever pissed. So we're standing on deck going forty miles an hour down the Mekong in a combat zone and he orders me to come to attention and shouts something like, 'Now listen up, asshole, and listen up good—you are not to touch any dope while you are under my command or I'll bust you myself. That's a direct order. Is that understood, Specialist McGill?'"

Art grinned and said, "So I clicked my heels gave him a Nazi salute and yelled, '*JAWOHL, Lieutenant Mulligan Man, sir*!' Ha, now that I think about it, it was right before I told him he was going to be a father."

"Please tell me all about it, Art, everything. My therapist says it will be good for me, and probably good for you too, and for Little Mike when he's older if Mike doesn't…well, you know."

Catherine watched as McGill slumped back in his chair, lit a cigarette, swigged on his beer, and said, "Okay."

Chapter 24

Holidays

Sunday, December 31, 1972

On cold, wintry nights over Christmas break Jenny had insisted that Arty get up with her when she needed to go. His job was to pull his grandmother's goosedown comforter off the bed and follow along while she led the way with the flashlight. They would put on their robes and shoes and crunch over the gravel path to the two-holer outhouse and huddle under the comforter. When she finished, they would sit for a while and watch the ice floes bobbing down the half-frozen creek in the moonlight.

They kept the window by the bed cracked open despite the cold so they could hear the soothing murmur of the creek and the spooky sounds of ice creaking and cracking in the current. In the deepest hours of the night, a barred owl often hooted his famous mating call: "Whoo cooks for you? Whoo cooks for you-all? Whoo cooks for you? Whoo cooks for you-all?"

It was snowing early one morning as they were returning from the outhouse when the clouds parted and the moon lit up the night in an iridescent, sparkling snowscape. She switched off the flashlight and they stood transfixed in the frosty air until she shivered, "Brrrr." He pulled her close, wrapped the comforter around them—tight, like a cocoon—and eased her down on the new-fallen snow and made love to her like they were a couple of Vikings.

The next day Jenny confided to her diary how much fun it had been sitting side-by-side like the early pioneers, pooping and pissing and farting and keeping each other warm as they watched the creek flow by. She leafed back through her diary, remembering the men she'd been with since that first time with Arty. They were all either stronger, smarter, cuter, or richer than Arty, but none was as interesting. She finally admitted to herself that she might—just might—be in love with him. Only her diary knew that it was his ability to make her break into belly laughs in the outhouse that had finally done the trick.

She had flown home for Christmas break planning to stay with him at the cottage and study for finals while Cate and the baby spent the holidays in Michigan with her parents. She couldn't help wondering if Arty had slept with any groupies since she'd last seen him, but their no-commitments relationship meant that neither could ask any questions.

She had been on a few dates herself that she would rather not mention. After they spent last summer learning what great sex any time you were in the mood was all about, she was suddenly four hundred miles away and she missed it. She felt conflicted, but not quite guilty, when on a whim she indulged herself a few weeks later. In an open relationship she didn't have to tell, so it wasn't really cheating, but it chilled her to think what old Father Zyhowski would say if she ever went back to confession.

One Saturday morning she had come back after a one-night stand and found Cate sitting on the couch cradling the baby. She flopped down next to her, sighed and said, "I can't believe I didn't see what an asshole he was until this morning. Why do I do these things?"

"I've told you before, Jennifer, you can't help yourself. You're a Scorpio, it's the sign of sex and passion. You can try to control it, but you can't fight it."

"Please Cate, you know I don't buy that stuff."

"It doesn't matter if you buy it or not," Catherine said as she put a towel on her shoulder and positioned the baby for burping. "I mean, look at me—I'm a Cancer, the sign of motherhood. You can't escape it."

Jenny was now just eleven months from turning twenty-five—*a quarter century old!* She would graduate in June and nothing was firmed up after that. Would she get a clerkship? Would she work in a law mill? If so, where: New York, Paris, Washington…Pittsburgh? Could she really live in Pittsburgh after Bryn Mawr and Yale? How would she repay her loans wherever it was? Could she be a lawyer and a mother? Did she even want to be a mother *or* a lawyer? For the first time ever she was a little afraid of the future.

The news since she had last seen Arty had been mostly bad:

—Terrorists had attacked the Olympics in Munich killing nine Israeli athletes.

—The last mill in Milltowne, Babcox Tubing, where Arty had worked on summer vacations to pay his college tuition, closed down, putting Mike's father out of a job. Arty mailed her an editorial in the *Milltowne Gazette* lamenting the closure: "If Nashville is 'The Buckle of the Bible Belt,' then the Pittsburgh area is 'The Buckle of the Rust Belt.'"

—Even good news turned sour: the Pirates had won their division and Roberto Clemente became only the eleventh player in the history of baseball to get 3,000 hits in the regular season, doing it in his very last at-bat, but they lost in the playoffs and missed the World Series. The Series marked exactly a year since Mike had gone missing. She could hear the ache in Arty's voice when he talked to her on the phone, "We were gonna listen to the sixth game together that night when the shit came down. I keep wondering if he even knew the Pirates won last year."

All she could say was, "Try not to think about it, Arty."

—With only weeks to go before the election, Henry Kissinger dropped an "October Surprise" at the peace talks in Paris when he announced: "We believe peace is at hand."

"Yeah," Arty told her, his voice rising in anger, "it's Tricky Dick's 'secret plan to win the war' just in time to guarantee his re-election. The fucker could have ended it four years ago and Frankie would still be alive and Mulligan wouldn't be missing."

—After Nixon crushed McGovern in the election, all Arty could say was, "We get what we deserve, Jen. Four more years of Nixon. I think I'll give up on political songs for a while. Love songs and dance songs and weepy country ballads are where it's at."

—But peace was not at hand, and after the election was over Kissinger issued a long list of new demands and negotiations broke down. A month later, Nixon unleashed waves of B-52 bombers over Hanoi and Haiphong that would become known as the "Christmas bombing" to try to compel the communists to return to the table.

—A massive earthquake in Managua, Nicaragua, killed 12,000 people, and reports were all over the news about how the officials of the Somoza dictatorship in Nicaragua were skimming relief supplies to enrich themselves at the expense of the victims.

On the home front, things had been going surprisingly well. Christmas Eve with his family and Christmas Day with hers had been fun. She tried not to show how disappointed she was that he had not even looked into applying to law school or graduate school. He had ten years to use up his GI Bill when he did go back, so she wasn't too worried about his long-term future, career wise. Or was it *their* future? Was she in love, or wasn't she? Did she want his babies? Tonight was New Year's Eve, a time for resolutions.

Arty's unemployment checks were due to end next week, but he had not applied for even a single job or looked at the want ads for a temporary job to tide him over—maybe bartending, or waiting tables. He had enough in the bank from his Army pay and had been making some money gigging as a solo act, but it was only one night a week and it wouldn't be enough once his savings ran out.

When he picked her up at the airport, he had what he seemed to think was great news. "I auditioned for an oldies band last week, Jen, and nailed it. We've been rehearsing like crazy. They're called The Keystoners and they gig almost every weekend. It's like a real job. And you can help."

She had heard good things about the band, which had played around the Pittsburgh area for several years. "Help? How?"

"I've got to learn a bunch of songs. Lots of Beatles and Elvis and Buddy Holly and Motown. We'll learn 'em together. It'll be great!"

She pretended to happy, but it wasn't a healthy lifestyle. Janis Joplin, Jimi Hendrix, and Jim Morrison were all dead at twenty-seven. Just playing in a local band meant getting home at four in the morning, sleeping past noon and lots of drugs. "I'm happy for you, Arty, but what do you really want to do? There's no future in an oldies band. You've been back for six months. You've got to start planning."

At first, she hadn't been sure about his ponytail. It took her a few days to conclude she liked him with his hair pulled back and showing his full face. It was more dignified than a shaggy mop-top, but both his and her parents hated it. "Loathed" was not too strong a word.

Two days before Christmas, a lightning bolt of great football news had super-charged the tri-state region and lifted the rusty gloom. The Steelers won their first-ever playoff game with a miraculous shoestring catch that would go down in football lore as "The Immaculate Reception." But no one in the area who wasn't in the stadium saw it except in reruns thanks to a TV blackout that kept it off the Pittsburgh stations. The next playoff was today, and it would be on TV, with the winner going to the Super Bowl.

Arty's father decided to throw a game-watching party for the employees and their families in the McGill Motors' showroom. The game was on a Sunday, and because Pennsylvania's strict "blue laws" decreed that it was immoral and illegal to sell either alcohol or cars on a Sunday, all the bars and car dealerships had to be closed for business. But there was no law against a car dealership throwing a party.

His mom said, "Arthur, maybe you and Jennifer can sing a few songs. We haven't seen you perform for a long time."

"No, that's not a good idea," said his father. "He pisses people off."

His mother glared at his father. "Well *I* want to show him off."

His father rolled his eyes. "It seems your mother wants to see you perform, Arthur. Very well. On one condition—you have to promise not to do any of that political crap of yours. Just do songs people like."

Arty grinned. "How about 'Jingle Bells,' Dad? Is that okay?"

His mom cut the argument short. "That will be fine, Arthur. There might be children there who don't care about football. You can get them to sing along like you used to do at those hootenannies. You were so good at that."

"Just remember," said his father, "those people work for us. Some of them are very religious, so you can't do anything dirty. Understand? And don't talk about the war. Nixon's bombing the bastards back to the peace table and nobody wants to hear about it. That's why Nixon won so big. Everybody's sick of hearing about the war."

"Your father's right," said his mom. "And please don't play that guitar you brought back with that peace-sign thing. It will only make people uncomfortable."

"Okay," Arty said, "you got it. It's 'Jingle Bells' and 'Auld Lang Syne.' No politics, no sex, no peacenik guitar, just New Year's cheer."

Today would be very busy. In addition to the Steelers game in the afternoon, that night Arty's college team was playing in the Sugar Bowl, but he was resigned to missing that game to play rhythm guitar in his first gig with the new band at a New Year's Eve bash.

"I'll go to the store and gas up," he said as he picked up the shopping list and gave Jenny a kiss on the cheek on his way out. "Nothing will be open tomorrow."

"What should I wear for this afternoon?" Jenny asked.

"It's just a football game. I'm going like this," he said, indicating his sneakers, jeans, Penn State sweatshirt and Army field jacket. "I'll be back in a couple hours to pick you up. We'll have plenty of time after the game to come back and change for the gig."

For working musicians, New Years Eve was always the most lucrative night of the year, and the band had rented tuxedos for the gig at an estate in Sewickley Heights for Pittsburgh's trust-fund crowd. Jenny had never seen him play in a band, had never seen him in a tux, and had never been anywhere with him where she could wear heels and pearls. On top of that, the bandleader had told Arty that she might be able to sing back-up on a couple of tunes. She hadn't sung in public in years and couldn't wait.

She was warming up on the piano when she heard someone knocking and a female voice calling, "Hello, anybody home? Hello." She peered out the kitchen window and saw a blonde in a ski-jacket and a stocking cap with a *Cal* logo. Where had she seen her before?

The woman was about her age and very pretty, but her face was drawn and tired, her makeup in need of serious attention. "Hi," said the woman when Jenny opened the door. "I'm looking for Art McGill. Is this the right place?"

Jenny sensed trouble. "He just left. Can I help you?"

The woman smiled. "You must be Jenny. You look just like your picture. He told me all about you."

"And who are you?"

"Maggie Lindquist," the woman said as she extended her hand. "I met him in California when he got back from Vietnam."

"Jenny Abruzzi," she said, accepting the handshake and recalling his photos and the tapes with the woman with the houseboat. The one he'd been fucking. "Are you the singer on those tapes he made?"

"Yup, that's me. Maggie of Maggie and McGill, or what's left of me after a week on the road."

As McGill pulled up to the cottage he was surprised to see a salt-splattered VW Squareback packed with luggage parked in the driveway. A sleeping bag and a guitar case were in the front seat. As he parked he saw the California plate and the DayGlo daisy. *Maggie*? What the…?

He opened his trunk and took out the tuxedo, picked up the bags of groceries in the front seat, and used his knee to slam the car door shut. Jenny appeared at the kitchen window and put her index finger to her lips signaling him to be quiet. Seconds later she slipped out the door and half-whispered, "The other half of Maggie and McGill is crashed in the guest room."

There was no mistaking the edge in her voice. Was that jealousy he heard? He had never known her to exhibit even a hint of jealousy, but then she was usually the most beautiful woman in the room so it was never an issue. He asked, "But what's she doing here?"

"She's moving to New York for grad school at NYU and got caught in a blizzard. I offered to make her breakfast but she'd just eaten and asked if she could get some sleep. She made me promise to wake her up as soon as you got back."

"I had no idea she was coming."

"So I've heard," Jenny said as she held the door open for him. "I told her about the game and the party tonight and invited her to stay."

"Great. What did she say?"

"She said she should probably just shower and keep on going."

"Well, we'll talk her out of that real quick," McGill said excitedly. "You don't mind if she stays, do you? I…uh, I kind of owe her."

"Owe her for what…a week of mercy fucks?"

McGill had never seen Jenny acting catty before, and boy was he thankful he had come clean about Maggie months ago so he didn't have to keep any lies straight.

"Come on, Jen. I told you all about it. It was nothing. I'd just got back from Vietnam. She's a friend, that's all."

"Yeah, so what's a friend for if not a mercy-fuck now and then?"

He put the groceries on the counter, tossed the tux over the back of the couch, and opened the door to the guest room. He gently shook her shoulder. "Maggie."

"Oh, hi Art." She got up and they embraced in an asexual, hippie hug, and she reached behind his head, jiggled his ponytail and giggled. "Would you look at this. And I like the beard. The last time I saw you, you were a sergeant. This is much better."

"You're as beautiful as I remember. Jenny says you're going to NYU. Congratulations."

"Thanks. It's a really unique program."

"I'm thrilled you're here," he said, "but why didn't you call?"

"My plan was to drive straight through and move in a few days early, but the blizzard closed the Interstate and I got stuck in a motel in Nebraska. Now the rental office is closed and I can't get the key until Tuesday. When I saw the 'Welcome to Pennsylvania' sign, I remembered you were from around here somewhere. I had your address and number from your letter, and the map showed Milltowne was pretty close. I tried to call, but it was busy. But that meant somebody was home, and the truck stop had a big truckers' map-book that showed your road. So I wrote down directions and took a chance."

McGill said, "Your timing couldn't be better. I'm in a new band and we've got a huge gig tonight. You and Jenny can sit in and sing backups. It'll be great."

Maggie said, "I don't think so, Art, I—"

"So what are you going to do?" McGill said. "Drive eight hours in the snow and ring in the New Year in a motel in New Jersey. Whoop-dee-doo. Come on, Maggie, we've got a guest room, and you'll get to see me in a tuxedo. The chance may never come again."

"I don't want to impose, I—"

Jenny said, "Don't be ridiculous. It'll be fun."

McGill gave Jenny a smile to let her know that he appreciated the gesture. "See, Maggie, you're not imposing, you're honoring us with your presence. I've been dreaming of getting you two together ever since I heard you at the open mic. We'll have a blast tonight and jam tomorrow, you and me on guitar and Jenny on piano. It'll be great."

Arty's "friend" agreed to stay for the party but begged off the football game to get a little more sleep, which was just fine with Jenny. She was flying back on Tuesday and she wanted time alone with him. She hadn't planned on a "friend" he'd been screwing dropping in from California. They needed to talk, but he kept being evasive. She had major decisions coming up and so did he, but he didn't seem to know it.

The day was sunny and balmy, almost seventy, more like the middle of May than the last day of December.

"Let's put the top down," Arty said as he put his Guild guitar in the back seat.

Jenny always enjoyed the drive into Milltowne through the gentle countryside of silos and barns and horse-drawn Amish buggies. She tied a scarf around her hair and sat in the middle, close to him, like teenagers going steady, and asked, "So what should I expect at this party?"

"It'll be like company picnics," Arty said. "The salesmen and mechanics will be bullshitting and boozing and the wives gossiping and lots of kids running around and Dad telling war stories."

Jenny had her own issue with his father and his stories. Last summer, she was at a party at his parent's house when his father introduced her to some guests, and when he told the story of "the girl with the secret nose-job" the guests all stared at her nose. The first chance she got she took him by the sleeve, tugged him aside, and growled in a fierce whisper, "Mr. McGill, if you say one more word about my nose ever again I swear I'll take the nearest drink and I'll throw it in your face and I'll never speak to you again. Never!"

He hadn't done it since.

They came to a farmhouse they had passed many times, but today it was surrounded by a dozen Amish buggies with the horses tethered to a railing like in a TV western. Several more buggies were lined up on the shoulder on the other side of the road waiting for a break in the traffic to cross the busy two-lane highway into the driveway. "What do you know," Arty said. "An Amish traffic jam."

"It's looks kind of dangerous," Jenny said.

"Yeah, buggies and cars don't mix. They need professional help."

He used the hand-signal everybody learned in Driver's Ed class to show the car behind him that he was slowing down. He came to a stop, shut the engine off, ran to the center of the other lane, and took charge by waving his hands high in the air and signaling "Halt!" in both directions. His Army field jacket seemed to give him an air of authority, almost like he was still directing traffic at the Pentagon.

When Arty was sure traffic was stopping, he put his hand to his mouth, gave a shrill, two-fingered whistle, pointed at the bearded driver of the lead buggy with one hand and at the entrance to the driveway with the other, and began vigorously waving for him to get going. The driver gave him a nod, flicked his reins, and the horse started across the road. The other buggies followed as Arty kept one hand pointed at the driveway and continuously motioned hurry-up-keep-going-hurry-up-keep-going with the other.

It was almost magical watching as six Amish families crossed right in front of her, not twenty feet away. She loved hearing the whinnies of the horses and the clippity-clopping of their hoofbeats on the pavement and watching the fresh-faced boys and bearded men in black coats and pants, white shirts and broad-brimmed black hats and the women and girls in white bonnets, black shawls and black dresses. It was as if they were having an Amish parade just for her.

When the buggies were safely across, Arty signaled for the cars in the other lane to proceed, gave a high thumbs-up to the cars behind them in their lane, hopped into the driver's seat and said, "Damn, Jen, that was fun."

As he started to drive away she squeezed his arm and said, "You did great, Arty. And they were fascinating. Both the men and the women. I'd never seen them up close before. I thought the women always wore blue dresses."

"I'm pretty sure it depends which sect they're in. I think the ones around here like to get dressed up in black on Sundays."

"So is that a church?"

"No, they don't have churches. They meet at somebody's house, a different one every week. That's probably what's going on."

She remembered an article in *Cosmo,* or maybe *Glamour,* about Amish life called "The Plain Folk," and asked, "I've read Amish men have to grow beards when they get married, but why don't they have mustaches? What's that all about?"

"It's because they're pacifists and hate the military," Arty said. "They were persecuted in Germany for refusing to be in the army. Back then, German soldiers all had mustaches, the fancier the better, so the Amish shaved theirs off just to show they were different."

"They do seem so different. I wonder what it's like being Amish."

Arty laughed and said, "*Boorrr*ing. I'd bet none of them know there's a Steelers playoff game today. And they can't smoke or drink or dance or go to movies or watch TV or play guitar or piano or anything."

"So they don't have any music?"

"Well, they're allowed to sing, but they think playing an instrument is a big ego trip to draw attention to yourself. And they only sing in unison. No solos to make you prideful because you have a better voice. They're big on humility."

As they drove away she noticed two teenage girls standing in the yard and staring at them from under their white bonnets. Jenny wondered what they felt at the sight of two young lovers in a jaunty convertible. Was it envy…or pity?

She remembered that Amish women were usually married by twenty and had an average of seven children, so if she'd been Amish, she'd have at least three by now. And they never cut their hair and were forbidden to wear make-up, jewelry, or bright clothing as it could make them prideful. She remembered the magazine photos of the hand-sewn Amish dolls with no facial features—no eyes, no ears, no mouths, no noses—so even Amish dolls would not be prideful. Amish women were definitely not the *Cosmo* type.

She suddenly flashed back a dozen years to the crinkled face of old Father Zyhowski poking his bony finger at her nose as he invoked the deadliest of the seven deadly sins: "Vanity is the root of pride, my child, and false pride has led many of God's children into the arms of Satan, and to the eternal damnation of the immortal soul."

The Amish went to far greater lengths than even old Father Zyhowski to quash the deadly sin of vanity before Satan could do his dirty work. If she'd been Amish, a nose-job would have been completely out of the question.

Chapter 25

Auld Lang Syne

THEY PASSED A MCGILL MOTORS' BILLBOARD WITH A PHOTO OF HIS FATHER decked out in a Santa suit sitting behind the wheel of a sporty red Chevy convertible with boxes of presents and a Christmas tree in the back seat. Five salesmen in coats and ties and red Santa hats stood around the car, smiling and waving. The banner headline read: *Santa says, When it comes to cars, Milltowne is McGilltown.*

"Can you see me up there, Jen?" Arty said. "Hawking Chevys in a Santa hat. Can you imagine me working for Dad doing *anything*?"

"No, Arty, I can't. The way you two go at each other I think you'll be much happier if you do something else." And if she were going to spend the rest of her life with him, so would she. She hadn't spent four years at Bryn Mawr plus three more at Yale and racked up almost a hundred thousand in student loans just to become the wife of a small-town car salesman with an overbearing father-in-law.

They pulled into the McGill Motors lot and saw *GO STEELERS!* filling the showroom display window in gold and black. A few young children, dragged to a boring party by their parents, were playing among the rows of cars. Eight or ten middle-aged men were standing outside the showroom enjoying the unseasonably warm day with drinks and cigarettes.

"Free booze brings them out early every time," Arty said as they parked. "They want to make sure they get theirs before it runs out."

As soon as Arty had turned fourteen and could legally work his father had him washing cars and changing tires after school and on Saturdays at "the garage," so he knew most of the employees by name. He grabbed his guitar case, took her by the hand, and as they walked up to them he said, "Hey, everybody. This is my good friend, Jenny. Jenny, say hi to the guys."

Somebody yelled, "Good is *right*!"

Jenny smiled, gave a little wave, and said, "Hi guys."

They all gave her a friendly greeting and one said to Arty, "Your mom says you're gonna sing for us."

Another guy yelled out, "We'll double what she's payin' if ya don't!"

Everybody laughed as Arty grinned and gave the guy the finger.

The doors of the showroom were swung wide open and a crowd was milling around inside. Gone were the shiny new 1973 Chevys and Caddys, and in their places were vinyl couches and chairs from the customer lounge and folding chairs from A-1 Rentals. Four men were hoisting a heavy console color TV with giant rabbit ears up onto the top of a desk. Two long folding tables were covered with tablecloths, paper plates, plastic utensils and lots of food: potluck dishes, pretzels, chips and dips. There was a keg of beer in a tub of ice beside two desks which had been pushed together to create a makeshift bar, with plenty of plastic cups, mixers, a bucket of ice and several fifths of cheap whiskey, gin and vodka from the State Store. The only wine was in a big punchbowl with a sign proclaiming it to be "Vinnie's Finest Dago Red."

Arty set his guitar case in a corner and got them each a beer. Jenny was politely listening as he joked around with a couple of salesmen when his father and mother came out from the back. "There you are, Arthur," said his father. "We need you to run down to Augustino's and pick up the pizzas. They're supposed to be ready at one."

"Where's Tommy?" Arty said. "He's the gofer now."

"He helped set everything up," said his mother, but he wants to be with his friends. I told him they could watch it in the den."

"Yeah, if I was sixteen I wouldn't want to be here either," Arty said. "Okay. Let's go Jen, it won't take long."

"No, let her stay," said his father. "She's never seen the garage. I want to show her around. Better get going, Arthur, or you'll miss the kickoff." His father took her by the arm and said, "Come along, Jenny, and I'll give you the grand tour. We'll start in the body shop."

It was apparent his father was much more interested in pumping her for information than showing her around. He quickly walked her through the lot, pointing out the wash bay, the twelve-stall shop with six hydraulic hoists, the parts-counter and the offices and led her down a hall to a door with a brass nameplate reading: Arthur B. McGill, Jr.

His office was about sixteen by twelve, with a large mahogany desk, a swiveling executive chair and two matching leather chairs in front of the desk. On the wall behind him was a framed aerial photo of McGill Motors along with photos of him in his Army uniform in front of the Eiffel Tower, his BA degree from Bucknell, a "Chevrolet Dealer of the Year 1965" plaque and various other family photos. On the desk next to the phone and the intercom were two framed photos, one of Arty's mom and a one of Arty with both his father and grandfather with Bob Hope and Bing Crosby at the World Series. She remembered her father snapping the picture with Arty's grandfather's Polaroid. It was odd how it made her feel connected. "Didn't my father take that, Mr. McGill?"

"I think that's right. Sit down Jenny, and make yourself comfortable."

Jenny had never truly talked to him one-on-one. There was a strong family resemblance between the three McGills in the photo—Arty had been twelve, his father in his forties and his grandfather in his sixties. Is that how Arty would look when he was older? She tried to imagine his father and grandfather with beards and ponytails but she couldn't.

After a few feeble tries to get her talking with questions like, "So how's it going with you two?" he got to the point. "Jenny, we're worried about Arthur. He doesn't seem to have any goals any more. Any drive."

"So is that why you arranged this little chat?" she said with a smile.

"We've never really had a chance to talk," he said, "you and I, and if I didn't corner you today who knows when I might get another shot at you. So can we talk?"

He had her cornered all right. "Of course."

"We just don't understand what's gotten into Arthur, he's—"

"Mr. McGill, he just got back from the war."

"It's been six months, Jenny. It seems to us he's lost his…his I don't know what. He used to dream of becoming a lawyer. He never missed an episode of *Perry Mason* and he read all the novels. Being a lawyer was all he ever talked about wanting to do. We encouraged him. We thought it was an incentive for him to do well in school. And for the most part, he did. Except for math of course. He was always reading newspapers and history books and playing that damned guitar but never cracked his math book. So a career in law made sense to us. But now he's a hippie who doesn't want to do anything."

"That's not true, he's—"

"Why with his military record in the MPs and his medals he could walk into any law-enforcement organization in the country and get a job tomorrow."

"I'm certain he never wanted to be a cop, Mr. McGill. And the war changed him. It's not that he doesn't want to be a lawyer, he doesn't want to be part of the system."

"The system? Just what the hell does that mean, Jenny?"

Something Arty said to her on the beach in Wildwood on their very first date popped into her head. "I remember him once telling me he didn't want to spend his weekends riding on a power lawnmower, Mr. McGill. And this was years before he went to Vietnam. I think he's afraid of going into business because it would make him ordinary. He's always wanted to be something…something more than that."

"Every boy wants to be Superman or President when he's young, Jenny. That's beside the point and you know it. He needs to grow up. He can pay someone to mow the damn lawn until his kids are big enough and then he can put them to work, teach them responsibility like I did with him and Tommy. Hell, he could learn the business so his mother and I can spend winters in Florida like his grandparents do. I'm fifty-four and not getting any younger, Jenny. He could be running things here sooner than he thinks. It's not glamorous, but it's steady and you're your own boss."

Arty had often told her that when his father got wound up he talked in circles, jumping from subject to subject and conflating everything into gibberish. This was the first time she had experienced it. She tried to be truthful but diplomatic. "I don't think that's what he wants to do, Mr. McGill. He's always told me that Tommy would be better at it."

"Of course Tommy would be better at it. Tommy's better at everything but that damned guitar. Thank God he didn't get into that. That's the point. Tommy's a real competitor—golf, tennis, basketball. Arthur never was. Arthur was a bullshitter, which is why he'd be a great salesman. But it doesn't matter because Tommy's still in high school and Arthur has to start doing *something* with his life."

"Mr. McGill, he just got back from the war. He doesn't have to make that kind of commitment right now. He can go to graduate school on the GI Bill and—"

"And do what? Teach history or poetry to a bunch of pimply college kids? If he's not going to go to law school or get an MBA he's just wasting his time. There's no money in teaching. He'll be twenty-five soon, and he's been out of the Army for six months and he's done nothing. Zero. That's not how he was raised. He's always worked. A day's work for a day's pay. I made sure he learned it just like my father made sure I learned it. I'm very disappointed in him, Jenny. He's a war hero, for crying out loud. If he'd shave and get a haircut, he could run for city council and he'd win. I wouldn't even care too much if he did it as a Democrat—at least he'd be doing *something*. He's got the whole world in front of him and he sits out there up the creek with that damned guitar and thinks it's a goddamned paddle."

"He's getting better, Mr. McGill. He's been writing and tonight he has a gig with a new band. He's even rented a tuxedo."

"So he told me," he said with a dismissive sneer and a shake of his head. "Do you know how banks and credit agencies evaluate risk, Jenny?"

"Uh…no, not exactly. Why?"

"I look at applications for car loans every day. Every buyer has to state his occupation, where he works, and how much he makes. Do you know what the *least* credit-worthy occupation is?"

"No, I—"

"Then I'll tell you what it is. It's 'musician,' Jenny. Musician. It's the least credit-worthy occupation. Dead last. Is that what you want in a husband?"

"We haven't said anything about getting married, we—"

"Well you damn well should be saying something about it. His mother and I are expecting it and so are your mother and father. Ever since they met last summer, my wife and your mother have been bickering about wedding details. You've been dating for how long now…five…six years?"

The news that her mother had been conspiring with Arty's mother about a wedding stunned her. "It's…it's really none of your business or my parent's business, Mr. McGill. But just so you know, he hasn't asked me and I don't expect him to. We have an open relationship."

"Then maybe you should ask him. Or tell him you're dumping him. That will get his attention. Sometimes he needs a good swift kick in the ass when he doesn't know it's coming to get him motivated. And what about you? What do you want? You're graduating, aren't you? Then what?"

"I'm not sure. I have interviews lined up when I get back to school."

"You'd better ask yourself if you're willing to be the breadwinner if he keeps up this musician crap. And what about him? What's he tell you he's going to do when you decide what you're going to do? Is he going to follow you around with his guitar singing in bars for tips? He hasn't said a word to us. You know his unemployment runs out next week and he hasn't even looked for a job."

"Yes, I—"

"He's using the war as an excuse, you know. He's always been on the lazy side and this just gives him an excuse. He—"

"That's not fair, Mr. McGill, he—"

"Fair doesn't matter. It's what I see with my own eyes that counts with me. If you're going to be with him you've got to give him direction. You've got a real head on your shoulders for a female, and you've got a bite behind your bark. I know, I've felt it. You've got to take the wheel. He smokes like a chimney and drinks like a fish. He always has at least two or three cocktails every time he comes to the house. And the last time I was out at his place, his trash was filled with beer cans."

He was right about the drinking, as Arty had acquired the Joe Six-Pack habit, but she came to his defense. "He's quitting smoking, Mr. McGill. It's his New Year's resolution. Today's his last day."

"Good, then he won't be bumming off me and his mother all the damn time. But I'll believe it when I see it. Tell me, is he doing drugs? Don't lie to me, Jenny, please. How bad is it? If you watch the news, it seems like everyone over there is into the bad stuff and then brings it home."

"No, he's not, I'm sure of it," she said, downplaying the pot and omitting any mention of the LSD they once dabbled in. "We both smoked a little marijuana in college, but he hasn't had anything illegal since Mike Mulligan gave him that order. He thinks that Mike won't come back if he disobeys."

"He's mentioned that, but it was so preposterous I thought he was bullshitting me like he always does."

"No, sir, he really means it."

"Then if that's what he really thinks, it sounds to me like he needs a psychiatrist. Now I'm even more worried than ever."

"Anything that helps to keep him away from drugs sounds good to me, Mr. McGill."

"But he's got some fantasy that his friend Mike is coming back. It's not healthy."

"My best friend is raising Mike's baby and she's not giving up."

"Yes, we've met her. Catherine. Nice young lady. We liked her a lot. I guess if I were her I wouldn't give up either. But at some point they'll have to."

"Mr. McGill, Don't take their hope away. They say there may be hundreds of POWs we don't know about."

A voice came over the loudspeaker: "The pizza's here and the game's about to start."

"Well, we'd better go," he said as he rolled back his chair. "I'm glad we finally had a chance to have a talk. It's time for Arthur to grow up, Jenny. His unemployment is ending and it's a brand new year. He's done his military service so that's out of the way. If he's not going to go to law school, then he needs to resolve to get a job or come to work here at the garage and learn the business. And as for the two of you, you both need to resolve to quit playing at being adults. Now it's not my place to tell you what to do with your lives, but the way his mother and I see it—and I'd bet the farm your mother and father do too—it's high time for the two of you to either shit or get off the pot."

At halftime the game was tied, and most of the men lit cigarettes as they headed to the restroom or to the bar and the food. Arty took out his guitar and led the kids and the mothers in singing "Jingle Bells" and "Over the River and Through the Woods." Jenny sang with him on "Puff the Magic Dragon," and at his mom's request, they did one of her favorites, "Jamaica Farewell," and even the mechanics and salesmen hanging around in the back by the bar applauded like they meant it. A few minutes before the second half was to start, his father called everybody together, gave a short speech, made a toast to a better year, and led everybody in singing "Auld Lang Syne."

When they finished Arty spoke up. "One last thing I'd like to share. As most of you know, I was in Vietnam at this time last year and our CO threw a party. At midnight everybody sang 'Auld Lang Syne,' and when it was over one guy asked, 'What's it mean, anyhow?' Most of us had sung it all our lives and didn't know what we were singing about. I remember when I was a kid and wondering just who this guy Old Lang Zyne guy was and why were we singing about him? I thought he must be an old geezer, kind of like Father Time with a long white beard.

"Well, one of the chopper pilots had taken a poetry class somewhere and told us it was a Scottish dialect and translated as 'old long ago' or 'old times gone by.' The song is asking if old friends should be forgot and never brought to mind, and it answers by saying we should toast old friends with a good stiff drink, which is what the Scots meant by 'take a cup o' kindness.' So now to me the song makes total sense like this:

For old long ago, my dear
For old times gone by
We'll take a cup o' kindness yet
For old times gone by.

"So when midnight rolls around, may we all take a cup of kindness as we toast old friends and old times gone by. It was great seeing everybody, and on behalf of Mom and Dad and my good friend Jenny, thanks for coming. *Happy New Year!* and *GO STEELERS*!"

The room was infused with gung-ho optimism as the game resumed, only to deflate like a punctured tire in the final minutes as the clock ran down and the Steelers lost, twenty-one to seventeen. There would be no Super Bowl for the Buckle of the Rust Belt this year. The magic of last week's Immaculate Reception had worn off.

"Well, at least it was an exciting game," Jenny said, trying to cheer him up as they walked to the car.

"It sucked and you know it. It's just like the Pirates. Best record in baseball and they blow it and miss the World Series, and now the Steelers blow it and miss the Super Bowl. *Fuck*!"

Dusk was falling and it was much cooler, and as Arty was putting up the convertible top his parents walked over and his mom handed her a Kodak Instamatic camera and two extra film cartridges. "Here's a camera for you, Jenny, but you've got to promise to take a lot of pictures. Leave the film with Arthur, and I'll get it developed and make sure he sends you copies. We've only seen him in a tuxedo one time, when he went to his senior prom. And be sure to have somebody take a picture of the two of you together."

"Thank you, Mrs. McGill. I will. I promise."

She and Arty's mom gently hugged and pecked each others cheeks, and his father reached out to shake her hand and whispered, "And remember, it takes a good swift kick in the ass to get Arthur moving. But don't let him see it's coming or he'll bullshit his way around it."

She squeezed his hand and said, "I'll remember, Mr. McGill," then she leaned in and shocked him with a peck on his cheek.

Arty was quiet on the ride to the cottage, almost sullen. "Are you okay, Arty? It was only a game."

"That's not it, Jen. Or it's only the half of it. Or something like that. Maybe it was 'Auld Lang Syne' and thinking about Mulligan and how his mom and dad are doing. And how Catherine's doing with the baby. And how Frankie's parents are doing."

"What I care about right now is how you're doing," she said as she snuggled up to him.

"I'm just pissed at everything, Jen. Frankie...Mulligan...fucking Nixon...the Pirates, the Steelers, the war—*my dad*!—everything's totally fucked."

"Even me?" she said as she snuggled closer.

He wrapped his arm around her and pulled her tight. "No, you're not totally fucked. You're totally *fuckable.* Big difference."

"I sure hope so."

"So how'd it go with my dad?

"About like you'd expect."

"What's that mean?"

"They're worried about you, Arty."

"Let me guess. I'm lazy and sitting on my ass and drinking and doing drugs and playing that damned guitar and don't have a job and look like a dirty hippie."

"That was pretty much it."

"Anything about us?"

She wanted to tell him their mothers were debating wedding plans but only said, "He told me it's time for us to either shit or get off the pot."

"Ha! My Dad actually said that? You're kidding, right?"

"He was very direct."

"He's not usually like that around women."

"It seems he and I have an understanding."

After nearly two weeks of evasions they were finally discussing the future. She might not get another chance, and one way or the other, something had to give. She told him, "He is right about one thing, Arty. We both have some big decisions to make."

"Yeah, but it's too soon to think about it," and he pushed in the lighter and pulled a pack of cigarettes from his field jacket.

"Too soon? Arty, you're unemployment is up and you don't have a job and haven't even looked into applying to grad school, and I'm about to graduate and have to start paying back student loans. We're not kids any more, Arty."

"But I have a job. I'm in a new band, Jen."

"That's not a real job and you know it."

"Sure it is."

"Don't try to BS me Arthur Bolton McGill the third. You've already told me everybody else in the band has a day job."

"Uh—"

"And what's with you calling me 'my good friend, Jenny' when you introduce me. You did it twice already today. What's *that* all about?"

He seemed stunned. "Uh…it's not about anything, Jen."

"That's what bothers me."

He sent a chill up her back as he scowled and said sharply, "Don't go getting strange on me, Jen. And I don't want to hear any more of that Arthur-Bolton-McGill-the-fucking-third shit. I'm not in the mood."

He never snapped at her unless he'd been drinking. How many beers had he had? She'd had two or three herself. She couldn't let it slide. "Arty, the way you're going you'll never be in the mood for anything."

Jenny could hear singing coming from inside the outhouse as they walked up to the cottage door carrying leftover pizzas and a box of half-empty liquor bottles. She recognized it as a vocal exercise Mrs. Scott had taught her back in the sixth grade. "La-la-la-la-la—"

"Maggie's really dedicated," Arty said. "She always sings on the john. She did it every day when I stayed with her on the houseboat."

Jenny wanted to gag but only said, "I've never tried it."

Arty shouted, "Yo, Maggie, we're back!"

Maggie yelled from inside the outhouse, "It's quite a ladies room you've got here!"

Maggie this and Maggie that. Maggie and McGill…was that where he was going? She had to admit that it was a good name for a duo, almost poetic. She felt pinched, constrained, frustrated, and more than a little scared. She was running out of time to get some kind of answer about *something* out of him before she went back. What the hell were they going to do? What was *she* going to do? What could she plan for?

A few minutes later Maggie came in with a suitcase and a guitar. "I'm wondering what to wear, Art. You said I'd get to see you in a tuxedo. Is it formal?"

"No, the band always wears monkey suits," Arty said. "But the guests will be decked out to the max. We're talking serious money. All the bigshot families have estates out there—Mellons, Fricks, Carnegies, Heinz. We're playing for their great-grand-kids."

He took the invitation off the coffee table, handed it to Maggie and said, "They told us the guests will be mostly in their thirties, so we've been rehearsing tunes from the Fifties that they grew up with. Elvis, Bo Diddley, the Everly Brothers, and lots of doo-wop stuff."

Maggie looked at the invitation and read out loud, "Fleetwood Farms, Sewickley Heights. What an interesting name—Sewickley. It's kind of musical."

Jenny said, "I did a report on local names back in junior high. Sewickley is the Indian name for the liquid that flows from maple trees in the spring that maple syrup comes from. It means 'sweet water.'"

Maggie's face lit up. "Wow, Art. Remember...*the Sweetwater*!"

"Uh, hey, yeah, that's right. *Far out*!"

Maggie clapped her hands and laughed. "Is that karmic, or what!"

"Absolutely," Arty said. "No doubt about it."

"What's so karmic about it?" Jenny said, trying to hide her irritation at some secret they shared of which she knew nothing.

"The Sweetwater's the bar where Maggie and I met where all the rock stars hang out," Arty said. "It was my first night back from Nam."

Jenny said, "So you think the name of a town just happening to translate into the name of a bar in California is karmic?"

"Sure," Maggie said. "Don't you? It's where Art and I met."

Arty smiled and said, "You can bet Catherine would think it's karmic. You know how New Age she is. I mean, think of the odds. They're *astrological!*"

Arty gave her a big grin, but sometimes Jenny couldn't tell when he was pulling her chain. Did he really mean 'astronomical' and just screwed up? Or was he serious about 'astrological?' The anxiety surged worse than ever. One more semester and she would be out of academia with a huge student loan debt, and meanwhile Arty was turning into a hippie. Or was he? What were they going to do? What did Arty want to do? What did she want to do? Neither of them were getting any younger. Who was this Maggie person?

Jenny was feeling...what? Threatened, or challenged, or...*something*. Irritable, for sure. She should be friends with Maggie. In any other situation they would have been instant sisters. She could hear Cate admonishing her to recognize the negative side of Scorpio in herself and control it. Could that be why she was so frustrated and so furious for no good reason?

Maggie said sprightly, "So how was your football game, Art?"

Arty groaned and said, "It totally sucked. The Steelers lost."

"But it was fun," Jenny said, trying to cheer him up. "You saw people you hadn't seen for a while and they got to see you play. And you made your mom and dad proud of you."

"It still sucked," Arty said as he took the liquor bottles out of the box and put them on the counter. "What are you drinking, Maggie?"

"Nothing, Art, and you shouldn't either. You're playing tonight. You know you lose it when you've been drinking, and you've already had a few. Make some coffee instead. If you stop now you'll be okay by the time you go on."

"I don't lose it," Arty said with grin as he unscrewed the top of a bottle of gin. "I get more personable."

"You're wrong, Art," Maggie said. "We don't know each other that well, but we've played together and we've partied together. Remember that tape we made before and after you'd been drinking? Remember?"

Arty lowered his head and said, "Yeah, kind'a."

"You remember all right. When I played it for you the next day you couldn't believe how bad you were. I've got it in the car. Maybe we should play it for Jenny and see what she thinks?"

"So what are you saying, Maggie?" Jenny said.

"I'm saying I've been in a lot of bands and seen how they screw up and it's usually because of drinking. This sounds like a really good gig and I don't want Art to screw it up. And if he doesn't stop drinking right now he's guaranteed to screw it up. He can hold his own playing rhythm, but put a few beers in him and his fingers get stupid. So Art, let's do those breathing exercises I taught you to help clear your head and get the energy flowing."

"Yeah, sure, okay," Arty said as he screwed the cap back on the gin bottle. "You're right. Coffee it is. Jen, would you put on a pot. And make Maggie some tea."

Jenny sneered to herself under her breath, "Put on a pot and make Maggie some tea" as she filled the teapot and the percolator. What was she, hired help? It occurred to her she had never really paid attention to Arty's proficiency on guitar. He had always played folkie stuff and his own songs, but he had never played lead or tried to impress her with a Hendrix or a Clapton virtuoso riff. He just played rhythm and sang. He had played her tapes of him with Frankie and the Dynamos when he was in high school, but she had never seen him play in a band; it had always just been him with his acoustic guitar. When they sang together, it had usually been just the two of them, or at occasional parties with his frat brothers or her friends in college. Maggie knew about performing and making a living at it, and she had a brain despite the gorgeous-but-dumb blonde stereotype. Jenny could play the piano well enough, and she knew she had a nice voice, but she had never considered being in a band. If Arty was going to be a musician instead of a lawyer, Maggie had something he needed that she didn't have. Would he be better off with her? Would it be best for him? And would it be best for her?

She was spooning coffee grounds into the percolator when Arty said, "You hungry, Mags?"

Jenny flinched as she angrily thought *Mags*? and spilled a tablespoon of coffee all over the counter.

Arty continued, "Augustino's makes the best pizza west of Rome. Cheese and mushroom, all veggie, like you like it."

He knows how she likes it? Jenny tried not to show her irritation and asked, "Want me to warm it up in the oven?"

Maggie took a slice. "No thanks. This is great. So come on Art. Let's get *you* warmed up.

Maggie was like a cheerleader—Rah rah rah! *Go team go*!

"Where's your guitar, the Gibson with the peace sign?" Maggie asked.

"Check *this* out," Arty said as he opened a guitar case and handed Maggie the Les Paul. "Like Dylan, I've gone electric."

Maggie's face lit up. "Wow! An original Les Paul Sunburst?"

"Yeah," Arty said, "it's a '61. It was my buddy Frankie's. We were in a band in high school, Frankie and the Dynamos. I think I told you about him. He was killed in Nam. His parents gave it to me."

"Oh, I'm so sorry," Maggie said as she went to hand it back.

"No no, it's okay," Arty said. "Frankie loved to show it off. I've been really getting into it. My dad would never let me have an electric. He didn't even let me have an amp. I always had to borrow Frankie's for gigs."

"So tell me about the new band," Maggie said as Arty plugged in the guitar and turned on the amp.

"Well, the bass player saw me at an open mic and asked me to audition and they liked me. It's mostly a cover band, Top 40 stuff, every song as close to the original as we can do it. I play rhythm and sing a few harmonies. Five of us have been rehearsing, but we're supposed to have a hot sax player with us tonight."

"What a nice sound," Maggie said as she noodled a few riffs on the guitar. "Have you played them your songs, Art?"

"No, I told them I write, but it's only been a couple weeks and all we've done is rehearse. This band is all about keeping 'em dancing. Nothing people don't know. No originals, nothing they've never heard. You want a classy party band in tuxedos that leaves everybody wanting more, you call the Keystoners."

He took a promo photo from the guitar case. "This is them without me. The rhythm player's got National Guard duty for the next six months, so if I don't screw up, it could be a regular gig till he gets back. They're booked almost every weekend."

"If you're not drinking, why would you screw up?" Maggie asked.

"We've only rehearsed a few times, and some of them are pretty freaking good."

"Well, so are you," Maggie said as she passed the Les Paul to Arty. "Let's hear something. You need to get loose."

"No, let's work something out together," Arty said. "The three of us. We might get a shot at doing a song by ourselves while the band's on break. I've been dreaming of getting you two together and this is my chance. What do you say? Jen?...Mags?"

Jenny hesitated, but she knew she couldn't say no. "I haven't sung in public in years, but I'm in."

Arty said, "It should be something from the Top 40 back before anybody ever heard of the Beatles."

There was a long silence. Jenny picked up the invitation and saw the address—Fleetwood Farms—which triggered a memory. "Hey, remember 'Mr. Blue?' by the Fleetwoods? It made Number One. It must have been, what, fifth grade? One guy and two girls."

"Yeah, sure," Arty said. "How's it go...

"I'm Mister Blue, when you say you love me

"Da da dat dah, dut dut dut daaa dat da da—"

"Wait a second," Jenny said as she pulled out the piano bench. "It will come to me if I play it." She loosened up with a quick practice scale, and sang, "I'm Mister Blue...."

It took just fifteen minutes to work up an arrangement. It went so well—the effortless vocal harmonies, with Arty and Maggie on guitars and her on the piano—that they kept going and worked up arrangements for two other oldies: "Come Go With Me" and "Breaking Up Is Hard to Do." They were having so much fun that they had to force themselves to quit and rush to change so Arty would not be late.

As they were leaving Arty put on his Army field jacket over his tuxedo, and Jenny and Maggie both broke out laughing and Jenny said, "Stop! Picture time." She reached into her purse for the camera and they took each others' photos. A volunteer would be needed to get the three of them together.

She was the last one out, locking the cottage door and racing up the path with the mic stands as Arty and Maggie loaded the back seat and trunk with guitars and amps. In the exhilaration of the jam session, Jenny had totally forgotten how uneasy, even fearful, Maggie could make her feel.

Arty closed the trunk and pulled out a cigarette.

Maggie said, "I can't be in the car with you if you smoke, Art. Being in the same house with a smoker is hard enough. I get physically ill."

"But I'm quitting at midnight. I've only got a few hours left."

"Smoke if you want to, Art," Maggie said, "but two seconds in a car with a smoker is two too many for me. I'll just follow you to the party."

"No, it's okay," Arty said, putting the cigarette back in the pack. "I'll tough it out."

Jenny was surprised how easily Maggie got Arty to do as she asked. Worried again, Jenny slid in the middle next to Arty. Maggie sat next to her, closed the door and said, "I can't believe how good we sounded. You know, Jen, you can really sing. Uh...can I call you 'Jen?'"

Jenny laughed and said, "Only if I don't have to call you 'Mags.'"

"You got yourself a deal," Maggie said and wrapped her arm around Jenny's shoulders and squeezed her in a hug.

Bunches of balloons floated above the wrought-iron gateposts of the Fleetwood Farms estate. Two valets in black uniforms with double-brass buttons and gold braided epaulets were on duty. One shined a flashlight on all the occupants' faces while the other checked a clipboard and questioned the drivers.

Arty flashed the invitation and said, "We're in the band and we've got equipment."

The valet directed them around the rear of the main house, an imposing stone structure with a turret.

"Sheeesh, Art, you were right," Maggie said. "This is quite a spread. It's like a medieval castle. All it needs is a drawbridge and a moat."

The stage was on a platform at the corner of a formal banquet room right out of *The Great Gatsby*. Huge nets filled with hundreds of balloons hung between the crystal chandeliers.

As they set up their equipment, Maggie said, "Jen, I don't know much about you, but please don't have anything to drink. We may get a chance to play if Art can talk them into it and I want us to be at our best."

"You're really serious about your music, aren't you Maggie?"

"You bet I am."

When the music started, she and Maggie, like the other women in the band's entourage, were open-season for guys on the make. They quickly became a formidable team, dancing with and fending off horny trust-fund Lotharios and their offers of exotic cocaine.

After a few songs, Jenny asked Maggie, "So what do you think of the band"?

"They're pretty smooth, and Art in his tux is the cutest guy on stage."

At the band's first break, Arty came up to them glowing with excitement. "They're going to let us do a song to warm up the crowd right before the band comes off break."

Maggie whooped, "Whooo, that's great!"

"Which one should we do?" Jenny said. "We only worked on three."

Without skipping a beat, Maggie said, "We're warming them up, so it has to be the one with the most energy."

They agreed that "Breaking Up Is Hard To Do" was the most energetic and found a back stairwell with great acoustics where they practiced vocals for a few minutes. As they were setting up on stage to play, Jenny recruited the drummer's girlfriend to take some photos of them with the Instamatic Arty's mom had given her.

Five minutes before the band came off break, Arty stepped to the mic and announced, "My friends and I are going to do a song before the whole band comes back. This is my Jenny, from right here in The Burgh. We play together a lot. And this is Maggie, who surprised us this morning by showing up out of the blue all the way from California. When I played with her out there, we called ourselves Maggie and

McGill. Now Jenny and Maggie just met today, and the three of us have played together for less than an hour and know exactly three songs, so for lack of a better name, this is the debut performance of the Surprise Trio."

Jenny twinged at hearing him say "my Jenny." He'd never used that before. But Surprise Trio? What a corny name.

She played the keyboard player's piano, Arty and Maggie played their guitars, and they sang "Breaking Up Is Hard To Do" harmonizing on the refrain, "Come-a-coma-a-down do-be-do-down-down."

They filled the dance floor, and the applause was enthusiastic. When the band came back the frontman said, "Not bad." Jenny and Maggie stepped down from the stage and went into the crowd, where they were congratulated with every superlative in the book.

At the band's next break, they rehearsed "Come Go With Me" in the stairwell, warmed up the crowd, and again left the stage to enthusiastic applause. As midnight came close the bandleader said, "Okay people, get ready, here we go. Ready. Set. Ten…nine…."

Everybody counted down together, and at the stroke of midnight, the band yelled into their mics, "Happy New Year!" The lights went down and hundreds of balloons and streamers of confetti fell from the ceiling to a cacophony of party horns and noisemakers as the band played "Auld Lang Syne." Everybody sang and hugged and kissed as Jenny and Maggie made their way on stage with the rest of the entourage and kissed and hugged Arty and various total strangers.

When the lights came up, Arty held up his Marlboros and said into his mic, "If anybody sees me with one of these suckers ever again, kick my ass!" and he crushed the pack in his fist and tossed it to the floor.

The frontman yelled into his mic, "Now, let's get *down!*"

Jenny and Maggie started off the stage with the other girlfriends but the frontman called out, "No—you two! Stay and help." Then he counted off, "Uh one and uh two and uh—"

As the bass and drums launched into "In the Midnight Hour" Arty motioned her and Maggie over to his mic. They improvised backup harmonies on the chorus and were soon working together and singing fills like they were soul sisters just in from Memphis. They were *hot*!

They sang backup for the entire set. The last encore ended at two-thirty, and afterward they and the band and the entourage partied for half an hour with champagne and joints and lines of coke. She and

Maggie had three glasses and a few tokes on a joint, and Maggie accepted a few lines of coke, but Arty just had champagne.

"What's with you, McGill?" said the sax player as Arty held up his hand to decline a toke on a joint. "Don't you get high?"

"I was the champion toker at a place called Dam Luc," Arty said as he poured another glass of champagne for himself. "Cambodian Gold, best you ever tasted, but now I'm under strict orders to do nothing illegal. The drill sergeants would have called it a 'personal problem.'"

The sax player gave him a wary look, suddenly cautious after being reminded that Arty was a Nam vet with an attitude.

While saying goodnight in the parking lot, the frontman said, "So what would it take to get you two ladies to help out once in a while?"

"Forget it," Arty said. "This was a one shot deal. Maggie's on her way to New York and Jenny goes back to law school."

The only downer of the entire night was Arty's college team losing.

"Can you believe it?" Arty said on the drive back as he angrily switched off the sports report on the car radio. "Our halfback wins the Heisman fucking Trophy as the best player in the country but he gets the flu and can't play and we get skunked. What a year. First the Pirates have the best record in baseball, then blow it in the playoffs and miss the World Series, then Steelers have the Immaculate Reception one week, but blow it the next and miss the Super Bowl, and now my team blows it in the Sugar Bowl. Fuck! At least there's nothing left to go wrong. Wait till next year! Ha. What bullshit. It already is next fucking year."

Maggie seemed surprised at how angry Arty was at the outcome of a football game. "You take your sports really seriously, don't you, Art? I don't understand. Why is that? It's just a football game."

"No, it's not just one game, it's two huge games on the same fucking day," Arty said angrily. "And as for why we take it seriously, nobody around here asks *why*. Everybody just does. Maybe it's something in the water. Sometimes it seems like it's all we got with all the mills shutting down and everybody out of work. It's not like California. There aren't any songs about the Pennsylvania dream."

In the morning, Jenny made a no-bacon veggie breakfast as Maggie showered and Arty washed the dirt and salt off Maggie's car.

"Where's Art?" Maggie said when she came out from the guest room and set her guitar case and suitcase by the door.

Jenny handed her a cup of coffee and said, "He's washing your car.

He says you need to be respectable when you hit the Big Apple."

"He's such a sweetheart," Maggie said in a wistful tone as she sipped her coffee and watched him through the window. "And cute, too. Skinny, but cute."

Once again feeling uncomfortable, Jenny changed the subject. "I think they liked us last night."

"Liked us? They didn't just like us, Jen, they *loved* us. You with that angelic soprano and me with my alto growl, and we didn't even have to work at it. Producers are always looking for a 'sound,' something unique. We've got it without trying. You're at Yale, right? How far is that from New York?"

Jenny said, "It's a couple hours on the train. Why?"

"That's practically next door," Maggie said enthusiastically. "We've just got to get together and tape some originals."

"That would be fun, but I graduate in June. I'm really busy."

Maggie said, "Jen, I...I have to ask, what's really up with you and Art? You know, relationship wise."

"Isn't that rather personal?" Jenny said, wincing at the question as she nervously flipped an omelet, a little too hard.

"Of course it is, that's why I have to ask. Look. I want you to come to New York for a few days, or at least a weekend. I haven't seen it yet, but my new place is supposed to have a couch that folds into a double bed for guests. Once I learn my way around, I'll find a studio where we can lay down some tracks."

That caught Jenny off guard. "You mean...without Arty?"

"If it's at a time when he can't make it I want you to come anyway. Our voices have a kind of chemistry. The kind that sells records. And we play different instruments, so we complement each other musically. We won't step on each other's toes, if you know what I mean."

"I...I think so."

"If we get some tracks down on tape I can take them around to producers and publishers, and Arty can always add tracks later. But it's really you and me that make the sound unique. I'll do everything I can to make it happen. That's why I have to ask what's really up with you and Art, so I don't make a mistake and screw things up for any of us, either musically or personally. I hope you can understand that."

Maggie totally reeked of innocent, hippie sincerity. Jenny's normally unerring BS detector was silent. She couldn't help trusting this Maggie, in spite of herself. "All I can say is that it's…it's up in the air."

Maggie sighed. "Look, Jen, I don't have my sights on Art, if that's what you think. He's a lot of fun and I enjoyed sleeping with him last summer, and who knows, maybe some day we'll do it again. Those things can kind of just happen."

Jenny said, "Yes, they certainly can."

"But he's not my Mr. Right, and it seems to me you two are kind of karmically stuck, what with that baseball thing and all."

Jenny thought to herself: *Karmically stuck with that baseball thing?*

"Trust me Jen, I'm not your competition, but I want to be your friend as well as his. So what do you say? Will you think about it?"

"Maggie, I graduate in June and I've got a full load and job interviews stacked up all semester."

"So what are you going to do after you've got your JD?"

"I have no idea. That's what the interviews are all about."

"And what about you and Art?"

"Like I said…it's up in the air."

"Well, if things don't work out job wise you can stay with me and I'll get us gigs so you won't have to starve while I shop our tapes around. I'm good at that part."

"I can tell," Jenny said, "but I'm up to my ears in debt. I have to start paying it back six months after I graduate. I need a real job or I have to keep going to school somewhere and taking out more loans."

Maggie nodded. "I know, if I can't make my music click I'll be in the same boat. But look, we just have to get some tracks down. One hit song could wipe out all of our student debts."

"You certainly are a dreamer," Jenny said.

"You have to be in this business. So what do you say?"

"I'll think about it."

Arty came in from the yard and Maggie thanked him for washing her car while Jenny dished up omelets from the cast-iron frying pan. She and Maggie flopped down on the couch with their plates on their laps while Arty wiped the coffee table with a wet dish cloth.

Maggie said, "I want to thank you both for a great time yesterday."

"I really had fun too," Jenny said.

Arty set his plate on the coffee table, pulled up a chair and said, "Except for the lousy football games, it was the all-time best night ever."

Maggie said, "So what's with that name, Art? The Surprise Trio? I don't know what to think."

"I don't know what to think either," Arty said, "It just came to me when I turned on the mic. What do you think, Jen?"

"It's kind of corny, Arty."

Maggie said, "Well, the Beatles started out as the Quarrymen."

Just then the phone rang. Jenny answered and said, "It's one of the guys in the band."

Arty talked for a minute, and when he hung up he shouted, "Jen, those rich bastards liked us so much they're thinking of booking us for a big Saint Patrick's Day bash at the Rolling Rock Club. And they want you and Maggie to sit in."

Jenny said, "Arty, we talked about your birthday a month ago and you said you'd come up to my place for it so I can go to that seminar that weekend. I've already signed up and paid."

"That was before I hooked up with the band, Jen. It's on a Saturday. You can bag the seminar, fly in on Friday and fly back on Sunday."

"No, Arty, I don't think so."

Arty said, "How about you, Maggie?"

"We'll see, but I kind of doubt it, Art," Maggie said. "So what's the latest weather report? Am I going to run into any snow?"

Arty said, "I don't know, but it's time for the news and the weather always comes on at the end."

"And what's the best route?" Maggie asked. "The turnpike?"

"No, not from here," Arty said as he flicked on the old Philco radio. "You should take the new Interstate 80. It's finally open clear through the mountains. Everybody says it's faster."

The radio's 1940's vacuum tubes crackled and hummed, warming up until the announcer's voice came to life:

> "Today, all of Pittsburgh is praying that the reports that Roberto Clemente was on a plane that crashed last night off the coast of San Juan, Puerto Rico, are wrong. Navy and Coast Guard seaplanes and a Coast Guard cutter and hundreds of private boats are conducting a massive search, but so far no survivors have been found, and no bodies have been recovered. The plane, which was carrying relief supplies for victims of the earthquake in Managua, Nicaragua, went down shortly after takeoff."

Chapter 26

Breaking Up Is Hard to Do

THERE WAS NO IGNORING THE GLOOM THAT HUNG IN THE AIR AS THEY drove to a farewell luncheon at Jenny's parents' house and then on to the airport for her flight to New Haven. The flags at schools and post offices were all at half-mast, and home-made signs like "Adios Arriba," and "Roberto, RIP," were in windows everywhere. It was all her father and Papa Carlo could talk about at lunch. They were almost crying.

The mood was even worse than when the Kennedys and Martin Luther King were killed. Those tragedies were not universally mourned in the same way, since lot of people didn't like the Kennedys or King. While those who didn't like them may have been appalled that such things could happen in America, few of them felt a personal loss. But nobody around Pittsburgh did not like Roberto Clemente. Republicans, Democrats, whites, blacks, even people who hated baseball liked, even loved, Roberto Clemente. "Arriba" had been Pittsburgh's brightest star for over fifteen years, beloved for his on-field hustle, his off-field charity work, and his shining sense of honor.

On the drive to the airport the car radio faded out as they crawled into the Fort Pitt Tunnel in a traffic jam just as the newscaster was saying, "Still missing and presumed dead...."

"Still missing and presumed dead," Arty repeated, bitterly, as he came to a stop behind a bus blowing oily black diesel exhaust right through the convertible's window cracks. "It's just like with Mulligan, Jen, except Nixon's official bullshit says Mulligan's missing in action. Nothing presumed about it."

After hearing about Clemente, Arty had gone from being ecstatic and excited after his success at the gig and regressed into the angry and morose Vietnam vet. She reached out, squeezed his hand and said, "Don't be so negative, Arty, please. There's still hope Mike is alive."

"Yeah, right. They say there's hope Clemente's alive too. Hey wait—I know...he'll wash up on the beach in an episode of *Gilligan's Island*."

"That's not funny, Arty. Please don't be like that."

"Hey, now that I think about it, he's just like Mulligan, MIA because of Nixon. He was only on that plane because Nixon's favorite dictator,

Somoza, has been stealing the relief supplies. Clemente hoped that his being there would keep from Somoza from ripping them off. It's just like in Nam, Jen. Kissinger says 'peace is at hand,' and after Nixon wins, they just start bombing away all over again. Everything fucking sucks."

She tried to calm him down. "Not everything, Arty, there's—"

"Jen!" he shouted. "*Wake the fuck up*! Nixon's in the White House for four more fucking years!"

"Why are you arguing with me, Arty?"

"I'm not arguing with you, not like with my Dad. It's just that sometimes you don't see how bad things really are."

He had a point. The national media was trumpeting the upcoming inaugural celebration as the triumphal vindication of Nixon's policy of Vietnamization that was ending American involvement in the war and had culminated in his smashing Electoral College victory, forty-nine out of fifty states. The Democrats were vanquished, the anti-war hippies crushed, and now Nixon was bombing the commies all over again.

Arty said, "So when will I see you again?"

"I don't know. I'll be really busy."

"You've got to meet me in New York when I go. Maggie says she's got plenty of room. We should really get some tracks down."

Jenny shivered, thinking about him staying at Maggie's if she couldn't make it. How would she feel about *that*? "I guess it depends on when you go, Arty."

"It will have to be in the middle of the week. The band's booked for the next month, so I can't just take off on a weekend. It's a real job, Jen."

She had to admit that if the band worked every weekend it would be almost like a full-time job. Of course it paid under-the-table, so in the I.R.S., pay-your-taxes sense, it wasn't a "real" job. Still, if he didn't go to graduate school right away, it was as good as tending bar, waiting tables, or selling cars for his father.

Her future was still up in the air. Her Plan B, studying international law at the Sorbonne while polishing her fluency in French and Italian, and then applying for a job with the United Nations or UNESCO, was looking better every day. A year at the Sorbonne would buff up her academic resumé, postpone having to repay her loans, and best of all, she would be in Paris, the City of Light! Would Arty follow her? Would she want him to? She had interviewed for clerkships on the Supreme Court as well as the Circuit Courts in New York and Washington, but the truth was no matter how well-qualified she might be, women never got those jobs. It looked as though her choices were coming down to clerking for the district judge she had interned with in Pittsburgh, accepting a job with Mellon Bank in Pittsburgh or a law firm in New York, or attending the Sorbonne in Paris.

"So Jen, will you come down for my birthday and the big gig at the Rolling Rock Club?"

"I've already signed up for the seminar, and I—"

"Oh, come on, Jen. This is the big one. I'll be halfway to fifty, a quarter century old—over a third of a lifetime—*gone*. We only live once. If Frankie were here, he'd tell you not to waste it on a stupid seminar. And Mulligan would too."

That pissed her off. "Screw you, Arthur Bolton McGill the *third*. I've been trying to get you to talk about what you want to do with your life so maybe I can think about what I'm going to do with mine but you keep putting me off and putting me off and putting me off some more. It's all about you–you–you. And I let you get away with it. That's my fault. Psychologists call it 'enabling.' Well that's over. You father thinks you're using the war as an excuse to sit on your ass and play guitar, and maybe he's right. Maybe we just shouldn't make any plans at all? To hell with the future. What do you say we give ourselves a break? Maybe that's *my* New Year's resolution—to give myself a break—from *you*!"

She was *steamed*. She had never lit into him like that...ever. She began shaking, almost shivering, stunned by her outburst. She waited for his reaction, but he just stared straight ahead, dumbstruck as the belching diesel fumes enveloped the car. When they finally exited the tunnel, they rolled down their windows, gasped for fresh air, and rode on in silence.

At the airport exit he sheepishly said, "So are we...are we breaking up?"

"Breaking up? How could we be breaking up? We've never 'gone together'...*remember?*"

Catherine made a multi-colored sign on the back of a box that read:

HAPPY FIRST BIRTHDAY!

Michael Patrick Mulligan, Jr.

January 17th, 1973

She hung it behind his high-chair, and using a light meter, set up lights and an photographer's umbrella to diffuse the shadows just right. The birthday-boy hadn't made any of his own friends yet, so the party would consist of her, Jenny, their favorite babysitter—Yolanda, who was a student at the local community college—and about ten guests, most of whom were fellow members of SAYL—S-A-Y-L—Sisters After Yale Law. It was set for Wednesday, from four to seven. There was a chocolate cake with raspberry filling, a single candle, floating helium balloons tied to Little Mike's high-chair, sodas, coffee, assorted teas, wine, beer, two large pizzas, a bottle of Remy Martin cognac, and two big fatties of Panama Red, a donation from a neighbor down the hall.

Her latest therapist had suggested her New Year's resolution should be to "Get your life back." She promised to try, and throwing Little Mike a birthday party seemed a good place to start.

Last year Yale had allowed her to be part-time due to her extraordinary situation. Her grades were good, so that wasn't an issue. And she was a DeWolfe, so it went without saying that if Yale expected further donations from the J.C. DeWolfe Foundation the university would do the right thing. Most of her classmates, including Jenny, would graduate in June, but Catherine could take whatever time she reasonably needed to fulfill her requirements.

She was enrolled in just one class for the spring semester, Civil and Political Rights, and only because Jenny would be in it too. The idea of sitting through courses like Advanced Contracts or Criminal Procedures depressed her. Her therapist assured her that getting her life back did not mean she had to cope with full-time law-school pressures. Other activities might be psychologically superior.

She decided to follow her heart, which included photography. She became a regular in the photo lab, printing film from shooting trips along the Connecticut seaside with Little Mike. She joined the judo club, the only female member, and began working out at Yale's world-class natatorium. Just this morning, an assistant coach on the Yale swim team, perennial NCAA, champions—the New York Yankees of collegiate swimming—had watched her doing laps. When she came out to dry off, he asked about her background, and when he learned she had been on the swim team at Vassar, he suggested she apply to be a graduate assistant for the soon-to-be Yale women's swimming team.

"It's not official," said the coach, "and there aren't enough undergraduate women on campus yet to fill a team, but the new Title IX law mandates equality of opportunity in sports. Here at Yale, that means swimming. They're already interviewing candidates."

Helping to coach Yale's first-ever women's swim team? *Wow.* That had never occurred to her. She couldn't wait to tell Jenny, who had been a diver on the Bryn Mawr team. If she could coach swimming, maybe Jenny could coach diving?

If Mike did not return, and she had to raise Little Mike by herself, Yale might be a good place to do it. And if he did come back, who could predict how they'd get along?

Her therapist helped her realize that it was okay if she no longer cared if she became a lawyer. Motherhood was a job, especially single-motherhood, and unlike Jenny with her loans, Catherine had no need to climb some greasy career pole just to earn a living.

Catherine was much more worried about Jenny than she was about herself. When she picked Jenny up at the airport, she'd cheerfully asked, "So how was Pittsburgh?"

"He's such an idiot, Cate. I don't want to talk about it."

Of course all Jenny really did want to do *was* to talk about it. By the time they reached the apartment, the whole story was out. Catherine had never seen her friend so agitated. She asked gently, "So what are you going to do, Jennifer?"

"Nothing. Not a goddamned thing. He's too busy doing his *thing* to pay attention to mine, so I'll make my plans and he can make his and that's *that.* Have you ever used an outhouse in the snow at four in the morning? It loses its charm real fast."

Jenny was upset that Art had given her future zero consideration; that a beautiful rival, a guitar-playing singer no less, had beamed-in from California; that she had interviews every week for the rest of the semester and a full class schedule; that she had not heard about her applications for a clerkship, or her application to the Sorbonne. For the last two weeks, Catherine could only watch and worry as Jenny brooded and festered.

The guests were crowded into Catherine's bedroom, sipping drinks while the babysitter snapped photos as Catherine brought Little Mike in from the bathroom. She removed the towel, finished drying him off, and hoisted him on the baby-scale for his official one-year weigh-in. His fidgeting made it hard to read the bouncing dial, so she gave up and said, "He's over twenty pounds of stubborn, goat-headed, Capricorn energy"

There was a click of a camera shutter and the babysitter said, "That's the last one, Ms. DeWolfe."

Catherine picked up the baby and said, "Okay, big guy, why don't you go with Aunt Jenny."

She passed him to Jenny, who grunted—*oomph*—and carried him into the living room.

The guests followed Jenny as Catherine put a new roll of film in the camera while the babysitter gathered up toys.

"I can't believe how huge he is," said a guest.

"His father is six-four," Jenny said as she set him down on the carpet where he could put on a show. "And Cate's about the tallest woman I know. He's going to be a big boy."

Little Mike sat up, surveyed the room, got his bearings, crawled to a chair, grabbed a leg and pulled himself to his feet for better visibility. While he was looking around at the guests, the guests were all gawking at his private parts.

"Oh, my," somebody gasped. "Why, he's not circumcised."

"No," Catherine said as she came in from the bathroom. "It didn't seem right for me to make that decision for him. It just seems so, I don't know, so unnatural. And it's not like it's too late. He can always decide for himself when he's older."

Seeing what he wanted, the baby squealed with glee and toddled toward his fuzzy blue dinosaur as Catherine snapped photos.

"Wow," said a guest. "He's already walking. Almost running."

Another said, "With his hair, Cate, he's just like you."

"And like his father," Catherine said, pointing to the Annapolis graduation photo on the end-table of curly, red-headed Ensign Michael Mulligan. They all knew there was a glimmer of hope he might be a POW and return when a peace agreement was reached, but that it was far more likely that he would never come back.

All of Yale knew the basics of the story: stunning heiress, weekend fling, MIA war hero, knocked-up, secret out-of-wedlock baby. There were dozens of variations and speculations about the heiress and her MIA lover and how an illegitimate son would affect the famously contentious DeWolfe clan, all of which made Catherine the toast of the Yale Gossip Society.

Finally, a guest had the courage to ask, "Cate, has there been any news about the father? It must be terrible for you. I can't imagine."

"There's been nothing for months," Catherine said, "but I talk to his mom and dad all the time. They'll call as soon as the Navy tells them anything. And the peace talks are starting up again, so I'm hoping there's something soon."

Two days earlier, the White House had announced that North Vietnam had agreed to return to the peace negotiations, and as a gesture of Christmastime goodwill, President Nixon ordered a suspension the massive bombings.

Someone asked, "Do you know if the communists even have him?"

"No," said Catherine. "He went missing in the Mekong delta, so it's probably not the North Vietnamese who have him, but the Viet Cong. There isn't much information on Viet Cong prisoners."

"So how long since you've seen him?"

"One year and nine months."

"And you knew him for how long?"

"Just a couple of days."

"So what happens if he...uh, I mean...*when* he comes back?"

Catherine tried to preempt the questions she knew were coming. "Will he want to marry me? Will I want to marry him? What if we hate each other? I just don't know."

After a long silence, somebody got up the nerve to ask, "Cate, what happens if he stays missing? Where does that leave you?"

Catherine took a deep breath and spit it out: "It leaves me raising my son and hoping for the best. I can't think further ahead than that."

A guest said, "You seem so, I don't know, philosophical about it. It's like you're some kind of a saint. How do you do it?"

"When you're a mother, you just do it."

"What about your parents? How are they taking it?"

"My mother was furious that I had a baby in secret, but she's come around and now she spoils him rotten. And my father and Mike's father were both in the Navy and have a lot in common. They even went on a fishing trip together."

"Cate, tell us...when was the last time you went on a real date?"

"A *real* date?" Catherine said with a chuckle. "Ha...that's easy. Exactly one year and nine months ago."

They'd finished singing "Happy Birthday" and were cutting the cake and opening presents when a Special Delivery package showed up. The babysitter opened it and passed her a card and a gift box. It was from Art, a fleecy throw-blanket with a Milltowne Tornadoes logo. Catherine unfolded it and said, "Look Mikey, it's from your Uncle Art," and she read the card out loud, choking up at the end:

> *Happy Birthday Mike!*
> *Your dad played football and basketball for Milltowne High. Everybody called him "Mulligan Man," and when he made a big play everybody would cheer Hey Mulligan Man, Hey Mulligan Man.*
> *Art "Stick" McGill*

Catherine saw Jenny quickly wipe a tear away as the guests went "Awwww." One guest said, "How sweet," and another asked, "Uncle Art? Is that Jenny's boyfriend?"

Before she or Jenny could answer, the babysitter called out, "Hey, Ms. DeWolfe, there's a bunch of pictures in here too, and an envelope and a tape with a note sayin' to play it right away. I'll put it on."

The babysitter passed her a thick stack of rubber-banded photos and an envelope and took the tape to the stereo. As Catherine opened the envelope, a guest took the photos, removed the rubber bands and said, "Wow, Jennifer. I didn't know you played piano."

"Pass them around," somebody said.

They divided up the photos, and soon everybody was exchanging snapshots in every direction.

"Is that your boyfriend, Jennifer?"

"He's kind of cute."

"Nah, it's the tuxedo."

"Who's the blonde bombshell?"

Catherine called out, "Quiet! Everybody," and held up the note and read it aloud:

> *"Jen!*
> *We got the New Year's gig on tape with you and Maggie and me and you two sitting in with the band. I just finished dubbing it. You sound great!"*

The babysitter said, "Here goes, Ms. DeWolfe," and she punched PLAY and Art's voice came on as the guests kept glancing back and forth between Jenny and the photos being passed around. When "Breaking Up is Hard to Do" came on, the guests were stunned. Nobody in the room but Catherine had known that Jenny was musical.

"Jennifer, is that you?"

"You guys sound great!"

Jenny flushed with embarrassment just as several guests started singing along and before long somebody said, "Let's dance!"

They moved the coffee table out of the way, took off their shoes, and turned what had been a quiet birthday party for a toddler into something closer to a junior-high sleepover, a girls-night-out with adult beverages. They jitterbugged, early-Sixties style, and as they danced to the tape of Jenny and the Keystoners they tried to remember the steps to all the hot dance crazes they'd grown up with—The Mashed Potato, The Twist, The Pony, The Stomp, The Frug, The Limbo, The Watusi—and when the band cranked up "The Locomotion," they formed a line and sang along as they danced in a train all through the apartment.

When the last guest said goodnight, Jenny and the babysitter did a quick clean-up while Catherine diapered Little Mike and put him in his crib under his new Milltowne Tornadoes blanket. Jenny drove the babysitter home, leaving Catherine alone for the first time all week.

She poured a nightcap, a hefty snifter of cognac, and sat back with her feet on the coffee table. The party could not have gone any better. Like most of the DeWolfe family, she wasn't very religious, but she prayed every day that Mike was alive. But was she in love with him? How long could she put her life on hold for news that might never come?

Chapter 27

Twenty-five & Counting

McGILL'S TWENTY-FIFTH BIRTHDAY WAS IN THE BOOKS, GONE FOREVER along with many pints of Guinness Stout and shots of Jameson's Irish Whiskey. Rather than spend the night totally alone, he let himself get picked up. There were usually wannabe groupies in every audience, but this one had once been a high-society debutante. What was her name, anyhow. Sally? Sue? Sharon? He was pretty sure it started with an 'S.' He wondered if Jenny were in the sack with some Yalie.

He slipped out of her bed and tiptoed to the bathroom, picking up his tuxedo jacket, pants and the kelly-green tie and cummerbund on the way. It was a special St. Paddy's Day rental, fifteen percent extra for the Irish colors, so he couldn't forget anything. He always carried a toothbrush in his emergency dopp kit in the trunk of the car, but he wanted to be out the door before she woke up. He stared at the mirror and splashed himself awake without waiting for warm water to wash up.

He stopped at a Wonder Boy for breakfast and bought the Sunday *Post-Gazette*, turning to the latest list of returning POWs. The peace agreement had been signed at the end of January, and for the last month Operation Homecoming had been bringing POWs stateside, about forty at a time on C-141 transport planes that the Pentagon dubbed the "Hanoi Express." He scoured the list for Mulligan and Dungy but didn't see their names. "Shit," he said out loud. The prisoners were being released mostly in the order in which they had been captured. If they were alive, they would be among the last to come home.

He and Jenny had talked on the phone once a week or so after she went back to law school in September, but since their blow-up on the way to the airport they had talked just twice in three months, and then only briefly. She had sent him the new Jackson Browne album as a birthday present, but signed the card "Jenny," not "Love, Jenny," like in previous years.

The Sunday after his birthday he got up feeling like shit, but not because of a hangover. He'd driven home alone, having turned down several groupies. His birthday was over, and dealing with an airhead in the morning didn't seem worth getting laid for the sake of getting laid.

It had been weeks since he'd talked to Jenny. It was as if they were in some kind of Mexican standoff—who would blink first?

He made coffee and sat by the window in his bathrobe watching the creek. The month of March had been rain and more rain; every day was a soggy gray. In like a lion, out like a lamb, this March was not. The ice was gone but the creek kept on rising. The Algonquin flooded every few years, and while his cottage was above the high-water mark, a neighbor had warned him that their road flooded, and he might need the canoe to get out, and to be prepared to be without power for days if it got bad.

The band was still just doing oldies, no originals, his or anybody else's. Oldies were getting old. Last night the bandleader, who owned the Keystoners name and called the shots, said he wanted everybody to buy red bow ties and matching cummerbunds for their wedding gigs.

McGill was the band's newest member, a musical FNG, and had done what he'd been told, just like in Nam, but he rebelled at the idea of having to buy his own uniform. "If you want me to wear a uniform, fine, just don't make me pay for it like the U.S. fucking Army does."

It was a minor dustup, but it was clear to the rest of the band that when the regular rhythm player got back from National Guard duty that McGill would be out of a job.

He spent that gloomy Sunday nipping at a bottle of gin and trying to write a song, but nothing sounded right. He did come up with half a verse: "The country ain't gravy without an old lady, it's no fun makin' love on your own," but he was too bummed, depressed, sad, despondent—whatever his shitty feeling was called—to keep writing about it. God did he ever want a cigarette. And a joint. Fucking Mulligan and his bullshit order.

It was seven that night when he finally worked up the courage to call Jenny. After the greetings he said, "Anything new on the job interviews?"

"No, nothing definite," she said, "but I have decided that I don't want to work in Pittsburgh. Mellon Bank offered me a job, and Judge Alford offered me a clerkship, but I'm going to turn them both down."

"But you interned for Alford last summer, and you liked him."

"Arty, I need a major change."

"So...so you won't be coming home after you graduate?"

"Only to visit. I've been accepted at the Sorbonne if I want to go, and Cate wants me to stay here and go for a PhD and help coach the women's aquatics team. I could be an assistant diving coach. And I may still take a job or get a clerkship somewhere, just not in Pittsburgh."

"But we had such a good time last summer. You loved the cottage."

"Things have changed, Arty. It's time to grow up and move on."

"So will you come back for spring break?"

"No, I have other plans."

"Other plans?"

"Arty, we've always agreed that we could both date others. Well, I am and I hope you are too. And you've always got Maggie to run to."

"That's not fair, Jen."

"No, you're right, it's not. I'm sorry. I liked her a lot too. But it's true and you know it. And of course you've got groupies to play with after your gigs."

McGill didn't even try to deny it. "So...so where are you going? What kind of plans? Who is he? Where's he from? Is he some rich Yalie? Tell me what I'm up against?"

"No, he's not rich. He's from Arkansas and his dad was a small town Buick dealer, so in that way he's kind of like you. He's going to work for Senator Fulbright. He wants to go into politics and change the world like you used to want to do."

"Come on, Jenny. Politics? We both know politics is bullshit. Jenny, you can't do this. I love you, Jenny. I think I want to marry you someday."

"Arty, that's part of the problem. Now don't make this any more difficult than it is. No matter what happens, I'll always remember you fondly. But it's time for me to move forward."

"You'll remember me *fondly*. Jen, after all we've meant to each other...how can you say that?"

"I'm sorry, but you have issues to work out and I have to move on with my life. It's better this way. We've both changed. I'll be twenty-five, Arty. Twenty-five! We have very different goals and responsibilities. Good night, Arty. It's late and I have a paper to write."

McGill went crazy when she hung up on him, screaming and pounding his fists on the pine-paneled wall. He threw some clothes into his duffle bag, grabbed his sleeping bag, took his stash of cash out of its hiding place and counted it up—$337. He grabbed the Gibson with the peace-sign, shoved it in its case, put the tape recorder under his arm, ran out the door, pulled out of the driveway and sped to Interstate 80. He gassed up at a truck stop, checked the tires and oil, bought two large coffees and roared through the coal-black Pennsylvania night. He kept the tape recorder next to him, singing into the mic, working up verses and trying to come up with a song that would win her back.

He drove until he was almost out of gas and stopped at a truck stop to fill up and catch a couple hours sleep in the back seat. He paid $3 to take a shower in the truckers' lounge and ate breakfast while reading the early edition of *The New York Times*. Operation Homecoming was coming to an end, and Mulligan was still not on the POW list.

He knew Jenny's class schedule, and when he got to New Haven he bought a map of the Yale campus. He found her chatting with some Yalies just before her ten o'clock class.

Jenny, cringing when she saw him, said, "Arty, what are you doing here? Why did you come? It won't solve anything."

He followed her like a puppy as she walked to class, pleading and cajoling with her as the Yalies, who knew better than to mess with a crazy vet in an Army a field jacket and a Vietnam boonie hat, kept safely away and glowered at him.

"Arty, you're only making it worse," she said as she went in the lecture hall door. "There's nothing more to say."

He shouted, "Yes there is!"

He jogged back to the car, got his guitar out of the case, strapped it over his back, Woody Guthrie hobo style, double-timed across campus to her classroom, marched down the amphitheater's stairs and right up to the podium and said to the stunned professor, "Excuse me, sir, but I need the floor. This is an emergency."

Jenny could only sit and watch, mortified, as he took the guitar off his back, slung it into playing position, and announced to the dumbstruck class, "This is the hardest thing I've ever done, so cut me a break. I wrote this song last night on the drive up here. Now parts of it of are not literally true, songwriting is like that, but that just makes the feeling behind it more emotionally true. It's for the love of my life, the beautiful Ms. Jennifer Marie Abruzzi, sitting right there."

McGill pointed so nobody could miss her, and everybody turned their heads and gawked. He strummed a G chord and said, "Jen, this is from me to you. I really mean it."

He whistled a few upbeat, chipper bars of a melody, strummed and sang:

"Well I told you that I love you

But you don't seem to care
You say you're going off to be with that
New guy somewhere
You say you like me but you love him
He's won your heart
It's okay honey, I'll be content
With a different part.
Duh doo bee doo

Save a couple o' eggs for me
I call first dibs on your ovaries
And when you're ready for me, honey
I'll come through
I'll save a couple hundred trillion
Sperms for you.

Yeah, save a couple o' eggs for me
I want to be there to sire your progeny.
Our genes belong together
Our kids will be cool
They'll get their attitudes from me
Their looks and brains from you.

You say you're sorry you've only come
To say good-bye
But there's one thing I want you
To keep in mind
I'll love you forever
And there'll come a time
When you'll see through him
And you'll want to be mine.
Duh doo bee doo

So save a couple o' eggs for me
Make sure to always use your spermicidal jelly
And when you're with him, honey
Never trust our luck
Make sure he always wears a rubber
No matter what.

Yeah, save a couple o' eggs for me
I got first dibs on your ovaries
And when you're with him, honey
Never trust our luck
Make sure he wears a big, thick, rubber
Every time you......

Save a couple o' eggs for me
I want to be there to sire your progeny.*

He finished by slowly whistling a few, forlorn bars of the melody and looked up at her as the class burst into wild applause. He took the guitar off his shoulder and knelt down, resting the guitar's lower bout on the floor while holding the neck upright—like Sir Galahad on bended knee. With his right hand, he gallantly removed his boonie hat and clasped it over his heart like a properly chivalrous suitor.

"Jennifer Marie Abruzzi, I love you. Will you please marry me? We'll drive down to Maryland today. Right now. They don't have any stupid blood tests or waiting period down there. We can be man and wife before the sun goes down."

Jenny could only sit, frozen and bewildered, as Arty added, "We have to do it right now, Jen, today, or our mothers will argue about corsages and gowns and cakes and all that stupid wedding crapola. Please, Jen, just say yes so we can get going."

She was incredulous at his audacity. What did *she* want? Did she love him? Sometimes it was yes, and sometimes is was no. And even if she had once loved him, did she love him still, and did she want to be the mother of his babies? Were they truly soul mates or just delusional victims of a Mickey Mantle foul ball? Did she love him? Yes no yes no maybe yes, maybe no. Yes. No. Yes. No. Maybe. How could she ever be sure if she didn't give it a chance? The shared history was there, and more often than not, the feeling was there, and she wasn't getting younger. It made sense to take a chance...and hope for the best.

"Okay, Arty, let's just do it."

McGill said, "Does that mean *yes*?"

She hesitated... "Yes."

He shouted, "*Fuckin' A!*" and slung his guitar on his back and bounded off the stage and up the stairs to her row as she made her way to the aisle. He wrapped her in his arms, pulled her tight, bent her over

*see Author's Notes, p. 323

like he was Clark Gable in *Gone With the Wind,* gave her a once-in-a-lifetime, Oscar worthy kiss as almost the whole class were on their feet, clapping and cheering.

Catherine, who had been sitting nearby, came over and gave them hugs and said, "Congratulations. You deserve it."

McGill took Jenny by the hand, and as he led her up the stairs a burly black guy in the back row started singing in a deep bass voice: "DA DOT DA DAH, DA DOT DA DAH" and instantly the rest of the class was singing along with him.

As they went up the stairs McGill felt her tug at his hand as she said, "Wait a second." They paused as she spoke softly to a guy with curly brown hair who did not seem to be as pleased with events as the rest of the class. McGill wondered if it was the guy whose father was a Buick dealer in Arkansas that she'd been dating. He didn't care. He wanted to get her out of there before she could change her mind. He pulled her away, and at the top of the stairs two students held the doors open for them like they were visiting royalty. McGill turned and gave the class two thumbs-up as Jenny beamed and waved.

They went to her apartment so she could pack a bag, then drove south and stopped for lunch and gas at a service area on the New Jersey Turnpike. As McGill studied the map he said, "Jen, we can either stay on 95 and go through the traffic in Philly, or we can take the Garden State Parkway down the shore to Cape May and catch the ferry and maybe stop in Wildwood on the way and have a beer at Pelican Bills."

"Will it take any longer?"

"Depends of the ferry schedule. Probably a couple of hours."

"It doesn't matter. Down the shore, Arty. Definitely."

Pelican Bill's was dead slow. McGill ordered the seven-mini-drafts-for-a-dollar special and went to play the juke box. He watched Jenny break into a grin as the organ intro to "Light My Fire" started up. It was their song, the first song they'd danced to on that final weekend of the Summer of Love.

He played three more of their favorites: "Hey Jude," "Bridge Over Troubled Water," and "Suite Judy Blue Eyes." Then they drove to Cape May and took the ferry across Delaware Bay. It was a choppy crossing, but with the sea gulls and the ocean breeze it was too romantic to even think about being seasick. They drove south, and as they crossed the Maryland line they saw a sign: *No-Wait Weddings—Cheap.*"

It was dusk when they rang the doorbell, which chimed the first few bars of "The Wedding March." A rumpled Justice of the Peace charged them $25 for the license, $25 to perform the service, with a $5 tip going to his wife who served as the witness to make it perfectly legal. McGill surprised her by pulling out a gold-colored metallic ring he secretly bought for $1.98 at the gift shop at the service plaza while she was in the ladies' room. As they were leaving, the Justice's wife handed them their only wedding gift: the Ocean City Honeymooners coupon book for discounts at local shops and restaurants.

They woke up in the honeymoon suite at the Surf King Motel with the waves breaking fifty yards from their balcony. They were man-and-wife.

The TV weatherman said the day would be sunny but cool, so they dressed in jeans and sweatshirts and wore their jackets. At breakfast, McGill bought a copy of *The Washington Post* from a vending machine. As the waitress was handing them menus he shouted, 'He's *alive*! Jen! He's on the list! *Mulligan Man's alive*!"

Jenny threw her arms around him. "Oh, Arty, that's wonderful."

"But Dungy's not on the list. Shit."

"Is he the one who pulled you out of the water?"

"Yeah. He probably saved my life."

They tempered their joy as Jenny said, "I'm going to go call Cate."

"And I'll call Mulligan's parents."

There was only one pay phone in the restaurant. Jenny went first, with Arty standing next to her, listening. But there was no answer at her apartment.

When McGill called Mulligan's house, one of Mike's aunts answered and told him that Mike's mom and dad, along with Catherine and the baby, were all on their way to Hawaii to see him.

"How is he?" McGill asked.

"The Navy said he had medical issues," said the aunt. "They wouldn't tell us anything more."

"So what's it all mean, Arty?" Jenny asked when he hung up.

"It means we have a couple of friends who'll need serious help."

Jenny rented a beach umbrella while McGill went to the motel for his guitar. Almost nobody came to the shore this time of year, so they had the beach to themselves—at least a fifty yards in each direction. They pitched the umbrella and McGill spread out his Army blanket.

They took off their shoes, held hands, and walked to the water's edge. They rolled up their jeans to their knees and waded in, but the water was shivering cold, so they walked along the waterline holding hands, picking up sea shells, and making tracks in the wet sand as the ocean gently lapped at their feet.

When they returned to the umbrella, McGill picked up his guitar and Jenny said, "Arty, play that new song again. I've only heard it once."

He sang it for her, and when he finished she said, "Everybody in the class thought it was funny, but…you know it's grammatically incorrect, don't you?"

"What's wrong with it?"

"It's not 'sperms,' Arty, it's 'sperm,' with no 's' at the end. Sperm is both the singular and the plural. It's like 'sheep.' You wouldn't say 'two sheeps,' would you?"

McGill was annoyed that her fancy Bryn Mawr and Yale Law education had caught him up on yet another minor point. It was one of the few things about her that irritated him. He tried it her way and sang, "I'll save a couple hundred billion sperm for you."

Shaking his head, he said, "Nope, Jen, it just doesn't work. It throws the phrasing completely off. Sheep and sheeps and sperm and sperms just aren't in the same league. Not even close. Have you ever seen them under a microscope? There's zillions of the squiggly little suckers in a single drop. And I don't care what Webster says is grammatically correct. He never tried to sing it."

The End

Glossary

Those unfamiliar with the military jargon and cultural slang from this era may need a reference for many terms used in this novel. (Note: The Air Force and Marines generally use Army terms for rank and the Coast Guard uses Navy terms.)

admiral — Navy and Coast Guard ranks. Pay grades O-7— O-10. Signified by silver stars (rear admiral, lower: one star; rear admiral, upper: two stars; vice admiral: three stars; admiral: four stars).

Agent Orange — an extremely toxic herbicide sprayed on the jungle canopy to denude vegetation and make it easier to locate the enemy.

AIT — Advanced Individual Training. Specialized training in a designated military occupational specialty (MOS), e.g., infantry, military police, cook, communications, artillery, etc.

AK47 — Soviet-made weapon of choice for North Vietnamese infantry troops and Viet Cong guerrillas.

AO — Area of Operations. A unit's geographic area of responsibility. Pronounced "A-Oh".

ARVN — Army of the Republic of (South) Vietnam. Pronounced "are-vin."

ASAP — As Soon As Possible. Pronounced "A-S-A-P" or "A—sap."

AWOL — Absent With-Out Leave. Pronounced "A-W-O-L" or "A-wall."

basic — common term for BCT (Basic Combat Training). Introductory course for Army and Air Force recruits. Equivalent to Navy and Marine "boot camp."

big brass — generals and admirals and Pentagon honchos.

bird colonel — a full colonel. Signified by a silver eagle. Pay-grade 0-6.

boo-koo — G.I. slang derived from the French "beaucoup," meaning "many," "much," or "very."

boonies — out in the jungle. Probably derived from "boondocks."

boot camp — (See "basic.")

BOQ — Bachelor Officers Quarters. On-base housing for single officers or those not with their wives.

brass — 1. military pins worn on collars and lapels identifying unit assignment (infantry, artillery, etc.) 2. officers of the rank of major and above authorized to wear the brass "scrambled eggs" on the brims of headgear (brass hats).

brassard — upper-arm band worn by military police with "MP" on it.

buck sergeant — nickname the lowest ranking Army sergeant. Signified by three chevrons. Pay-grade E-5.

butter bar — nickname for the lowest officer rank. (See "lieutenant.")

captain — 1. Army rank O-3. Signified by two silver bars. 2. Navy rank O-6, same as an Army colonel. Signified by a silver eagle.

Charlie — nickname for Viet Cong (VC) guerrillas. Derived from the phonetic alphabet V for Victor and C for Charlie.

chief — Navy honorific equivalent to the Army's and Marine's "sarge."

chief petty officer — Navy rank signified by three chevrons topped by a rocker and a symbol denoting specialty. Pay-grade E-7.

CO — Commanding Officer.

colonel —Army and Marine ranks. Pay grades O-5 and O-6. (See "bird colonel"; "lieutenant colonel.")

corporal — the lowest ranking Army & Marine NCO. Signified by two chevrons. Pay-grade E-4.

crossed pistols — the "brass" insignia of military police.

DD214 — Department of Defense Document 214. Record of the date and terms for separation from the armed forces (e.g. honorable, dishonorable, etc). Required as proof when applying for benefits.

Democratic Republic of Vietnam — official name of the government of North Vietnam.

DEROS — Date Eligible for Return from Overseas. In Vietnam, that was "three-sixty-five and a wake-up" after arriving "in-country." Pronounced "dee-ros."

donut dolly — female Red Cross worker.

doughboys — nickname for infantry soldiers of World War I.

dustoff — helicopter with a red cross on its sides and a medic and medical supplies on board. Tasked with transporting casualties.

EM — Enlisted Men (and women).

EM Club — a restaurant/bar/social venue for EM.

fifty — (See "M2.")

first sergeant — the "top" sergeant. Signified by three chevrons above three rockers with a diamond in the center. Pay-grade E-8.

FNG — Fucking New Guy. A raw, inexperienced soldier prone to making mistakes.

forty-five — .45 caliber pistol, the standard side-arm for officers and military police.

Freedom Bird — airplane that takes you out of Vietnam.

fuckin' A! — epithet or accolade, depending. Usually indicating strong agreement, good or bad.

general — Air Force, Army, and Marine ranks. Pay grades O-7 — O10. Signified by silver stars (brigadier: one star; major-general: two stars; lieutenant-general: three stars; general: four stars).

GI — Government Issue. Common term for Army enlisted personnel since World War I.

GI Bill — law defining benefits entitled to those honorably discharged.

gook — racial slur denoting people of oriental heritage.

grunt — infantry foot soldier or Marine. (See "REMF.")

hard stripe — nickname for U.S. Army ranks E-4 to E-9 signified by chevrons. (See "soft stripe.") Chevrons indicate command responsibilities.

head — 1. Navy, Marine and college fraternity term for bathroom. 2. someone who smokes pot (from "pot-head"). (See "straight.")

hooch — quarters for troops, usually a small hut sleeping a few men.

Huey — the Bell UH-1 helicopter in any of its many configurations.

HQ —Headquarters. Where decisions are made.

in-country — within the borders of Vietnam.

Indian country — enemy territory.

IV Corps — the southernmost military district in Vietnam comprising most of the Mekong delta. Pronounced "four-core."

JAG — Judge Advocate General. The military's legal department. Pronounced "jag."

KIA — Killed In Action.

klick — one kilometer. Overseas the military used the metric system.

KP — Kitchen Police. A lowly military duty consisting of peeling potatoes, cleaning pots, mopping floors, etc.

lieutenant — 1. rank of Army and Marine 2nd. lt. and Navy ensign. Signified by a single gold bar. Pay grade O-1. (See "butter bar.") 2. rank of Army and Marine 1st lt. and Navy lt. jg. (junior grade.) Signified by a single silver bar. Pay grade O-2.

lieutenant colonel — a "light colonel" as opposed to a "bird colonel." Signified by a silver oak leaf. Pay-grade 0-5.

lifer — career military personnel, often derogatory.

LZ — Landing Zone. Where a helicopter or plane is to land. Could be a semi-permanent base or a bare spot in the middle of nowhere.
M16 — the most common U.S. infantry weapon. Replaced the M14.
M2 — a fifty-caliber heavy machine gun.
M60 — a light machine gun.
MACV — Military Assistance Command, Vietnam. The headquarters of U.S. operations at Tan Son Nhut air base also nicknamed "Pentagon East." Pronounced "mack-vee."
major — rank signified by a brass oak leaf. Pay-grade 0-4.
master-sergeant — rank signified by three chevrons above three rockers, but without the diamond of a first-sergeant. Pay-grade E-8.
MEDEVAC — medical evacuation by helicopters. (See "dustoff.")
MI — Military Intelligence.
MIA— Missing In Action.
military time — The military has its own written and spoken protocols for time based on a twenty-four hour clock, e.g., midnight is written as 0000 but spoken as "twenty-four hundred," and five-thirty in the afternoon is written 1730 and spoken "seventeen-thirty" or "seventeen-thirty hours."
MOS — Military Occupational Specialty. The job for which you have been trained, e.g., the MOS designation for military police was 95B.
MP — Military Police.
NCO — Non-Commissioned Officer. The corporals and sergeants of the Army, Air Force and Marines and the petty officers and chiefs of the Navy and Coast Guard.
NCO Club — restaurant/bar/social venue for NCOs and specialists rank E-5 and above.
NVA — American term for North Vietnam Army. Used to differentiate the uniformed troops of North Vietnam from the Viet Cong guerrilla forces known as VC or Charlie.
O Club — Officers' Club. A restaurant/bar/social venue for officers, warrant officers and certain civilian personnel.
offed — past tense of "to off," meaning "to kill."
officer — a commissioned officer. Pay-grades 0-1 (Army and Marine 2nd lieutenant and Navy ensign) to 0-10 (general, admiral).
ossifer — derogatory nickname for "officer."
PACV — Patrol Air-Cushioned Vehicle. Pronounced "pack-vee." There are several YouTube videos showing PACVs in action.

PBR — Patrol Boat, River (or riverine).
PFC — Private First Class. Pay grade E-3. (Army only.) (See "private.")
POW — Prisoner Of War.
private — soldier in the Army's lowest ranks. Pay-grades E-1—E-3. E-1 has no insignia; E-2 is signified by a chevron; E-3 by a chevron above a rocker. (See "PFC.")
PX — Post exchange. Tax and duty-free stores for military families.
QC — South Vietnamese MPs with QC on helmets and brassards.
Quonset hut — half-oval structures of varying sizes made of cheap galvanized metal or canvass that could be put up quickly.
R&R — Rest & Recreation. Time off in exotic locales.
Republic of Vietnam — official name of the government of South Vietnam that had its capital in Saigon.
REMF — Rear Echelon Mother Fucker. Anybody who was not a grunt in the jungles chasing Charlie. Pronounced "remf."
ROTC — Reserve Officer Training Corps. A four year training program for college students leading to becoming a commissioned officer. Pronounced "rot-see."
RPG — Rocket-Propelled Grenade. A deadly, shoulder-fired weapon in the arsenal of the Viet Cong and NVA.
Sam Browne Belt — leather belt with supporting shoulder strap, pistol holster, loops for a nightstick and handcuffs and pouches for ammunition.
sarge — Army and Marine honorific for sergeants. (See "chief.")
sergeant — Army and Marine NCOs. Pay-grades E-5 to E-9.
soft stripe — nickname for patch worn by specialists.
specialist — Army "soft stripe" rank. Specialists did not have certain command responsibilities as did the NCOs with "hard stripes" (chevrons) worn by corporals and sergeants.
spec-4 — specialist 4 (SP4). Same pay-grade as a corporal (E-4) but not an NCO. Pronounced "spek-four." Signified by an eagle in a rounded-top (soft) shield. (See "soft stripe.")
spec-5 — specialist 5 (SP5). Pay-grade E-5. Signified by a patch with an eagle with a rocker above. (See "soft stripe.")
staff-sergeant — signified by three chevrons above a rocker. Pay-grade E-6.
straight — anyone who did not smoke marijuana was a "straight." It did not refer to sexual orientation as the term does today.

The World — any place that was not Vietnam, usually the USA.
time-in-grade — the number of months/years spent at current rank.
top — honorific accorded a unit's first sergeant. (See "first sergeant.")
USO — United Services Organization. A private, non-profit association of charitable groups including the Salvation Army and YMCA dedicated to making troops feel they have a "home away from home."
VVAW — Vietnam Veterans Against the War. Anti-war organization formed by Vietnam veterans.
VC — short for Viet Cong. Pronounced "vee-cee."
Viet Cong — guerrillas fighting the government of South Vietnam. (See "Charlie.")
y'uns — Western Pennsylvania equivalent to the South's "y'all." Probably a contraction of "you ones." Often mistakely written as "yinz."
warrant officer — not quite a commissioned officer but higher than a non-commissioned officer. Entitled to use officers' clubs. Helicopter pilots were often warrants. Pay-grades W-1 to W-5.
web-gear — load-bearing body-straps for a canteen, ammunition, etc.

Author's Notes

Luck of the Draw is a work of historical fiction set in the era in which I grew up. The main characters would have been my exact contemporaries, but they and their experiences are wholly fictional. I have tried to be as accurate as possible with the historical facts as I understand them as well as to evoke the social conventions and cultural conditions of that turbulent era as I remember them.

My first novel, *The Energy Caper, or Nixon in the Sky with Diamonds*, is set in a world in which there was no Vietnam war. In that luckier universe, these same characters live and love in an America that might have been. Neither novel is a sequel nor a prequel; I consider them to be equals. Together, they make a whole.

* A search on YouTube should bring up "Gotta Save Pittsburgh" and "Save a Couple of Eggs for Me," but you'll have to imagine them being sung by somebody decades younger and way cooler.

www.ingramcontent.com/pod-product-compliance
Lightning Source LLC
Chambersburg PA
CBHW032242010726
47494CB00002B/593

* 9 7 8 0 9 2 9 1 5 0 3 0 7 *